In her new novel, *Family Secrets – Divine Destinies*, Nancy Petrey crafts a poignant, unforgettable love story that seamlessly ties both the past to the future and Jew to Christian. And in the process, Petrey's readers get an unforgettable glimpse into the greatest love story ever told.

Joy Lucius
AFA Journal Staff Writer
and author of *Priceless Pennies: Rose and Odette, Unknown Children of the Holocaust.*

Nancy's writing brilliance shines in new and unexpected ways with this masterpiece. *Family Secrets – Divine Destinies* is her FIRST attempt at a fictional piece, and it has more than a hint of true-to-life circumstances. Being born and raised in a Jewish family, I see the plot as a bit unreal at times, but it is a super page turner. Anyone interested in Jewish Life would love this book. You never know, nor can predict, what will happen next. She kept my attention on every page, and I found that I could not put the book down. The characters were very believable, and you would probably recognize them as some people you know in real life. This is a romantic novel with a twisting plot that at times makes your head spin. People who love romance novels, as well as people who like the intrigue of the mysterious, will love this book. Delving into the dynamics of the Jewish family was obviously new territory for Nancy Petrey. However, she is a compelling author, and I am perfectly sure anyone who picks up this book will enjoy every second of the read. I can imagine several sequels coming our way. It's possibly a bit mushy, but all romantics will love it.

Janice Horowitz Bell
"Daughter of the King of the Universe,"
a Messianic Jewish friend, successful businesswoman, and Bible teacher.

FAMILY SECRETS
DIVINE DESTINIES

NANCY PETREY

*Dear Mack and Kathie,
I pray you feel the
joy, love, and presence of
the Lord as you read.
Love + shalom,
Nancy*

Energion Publications
Gonzalez, Florida
2021

ISBN: 978-1-63199-775-4
eISBN: 978-1-63199-776-1

Energion Publications
P. O. Box 841
Gonzalez, FL 32560

energion.com
pubs@energion.com

DEDICATION

To Jesus Christ – *Yeshua HaMachiach,* the Jewish Messiah –
King of the Jews, Savior of the World, King of the Universe –
Son of God - Second Person of the Trinity –
and my personal Lord and Savior,
to Whom I have given my whole heart.

ACKNOWLEDGMENTS

First, I would like to thank my son, Jim Petrey, for inspiring me to take up writing where I had left off years ago and to complete this novel. I thank him also for reading along as I was writing it and for his very helpful suggestions and corrections. His help with formulating my purpose made all the difference.

I needed several consultants for the Jewish terms and customs and other facts. I thank my Orthodox Jewish friend from New York and my Messianic Jewish friends, Mimi Finesilver, formerly of New York, and Janice Bell-Lewis of Alabama. Pamela Suran, a Messianic Jew living in Israel, who is also a licensed tour guide, advised me about touring Israel. Chaya Mizrachi, who has a ministry with her husband Avi in Tel Aviv, Dugit Messianic Outreach Ministries, advised me of the facts about Israeli citizenship requirements. My sister-in-law, Betty Petrey, formerly of Long Island, New York, gave me information about the area in which she grew up. Rainy Sepulveda also advised about the area. Marion Kohut, owner of Roberts Travel in West Point, MS, helped me with the policies of airlines. I am indebted to all these people for their help.

Prayer backup is invaluable to me whenever I write a book. I have a list of prayer warriors who pray for me and cheer me on, and I appreciate every one. I want to especially thank Debra Little, Hannah May, and Holly Shelton for their friendship, prayers, and encouragement.

A special thanks goes to Dr. Michael Brown for giving me permission to include him in the book. He is featured as the speaker at a conference in Trinity Church in the 19th chapter. In real life, Dr. Brown has authored more than 35 books and is widely considered to be the world's foremost Messianic Jewish apologist. My husband Curtis and I were blessed to have him speak at Faith United Methodist Church, Southaven, MS, in the 1980s and at Trinity

Church, Columbus, MS, in 1995, both churches of which Curtis was pastor. I have also been with Dr. Brown on other occasions, including once in Israel. It is a great honor that he consented to appearing in my book, and even more of an honor that he wrote an endorsement for my book.

I also want to thank Janice Bell-Lewis, my longtime Messianic Jewish friend and partner in ministry for her delightful endorsement. Joy Lucius, a staff writer for American Family Association, was gracious to take the time to read and endorse my book, especially considering its coinciding with the release of her new book, *Priceless Pennies: Rose and Odette, Unknown Children of the Holocaust*. I am thankful for Joy and also for another staff member of American Family Association, Randall Murphree who is the Editor of the AFA Journal. He is busy reviewing many books for the magazine, which makes me doubly thankful for his wonderful endorsement.

I am grateful to Henry and Jody Neufeld of Energion Publications for publishing this book, the sixth book they have published for me. It is a real blessing to have a Christian publisher. Henry and Jody are skilled in their trade, and I am blessed to have a great working relationship with them.

Not finally, but first and foremost, I thank my Lord Jesus Christ for giving me inspiration and great joy in writing my first novel. What a phenomenal adventure!

TABLE OF CONTENTS

CAST OF CHARACTERS

JEFF M. QUENTIN, JR., son of Jeffrey M. and Leah Quentin, Tupelo, Mississippi

Jeffrey M. Quentin, Sr., owner of Jeffrey M. Quentin Wholesale Grocery

Leah Quentin, daughter of Rabbi John and Rachel Cohen, Chicago

GLORIA ANNA SONDHEIM, daughter of Alvin and Sylvia Sondheim, New York

Alvin Sondheim, son of Samuel and Anna Berkowitz Sondheim, Chicago

Samuel Sondheim, son of Isaac and Ruth Levin Sondheim, Chicago

SARAH ZIPPORAH BERNSTEIN, daughter of Dr. Nathan and Naomi Bernstein, New York/Israel

CHAYA AND MAX BIRNBAUM, sister and brother-in-law of Sarah Bernstein, New York

PETER ("PETE") CARTER, roommate of Jeff Quentin, Columbus, Mississippi

JENNY SIMMONS AND REBECCA NORTH, roommates together, formerly roommates of Sarah and Gloria, respectively

PRISCILLA CALDWELL, desk clerk in Hamlin Hall, dormitory of Gloria and Sarah

GARY GRAYSON, friend of Priscilla Caldwell

KELILA – Messianic Jewish tour guide in Israel

RABBI LEONARD AND MIRIAM KATZ – Kehilat leaders in Katzrin, Israel

INTRODUCTION

This is my first novel, a book of Christian fiction. It may be the most enjoyable writing that I have ever done, creating characters and plot lines to carry forth marvelous truths from Scripture and to show how exciting life can be when God is orchestrating the relationships and events. Each day is full of joy, meaning, and purpose.

I began writing this in September 1997, while my husband Curtis was pastoring Trinity Church in Columbus, Mississippi. The first 24 chapters take place at Mississippi State University in nearby Starkville. Our daughter Susan was a graduate of Mississippi State, and our sons, Perry and Bert, also attended MSU, so I was familiar with the campus. The 19th chapter takes place at Trinity Church, located between Starkville and Columbus, where the real Dr. Michael Brown is featured as the speaker at a conference. He gave me permission to include him in the book.

After my initial writing in 1997, the manuscript was laid aside after a time and then resumed in 2002. It was again laid aside until April 2021, and 34 days later the first draft was finished. It is God's timing for the book to be released this year, as we see anti-Semitism on the rise and all kinds of attacks on Israel. Those issues in the book are especially relevant now. The book stresses "God incidents" and divine orchestration of events.

Three of the four main characters are Jewish. I became a teacher of Jewish roots, formed prayer groups, studied Hebrew, and visited Israel twice before beginning this novel. God called me to be a Mizpah for Israel in August 1995, and I have pursued that call as a "watchman and witness" for over 25 years now, having visited Israel nine times in all. Two of my six published books are specifically about the Jewish roots of the Church and about Israel.

1

INTRODUCTION

Readers who have little interest in the Jewish roots of the Church or interest in Israel will still enjoy the book because its overriding themes throughout are romance and friendship. Love, family loyalty, humor, and adventure will keep your attention. Answered prayers and acknowledgment of "God incidences" throughout the book will inspire you. Teaching nuggets from Scripture and history are interwoven in the plot. You will be blessed but challenged. Most of all, you will be stirred by young love, and you will learn a lot from Scripture and history as you read.

I pray the Spirit of God will touch you wherever you are in your spiritual development.

Blessings and shalom,

Nancy Petrey

CHAPTER ONE

AN OPEN DOOR

STARKVILLE, MISSISSIPPI, OCTOBER 1997

He was Jewish, but he didn't know it. Somehow, he did know that he was different. He liked the fact that he was different. His difference was an enhancement, and he accepted it gladly. If he had been a girl, you would say it was "feminine mystique," but there was definitely no effeminate quality in him. He could have passed for an American movie star with his dark hair, dark eyes, and golden tan, but he looked more like a Greek god. All the girls adored him. He was five-ten, athletic, and had a good build, having played football throughout high school, but he was not dependent on sports fame for his identity. A sophomore at Mississippi State University, he was pursuing a business degree. He had no use for fraternities. He was too busy making money, going to classes, studying, and trying to avoid being snared by cute co-eds.

Yes, Jeff Quentin was not your ordinary college guy. He was an ambitious young man, and he wanted to follow in his dad's footsteps, which meant making lots of money and being obligated to no one. The qualities he got from his mother took the sharp edge off his single--minded pursuit of success; otherwise, he might have stepped on others while climbing up the achievement ladder. But he was an "easy touch," and this cost him time away from his studies and, more importantly, making money. His roommate knew just how to make his petitions, the wording and the timing. More than once Jeff ended up giving away most of his week's profit from his birthday cake sales. Word got around the campus that Jeff had money, and there were ways to obtain some of it.

The summer before this school year Jeff went on vacation with his parents to Manila, and his eyes were opened to the truly needy

3

of the world. His mother couldn't ignore the constant cries of the beggar children as they swarmed around them in the airport trying to carry their bags, and Jeff couldn't either. Twenty little brown, grubby hands fought over each piece of luggage. His father kept saying, "There will be no end to this if you give them even one penny," but that didn't deter Jeff and his mother from emptying their pockets before they could even get in the taxi. They were rewarded with big smiles, laughter, and hands waving furiously as they drove out of sight.

When Jeff returned to college he wasn't such an "easy touch" any more. After seeing the poverty in a third world country, he realized that the "needs" of his fellow students were really petty. What's more he began to view his own life goals as selfish. This really came as a shock to him because all his life he had never questioned his dreams of wealth and high position. He no longer had the drive to excel in his business courses, nor did he relish making a profit from his money-making enterprises. The thrill was gone. What was the point? Was he just going to join the ranks of the rich and famous and be miserable when he had "seen it all" and "done it all," or was he going to make his life count by relieving some of the misery he had seen among the poor and the forgotten?

This was the way Gloria Sondheim found Jeff, when she sat at his table in the Mitchell Memorial Library. Gloria had just come from her Baptist Student Union meeting and was bubbling over with joy and brimming with energy. After being challenged at the meeting to share her faith with someone, she was "raring to go." What could it hurt if she picked out someone who looked intelligent and of the opposite sex? Surely it wasn't a negative factor if he happened to be handsome, too. She decided to sit down at the table with Jeff and pray silently first. He was alone, and talking wasn't forbidden on the second floor. She was serious about this, but she would wait for the Lord's timing. He would give her an opening line.

All she could think of were the glowing testimonies she had heard at the BSU meeting. Maybe she would mess it up. Maybe she wouldn't "catch her fish." Now this wasn't praying, she chided herself. *Lord, I've got to be honest. This guy is so good-looking. I confess that my motives aren't totally unselfish. I really wish he would notice me, maybe even be attracted to me. Please help me to talk to him about You. I can tell he really needs You. He seems to be worried about something. Maybe it's no accident I'm here at this time. I know that You are the answer to all of life's problems. Help me to be genuinely interested in him for Your sake, not for mine. If Your Holy Spirit is drawing him, and you set this whole thing up, then I know I can't mess it up. Now I'm going to open my mouth, and I know you will give me the words to say.*

Taking a deep breath and glancing heavenward, Gloria reached over and touched Jeff lightly on the arm. "Hello, I'm Gloria Sondheim. I see you are reading an economics book. I take economics, too, but I surely could use some help. Are you a business major?"

"Oh, hello. Glad to meet you, Gloria. My name is Jeff Quentin, no kin to San Quentin!" They both laughed and relaxed. "Yes, I'm a business major, and I love economics. I'll be glad to help you. What do you need to know?"

"Everything. My daddy suggested I sign up for this course, but I don't know beans about it. Maybe he thinks it'll help me when I go shopping. I keep overdrawing my account!" They both chuckled and began to feel more at ease with each other.

Jeff sensed that this girl wasn't like the others, and he wasn't anxious to get rid of her. Maybe she would understand the turmoil he was in. It was crazy, but she didn't seem like a total stranger. She seemed more like a sister, someone he could trust. But how wise was it to confide in someone he had just met? He had been going round and round in his thinking about his life's goals, his identity, his direction. He knew he was poised to make a 180 degree turn, but he couldn't do it without talking to someone first. His mother and father were out of the question. They had his future all figured out - he would graduate from college with honors and join Dad's firm, Jeffrey M. Quentin Wholesale Grocery, as full partner. What other alternative could there possibly be for their only son? His roommate had partying and girls on his mind. He and Pete, as well as the other guys in the dorm, were on different wave lengths. Jeff had led a pretty solitary life. He didn't even have many relatives. For some reason he couldn't fathom, here was this pretty girl who just happened to arrive at the juncture of a radical turning point in his life, and a voice inside him was saying, "Tell her about your struggle and the decision you are about to make." But what decision was he about to make? He only knew he wasn't going to pursue this present laid-out plan for his life any longer. The voice seemed to be encouraging him to go ahead and say what he did know, and the part he didn't know would come into focus.

So I'll take the plunge. What have I got to lose? I won't be staying at the University anyway, and I'll probably never see her again.

"Gloria, I'll make you a deal. I'll help you with your economics if you will help me with a decision I've got to make. Okay?"

"Well sure, Jeff. I'm all ears. One thing I've always been good at is listening. I'll try not to give advice till I've heard it all. Go ahead."

"You know, I've always thought that people who were searching for their identity and trying to 'find themselves' were emotionally unstable and also wasting time. But now I seem to be in the same place. I've always known who I was and where I was going and never doubted my ability to achieve my goals. I've had plenty of drive and willingness to work hard, even to the point of missing all the 'traditional' fun that college students have. I don't regret that now, but suddenly the drive is gone and the thrill of making money is gone. I don't even care about position and power in life. In short, I just **can't** fulfill the American dream. It's not in me anymore. I've got to find something in life to give myself to, something worthwhile. I know I have a lot to give, and I don't want to waste my life. That's where I am. Does that shock you?"

6

Gloria could hardly believe her ears. Truly, this was a divine appointment. *Now don't let me mess it up, Lord.* "Actually, no, it doesn't shock me nor surprise me." But it did shock and surprise her a few minutes ago. She could hear the Lord teasing her, "Oh ye of little faith."

Gloria felt like she was sharing with a close friend she had known for years. "Jeff, what you just said has renewed my faith in our generation. You see, over the last year I have become quite cynical and also judgmental about my peers. Their hopes and dreams seem shallow, self-centered. I was getting hardened and indifferent in my attitude toward school and social activities, and the zest for living had gone out of me. I saw this college life as being artificial, and I began to wonder why I was here. What was I preparing for? Was I just going to find a husband, get married, and have babies? Maybe I would work at a part-time job when they went to school and then look forward to grandchildren. After we saved up the money, we would travel and enjoy an early retirement. I'll have to tell you this, Jeff, I can certainly identify with what you are saying. I woke up from the American dream, and I had a hangover! Surely there has to be more to life than this."

Jeff felt like he had drunk an invigorating tonic. This girl was not only pretty, but she had deeper thoughts than any other girl he had talked to. As she talked, he found great enjoyment in observing both her outer and inner beauty. Some of her features reminded him of his mom, the olive complexion, straight Roman nose, dark brown hair and eyes, and erect posture. She was several inches shorter than he and about the perfect size. Perhaps she had been in beauty pageants because her smile was dazzling. In addition to all these ideal physical features her melodious voice had almost put him under a spell. *Jeff Quentin, this girl must be one in a million. Steady, boy. Don't scare her off.* He knew he better cool it or she wouldn't find him so interesting after all.

Jeff forced himself to be calm. "But now you certainly don't appear to be cynical, judgmental, hardened, or indifferent as you described yourself. Has something happened to you? What brought about the change?"

Here was the opportunity Gloria had been waiting for. This was the time her words needed to be "apples of gold in frames of silver" as the Bible said. "Jeff, I'm really happy that you can't see any of those negatives in me. I can't take the credit for the improvement though. I met someone about a month ago that has made all the difference. He gets the credit. Now I have a purpose in life, and everything I do has meaning. In fact everything that happens to me, good or bad, has significance, and it all works for my good. I don't worry anymore because I'm confident of the future, and I am not in control. I'm being guided every step of the way. It's really very exciting. Every day when I wake up I'm full of joy and grateful for what the day will bring. And it's all because of the man I met."

Jeff felt envy growing inside of him the more Gloria talked. It didn't seem fair that anyone could be this happy when there were so many problems in the world. On the other hand, she was probably an airhead, and he had his hopes up for nothing. If this guy was so great, where was he? Didn't he care that she was talking to a complete stranger about her deepest thoughts? Hoping his jealousy didn't show, he managed to ask, "So, I guess you're getting married soon, right? That's the reason you are glowing."

"No, Jeff, it's not what you think. The man I'm talking about is Jesus Christ. I attended a meeting at the Baptist Student Union one night and I heard a message about the life-changing power of Jesus Christ. I had always attended church, so the scriptures he used were not new to me, but I had never heard anyone claim to have a personal relationship with the Son of God. The speaker told what his life had been like before he met Jesus and then what it was like afterward. He was one mixed-up individual who had indulged in every vice imaginable. When he was ready to take his life, he had a supernatural encounter with God that totally transformed him. As he was describing the peace that came over him and the love that filled his heart, I said to myself, 'I want that. I'm sick of the way I am. I want to give my life to God, and see if he can do anything with it. I sure can't.' When the man asked who wanted to receive Jesus Christ as his personal Savior, I didn't hesitate. Neither did six other people. We walked forward to the altar and knelt. This man and several others began praying with us. The scripture that said it all for me was Revelation 3:20 - 'Behold, I stand at the door and knock. If anyone hear my voice and open the door, I will come in to him and dine with him and he with me.' I knew Jesus was asking entrance into my heart, but it was up to me to respond and invite him in to take over my life. Right then I asked Him to come into my heart, forgive me of my sins, and be my Lord."

Jeff had become engrossed in Gloria's story because the light in her eyes kept increasing as she got to this point. Now she seemed to be far off somewhere and had forgotten he was sitting there. He felt a reverence he had not experienced before, and he didn't want to ruin it by talking. He didn't know what to say anyway. The silence was not uncomfortable; it was peaceful. All the things he had been pondering didn't seem important now. But there was something important about this moment, and he didn't want it to end.

CHAPTER TWO

MEMORIES OF GRANDFATHER

Jeff had never been religious. He didn't know the language. His parents weren't religious either, but his grandparents, his mother's parents, were very religious. Unfortunately, they were both killed in a car wreck when he was only five years old, so Jeff had no memories of being in church. He did remember his grandfather wore a little black cap when he read the Bible, but it wasn't a pleasant memory. It had something to do with a lot of arguments between his mother and his grandfather. Then that led to arguments between his mother and father. He remembered the tension in the house every time Papa and Mama Cohen came to visit. He knew they all loved each other because there were plenty of kisses and hugs when they first came and also when they left, but there were some late-night debates while they were there. Jeff could hear angry voices coming from the kitchen, and he knew better than to leave his bedroom. He had been warned that adults have things to talk about that children don't need to hear. He wanted so badly to just go and plop in his grandfather's lap and give him a big kiss. Surely that would stop the arguing.

Papa Cohen was like a magnet to Jeff. As soon as he walked in the door, Jeff would run and jump in his arms, and Papa would smother him with warm kisses. Jeff would follow him around the house and sit next to him at the table. He liked to sit in his lap and stick his head between Papa and the newspaper. The newspaper always lost because Papa was a pushover for his only grandson's wide grin. What Jeff didn't understand was why he couldn't sit on Papa's lap while he was reading the Bible. Papa always said, "Now run along. Your mother needs you to help in the kitchen." He would scamper away, but he would peep around the corner and see that Papa had put on his little black cap and shawl, had his Bible open, and was bending back and forth. He knew he better not watch long, or his mother would be snatching him up, and there would be another argument.

As Gloria was reliving her divine encounter, Jeff began to think back about his poverty of religious experience. The only person in his family who appeared to have a relationship with God was Papa Cohen. It was a way of life for his grandfather, but it was upsetting for his mother. *There must have been something important in that book because Papa would risk his daughter's displeasure every time he read it in her house. Who was right, Mom or Papa Cohen?*

"Well, who was right?" Jeff interrupted Gloria's reverie.

"What do you mean, who was right? I was right with God, and I knew it instantly. Jesus had washed away my sins, and I felt clean, like I just had a shower on the inside! When I opened the door of my heart, He definitely came in. I felt brand new. My life was just beginning. I was born again, and immediately I had a thirst for the Word of God. That man said, 'The Bible is God's love letter to you,' and I wanted to know everything He had written to me. I knew He loved me because He laid down His life for me. Now I wanted only to please Him."

This is way out. "I've never heard it said that the Bible is a love letter. On the contrary, it caused nothing but arguments in our house. My parents never had a Bible, and I've never read it. Of course, I've heard it quoted many times, especially from my high school English teacher at Tupelo High School, and I've read passages from Psalms and some other parts of the Bible in textbooks through the years. Have you read it through yet? What's so great about it? I've always been ignorant about its contents, but it hasn't mattered to me until now."

Jeff suddenly felt like he was five years old again with an intense curiosity to know what was so important about the big black book his grandfather was always reading. He could see himself climb up in his grandfather's lap and ask, "Papa, would you read to me out of that book you like so much?" Yes, it did matter to him.

Gloria responded, "No, I haven't read it all the way through yet, but it has been a part of my life since I started going to church with my friends when I was in the sixth grade. When I was twelve years old and struggling with an inferiority complex, I decided that reading the Bible a little every night before I went to bed would help me feel better about myself. In my own way I was reaching out to God, and that's all I knew to do. But now at nineteen years of age I realize that the Bible is not a self-help book, it's a history book. It is His Story. In all 66 books of the Bible the Living Lord is reaching out to His creation and saying, 'I love you. Receive my forgiveness, and you can live with Me forever.' I did that, and now I'm certain of my destination after I leave this earth. That's why I have peace and joy. The death question has been settled for me."

"So I'm beginning to read it from beginning to end, and I can't get enough of it. This book means everything to me. I hope you'll let me share with you some of what I'm learning, since you seem interested." Gloria ran out of words at this point. Up to now the words had flowed effortlessly. She knew God had answered her prayer by putting words in her mouth she hadn't planned. Some of the things she said surprised her, so it had to be God. Now it was up to God's Spirit to do the work in Jeff's heart.

Jeff could see that this girl was way out ahead of him in this whole religious thing. He figured he better not reveal any more of his ignorance, so he would put this new information on the back burner of his mind and change the subject to something more comfortable. Hadn't she said she wanted help with economics? It was getting late, and he felt an urgency to close this conversation and get back to the dorm. He hoped no one had tried to call him while he was gone. He needed to sell more birthday cakes. *Goodness*, he thought. *I've been fooling around long enough here. This girl is breath-taking, and there is something being stirred up inside me, but I can't go bankrupt. I've got bills to pay, some bookkeeping to do, a few orders to make, and an English Lit. exam to study for. If I'm going to withdraw from the University, it's got to be done gracefully and with the loose ends tied up. Anyway, I can think better if I can pull myself away from these dark tantalizing eyes.*

Jeff's strong sense of responsibility went into high gear, and he took control of the conversation. "Gloria, I must get back to the dorm. Duty calls. I tell you what, let's set a definite time and place to meet each week. What about Thursdays? I'll give you a 30-minute lesson in economics. I guarantee you'll pass your course with flying colors. Is that a deal?"

Gloria was relieved. She had never gone this far before in sharing her faith, and she was glad God had not required any more. She wasn't sure what decision Jeff was struggling with, but whatever it was, she knew everything she shared was relevant.

"Thanks, Jeff. That's super. How about the chapel at 4:30 p.m.? I don't think anyone will be there at that time. We can have privacy and quiet. Or at least I hope so because there are so many events all over the campus this whole week for Homecoming. In fact they are showing the movie, 'Jurassic Park,' on the Jumbotron at Scott Field tomorrow night, but I have no interest in it. Do you?"

Jeff picked up his books and said, "None at all. I'll be through with my English Lit. exam right about that time tomorrow, so I'll meet you there at the chapel at 4:30, and we can keep meeting on Thursdays at that time." He wanted to offer to take her books and walk her to the dorm, but his practical side knew better.

As Jeff walked on ahead of her, Gloria called out, "Jeff, I haven't forgotten about the decision. I'll be praying for you to make the right one, okay?"

Jeff looked back and politely smiled. "Sure. I'll see you tomorrow." He didn't see what difference prayer would make, but he figured that's how religious people think, so it couldn't hurt anything.

CHAPTER THREE

WORSHIP SERVICE FOR ONE

While getting into bed, Jeff pondered Gloria's words. *What was that phrase she used? The death question. M-m-m, certain of her destination, the Bible, His story. I've never heard anyone talk like that, never heard anyone speak with such... I guess the word is... faith. She really believed what she was saying. The question is, do I believe it?*

Jeff couldn't sleep. That smiling, other-worldly face with the brown twinkling eyes was pervading his thoughts. *I need to think about my future, but I can't get Gloria off my mind. She said Jesus Christ washed away her sins. What sins? That girl looks as pure as the driven snow. If she needed forgiveness, where does that put me?*

She said she was confident of the future, that she was not in control, and He was guiding her every step. How could she say that? It sounds pretty irresponsible to me. Some of the guys who get drunk on Saturday night and go to church on Sunday say, "Whatever will be, will be." I wonder if she believes that. That makes life sound like a roulette wheel, a cop out on responsibility.

I've got to ask her how she gets His guidance. Does she hear Him speak? Or does she figure it out herself from reading the Bible? But what about making decisions? Does she put her mind on auto-pilot? It sounds risky to me, and weird, too. You might wind up making some big mistakes and doing something stupid. Surely you can use your own abilities and reasoning. I don't want anything to do with a God that takes over your life, and you have no say in it.

Right when I was about to take action and make big changes in my life, I run into this starry-eyed girl, and now I find myself having to deal with these religious issues I am not equipped to deal with. I need to get on with it. I've got to make a decision.

Jeff finally fell into a fitful sleep about 2:00 a.m. He had not been able to concentrate enough to study for his exam, but he had managed to take care of his business, and he planned to mail the orders and bill payments tomorrow. He set his alarm clock at 8:00 a.m. That would give him enough time to study for twenty minutes, stop by the post office, and make it to his nine o'clock class. He could get a snack at the Union after class, go back to the dorm, and have time to drum up some business on the phone before his next class. His bank balance was getting dangerously low, and all his fees weren't paid. The decision could wait one more day.

◆

Gloria floated back to her dorm. Hurrying to her room, she found that her roommate had left a note, saying she was spending the night with a friend off campus so they could study together. "Thank you, Lord!" she exclaimed as soon as she had closed the door behind her. She had her own little sanctuary, and she couldn't be happier. She could pray and sing out loud and do whatever she wanted to.

She whirled around the room as if waltzing with an invisible partner. Bowing, bending, swaying, lifting her hands up high, she improvised a dance of delight before the Lord. No one had instructed her, but she felt free to express herself in worship in this way. The joy coursing through her must find release. Then she began to sing, the Spirit within her supplying the melody and words, "a new song" to the Lord. She didn't know how long she danced and sang, but she instinctively knew when the "benediction" had come. She gracefully fluttered to the floor like an experienced ballerina, spent but not tired.

Kneeling at her bed, Gloria poured out her praise and thanksgiving to the Lord for the sheer joy of witnessing to someone God had drawn her to. Then she got down to petitioning the Lord specifically for Jeff to make the right decision, whatever it involved.

Having done that, she got out her Bible and resumed reading where she had left off the night before, I Kings 18. It was the story of Elijah and the prophets of Baal on Mt. Carmel. The 24th verse really struck her - "Then you call on the name of your god, and I will call on the name of the Lord. The god who answers by fire - he is God..."

I know what I'll do, I'll challenge Jeff to ask God to reveal Himself to him. On the other hand, I can't convince him intellectually that God is real and that he needs Jesus Christ. Probably he doesn't even have a consciousness of sin yet and of his need for forgiveness. But God surely set up our meeting. He will orchestrate the next step also. I'm just going to wait and see what God does.

"Please let me stay on this case, Lord. You can see my heart, so you know what I'm feeling for this guy. Please let me be right in the middle of his being born again. I promise you I'll only do and say what you lead me to do and say. After all, we have a 'date' tomorrow in the chapel! Thanks again, Lord, for this exciting experience. I love you, Jesus. Good night."

Gloria had just had a full-fledged worship service in her dorm room with two people present, she and Jesus. It was only 11:57, and by 12:07 she was in a deep, restful sleep.

CHAPTER FOUR

GLORIA'S JEWISH BACKGROUND

The girls on third floor of Hamlin Dormitory were gathered around the TV in the lobby when Gloria floated in that night after her encounter with Jeff Quentin. No one could accuse her of being drunk, but they might accuse her of blissful ignorance, not noticing that the "third-floor gang" was talking about her. She was pretty, but her nose was a little long. She didn't drink, so she probably looked down on those who did. She didn't date. Maybe no one was good enough for her. She wasn't a Southerner. Didn't she know that sororities were important? No one wanted to appear jealous of Gloria Sondheim. Why would they be jealous of a Jew? If she were not so friendly and cheerful, always asking if she could help them with homework or run an errand, they could speak openly of their dislike. As it was, they only whispered "the facts" as they saw them.

Gloria had been searching for a close friend ever since she came to Mississippi State last year. She liked the University, her professors, and the teachers, but she still didn't seem to fit in. Some girls invited her to the Baptist Student Union, and it had become her home away from home. She had made friends there, but still she had not found that special friend that she needed.

Being from New York could have been the problem. She was teased about being a Yankee. No one ever mentioned her Jewishness though. She never thought about it herself because she didn't go to temple or keep Jewish customs. Her family was surrounded by Gentiles in Belle Terre Village of Port Jefferson on Long Island. Her parents allowed her to join the First United Methodist Church with her friends when she was twelve years old, so all her friends were non-Jews. Mr. and Mrs. Sondheim never attended temple, but they occasionally attended Gloria's church when the young people were having a special program.

Alvin Sondheim had political ambitions, and he must have felt that being Jewish could be a liability, so he and his wife Sylvia kept their distance from the Jewish community. They weren't ashamed of being Jews, but they were more interested in the present and future than their past heritage. When Gloria tried to probe into her Jewish background, her parents discouraged her, saying that it was a waste of time and unhealthy to look back. They always said to her at these times, "All men are created equal and are endowed by their Creator with certain unalienable rights. We must live in harmony with each other because God is our Father, and we are all brothers, no matter our race or creed."

They said it didn't matter where they came from. What mattered was where they were going. Alvin and Sylvia Sondheim had big plans for their beautiful, intelligent daughter, and being Jewish wasn't going to get in the way. So far they had been successful in shielding her from prejudice by enrolling her in a prestigious private school, The Knox School, in Port Jefferson. However, in her senior year, she had become inquisitive about her Jewish roots, and they knew they needed to divert her attention elsewhere. Therefore, they sent their daughter down South to college, precisely because they knew there were few Jews there.

No, the Sondheims were not ashamed of their Jewishness, but they desired to be known for their achievements and their character, not for their pedigree. Gloria was a second-generation Jew, born in the United States.

Alvin's grandfather, Isaac Sondheim, was born in Germany. He married his next door neighbor, Ruth Levin, whose parents had moved to Germany from Poland. Their first child was Samuel. He was only nine years old, when they were taken to a concentration camp in 1942. In the camp he became friends with Anna Berkowitz. Her parents died not long before liberation. In 1945 when the Americans, as well as the Russians and the British, liberated all the

Jews in concentration camps, Isaac and Ruth, their son Samuel, and his friend Anna, made their way to the United States. Anna had relatives in Chicago, so it was there that the Sondheims settled down. Samuel and Anna continued their friendship throughout high school and decided together to enroll in the University of Chicago. Samuel was an exceptionally bright young man. From his childhood he was fascinated with the heavenly bodies, so he determined to get a degree in physics and astronomy. His goal was to do research. That way he could spend his days gazing at the skies through high-powered telescopes.

Anna chose to get a degree in history, but she made sure to take the same astronomy class as Samuel. One day in class their professor began to present the creation story from Genesis. Being non-religious Jews, they had never read the Bible, so they listened with great interest. The other students sneered at this non-intellectual explanation for the origin of the universe, but Samuel and Anna wanted to explore the subject further. They decided to purchase a Bible for themselves.

They were shocked to find so many references to the Jews. They didn't realize that Jews only had the Tanakh,[1] or Old Testament, so they bought a Bible with both Old and New Testaments. After reading the story of Creation, they went on to read all of Genesis. When they read the 15th chapter, they were excited to see the words of God to Abraham, "'Look at the heavens and count the stars - if indeed you can count them.' Then He said to him, 'So shall your offspring be.' Abraham believed the Lord, and He credited it to him as righteousness."[2] Samuel was thrilled to know what God said about the stars. Maybe it wasn't his own idea to study the stars, but maybe God had put it into his heart!

They continued to read about God's everlasting covenants with Abraham, his son Isaac, and his grandson Jacob, whose name was later changed to Israel. To Isaac, God said, "I will make your descendants as numerous as the stars in the sky and will give them all these lands, and through your offspring all nations on earth will be blessed."[3] Samuel wished his father Isaac knew this!

To Jacob, God said, "A nation and a community of nations will come from you, and kings will come from your body. The land I gave to Abraham and Isaac I also give to you, and I will give this land to your descendants after you."[4]

Samuel and Anna began to spend their weekends reading the Bible together, and their friendship attained a new depth. They were thrilled with the Exodus from Egypt, the miracles in the wilderness, the conquest of Canaan, and the love story of Ruth and Boaz. Again, Samuel longed for his parents to read this wonderful Book of books, especially for his mother Ruth to read about the Ruth of the Bible. Samuel and Anna read that the first prophet after Moses was Samuel. "Hey, that's my name!" Samuel exclaimed.

They especially loved the stories of Saul, David, and the other kings, but the prophets Elijah and Elisha set them on fire. "That's what we need around here, some real men of power!" laughed Anna.

They saw that the Bible was indeed the history book of the Jewish people. Why did they not know this before? They both had been raised in non-religious homes where there were no religious books. They had rarely attended the synagogue. Very few of their friends were religious. Suddenly they realized that they had been in a spiritual desert.

One Friday night as they sat on the bench outside Anna's dorm, they both had the same idea and practically said it simultaneously, "Let's pray. What could it hurt?" They laughed, but it was obvious they were having the same thoughts more and more. So they did pray. They addressed God as the God of Abraham, Isaac, and Jacob. They didn't get on their knees. They didn't want anyone to notice them, so they bowed their heads and whispered. Anyone passing by would only think they were being intimate.

Faith had grown in their hearts, and they had no doubt of God's existence. They had read the stories of faith and of prayers answered. It was a simple matter now of joining their ancestors in a faith based on history, not legend. They fully believed this book was an accurate account of the lives of their ancestors. No one had to convince them. They were convinced by reading for themselves. Also, the fact that Israel had been established as a nation in 1948 gave them more proof that the God of Israel was keeping the many promises they read about in Isaiah, Jeremiah, Ezekiel, and Zechariah.

Their faith was beginning to bud, but it would never see completion that night. As they sat on the bench praying, oblivious to the present world, they were startled by an angry voice. Samuel felt a rough hand on his shoulder shaking him. He looked up, and it was his father Isaac!

Red faced and trembling, Isaac shouted at them, "What are you doing with that Bible? Don't you know Jews don't read the Gentiles' Bible? We have the Tanakh, not the New Testament!" He snatched the Bible from them and began to tear out pages in the back of the book, crumple them up, and spit on them.

Samuel and Anna stood up, trying to pull the Bible out of Isaac's hands. Samuel was devastated. "Don't! We love that book! It's the history book of the Jews. We haven't even gotten as far as the New Testament, but we don't see any reason why we can't read that, too. How dare you do this to us!"

Anna began to cry. People noticed the commotion and were coming over to see what was going on. She ran inside the dorm to her room and slammed the door. Then she sat on the bed and sobbed. "How could he do that? How could he do that?"

Isaac threw the Bible in the grass after he had torn out more pages. Then he walked off shaking his head wearily.

Samuel picked up the book and salvaged what he could of the pages, then sat down on the bench. He was so distraught, he didn't know what to do. He sat there for a long time, paralyzed by his father's vicious attack. *Why would he do such a thing? Why? I don't understand. I've never seen him get this angry. Why does he hate the New Testament so much?*

Samuel decided he needed to pray more than ever now, so he did just that. He poured out his heart to God. This was his first effort at communicating with God, but it seemed like he had done it all his life. It gave him as much pleasure as looking up in the sky on a starry night and trying to count the stars, like he did when he was a child. He felt that God was listening, and that God would give him an answer about all that had happened that night. The bud on his flower of faith was not crushed. It would bloom in time.

CHAPTER FIVE

THE CHAPEL

What a gorgeous October day, thought Gloria as she walked out of her dorm and headed to the chapel for her meeting with Jeff. She had timed it just right, so she could make it by 4:30. Fall with its accompanying nostalgia was her favorite time of the year. It never failed to bring back memories of her childhood days in school. As she enjoyed the beautiful fall colors and reminisced, her thoughts turned to the time when she was ten years old, backstage in the school auditorium, nervously awaiting her performance in the Recital. She waited for her piano teacher to say, "Your time, Gloria." And now it seemed the Lord was saying the same thing, although the two situations really had nothing in common except for the intense emotions and the alternating feelings of excitement and dread. God had obviously set up this time, and she didn't want to fail at introducing Jeff to his Savior. However, she could sense that this meeting would be just as much of a turning point in her life, as she hoped it would be in Jeff's life.

As she reached the chapel, Jeff came striding toward her with a big smile on his face. "Hey, Gloria. Keep praying. So far so good. The English Lit. exam was easy, and I think I aced it! I'm feeling more confident about making that decision now. Maybe after we study economics I can share with you more about it, and you can help me look at the ins and outs objectively, so I'll know what to do. Okay?"

He's talking about one decision, and I'm thinking about another one he needs to make. Lord, what is it You are doing? Please keep me on the same page with You.

"You bet, Jeff. I'm a good sounding board. Well, let's go in. Hopefully, we'll have it to ourselves."

It was dark inside except for a single lighted candle on the altar. "Now where are the lights?" asked Jeff, feeling the walls.

A faint, sorrow-tinged voice came from the front pew. "Oh, I'm sorry. I didn't want to turn them on. The switch is farther to your right. I better go." In the light they could see a skinny, pale brunette dressed in black, rising from the pew. She quickly extinguished the candle, gathered up her books, and walked quickly up the side aisle, her head down.

Gloria couldn't let her leave without a kind word. The girl looked like she needed a lot of kind words. "My name is Gloria, and this is Jeff. We are studying together and thought this would be a quiet and private place. Of course, that's not the main purpose of a chapel, and we certainly don't want to run you off."

"Glad to meet you. My name is Sarah. I came in here to be by myself. I have to go now, so you're not running me off."

When Sarah brushed past them, they could see the pain in her tear-streaked face and could almost touch the grief surrounding her. Gloria, moved by the hopelessness in Sarah's eyes, caught up with her and blurted out, "Please don't go. I want to pray for you. You are hurting so bad, and I can feel it."

Anger flashed in Sarah's eyes. "Thank you, but I've already prayed. I need to go now." She was out of sight before Gloria could think of what to say.

Jeff took Gloria's hand and led her to the front pew where Sarah had been. "Don't worry about it. Some people don't want anybody invading their space. She probably wouldn't have let Billy Graham pray for her."

That broke the tension, and they both laughed. *What a gentle, understanding guy he is. I'm supposed to be helping him find the way, but he's wiser than I am. Oh well, I'll just relax, and let God do His thing. I'm not making anything happen. After all, I didn't plan that scene with Sarah, and I certainly don't know how it fits in, but I'm sure God does.*

"Are you ready for the economics lesson, my Yankee friend?" Jeff used his most business-like manner.

"Hey, wait a minute, we're not getting off on the wrong foot with that little jab! Besides, how did you know I'm a Yankee?"

"You don't exactly have a southern accent, you know. I'd guess you are from the Big Apple. Am I right?"

"You must be a detective. Well, I haven't been snooping, but your accent tells me you are from the deep South. If I'm a Yankee, then you are a red-neck! Aha! Gotcha!" Gloria crowed.

Jeff grinned wide. "As you said, we don't want to get off on the wrong foot, so I'll just shorten your name to 'friend', okay?"

"I guess you can say we are cross-cultural friends. I'm from New York, and you are from?"

"None other than Tupelo, Mississippi." Jeff stuck out his chest.

"Pleased ta meetcha again." Gloria grinned, as they ceremoniously shook hands. "Teach me, friend." Gloria spread out her textbook and class notes on the pew, and Jeff took charge.

Thirty minutes seemed like thirty seconds to both of them. Jeff, ever the practical one, checked his watch and suggested they walk to the Union to get something to eat, and they could talk about his upcoming decision. Gloria agreed. As she stopped by the restroom, she silently prayed that the Lord would direct the conversation. She hoped she had not already missed an opportunity to witness to Jeff in the chapel, the ideal location. *What was all that business about Sarah, Lord? Did I say the wrong thing? And with Jeff, did I get so engrossed in Economics that I missed Your voice?*

When she came out of the restroom, Gloria's face gave her away. "Friend, what is bothering you?" gently inquired Jeff.

"Oh, nothing really. I was just concerned about Sarah."

"I don't mind if you want to pray for her right now. Maybe that would make you feel better." Jeff guided Gloria to the altar.

"Of course. Thanks, Jeff, for your sensitivity. Do you want to kneel with me here?"

"You go ahead. I'll be right outside waiting for you."

27

Gloria was more than ready to fall to her knees and unburden her heart to the Lord. First she would light the candle as Sarah had. As soon as she lit it, surprisingly, the lights went out. How thoughtful of Jeff. He stayed in the chapel, anticipating the need to flip the switch. Then he went out.

"Oh, God, what a caring guy You have introduced me to. I'm the one with the answers, or rather, THE Answer, but he's the one with an understanding heart. You are teaching me, Lord, that Your ways are not my ways; Your thoughts are not my thoughts.[5] Reveal Yourself to Jeff, Lord. I don't know how to do it. And Lord, tell me what caused Sarah's anger. Please help her find comfort in You. Help her believe that You do answer prayer, and You do heal broken hearts. Yes, Lord, You do answer prayer. What an adventure I'm having with You, and how I love You. In Jesus' name, Amen."

Gloria blew out the candle and walked out of the chapel with victory in her heart. When Jeff saw her, he knew something had happened at that altar, and it made him just a wee bit jealous. In the intervening time he had been stewing again about his decision, and now it was his worried look that brought his previous question to Gloria back to him.

"Friend, what is bothering you?" sweetly asked Gloria.

Jeff had to chuckle at himself. Both were thinking, *How good we are for each other.*

CHAPTER SIX

A SONG

The Union was full of cozy sofas and chairs and would be ideal for discussing Jeff's decision. They got their food and sat down in an area that was practically empty. Jeff had helped Gloria. Now it was time for Gloria to help Jeff. The hamburgers disappeared fast as the two young people concentrated on looking at each other and pondering what the other one was thinking. *Goodness, how did such a prize of a girl come my way? She's the first girl I've seen on campus who doesn't wear gobs of makeup and skimpy, sexy clothes. Her blouse buttoned up to the top and her long skirt only add to her feminine allure, not take away from it. She obviously isn't even aware of her beauty but seems genuinely interested in other people – like Sarah – and like me, of course. I'm used to girls going after me, but this time I'm ready to get caught. I hope she really is interested in me just for myself and not for how she can help me.*

Gloria broke the silence. "A penny for your thoughts, southern friend."

"Are you sure I can trust you with my thoughts, northern friend?"

"Okay, it is now established that we are friends, but could we please drop the adjectives? It's getting a little corny," pleaded Gloria.

"Hey, don't take the fun out of everything. My next adjective was going to be even better, and it's the best one of all – gorgeous Gloria." Jeff laughed.

"Well, thanks. A girl never tires of that kind of superlative, but seriously – yes, you can trust me with your thoughts, and I'll try to refrain from saying something like 'jovial Jeff.'" Gloria giggled.

"Touche! You win. Well, here goes, and please hear me out before you think I'm crazy."

"Last summer I went to the Philippines on vacation with my parents. We had a fantastic time, and I fell in love with the Filipino people. They are so gentle and servant-hearted, and it ignited something in me I didn't know was there. I've heard it said that when an American goes to a foreign country, he returns home with a greater love for America than ever. Honestly, that wasn't how it affected me. I got a whole new perspective on life. We have so much in this country and take so much for granted, that it is a jarring experience to see the poverty in a third world country. I want to go back and help those people, but I don't think I can do it as a businessman, and that's what I'm studying. Here is the conclusion I have drawn. Are you ready for this? I want to leave college, cash in my trust fund that comes due next year, and simply get on a plane to the Philippines."

Gloria was not expecting such a plan from an all-American guy like Jeff, and her face couldn't hide her confusion. She thought she had made a radical change in her life just a month ago, but Jeff was contemplating something even more radical. "Jeff, I think I can understand your disillusionment with the quote 'American way of life,' but I'm not sure this is God's plan for you. Besides, who do you know in the Philippines, and what would you do when you got there? I do believe that one person can make a big difference, and I know you have gifts and talents, not to mention a work ethic, but it's a question of being in the right place at the right time." She hoped her words weren't discouraging, but this was her gut feeling, and she had to express it.

"Gloria, you're doing exactly what I need. It's testing my resolve, but it only challenges me to think ahead and work out the details. Yes, I need wisdom, not just facts, and one very important thing I need is my parents' approval. I have an idea that Dad is going to give me the 'third degree' on this, and if he can, he may even stop me from getting the money from my trust fund. My mother is another matter. She will be very sympathetic with my desires, but she won't be so quick to give up her son to an unknown future. She's a softie, though. I saw how moved she was when a mob of children rushed us at the airport in Manila. Hardly anyone paid them attention, but my mother rewarded them with smiles, money, and kind words. I was drawn to do the same thing. Dad just walked on ahead and got us to the taxi as fast as possible. But, Gloria, you should have seen their rags and dirty faces that lit up with wide grins when we responded to them. I had to wipe away a few tears, and I still can see them, standing there waving to us as we drove off."

"But Jeff, aren't there missionaries over there doing all they can to help the people? Jesus said, 'The poor you will have with you always,' so it's like trying to drain the ocean with only a bucket and a spoon."

"Gloria, you weren't there. After seeing how you responded to Sarah, I'm sure you would be even more touched than I was to see children living in such poverty." He liked the way she was challenging him. He didn't need someone who would react on a surface level and only give him the advice he wanted to hear.

Gloria didn't want to give in too soon. After all, what if this wasn't God's will for Jeff, and he wasted a lot of valuable time and money pursuing the wrong dream? She didn't want to be responsible for agreeing to something that would be harmful to Jeff and would not further the Kingdom of God. But, wait a minute, if Jeff had never said yes to Jesus, could he even hope to go in the right direction? She had to bring it up. She had to risk rejection. Jeff was becoming more precious to her by the hour, but if he wasn't going to give his life to God, then she, too, would be pursuing the wrong dream. She couldn't advise him any further until he gave honest consideration to the gospel. It was her responsibility. God had brought them to this point, and she had to be faithful.

She sent up an anxious prayer and proceeded to open her mouth, knowing that God would fill it as He had promised.[6] As she began to speak, she was astounded to hear, not words, but a song, flowing like a river from her mouth! Amazingly, she had no sense of embarrassment, and as she boldly delivered her message, her eyes locked with Jeff's eyes. It seemed entirely appropriate to be singing this old hymn. It had to be God. She never would have thought of it herself.

> *The love of God is greater far than tongue or pen can ever tell;*
> *It goes beyond the highest star, and reaches to the lowest hell;*
> *The guilty pair, bowed down with care, God gave His Son to win;*
> *His erring child He reconciled, and pardoned from his sin.*
> *Could we with ink the ocean fill, and were the skies of parchment made,*
> *Were every stalk on earth a quill, and every man a scribe by trade,*
> *To write the love of God above would drain the ocean dry.*
> *Nor could the scroll contain the whole, though stretched from sky to sky.*
> *O love of God, how rich and pure! How measureless and strong!*
> *It shall forevermore endure the saints' and angels' song.*[7]

"Wow!" shouted Jeff. I didn't know you could sing, too. You are beautiful; you have an intellect, and you can sing! I must have done something right, or God wouldn't bless me like this. Wait a minute, what did I say? I've never talked like that before. The words 'God' and 'bless' aren't in my vocabulary. Please forgive me for such a gushy outburst. We've just met, and you probably think I'm strange." Jeff was so emotional that he couldn't hold back the tears, and his words were coming fast and furious as he tried to cover up his wide open heart. It wasn't working. He felt exposed, so vulnerable, so stupid. But he couldn't stop his heart from racing, and he couldn't stop his hands from grabbing Gloria's hands. In just a few minutes she had become the most precious thing to him in his whole life. How was that possible? Surely these feelings couldn't last. Maybe he needed to see a shrink.

Gloria felt an overwhelming sense of God's presence singing that song. She hadn't planned to sing it, but, evidently, God had. Jeff's heart was ready for the seed. She knew it. She could discern that it was seedtime and harvest right now. She didn't dare manipulate things. His hands felt so strong and caring. Her heart was on fire with love for God, but she knew also that she had fallen in love with this man. Tears began pouring from her eyes, too, and she couldn't stop them. As their hands and eyes connected they both felt charged with the desire to draw closer. Jeff looked around and saw no one in the whole area. Then he reached out to Gloria with both hands on her face and tenderly kissed the lips that poured forth such glory. Gloria welcomed Jeff's handsome face and simple kiss.

I've got to keep my mind on You, Lord, but it's awfully hard with this man's warm lips on mine. Quick, God! What am I to say? Here I go again. I'll just open my mouth like before, Lord. But what she heard herself saying, she wasn't expecting. *God is so unpredictable.*

"Jeff, what time is it?" asked Gloria, dreamily. "I don't think I can do anymore to help you with your decision now because I'm not thinking straight." She looked at him and coughed nervously. "I'm glad you liked my song, and I liked your way of showing appreciation. I hope we can keep meeting like this. If you don't mind, I need to say a quick prayer, and I better go."

Gloria didn't ask Jeff if he wanted to pray. She knew that the powerful emotions evoked in both of them had to be contained by the blessing and supervision of a loving heavenly Father. She didn't wait for Jeff to agree. She began, "Dear loving Father, I thank you for my new friend, Jeff Quentin. You are the giver of all good gifts, and Jeff's friendship is Your gift to me. I respect this gift and highly value it. Please show me how to be a blessing to him. You have a plan for every life, and You have a plan for Jeff. He needs Your guidance and the experience of Your great love as shown through the gift of Your only Son, Jesus Christ, to die for our sins and give us eternal life. We both felt Your love just now, and we thank you for that wonderful experience. Help us to glorify You in our everyday lives. In Jesus' name we pray. Amen."

Jeff rose from the sofa, took Gloria's hand, and walked with her to the dorm. Neither of them spoke. Their hearts were still burning, and they knew they would keep meeting. Their lives would never be the same again. Before they parted, Jeff squeezed Gloria's hand, and said, "We need more than a weekly meeting. Let's meet at the chapel again tomorrow at 4:30. Then we can go eat afterwards, okay?"

Gloria nodded, her eyes aglow and heart racing. "I'll be there. In the meantime I'll be praying for you. Good night."

"Good night. Oh, wait, tomorrow I want you to explain the words of that song to me, please."

"Sure thing. I'll bring you a copy of it. Bye now." Jeff stood looking at her as she walked up the steps, turned and waved and flashed her brilliant smile.

CHAPTER SEVEN

A New Friend

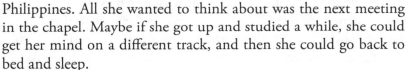

Gloria couldn't sleep that night. Her heart wouldn't be still, and her mind kept replaying over and over that ecstatic moment when Jeff kissed her. She didn't want to think about the future, especially if it involved Jeff taking off for the Philippines. All she wanted to think about was the next meeting in the chapel. Maybe if she got up and studied a while, she could get her mind on a different track, and then she could go back to bed and sleep.

History usually put her to sleep, so she'd try that. She got her textbook and began to read about the Roman World in Chapter Six, "Pax Romana," but Jeff's face was still so vivid in her mind's eye she could hardly concentrate on her homework. After backtracking over the same few paragraphs several times, Gloria realized that anger was building in her spirit. *All this stuff is boring. Besides, I haven't gotten over the first chapter yet, which states that mankind started out as cavemen. How can I believe what this textbook states as fact, when the facts must have been written by people who don't believe the Bible? I believe that Adam and Eve were real people, created by God on the sixth day, just as the Genesis account says. Jesus talked about Adam and Eve, and so did Paul. You can't expect nonbelievers to care about that, but Christians certainly should. Why can't all Christians agree that the Bible account of Creation is accurate?* Gloria knew people at the BSU that assumed evolution was true because they had been taught it in school from an early age.

She wondered if Jeff believed the theory of evolution. She had to talk to him about it and find out if this was discussed in his history class. Studying history to get her mind off Jeff hadn't worked. Her thoughts were just as intense now as before she picked up the history book. She was still running on the adrenaline that kicked in when he kissed her. *How am I ever going to cool down?* Gloria was in agony.

She envisioned herself challenging Jeff. "Why is evolution so appealing as an explanation of our origins? Coming from monkeys isn't a concept that inspires me to achieve something in life. If we weren't made in the image of God and designed by Him for a unique purpose, then what goal can we set in life that is meaningful and worthy of aspiring to?"

Gloria continued her imaginary debate with Jeff. "Being accountable to our Maker must be the reason that evolutionists deny the existence of God. Wanting to run their own lives, they manufacture a belief system that insures no guilty feelings for their sins. They convince themselves there is no God, so there can be no such thing as sin. How convenient for them. But what about Christians? Why do they buy into the foolish lie of evolution?"

On second thought maybe she had better not bring up this issue to Jeff. It could complicate matters, and she knew that the Bible taught her to avoid foolish disputes, and a servant of the Lord must not quarrel. Everything would fall into place in Jeff's life once he surrendered completely to the Lord. Besides, wasn't she jumping to conclusions about Jeff's beliefs anyway?

Gloria decided it was useless to continue studying. Instead she would do some walking in the dorm and transfer her mental energy to physical energy. That would make her body beg for sleep. Going up and down the stairs and walking the halls at a brisk rate was a sure cure for insomnia. Sleeping pills always gave her a hangover, so she would have to try the exercise angle. For better or worse, the romantic feelings had almost dissipated. All she could think about now was getting some sleep.

After several laps up and down the stairs and through the halls, she needed to catch her breath. The plush sofa in the lobby looked inviting, so she plopped down and sighed with relief. It was 1:00 a.m., and it looked like everybody had gone. Her mind was clear at last. Then she heard sobbing. She turned around and caught her breath. It was Sarah, the girl they met at the chapel, and she was almost bent double in anguish, so distressed she didn't even notice Gloria at the other end of the room.

Surely this is no coincidence, Lord. Help me to understand her problem, and give me your wisdom. I can't help but try to comfort her, even if it means being rejected again. Gloria approached cautiously and spoke softly. "You are not alone, Sarah. There is someone who cares."

Startled, Sarah looked up, her face awash with tears. "It's you again. Please let me be alone."

Gloria felt boldness rise up within her, the same as when she broke out into song for Jeff. "Sarah, don't you realize that my meeting you here is no coincidence? Twice in one night? I saw you praying, and if you believe that God answers prayer, then you ought to consider that He might have sent me to you at least as part of the answer to your prayer. Won't you please share your burden with me? You can trust me."

"You surely think a lot of yourself. We don't have anything in common, and I'm sure you wouldn't understand."

Gloria would not be put off this time. "What have you got to lose? My prayer added to your prayer has got to help. The Bible says, 'If two of you agree on earth concerning anything that they ask, it will be done for them by My Father in heaven.'"[8]

Sarah's eyes blazed as she raised her voice. "What Bible did you get that out of? It sounds like the New Testament to me, and that is not part of the Holy Scripture!"

Gloria never expected this. What kind of religion did Sarah practice? If it wasn't Christianity, then why was she in the chapel? Gloria assumed that only Christians used the chapel. Sarah didn't look like a foreigner. Surely she wasn't a Hindu or Buddhist. Gloria refused to be drawn into an argument and gently replied, "Would you tell me what kind of religion you practice?"

"Judaism!" replied Sarah, scornfully.

"Oh, that's great. Then we are kin. I'm Jewish, too, but I now believe in Jesus as the Messiah. He is Jewish, you know. Think of it, Sarah, we share the same Scripture, the Old Testament. We do have a lot in common. Our country is built on Judeo-Christian foundations, which gives us even more in common. Listen, if you don't believe that Jesus is your Messiah, then I respect your belief. Please respect my belief in Jesus and the New Testament."

"You Christians! You have persecuted my people throughout history, and you want me to get over it in a few minutes? If you were really Jewish, you would identify with the Jewish people in their suffering and not with the arrogant WASPs who hate us!"

"I don't even know what 'wasps' are. You surely don't mean flying insects. But your words are stinging me like wasps! Who are these 'wasps' who hate you?"

"White Anglo-Saxon Protestants like you!" Sarah's eyes were blazing.

Gloria was devastated by this accusation and knew there was absolutely nothing she could do to bridge the gap between her and Sarah. She had tried, but she had failed. Suddenly, without warning, she broke down and started to cry. She couldn't stop the raging currents of sorrow coursing through her being from the pit of her stomach. Loud groans spilled out of her mouth. As she looked at Sarah's shocked face, she felt overcome by waves and waves of helplessness, and she cried all the harder.

Sarah couldn't move as she witnessed this phenomenon which continued for over ten minutes. Gradually, her heart began to soften, and she drew closer to Gloria. As her heaving sobs subsided, Gloria looked up and was surprised to see Sarah still there. Bewilderment now replaced the anger in Sarah's face. She pulled a Kleenex out of her purse and offered it to Gloria.

"Oh, please forgive me, Sarah. I have no idea what happened to me. It was so gut-wrenching, and I couldn't stop it, no matter how hard I tried. You must think I'm crazy, and maybe I am. I apologize."

"No, no, don't apologize. I must have caused it when I tore into you like I did. You're the one who needs to forgive me. I'm so sorry. I get caught up in my pain, and I forget that other people have problems, too. While you were expressing your own pain, I realized that you probably don't know what I was talking about. I've found that Jews know the history of Christianity better than Christians do. Anyway I don't hold you responsible for what Christians did to Jews hundreds of years ago. You were only expressing human kindness. My pride wouldn't let me accept your help. Will you forgive me?" plaintively asked Sarah.

"Of course I forgive you, but that outbreak of sorrow was not caused by you. I'm at a loss to explain it. One thing I know is that I feel a tremendous relief now, and at the moment I have one burning desire, and that is to be your friend."

Sarah's eyes brimmed with tears as she reached out for Gloria's hands, and her face was wreathed with a big smile. "Gloria, I will be honored to have you as a friend. I haven't made a single friend since I transferred from Yeshiva University in New York this year, and I have been lonely."

"New York? Really? I'm from New York, too, the Long Island part. Wow! We have plenty in common. Hey, you know what? I've been praying for a good friend ever since I enrolled last year, and at last God has answered my prayer!"

Sarah laughed. "Girl, you are one praying dude! I may not agree with you on the Scripture and the Messiah, but I really like your faith. Yes, we certainly have a lot in common. And we're both girls." Sarah giggled. "And we both live in America, and we both live in Hamlin, and we both frequent the chapel, not to mention both being Jewish and from New York. Wonder what else we'll find in common. I think we're going to be a great pair!"

Gloria felt like dancing all over the lobby. *What a transformation! How did you do that, God? Was my groaning part of it? Will you explain that to me? But don't do it now. Right now I only want to rejoice with my new heaven-sent friend.*

Gloria began to dance and sing as she grabbed Sarah's hands and swung her around.

We're a great pair, and we don't have a care!
With a friend to share, we are dancing on air!
Banishing sorrows in the middle of the night!
Look at us twirling, we're a crazy sight!
Joy from above has invaded our hearts!
We're friends forever, and we'll never part!

Sarah was grinning from ear to ear. "I haven't had this much hilarious fun in years. Gloria, you are a character. You know, this has done wonders for me. I'm not worried any more, and I'm just going to trust God in this situation I've been in turmoil over. We never did actually pray together, but I sense that you touched heaven for me because I'm different from what I was just thirty minutes before. If only we had become friends before roommates were assigned. My roommate doesn't like me ever since she found out I'm Jewish."

"Hey, my roommate isn't crazy about me either. Maybe it does have something to do with being Jewish because I've bent over backwards trying to be nice to her. In fact quite a few of the girls on my floor don't seem to like me. I call them the 'third-floor gang.' Since I know that the Lord likes me, being rejected by them doesn't bother me."

"Do you suppose we may be able to swap roommates? I live on third floor, too. Maybe our roommates are in the same clique or gang, as you say, and they would like the change as much as we would."

"Good idea! What's your roommate's name? I'll bring it up to Rebecca in the morning."

"Jenny Simmons. Could we get together for lunch and compare notes? I'll ask Jenny if she knows Rebecca. What's her last name?"

"Rebecca North from South Carolina." Gloria giggled.

They settled on a plan of action to query their roommates in a tactful manner and then report to each other at the cafeteria at 12:00 noon. Prayer was part of the plan, the key part, they agreed. It was 2:00 a.m. when they left the lobby. Both of them were out like a light and had a refreshing night's sleep. A miracle had happened, and they both knew it.

CHAPTER EIGHT

BUSINESS VENTURE IN COLUMBUS

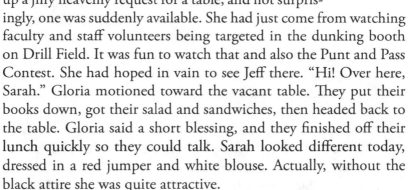

Gloria was prompt for her meeting with Sarah for lunch. Because it was Homecoming week, the cafeteria was really crowded. Gloria sent up a jiffy heavenly request for a table, and not surprisingly, one was suddenly available. She had just come from watching faculty and staff volunteers being targeted in the dunking booth on Drill Field. It was fun to watch that and also the Punt and Pass Contest. She had hoped in vain to see Jeff there. "Hi! Over here, Sarah." Gloria motioned toward the vacant table. They put their books down, got their salad and sandwiches, then headed back to the table. Gloria said a short blessing, and they finished off their lunch quickly so they could talk. Sarah looked different today, dressed in a red jumper and white blouse. Actually, without the black attire she was quite attractive.

"Hey, Gloria. I've got good news."

"So do I," chimed in Gloria. "You see – prayer works. As we guessed, Rebecca and Jenny do know each other, and they had already discussed the possibility of a roommate swap. They figured two Jewish girls could be convinced to room together, Rebecca said."

"Yep, I found that out, too. So when is the move? I'm ready this Sunday if you are. I keep Shabbat, so I can't do it then. Jenny wants to keep our room, and she knew Rebecca would agree, so I'm the one who has to move... and, of course, Rebecca. Neither one of them go to church, so they don't mind moving on Sunday. I'll be all moved in when you get home from church. No sweat. What do you say?"

"That's fine with me. Oh, by the way, we never fully introduced ourselves. My name is Gloria Anna Sondheim. My parents are Alvin and Sylvia. I wish they could have come for the Homecoming game tomorrow and festivities, but it's just as well because football is the last thing on my mind at this time."

A cloud passed over Sarah's face. "My name is Sarah Zipporah Bernstein. My parents, Nathan and Naomi, are deceased," Sarah stated flatly.

Gloria put her hand over her mouth. "Oh, Sarah. I'm so sorry. Does that have something to do with your visit to the chapel?"

"Yes, I was saying Kaddish, a prayer for the dead. The nearest temple is in Columbus, and I don't have a car, so that's why I went to the chapel. I know there should be ten people, but I can't get to temple, so I had to say it by myself. They died two months ago, and I say Kaddish for them every week. They were killed in Israel."

"Were they on a tour?"

"No, they had made aliyah; in other words, they had moved there. Since 1995, they lived in Katzrin on the Golan Heights but were in Jerusalem when it happened. A suicide bomber boarded their bus and blew himself up. Twelve people died, and fifteen were injured. My family in the U.S. flew over there for the funeral. Our parents loved the land of Israel, so we knew that's where they would want to be buried. The family insisted I stay at MSU, since I had just enrolled. So I didn't get to say a final goodbye." Sarah headed for the restroom, not able to keep the tears back any longer. Gloria followed her, praying hard she could give her new friend some comfort.

As soon as Sarah got inside and found the restroom empty, she let go of her grief, and this time she allowed Gloria to hold her and comfort her. *What a blessing this is*, thought Gloria, *to really do some good for somebody. How fulfilling, to be needed. Nothing is more important than relationships. That's what Jesus was trying to tell Martha when she criticized Mary for sitting at Jesus' feet. Lord, help me to really make a difference in Sarah's life and also in Jeff's life. Please comfort Sarah.*

Sarah and Gloria walked out of the restroom, both smiling, and Jeff walked in the front door. "There's Jeff. Come on, Sarah, let's tell him what's happened about our being roommates." She took Sarah's hand and started toward Jeff.

Jeff was astounded that Gloria had Sarah with her, and Sarah looked happy. She didn't look like the same person. This Gloria was an amazing girl. There was never a dull moment with her. This must be another evidence that prayer worked. *I think I'm about ready to pray with Gloria. Things happen when that girl prays.*

As their eyes met, the feelings they had the night before rekindled. It seemed entirely appropriate to greet each other with a hug, but when they did, a warm tingling sensation engulfed them both. *Lord, I wish Jeff and I were alone again, but Sarah is here, and, Lord, I need you to take control of my emotions. Please help me to quit reliving that kiss in my mind. Be in the midst of us right now.*

"Jeff Quentin, I want you to meet Sarah Bernstein. We both happened to be in the lobby of the dorm in the middle of the night, and we have become fast friends. In fact by Sunday afternoon we will be roommates!"

"Any friend of Gloria is a friend of mine. I guess we first met last night at the chapel, Sarah, but now we know each other's last names, so the introduction is complete." Jeff extended his hand.

Sarah couldn't help but be impressed at what a good-looking couple she was getting to know. *It's nice to be included in first-class company like Gloria and Jeff. Another Christian, though, but I guess I might as well get used to it. At least Gloria is Jewish, and Jews are few and far between on this campus.*

"Glad to know you, Jeff. Please forgive me for my behavior at the chapel. I was rude and self-centered, but Gloria has lifted me out of the doldrums." Sarah's face brightened as she shook Jeff's hand.

"Don't think anything of it. We invaded your privacy, and we're sorry about that. You and I are both the fortunate recipients of Gloria's gracious ways, I can see." Jeff looked straight into Gloria's shimmering eyes and spoke to them both. "I'm sorry I can't eat with you. I was coming in here to get some food to take with me on my deliveries. I tried the Union, but the Homecoming crowd was lined up for miles. I need to get started 'cause I've got a lot of deliveries, and they're in Columbus."

"We've already eaten anyway. You're going to Columbus, Jeff? That means you have wheels. You lucky guy!" Gloria had an excuse to look at Jeff, adoringly. How she longed for him to sit beside her.

"I guess I am. I have the best parents in the world, and my new wheels are a gift from them. But I think they overdid it because it's hard to back in and out of parking places with this SUV. But listen, I've got an idea. Do you girls have anything scheduled this afternoon? Did your parents come to Homecoming?"

"No to both questions," Gloria hastened to answer. "You're available, too, aren't you, Sarah?" Sarah nodded in agreement.

"Would y'all like to go with me on my deliveries? It's birthday cakes, and I'm going to MUW. The work will go much faster with two more pairs of hands to deliver the cakes to the rooms." Jeff was excited. "I can have you back for the Pep Rally at 4:00 if you want to go."

Gloria and Sarah looked at each other and grinned. "It's a deal!"

"Follow me." The girls scurried back to the table to retrieve their books as Jeff opened the front door for them. Jeff's beautiful, brand new, golden Ford Expedition SUV was parked right on Lee Boulevard. They climbed in, and Jeff pulled Gloria in beside him. Sarah took note of this and covertly elbowed Gloria in the side. She realized that internal fireworks had just gone off in Jeff and Gloria. Maybe her role would be chaperone. Now she could return the favor of helping a friend. Sarah chuckled to herself.

Jeff explained the birthday cake operation. There were thirty cakes in the back, labeled with the name of the recipient, name of the dorm and room number. Each one would be a surprise from the parents to their daughter or, in a few cases, their son. The method of delivery included a knock on the door and a birthday song, if the intended recipient was in the room, and today was her actual birthday. If not, the cake had to be taken to the contact person Jeff had lined up in a particular dorm. If the contact person was out of the room, the cake would be taken to the person at the desk who would be sworn to secrecy. The cake must be a surprise. The contact person could pick it up at the desk and deliver it on the right date.

Gloria marveled at Jeff's ingenuity. "What a complex operation this is. You must stay on the phone a lot to get all this arranged. I hope you are amply rewarded for this service, and I hope the bakery gives you a good price and a good product."

"Positive on all counts of your observation, Gloria. Another positive is that I have two of the finest delivery personnel anyone could ask for." Jeff winked at them.

"And we're free, too," laughed Sarah.

"Now don't be too hasty, Sarah," chided Gloria. "I was thinking of having a cake at some point in time!"

"You'll do the work first and see what you've earned. Maybe your experience of working in this cutting-edge corporation is your reward, not to mention hobnobbing with the CEO and taking an excursion in the Golden Triangle on my brand new wheels."

Their light banter continued as they drove the twenty miles to Columbus and Mississippi University for Women. Youthful exuberance and the sheer joy of being together on what Sarah considered an adventure was the greatest thrill she had experienced since coming south.

As for Gloria, sitting next to Jeff and hearing him talk eclipsed any previous experience, except for the song capped off by Jeff's kiss. However, as intoxicating as the kiss was, nothing could ever measure up to the explosion of life inside her when she accepted

Jesus Christ as her personal Lord and Savior and began living every moment under His direction. Jeff was occupying more and more of her thoughts and emotions, but she was depending on the Lord to reign over their relationship in every dimension. Her new life in Christ was like a quiet, flowing stream in the depth of her being. Heady emotions on the surface waters of her life could not touch or change this dynamic flow of divine presence and power. She was forever settled in her commitment to the heavenly Bridegroom. Gloria resolved that there would be no compromise with His pre-eminence in her life.

CHAPTER NINE

FINDING RELIGIOUS COMMON GROUND

The cake deliveries went smoothly, and all was accomplished by 2:00, which was necessary, since most students would soon be leaving campus for the weekend. All three met back at the parking lot, Sarah the last to come. When she walked up, Jeff and Gloria were already in the SUV with the air on and sitting as close as possible. Their faces were turned toward each other, but Sarah could observe no kissing. She was glad because she didn't want to embarrass them.

Sarah had an idea. "Hey, guys, what do you say we spend a few minutes touring the ante-bellum homes, not stopping, just driving around?"

"Sounds like a good idea to me," Jeff replied. "What do you think, Gloria?"

"Sure thing. My parents would disown me if I didn't see the splendor of the Old South when I had the opportunity. This kind of thing really turns them on. I'm kind of interested, too."

They followed the signs, going down several streets, and gawked at the magnificent homes. Then Jeff had the idea of looking at the churches of the city, so he turned toward downtown. As they went past the First United Methodist Church with its sprawling additions, Main Street Presbyterian Church, and the First Baptist Church, all huge buildings, the three of them agreed that Columbus should be quite a righteous city if all the pews were filled every week. They knew there were perhaps a hundred more churches within the city limits, so it was an impressive sight for the girls from New York, where church-going wasn't popular and church buildings were scarce.

Spotting a building right next to the First Baptist Church, Sarah spoke up, "Slow down. That's the temple, Temple Bnai Israel."

"What kind of church is that?" Jeff asked, taking the empty parking space right in front of the building.

"It's not a church. It's a temple, or a synagogue, same thing," Sarah explained.

"It's so small," Jeff commented.

"That's because there are few Jews here. This temple serves the whole tri-city area. I knew about it before I moved down here, but I haven't been able to go yet. I don't have a car, and I don't know anyone Jewish who goes to Temple."

"You mean you are Jewish?" Jeff was curious.

"I thought you could tell by this nose of mine." Sarah laughed. "You can't tell Gloria is Jewish though, can you? She has a beautiful nose."

Jeff was shocked. "Gloria, you didn't tell me you are Jewish."

Gloria felt embarrassed, but she didn't know why. "I guess I took it for granted you knew when I first introduced myself to you as Gloria Sondheim. That's obviously a Jewish name. You haven't told me much about yourself either. And Jeff, we haven't told you why Sarah was grieving in the chapel yesterday. Her parents were killed in Israel only two months ago."

"Oh, Sarah, I'm truly sorry. That's awful. What can we do to help?" With great compassion Jeff reached over to put his arm around her. Gloria joined in the hug, and Sarah allowed them to comfort her as hot tears came to her eyes. Gloria pulled out a Kleenex as she remembered that Sarah had done the same for her last night. Sarah clung to Gloria intensely, and they could both feel the bonds of friendship growing tighter.

Jeff needed more time to process this heavy new data. "Hey girls, why don't we go get an ice cream and head back to State?"

"Sounds like a winner," said Gloria.

"Ditto," said Sarah. Jeff cranked the car, found McDonald's on Highway 45, picked up the cones at the drive-thru, exited to Highway 82, and they were on their way back to Starkville.

"Well, girls, how did you like your first day on the job with Quentin Services Unlimited?"

"It was fun and good exercise, too." For emphasis, Gloria panted. "Going up and down stairs is the quickest way to lose weight, and in air-conditioning comfort to boot. Thanks, boss, for the opportunity. Now where is my cake?"

"Hey, I thought you wanted to lose weight."

"Well, **I** don't." Sarah chuckled. "Give **me** the cake. I'll make sure Gloria only gets a small bite."

Gloria elbowed them both. "Take that!"

"Seriously, girls, I could use your help every Friday. That's when I make the deliveries at MUW. I already have helpers at State. You'll get a small check at the end of every month."

"Ooh!" Gloria squealed and rolled her eyes. "My daddy will be proud of me. He's always saying, 'If your outgo exceeds your income, your upkeep will be your downfall!' Ha!"

Sarah had a sober attitude. "Jeff, I'm most grateful for this offer. I need the money, and if you need help with bookkeeping, I can do that, too. Accounting is my major. "

Jeff's face lit up. "As a matter of fact, I **do** need a bookkeeper. The business is getting over my head. Thanks, Sarah. Can the three of us meet at the State Fountain Bakery for a late breakfast? I'll bring the books and explain everything to you, Sarah. We'll be through in plenty of time for the game. You can start right away, I hope?"

"I'm sorry, Jeff, I can't. Tomorrow is Shabbat. I don't work. I just rest and study the Tanakh and the Talmud."[9]

"What about tonight then? I'm not planning to go to that Bob Dylan concert." Jeff wondered what these terms, Shabbat, Tanakh, and Talmud, meant.

"Shabbat starts at sundown tonight, so that's not a good time either. I'm sorry to disappoint you."

"Well, I don't mind getting together Sunday morning if that suits you."

Sarah looked confused. "You don't go to church on Sunday morning?"

Gloria had been silent while Jeff and Sarah talked, but she couldn't hold back any longer. "What's going on here? God really has a sense of humor, doesn't He? Bringing three people like us together? Here I am, wild about Jesus and in church every Sunday. Sarah, you are a loyal Jew, following the religious traditions of your people, and Jeff, you don't have any religious background at all. If we're going to be working together every week, we've got to make an effort to meet on common ground. I say we pray together right now in this car and ask God what His plan is in all this. Do you two agree?"

Neither Jeff nor Sarah could argue with Gloria's simple logic. Both of them had seen Gloria in action, and they knew God listened when she prayed.

Jeff had a suggestion. "I've got one thing to say, Gloria. I'm keeping my hands on the wheel and my eyes wide open. You two can close your eyes if you want. Go right ahead and pray."

Sarah agreed. "Yes, Gloria, pray for us."

Gloria took a deep breath and pictured the Lord Jesus in her mind as she addressed God. "Father, this has been an exquisite day, and You gave it to us! Thank you, thank you. You are the master designer of this beautiful creation, and you are our Maker. We are Your workmanship, created in Christ Jesus unto good works, which You have before ordained that we should walk in them.[10] O God, help us to walk in them. You have a plan here in bringing the three of us together. Speak to us and show us how to honor You and give You pleasure as we make choices in our everyday lives. We submit all our plans and dreams to You, Lord. You are our Shepherd. We shall not want. You make us lie down in green pastures. You lead us beside the still waters. You restore our souls. You lead us in paths of righteousness for Your name's sake. Even though we walk through the valley of the shadow of death, we will fear no evil. Your rod and Your staff, they comfort us. You prepare a table before us in the presence of our enemies. You anoint our heads with oil. Our cups run over. Surely goodness and mercy will follow us all the days of our lives, and we will dwell in the house of the Lord forever.[11] We love You with all our hearts, Father. In Jesus' name we pray."

Sarah squeezed Gloria's hand tightly, and Jeff, with hands gripping the wheel, turned toward Gloria and lightly kissed her on the cheek. It was a holy moment, and they were comfortable with the silence for the remaining minutes as they approached the campus.

"While you were praying, Gloria, I had this idea. See what you both think. If they have a service at the temple tonight, I can take all of us there. Then on Sunday morning the three of us could go to Gloria's church. Is this crazy or what?" He figured there would be plenty of time later to discuss business.

Conflicting emotions and thoughts tumbled over each other in Sarah's mind, but before she could state her reservations, she found herself saying, "Of course that is a great idea. Shabbat service starts at eight o'clock. Let's do it!" *Did I really say that? We will be driving back after sundown, and that breaks the Sabbath. What has come over me? After being around Gloria, my mind doesn't function the same. Forgive me, HaShem,12 for this one exception.*

Gloria was overjoyed that Jeff had agreed to, not one, but **two** worship services the same weekend. On top of that, she could finally explore her Jewish roots. Wow! God was up to His same old tricks, answering prayer in the strangest of ways. "Jeff, you are wonderful. God has spoken through **you**. How can we refuse? Two trips to Columbus in one day and with my two favorite people. How blessed I am."

"Okay, girls, I'll pick you up at---?"

"Hamlin dorm," they both answered.

"I guess it goes without saying that we won't meet in the chapel today." Gloria was thinking it was probably just as well anyhow, since it was getting harder to trust herself around Jeff. God was protecting her. There would be other times when they could be alone, she knew.

"Right," agreed Jeff. "Maneuvering in this traffic on Home-coming weekend won't be easy, but I'll see y'all at 7:20. Meet you at the desk, okay?"

"I'm not going to the Pep Rally. We'll have plenty of time. See you soon." Gloria answered enthusiastically, and Sarah heartily agreed.

As they parted company, they were aware that Gloria's prayer had launched a whole new dimension in their lives. God was real, and He was interested in them, this they knew.

CHAPTER TEN

TEMPLE SERVICE

Jeff went to the dorm, intending to spend some time studying World History, but he kept thinking that this would be his first date with Gloria. Someone else would be along, but it still was an official date, even though they were going to a worship service. Of all things, a worship service! How unproductive, he thought, in light of all the school work and the business piling up on him. Gloria's face kept parading in his mind, and he also saw himself wrapping his arms around her and kissing her.

What has come over me? I'm a pushover for that little beauty. It is so out of character for me to be spending my Friday night going to a temple and my Sunday morning going to a church. Besides, I was looking forward to being with Gloria alone at the chapel this evening. That song she sang did something to me, and I want to know more about the meaning and why it affected me the way it did. Of course I believe in God. I always have. Now Jesus, I hadn't given him much thought, but if he's important to Gloria, I've got to understand more about him.

Jeff made a supreme effort to begin studying, but his thoughts were continually drawn back to Gloria. *So she's Jewish, huh. And Sarah, too. I don't think I've met any Jews before. I've heard people make jokes about them, but I don't see why people are prejudiced against them. After the Holocaust it looks like people everywhere should consider that the Jews have suffered enough, but now the Palestinians in Israel are trying to 'drive them into the sea,' as they say. Their hatred of the Jews reminds me of the Nazis. I wonder if Sarah's parents were killed by a suicide bomber. How gruesome. I'm not going to bring it up. Gloria can fill me in later.*

Jeff needed to read about the Romans, but he couldn't concentrate on history. He only wanted to daydream about Gloria. Her

radiant face, effervescent personality, and reverent prayers filled
him with wonder. But the kiss, that took him into another realm.
He had kissed girls before, but no one had captivated his heart like
Gloria. He had never gone farther than a kiss with anyone, a rare
thing in sex-saturated American culture, he realized. Hopefully,
Gloria had never given herself to anyone in that way either. *But wait
a minute, why would I care about that, unless I want her as a wife?
Whoa, Jeff! Don't go there. You've got plans to go to the Philippines, to
do something significant with your life.*

That reminded him of what Professor Holder had said in history class last Wednesday. It caught Jeff's attention when he said,
"You may be thinking, 'Why do we have to learn what happened
hundreds of years ago? How does that affect my life today?' Well,
history repeats itself, and if we don't learn from the mistakes of
those who have gone before us, we are doomed to repeat the same
mistakes. The Romans made many lasting contributions to civili-
zation. They built roads. Their architecture was magnificent. They
gave the world some of the finest literature known to man, and they
produced many outstanding thinkers and scientists. Unfortunately,
they became a decadent society, and within that decadence were
the seeds of their destruction."

Professor Holder could see he wasn't getting through to the
class, remembered Jeff, but the class was jolted awake when he
said, "I have an assignment for you that will help you to see the
value of studying the civilizations that have gone on before us. But
instead of focusing on the many, I would like for you to focus on
only one of the many. If you study what people of the past have
done, how they succeeded, and how they failed, it will help to
shape your own life. Learn from them. Then make your plans if
you want to do something significant in life. Who knows? Maybe
you can change the world! I have a list of famous people to hand
out to you. This is your homework. Choose one, find out what one
significant contribution they made that is affecting your life today,

and write a three-page paper on it. It will be due next Wednesday. Class dismissed."

That phrase, "if you want to do something significant in life," stirred Jeff's heart. Yes, that is exactly what he wanted to do. He hoped there was a person on the list that would inspire him. Maybe he was about to get some concrete answers. He needed to go to the library for this assignment, but it would have to wait till tomorrow. There was only enough time now to take a shower and get dressed.

Jeff stood in front of the mirror. *Not a bad looking guy. Wonder how I look to Gloria. I'll ruffle up my hair – I don't want to look too neat. Oh, yes, the perfect after shave. The girls love it. Hey, Jeff, get ahold of yourself. You don't really care – you can take 'em or leave 'em.* He laughed at himself for such juvenile thoughts and said out loud, "Get real, Jeff. Let's go."

It was 7:15 sharp, and Jeff walked in Hamlin Dormitory as Gloria and Sarah walked up to the desk. They signed out, noticing that the girl at the desk had dropped her jaw. Priscilla Caldwell could hardly believe that a boy as gorgeous as Jeff would be taking two Jewish girls out on a Friday night. "Y'all have fun now." She winked at Jeff. "Be careful." she winked again with a mischievous grin.

Gloria set her straight. "We're going to worship, and we **will** have fun, but we don't have a care in the world. She fluttered her eyelids at Priscilla. "Come on, y'all." Gloria used an exaggerated southern drawl, milking the scene for all it was worth. "Bye now," she threw back at Priscilla, as she linked arms with Jeff and Sarah and made a grand exit. Priscilla was left with that "Well, I never" expression on her face as the threesome scampered down the steps and into the SUV.

They were soon on their way to Columbus with the usual seating arrangement and accompanying warm feelings. Gloria showed Jeff a music sheet. "I brought the words to the song you wanted."

Jeff smiled. "How about reading it out loud so Sarah can hear it, too?"

"Okay. Here it is." Gloria read with expression:

The love of God is greater far than tongue or pen can ever tell;
It goes beyond the highest star, and reaches to the lowest hell;
The guilty pair, bowed down with care, God gave His Son to win;
His erring child He reconciled, and pardoned from his sin.
Could we with ink the ocean fill, and were the skies of parchment made,
Were every stalk on earth a quill, and every man a scribe by trade,
To write the love of God above would drain the ocean dry.
Nor could the scroll contain the whole, though stretched from sky to sky.
O love of God, how rich and pure! How measureless and strong!
It shall forevermore endure the saints' and angels' song.

"That is beautiful," commented Jeff. Sarah agreed outwardly, but inwardly the thought of God having a Son was repugnant to her. "But who are 'the guilty pair'?" Jeff wanted to know.

"That means Adam and Eve. You both know the story in Genesis, don't you?"

This was Sarah's territory. "Yes, I've read the first book of Moses many times. Genesis is called 'Bereshit' in Hebrew. It means 'In the beginning.'"

At that moment Jeff hated his ignorance. "I vaguely remember it. Refresh my memory, Gloria."

"I realize that most people don't believe this is literally true, but I do. I'll tell the story. After God created all there is in six days, he rested on the seventh day. Adam was formed by God's hands on the sixth day and was the crowning masterpiece of all His creation. He was given the job of naming all the animals and of tending the garden God planted and put him in. Adam noticed that all the animals had mates, but he did not have one, and he was lonely. God decided to make a helpmate for him, so He put Adam to sleep and did surgery, forming Eve as a wife for Adam out of a rib in his side. When God brought Eve to Adam, Adam said, 'Wow! She's perfect!' Actually, that's not in the Bible, but surely the 'designer original' woman must have been a knockout." Gloria laughed. Sarah covered up her disgust.

Jeff went with the flow. "If Eve was so great, then Adam must have been an Atlas."

"You Christians really do take a lot of liberties with the Scripture," scolded Sarah. "The Jews treat the Scripture with such reverence that if a scribe who copies it by hand makes only one mistake in a section of a scroll, the entire section of the precious parchment is destroyed. If, after a scribe has copied the entire five books of the Torah, it is discovered that he himself does not believe the Scriptures are divinely inspired, the parchments are taken out and buried! And a worn out Bible is never thrown away, but is given a sacred burial in the ground."[13]

Gloria knew she needed to apologize. "Sarah, thank you for setting us straight. I really do love God's Word, and I don't intend any disrespect whatsoever."

"Go ahead, Gloria. You were telling the story right, and we can discern when you're reading between the lines," chided Sarah.

"Okay, here is what Adam really said: 'This is now bone of my bones and flesh of my flesh; she shall be called Woman, because she was taken out of Man.'" As Gloria continued, she looked at Jeff, "Therefore a man shall leave his father and mother and be joined to his wife, and they shall become one flesh." Jeff was looking straight ahead at the road, but she could see his face turning red, and she knew she must be blushing, too. Sarah was not unaware of this emotionally-charged moment.

"Keep going, Gloria. What about the 'guilty pair'? I know what they did, but I want to hear you tell it," insisted Jeff.

"God had given them **everything**, plus fellowship with Himself on a daily basis, but in order to test their love for Him, he gave them a command, only **one** command. He wanted them to obey Him because they loved Him, not because they had no other choice. It's hard to understand why the God of the universe needs anything from us humans, but this shows us that He has a great need for our love, which is demonstrated by our obedience. Adam and Eve were perfect creatures in a perfect environment with their every need met, including fellowship with the One who made it all, but they failed the test."

"They were warned not to eat of the tree of knowledge of good and evil, but when Satan in the form of a serpent tempted them, they used their free will to disobey God and satisfy their own desires. They sinned, and shame filled their hearts. God came looking for them, knowing they needed to confess their sin in order to be forgiven. They did just what we do today. They played the blame game. God brought them up short by pronouncing judgment on the three of them, beginning with the serpent."

Gloria's audience was rapt. Sarah ventured, "I've never heard it quite like this before, but everything you have said is true, even though it is not the exact wording of the Scripture. Please go on."

"Even though God's judgment has affected all mankind up to this very day, He gave us hope of a Redeemer who would come, and paradise would be regained. That hope is stated in Genesis 3:15, and it is the first promise of the Messiah. It's amazing that it was made in the context of the curse on the serpent. I had to memorize it in my BSU Bible study. Here it is:

"And I will put enmity between you [Satan] and the woman [Mary, the mother of Jesus], and between your seed [Satan's kingdom of darkness] and her Seed [Jesus]; He [Jesus] shall bruise your [Satan's] head, and you [Satan] shall bruise His [Jesus'] heel."

Sarah was aghast. "Gloria, you don't know what you're talking about! I don't want to argue, but you have interpreted that wrong. The woman represents Israel, not Jesus. I know that Christians use many of the prophecies of the Messiah in the Tanakh to point to Jesus of Nazareth, but the writers of the New Testament were just trying to make what Jesus said and did **FIT** the prophecies. There is simply not enough evidence that the New Testament is a valid document," blustered Sarah.

Gloria held to her convictions and refused to be offended, but she could see she had touched a nerve and knew she was treading on dangerous ground. "Oh, Sarah, please forgive me for being so insensitive to your beliefs. I already knew that you don't believe Jesus is the Messiah, so I should have just quoted the verse and not inserted the commentary. Will you forgive me?" Gloria pleaded, looking at Sarah with utmost kindness.

Sarah hesitated, her feathers still ruffled. "Well--- yes...., I will," replied Sarah in a tentative tone.

Jeff felt like he ought to be the referee, but he also knew he was way out in left field. He didn't want to cause more damage, so he remained silent.

After a few more miles, Gloria made a statement in her most enthusiastic voice. "We're almost there. I can't wait to experience the Shabbat service. Mom and Dad never would let me explore my Jewish roots, but now at last I can! I'm depending on you, Sarah, to explain everything to me."

Brightening, Sarah replied, "Sure. It won't be hard to follow. The service is in English and Hebrew, but mostly English. Some of it will be sung. I'll keep you on the right line in the Siddur – that's the prayer book. Hope the people are friendly. It will most likely be a rare thing to have visitors, so we should get a lot of attention."

Jeff parked the SUV right in front of Temple B'nai Israel. Sarah noted, "The sun has set, so it is now the Sabbath. Shabbat Shalom!"

"Huh?" said Jeff.

"That's the Sabbath greeting in Israel at sundown every Friday evening. My brother in Jerusalem went to the ulpan, which is a school for learning Hebrew. He writes us regularly, so when we visit Israel we will know some of the Hebrew phrases. This one means, 'Have a peaceful Sabbath.' You're supposed to answer, 'Shabbat Shalom!'"

"Shabbat Shalom!" chimed in Jeff and Gloria, as they all got out of the SUV.

The people were gathering outside the temple as the visitors walked up. Introductions were made, and soon they were ushered inside. Jeff was handed a kippah. He looked puzzled. Sarah leaned over and whispered, "Put it on your head. All the men wear them. It's a kippah, Hebrew for 'covering.'"

Jeff whispered back. "I've seen it on T.V. – the Jews at the Wailing Wall in Jerusalem."

There were about twenty people in attendance. They all looked like normal people to Jeff, except for the men wearing the little caps. Then he spotted the elaborate, lighted cabinet at the back of the stage with some things covered in blue velvet and gold displayed. As they waited for the service to begin, Jeff asked Sarah for an explanation.

"That cabinet is called the Aron Kodesh, or Holy Ark. Remember the Ark of the Covenant that God instructed Moses to make? It houses the Torah scrolls, the Word of God, just as the Ark in the wilderness held the stone tablets of the Ten Commandments."

"I remember the movie, *Raiders of the Lost Ark*, and how God's power was connected with that little gold box." Jeff was glad he wasn't completely clueless.

Sarah frowned. "That movie raises a lot of questions as most Bible movies do. I prefer to get my truth right out of the written Scriptures."

"What exactly is the Torah?" asked Gloria.

"That's the Hebrew name for 'instruction.' It consists of the five books of Moses – you call them Genesis, Exodus, Leviticus, Numbers, and Deuteronomy. The Greek equivalent is Pentateuch. It is the most revered part of the Tanakh because it came directly from God to the Israelites, His chosen people. It has the same books as your Old Testament. God spoke the Ten Commandments audibly to the people at Mt. Sinai. The rest of the Torah is what God spoke only to Moses, who wrote it down and relayed it to the people. Also God instructed him to write about everything that took place in the wilderness journey and put that together with the parchments that had been passed down from the time of Adam. The Rabbi will read from the Torah tonight in the original Hebrew." Sarah was excited.

"Sarah, why are the coverings on the scrolls so ornate?" asked Gloria.

"The Torah scrolls are treated reverently. They are even dressed like a person, with a crown and a breastplate. Some of them are worth thousands of dollars. Many Arks, too, are elaborate and costly. The largest one in the world is in Jerusalem. It is 40 feet high, weighs 18 tons, is partially gold-plated, and will hold 70 Torah scrolls! My parents saw it and told me about it. But the appearance of the Torah scroll and the Ark is not what counts. It is the Word of God that is contained within it. We have to remember that." Sarah was in her element now. Jeff and Gloria were giving her their undivided attention.

The rabbi came up on the stage donned in his tallit and kippah. Jeff stared at the rabbi and his tasseled prayer shawl, straining his brain to remember why this sight was familiar. Then it hit him. *So that's what my Papa Cohen was, a rabbi!* He almost gasped audibly. *Oh, God, I wish he were here. Why did he have to die?* Then it began to dawn on Jeff that he had a heritage he knew nothing about. He had better pay attention to what went on here tonight. He could get some clues to his past that his mother had withheld from him. *Why did she do it? She loved her father, but she resisted his Jewish ways. Why?* Jeff agonized in his thoughts.

The rabbi walked toward the Aron Kodesh, and the people stood. Then he prayed:

"Avinu sh'baShammayim – Our Father in heaven, Yitgadal v'yitkadash – Magnified and sanctified – be his great name throughout the world which he has created according to his will, and may he establish his Kingdom in your lifetime and during the life of all the house of Israel, speedily and at a near time; and say ye, Amen."

The rabbi opened the Ark, took out a Torah scroll, and handed it to his assistant. The man took the Torah out into the congregation and walked down the aisles. The people reached out to touch it with their prayer books or prayer shawls and then touched them to their lips.

Jeff made sure he touched that precious thing that meant so much to his beloved grandfather. At the moment he touched his hand to his lips, he felt a prayer rise up from the deepest place inside him. *Our Father in heaven, open my eyes to the wonders of Your Word, and help me to reconnect with my heritage.* Gradually, he realized that He could talk to God about anything, just like Gloria did. He continued. *And God, show me if Gloria is to be my wife. If she is, then show it to her, too, please. As Gloria says, "In Jesus' name."* This was his first attempt at prayer, and it amazed him how natural it was, how easy. He felt much better.

The assistant returned to the stage and helped the rabbi remove the covering and place the scroll on the pulpit. Sarah whispered, "The raised platform is called the bimah."

The rabbi began to read the Scripture in Hebrew, then in English. The reading was Deuteronomy 34 and selected portions from Genesis 1:1 to 6:8. Jeff and Gloria gasped. As the rabbi read the very words that Gloria had just quoted in the car, a tingle went up Gloria's spine. She squeezed her companions' hands. Sarah whispered, "I'll explain that later."

A woman was called up from the congregation, and she read I Samuel 20: 18-42, a passage about David and Jonathan and King Saul's pursuit of David. Jeff paid close attention because he had never heard the story before, and it appealed to him.

Many responsive readings followed, and Sarah kept her charges right in sync with the congregation. Gloria noticed that the readings, minus the Hebrew, were similar to those in the churches she had attended, only longer. Then the rabbi began his message which was entitled, "True Friendship." He talked about the bond between man and wife, the bond between friends, and the bond between God and man. The examples were Adam and Eve, Jonathan and David, and, finally, God and Enoch. Although the rabbi's delivery was low-key, his content was well organized and thought-provoking. Gloria was delighted that she would have a lot to talk about later with Jeff, and she anticipated he would have questions. She prayed earnestly that the Holy Spirit would inspire Jeff to read the Bible diligently, and that God would speak to him right out of its pages.

Gloria missed the spirited singing she had been enjoying at the BSU and at Adaton Baptist Church outside Starkville. The Jewish service had songs and chants in Hebrew throughout the readings, and the music was unfamiliar to her. Her heart longed to break out in song. She decided she would make melody in her heart instead, while the people were singing.

> *I worship You, Almighty God. There is none like You.*
> *I worship You, oh Prince of Peace. That is what I want to do.*
> *I give You praise, for You are my righteousness.*
> *I worship You, Almighty God. There is none like You.*[14]

Her heart began beating faster as she sang silently. Then the tears started coming. She loved the Lord so much. If only she could impart her love for God to Jeff. Sarah seemed to be content in her Judaism, but Gloria knew there was a place in her heart that only Jesus could fill. She resolved to pray more fervently for both Jeff and Sarah.

Jeff noticed Gloria's tear-stained cheeks and handed her his handkerchief with a questioning look in his eyes. Sarah was engrossed in the prayer book and didn't see. Gloria squeezed Jeff's hand extra hard. He wanted to hold Gloria so much he could hardly restrain himself. *Down, boy*, he admonished himself.

Sarah whispered, "Stand up. This is the closing prayer of the Kaddish."

The rabbi intoned, "May He who makes peace in His high places make peace for us and for all Israel; and say: Amen."

As in most churches, the people here also came alive after the benediction. Several made a beeline for the visitors to give them warm handshakes and encouragement to come again. The visitors felt very welcome among these people. Sarah explained to several that she would be coming as often as possible, but her two friends were churchgoers. When she said this, the smiles grew wider and handshakes heartier. They made sure no one could accuse them of being narrow-minded or exclusive.

After they had returned to the SUV, Jeff said, "I really did enjoy that, and I learned something, but I have a lot of questions. Could we go to a restaurant and talk it over?"

Sarah was first to answer. "I already ate dinner, but a piece of pie and coffee would be great."

Gloria nodded vigorously. "You bet!"

"I know just the place, girls – Harvey's, and it's close by. All agreed?"

"Drive, James," Gloria commanded.

"Yes, ma'am!" They all laughed as Jeff cranked up the SUV.

CHAPTER ELEVEN

JEFF'S HERITAGE REVEALED

The place was dark except for candlelight. The booth also contributed to privacy, so Jeff was anxious to get started on his questions. As soon as the waitress got the orders he began. "There is so much I want to ask about the service and also about you two girls. We've got a lot of getting acquainted to do. First, what was that you wanted to say about the Scripture reading, Sarah?"

Sarah loved the role of teacher. "Yes, it was quite a coincidence that we had been discussing Adam and Eve in the car, and then the rabbi read that same Scripture."

Gloria was excited. "I have to tell you, that we shouldn't think it as a coincidence. It is a **GOD** incidence. I am sure of it. He is making all this happen."

Sarah agreed. "You must be right, Gloria. These coincidences, or rather God incidences, keep happening, and it makes me more aware of God's presence than ever before in my life. Anyway, on the Jewish calendar, Sukkot, or the Feast of Tabernacles, was celebrated this week, ending the High Holy Days. Rosh HaShanah, which is the Jewish New Year, and Yom Kippur, which is the Day of Atonement, preceded Sukkot. The Torah readings were completed tonight on Simchat Torah, which means 'Rejoicing in the Law.' Deuteronomy 34 is the last chapter, and we begin the cycle again at Genesis 1, reading through the Torah each year. The Jewish year is 5758. Today is the 18th day of the month of Tishrei, which is the first month on the civil calendar."

Gloria marveled. "Wow! That's a lot to take in, Sarah. I'm Jewish, but I'm ashamed to say that is new information to me."

"Yes, it's all very interesting," pondered Jeff. "How did the Jews arrive at that number 5758?"

Sarah was glad to answer. "That's how long it has been since God created man, five thousand, seven hundred and fifty eight years."

Gloria's eyebrows went up, and Jeff began to object. "That can't be right. Scientists know that the earth is millions of years old because of the fossils and strata in the earth."

Gloria was alarmed. *Oh, no, I hope he doesn't believe in evolution, but I'm sure God doesn't want me to talk about that now.* "Very interesting, Sarah. You mean the Jews believe that man was created less than 6,000 years ago? That's neat. I learned in Bible study that in the 17th century an Archbishop in Ireland, James Ussher, computed the age of the earth, arriving at the date of creation as 4004 B.C. He added the ages of the 21 generations of people in the Old Testament, beginning with Adam and Eve. He used other facts from the Bible itself, and it took him twenty years.[15] He also used Babylonian, Greek, and Roman sources.[16] That means 4004 B.C. plus A.D. 1997 equals – let's see–" Gloria drew on her napkin. "That's 6001. Pretty close, I'd say. Amazing!"

"We call it B.C.E., though, not B.C.," corrected Sarah.

"B.C. means 'before Christ.' What does B.C.E. mean?" Jeff was impressed with Sarah's knowledge.

"It means 'before the current era.' Also, Jews use C.E. instead of A.D."

Gloria knew this was a delicate matter, but still she ventured to explain. "B.C. means 'before Christ,' that is, before His birth. I used to think A.D. meant 'after death,' until someone explained to me it stood for Latin words, Anno Domini, meaning 'in the year of our Lord.' You'll have to admit that the life of Jesus Christ, whatever you believe about Him, was the dividing point of history, since all dating systems are affected by the time He was born."

Jeff could see red flags, as he observed that Sarah was getting ready to reply, but the waitress came just in time. *Must be a God incidence, as Gloria would say.* "Here comes our pie! M-m-m, my favorite, pecan pie." Jeff licked his lips.

"And my favorite, apple pie with ice cream," said Gloria.

"Mine's the best of all, blueberry cheesecake." exclaimed Sarah.

After the happy threesome devoured their desserts and coffee, they settled back in the booth, ready to find out more about each other. Jeff started the conversation. "Let's leave all the issues and talk about our individual lives. We seem to be pretty different from each other, so this should be interesting. I'll start with myself. I was born in Tupelo, Mississippi, to Jeffrey and Leah Quentin. I'm a junior. My dad, Jeffrey M. Quentin, Sr., is the son of Everett and Joyce Quentin of Tupelo. They died five years ago within six months of each other. My mother is the daughter of John and Rachel Cohen, and she grew up in Chicago."

Sarah and Gloria looked at each other in surprise. Sarah said, "Then your mother was Jewish! That means you are Jewish, too!"

Jeff felt like a bombshell had been dropped. "Cohen is a Jewish name?"

Sarah replied, "Of course. It's the Hebrew word for 'priest.'"

"Oh my, gosh!" Jeff clapped his hand over his mouth. "I didn't realize that. Living in the South hasn't brought me in contact with Jewish people, at least not until now."

"Well, join the club, Jeff. We're all Jewish. First, I don't know any Jewish people down here, and now all my friends are Jewish." Gloria was clearly delighted.

Jeff was puzzled. During the Shabbat service it had been revealed to him that his grandfather was possibly a Jewish rabbi, but he hadn't yet figured out that he, too, was Jewish. Jeff protested weakly. "I thought you were Jewish if your father was Jewish."

Sarah was glad she could tutor these two ignorant Jewish people. "Well, in Israel's Law of Return of 1970, "a 'Jew' is a person who was born of a Jewish mother or has become converted to Judaism and is not a member of another religion."[17] However, the Israeli government today accepts those born to either a Jewish mother or a Jewish father as qualified for citizenship.[18] In fact, my brother Abe told me this is a hot topic in Israel among the religious parties. But even the most ultra Orthodox rabbis today say that if you would have been sent to Hitler's gas chambers, you can come live in the state of Israel. Hitler killed anyone with even a trace of Jewish ancestry!

"You mean if my father is a Gentile, and my mother is a Jew, as their child I am considered Jewish?" Jeff had to get this right. This was going to change his life. "Even if my mother didn't want to be Jewish and didn't practice Judaism?"

Sarah explained patiently. "Yes. You are bona fide Jewish. What do you know about your grandparents? Surely you were exposed to their Jewish lifestyle, or were they assimilated Jews like your mother?"

"Assimilated Jews? You got me again, Sarah. I don't have the foggiest idea what that is."

"Assimilated Jews are those Jews who want to hide their Jewishness. They want to blend in with the Gentile world. They don't keep the Jewish holy days, don't keep kosher – that means the dietary laws and customs about food and the kitchen – and don't attend temple or synagogue. In short, they act like Gentiles, whether they go to church or don't go anywhere. They often marry Gentiles and raise their children in a Christian or non-religious home. Several generations later some of these Jews don't even know they are Jews."

Gloria eyes were getting wider and wider. "You have almost described my parents, Sarah, but not quite. They know they are Jews, and they don't exactly hide it, but they move around in the Gentile world with ease. In fact, so do I. All my friends in high school were Gentiles, although I didn't think to label them that way. It was natural for me. The only holiday my parents ever pay attention to is Passover, but that is because my grandparents, Samuel and Anna Sondheim, invite us to their house every year for Passover."

Jeff was beginning to understand. "It looks like my mother is a classic assimilated Jew, to the point that she even hid my Jewishness from me. As for my grandparents, they died in a car wreck when I was five years old, so I didn't get to know them very well. I really regret that. At the temple tonight when I saw the rabbi in his prayer shawl and kippah, an image of my grandfather came to mind. Papa Cohen looked just like that. I loved him. Mother wouldn't allow me to go to the funeral, and I cried for days and days."

"Oh, that's terrible." Gloria was indignant. "My parents would never do that. Our visits to Chicago have been few and far between, but if anything happened to Mama Anna and Papa Sam, I know my parents would have all the family members at their funeral, no matter how young. I can't imagine why your mother did that. I guess she didn't want you to have to deal with death, but it turned out to be more traumatic for you not to go." Gloria wondered if Jeff was feeling the effects of it even now. She reached over and patted his hand.

"I appreciate your caring, Gloria, but that was fourteen years ago. I dearly loved my grandmother Rachel, too, but I don't re-member as much about her as Papa Cohen. The thing that stands out in my memory the most is the way Papa would put on his kippah – now I know the name of it, thanks to you, Sarah – and prayer shawl and sit in the big chair with what must have been the Bible – or maybe you would say Torah or Tanakh, Sarah. He would read a while, then close his eyes, and start rocking back and forth. He wouldn't let me in his lap at those times, so I just watched. If my mother came in the room, she would frown and tell me to go outside and play. Sometimes when the grownups didn't know I was listening, they would get into heated arguments. Most of it was between Papa and my mother, and I think it had to do with the Bible. After that it would be a long time before Papa and Mama would come for another visit. And you know what? I don't remember one single time that we went to visit them. That's kind of strange, don't you think?" Jeff looked at Sarah.

"Well, from the way you have described it, Jeff, I would say that your grandparents were Orthodox Jews, and your mother wanted no part of it for herself or for her children," explained Sarah.

"I'm an only child," added Jeff.

71

"You are? I am, too." Gloria was engrossed in Jeff's story and finding out that they had more in common than she ever suspected.

Sarah continued her insights. "Something must have happened to your mother, perhaps in her childhood, which caused her to rebel against her parents and their beliefs. It could have been a reaction to the Holocaust. The Jews who went through the Holocaust were mainly Orthodox from Eastern Europe and Russia. That means that most of the six million Jews that Hitler destroyed were religious. There is now in Israel and the rest of the world a whole generation of atheistic Jews who were born to Orthodox parents. The vast majority of survivors of the Holocaust became atheists or agnostics. Their reasoning was this: If a God such as described in the Bible exists, He would never have let the Holocaust occur."

Gloria couldn't help but interrupt. "I have struggled with that, too, but I won't let myself dwell on it because I know that Jesus suffered more than any other person ever suffered. God allowed that, even planned it, and Jesus obeyed the Father's will. He was resurrected, and His death brought us life, so there's a happy ending to the story. Please don't be offended, Sarah, but I couldn't help but say that. It is the very core of my beliefs, and you already know I believe it strongly."

"It's okay, Gloria. I won't interfere in your love affair with Jesus, but I will say that 'love is blind.' I've heard Christians try to prove that Jesus is the Messiah from Isaiah 53, but any religious Jew will tell you that the 'Suffering Servant' refers to Israel, not Jesus. Who could have suffered more than the Jews?" challenged Sarah.

"Sarah, I haven't been saved but a month, so I don't even know what Isaiah 53 says. I've been to church all my life, and my parents approved and even encouraged me, but I've still got a lot to learn, especially about the Old Testament. I'll be sure to read that chapter. Maybe the Lord will show me something. I won't do it just to argue though. I only want to learn more about my Savior. Whether that chapter refers to Him or not, He certainly was a suffering servant. I want to be more like Him every day." Gloria's sincerity touched Sarah.

Jeff was in deep thought. "Yes, I've always known that Mother was troubled about something. She has a heart of gold, but there is a wounded part of her. My Dad has been an anchor for her. They love each other very much, and they have showered me with love. I am thankful for my parents and the happy home they've provided for me. I guess there's only one thing I have lacked, and that is religious understanding. My folks never took me to church or taught me the Bible. As a consequence, I didn't see the need because my parents seemed to be fine people without it. They aren't atheists. They believe in God, but Jesus has never been mentioned. Sarah, you've given me a lot to think about. You, too, Gloria. I'm so much richer than I was three days ago."

The three gave each other 'high fives' just as the waitress brought the check. Jeff boasted, "The rich guy will pay for it."

Gloria and Sarah dug into their purses, and with Jeff's contribution, they left the waitress a fat tip. Yes, rich was the word for it. Their relationship was paying rich dividends. They all wanted more and soon. The ride back to Starkville went swiftly as the conversation was light-hearted and free, centering on the rabbi's message of "True Friendship." Talking about Adam and Eve and David and Jonathan was educational for them, especially Jeff, who had had no previous Bible knowledge. However, the word 'covenant' pertaining to all types of friendship bonds, whether marriage, filial, or spiritual, really resonated in Jeff and Gloria. Their stolen glances increased as did their heartbeats. Sarah always felt included and valued, but she wisely planned to give them more space at the end of the journey.

"It was a wonderful evening. The Orthodox don't permit driving on the Sabbath, but it was the only way I could go to temple, and I feel no condemnation from HaShem at all. Jeff, I can't thank you enough for taking us to the temple service." Sarah jumped out of the SUV. "Gloria, you are a gem. I love you both and can't wait to see you again on Sunday. I better get to my room. Biological necessity, you know." They laughed.

"We love you, too. See you Sunday morning at ten o'clock," shouted Gloria. "We're going to Adaton Baptist Church, and the service starts at ten-thirty. Meet you at the desk." Sarah was soon out of sight.

Jeff inclined the front seat slightly, intending to sit there with Gloria for a while. "Now I can feast my eyes on you, sweetheart, without having to watch the road. Do you feel like singing?"

"Ha! Ha! I know what you're thinking, and I'm thinking that, too. I love what you called me," cooed Gloria as she looked at Jeff with unabashed longing.

"There's no doubt about it. You are sweet as they come. If Jonathan and David could make covenant, why can't we?"

"Jeff, darling, we already have. Remember, we've been calling ourselves friends for three days."

"Did you say 'darling'? I love that. Keep saying it. And could we upgrade our relationship from friend to sweetheart?" Jeff's face inched closer to Gloria's.

"Does that mean sweethearts to each other and to no one else?" asked Gloria, dreamily.

"No one else, darling. I know the term is a very old-fashioned word, but I like it better than calling you my 'steady girlfriend.' I look at it as sort of a covenant thing. So I'm asking you, will you be my sweetheart now and forever?"

Gloria wanted to give her response in a "designer original" way, so with her heart thumping wildly she put her arms around Jeff's neck and kissed him with all the passion she could summon.

Jeff felt like he had just knocked a home run. His lips met hers eagerly. Then he kissed her eyes, her cheeks, her forehead, his arms holding her tightly. Coming up for air, they continued embracing and kissing. *This is a greater* **DELIGHT** *than Adam ever had.*

Gloria sighed. *I want this man forever. I don't know if this is romance or love or what, but it's just got to be perfect in God's sight.*

"Bone of my bone and flesh of my flesh" – that's what I want. That's what we are destined for.

Five minutes passed, and Gloria called halt. "Jeff, sweetheart, you know I have to go now. There's no one I'd rather be with than you, but God says there's a time and place for everything. Let's do it God's way."

"You are absolutely right, sweetheart. You go to my head, and God must be in charge. Let's talk more later about the covenant thing. I truly love you, and I want it to be forever."

With as much self-control as she could muster Gloria got out of the SUV and waved goodbye. "See you Sunday morning at 10 o'clock, sweetheart."

"I won't breathe till I see you again, sweetheart." Jeff waved goodbye.

CHAPTER TWELVE

PERSECUTION

Rebecca North and Jenny Simmons were delirious with joy that they could finally be rid of their Jewish roommates and be together night and day. There was only one fly in the ointment – they had to wait until Sunday afternoon to make the move. Saturday morning early would have been the logical time, and it infuriated them to have to wait. As Jenny aired her feelings to Rebecca, she spit on the floor in disgust. "How stupid that Jews have to keep those old outdated laws in the Old Testament. They're still living in the Middle Ages!" Her voice got louder and louder. "God, if there is a God, doesn't care what day you worship him. Sunday is the holy day anyway. That's the day some businesses close, but that's archaic, too. If you ask me, fundamentalist Christians and Jews are not very different – they're both narrow-minded."

Rebecca couldn't agree more. "You said it. I came here to get away from my narrow-minded parents, and then I got saddled with a narrow-minded roommate. Yuck! My roommate is worse than yours when it comes to religion. Gloria is Jewish, but she behaves more like a Fundy than a Jew. She goes to church or that other religious place on campus every time the doors are open. When she gets back, she sets her sights on getting me 'saved.' That's what she calls it, but I call it 'get put in prison!'"

"Well, at least I haven't had to put up with that," said Jenny. "Sarah doesn't have much to do with me at all. But it's worse. She tries to make me feel like scum with all her holy stuff. She puts a scarf over her head and prays. I think it's Hebrew. She mutters under that scarf and reads her holy book. I don't think it's a Bible. I can't tell, and I'm not about to ask. She cries a lot, too. I've tried to talk to her, but she only answers my questions and doesn't say anything else. I found out she transferred here from a university in New York."

"Yeah, my roommate's a Yankee, too. And she's also from New York. No wonder they wanted to get together. Well, all I got to say is good riddance!" scoffed Rebecca.

The two girls were sitting on Jenny's bed. Knowing that Sarah would spend the whole day in the chapel, they felt completely free to get on with their relationship. It wasn't long until their hand-holding progressed to kissing and intimate conversation. Rebecca got up to pull the blinds and lock the door. They were determined to get the full benefit of their private love nest.

In Suttle Dormitory, Pete was trying to sleep. It was 9:00 a.m., but he had planned to stay in bed until noon. The only thing on his agenda was the Homecoming game with Central Florida at 1:30. Unfortunately, his conscientious roommate had awakened at 7:30 and interrupted his sleep, which was more drunken stupor than sleep. Jeff Quentin was one weird guy, always working or studying, never taking time out to party, Pete thought. He didn't really care. They went their separate ways, but on Saturdays sleep was a priority with Pete, and Jeff's agenda was anything but rest. He talked on the phone, he pulled drawers in and out, and generally made a lot of racket. Pete had just about had enough. "We're not compatible, let's face it!" he blurted out, suddenly slamming his feet on the floor and standing up.

Jeff had been doing his bookwork, getting ready to turn everything over to Sarah. He had tried to be as quiet as possible, but soon he had forgotten that Pete was still in bed. He knew Pete had a reason to be angry, although his noisiness was not intentional. "Hey, don't lose your cool, Pete. I'm sorry I've been disturbing your sleep. I thought I could sit right here at the desk and finish up my bookwork, as well as make contacts for the business, and catch up on my school work. Saturday morning is the only time I have to do the accounting, but I can see I'm not being fair to you, Pete. I'm really sorry. Tell you what, if you can get another roommate,

I'll see what I can do about getting myself an apartment. What do you think?"

Scratching his head and rubbing his eyes, Pete straightened up and smiled. "Now ya talkin'. Sounds like a good idea. I've got a friend that wants to move out of an apartment and into the dorm. He says it's too crowded. I'll talk to him about it today. Thanks, Jeff. I didn't expect you to understand my dilemma, since you aren't a party animal like me." Extending his hand to Jeff, he said, "Let's shake on it."

Jeff had nothing against Pete, but he knew they had totally different lifestyles, so he might as well make the break. He could afford the apartment. He'd look for one today. "Sure, Pete." They shook hands.

There was at least one person on campus who was oblivious to Homecoming. It was 4:30 in the afternoon and time for Sarah to get back to the dorm. She had been at the chapel since 11:30 that morning, and her hunger was getting unbearable. Maybe she could take a quick nap, and then it would be time to go eat. The Sabbath would be over, and so would her fast. Fasting was a spiritual discipline she had learned at Yeshiva University. She had to do something to reach God. She could not continue to bear this heavy weight of grief. HaShem had to give her some relief and some answers. Why did He allow it to happen? What good could possibly come from it? Her parents had feared for their lives in New York only to meet their fate in the Land of Promise.

She had studied her Tanakh and Talmud and prayed from the Siddur for five hours. This was a record for her. She did this not only for her grief but also because she needed spiritual stamina for the big change she was facing. A Christian roommate. She already loved Gloria and even admired her, but she knew Gloria would try to convert her to Christianity, and she needed strength to resist. She hoped she had made the right decision to room with a Christian. At least Gloria had a Jewish background, although it looked like her life wasn't affected by it. On the other hand, Jenny was a worldly person, and she and Sarah had nothing in common. Rooming with her only deepened the loneliness Sarah felt since coming to Mississippi State. So, evidently, it was HaShem's will that she room with Gloria. She brightened at the thought that she could help Gloria explore her Jewish roots.

Oh, how she missed her friends at Yeshiva University and her sister Chaya and husband Max in New York. Sarah was the youngest of six children, and her brothers and sisters were protective of her, especially since their parents were gone. Her oldest brother Abe and his wife and children lived in Israel. Except for Chaya, the others had spread out all over the United States, choosing small towns with low populations of Jews. There was no danger of any of them being assimilated, however. They would always follow the Jewish traditions. That was the result of their strict upbringing and the strong community they enjoyed before February of 1993. They would keep their Jewish identity, but not so openly.

Since the bombing of the World Trade Center in 1993, the Jews of New York had suffered an increase in anti-Semitic attacks. Her family was especially affected because her father, Dr. Nathan Bernstein, professor of Jewish history on the Wilf campus at Yeshiva University, had been in the World Trade Center on that fateful day. He was called as a witness at the trial. This subjected the entire family to persecution throughout the ordeal of the trial which lasted for six months until the conviction on March 4, 1994, exactly a year after Mohammad Salameh's arrest. But that wasn't the end of it. More conspirators were arrested, and it was still dragging on into 1997. Ramzi Yousef, the mastermind, was on trial, and his vitriolic speech was primarily vented on Israel.

Sarah's parents had been visiting Israel regularly even before the 1993 WTC bombing, learning all they could about the country and studying Torah with Rav Nachman Bulman at the Kiryat Nachiel community in Migdal HaEmek.[19] It was at this beautiful area in the upper Galilee where their love for Eretz Yisrael grew. Nathan and Naomi's faith kept them strong during the trial, but the continuing persecution finally wore them down. The last thing they wanted to do was leave New York because that would mean abandoning Dr. Bernstein's work at the University. But after Salameh was convicted in 1994, they made the radical decision to move to Israel the next year.

Sarah moved in with her sister Chaya. She had begun to develop her independence a year before her parents made aliyah. She enrolled at Yeshiva University High School in Queens, having a subway commute each day.

It seemed the whole family became paranoid after their parents were killed in Jerusalem, and Sarah was the focal point of their concern, being the youngest member of the family and unmarried. Sarah insisted that she wasn't afraid, living in New York. After all, her parents weren't killed in New York but in Israel. Nevertheless, right after the funeral the family got together and made a radical decision to send Sarah as far from New York as possible, both geographically and culturally. What better place than Mississippi State? They reasoned that Jewish life was not pronounced, although there were Jewish people in Starkville and a temple close by in Columbus. It was regretful there was no conservative synagogue, but a reform temple would have to do. Surely it would be harmless to Sarah's spiritual growth as long as she continued the disciplines she had learned at home and at Yeshiva High School and University.

Sarah had demonstrated her independence, and they felt she would be much safer in Mississippi than in New York. Everyone knew that the highest concentration of Jews in the world was in New York, and after what they had learned about the Islamic terrorists' plots against them, it seemed that Mississippi would be the perfect haven for Sarah. That left Chaya and Max as the only part of the family still remaining in New York. Max was adamant that New York would always be his home.

The game wasn't quite over, but people were beginning to leave the stadium. Sarah decided to run to the Union and get a drink. As she left the chapel, she realized someone was right on her heels. Sensing danger, she walked faster, and made it across the street just in front of a passing car. Looking behind her, she saw a dark-skinned man, impatiently waiting for the car to get by. He ran across the street, and before Sarah could get in the door of the Union, he grabbed her arm and shoved something hard in her side.

"This is a gun. Act like you know me, and keep walking in the direction I'm leading you. If you keep quiet, you won't get hurt. I only want to ask you some questions. Then I'll let you go." The man looked like a Palestinian or some other Middle Eastern type, similar to the faces of the WTC bombers she had seen in the newspaper. His voice made her cringe. His face was contorted with hate, and she felt an immense evil in his presence. She was smart enough to know that he wouldn't shoot her right here in broad open daylight with students milling around. With all the courage she could muster, she made her decision.

"I'm calling your bluff, you deranged idiot. You don't scare me. I'm about to yell my head off, and you'll soon be behind bars, if you don't let me go. Run for it, and I'll be quiet," she dared him.

"You Jewish slut! I'll find you alone somewhere. You can bank on that," he retorted in an acid tone, as he hurried off.

Sarah was running on pure adrenaline as she chased him until he was out of sight. She was hoping to see if he got into a vehicle. Her eyesight was excellent, and she may have been able to read the license plate or at least recognize the make and year of the car. Unfortunately, there was not a sign of him.

Out of breath and near the point of collapse, Sarah managed to get inside the Union, get a cup of water, and plop down on a sofa. Jeff's roommate, Pete, had left the game early, and he had seen what happened to Sarah. Now he approached and asked if he could sit down by her.

CHAPTER THIRTEEN

A SHIELD

Pete was studying Criminal Justice, so maybe he could do some on-the-job training right here. His investigative skills could be honed on this case with the first step of interrogating the victim. Yes, he had an ulterior motive in what he was about to do, but his overriding emotions were anger at the attacker and concern for the frail girl who was about to come apart at the seams.

Sarah had run out of fuel by the time she downed the water, and now her whole body began to shake. She thought no one was noticing her, so she would just sit here and try to get hold of herself. Conflicting thoughts were colliding in her head, and she couldn't make her limbs stop trembling. A gentle voice interrupted her thoughts.

"May I sit down here?" asked Pete, his eyes showing compassion.

Ordinarily, she would have said, "Sure, but it's time for me to leave now." Somehow she couldn't make her body move, and the stranger looked non-threatening. His presence even brought a measure of relief, due to his kind eyes and gentle voice. *He must be close to seven feet tall!* Sarah thought.

"Yes," she answered as steadily as possible. She couldn't let this stranger see her fear. She could handle it, if she had just a few more minutes to relax.

Tenderly, Pete began, "I saw what just happened out there with that evil-looking guy. I want to help." He sat down next to Sarah, but not too close.

Sarah was surprised and grateful. "You did?" Relief swept over her, and she couldn't hold back the tears any longer. She was embarrassed, but it felt good to cry.

83

Pete's heart was moved, and he wanted to reach out and hold this fragile little girl in his arms and assure her he would see to it that she was absolutely safe. He didn't dare do it though. He had such a bad reputation when it came to women, and he knew one of his buddies might see him and misinterpret the whole thing. He had to be real clinical about this, like a policeman – detached and objective. That's what they were teaching him in the criminal justice classes. But surely a little human kindness wouldn't hurt.

Patting her arm, he said, "Go on and cry. Those emotions must come out, so you can think clearly. I could tell the man intended you real harm. I don't know what you did or said, but it sure did the trick. He was running like a scared rabbit. Do you mind telling me what happened? This probably needs to be reported to the Campus Police."

Sarah sat up straight, alarmed at his suggestion. Her voice trembling, she insisted, "Oh no! Please don't report it to the police. That will put me in more danger. He may be only one of a whole group of violent men."

Pete hadn't expected this response. It went against all his pre-conceived ideas of handling crime. "But you need protection. That man is still at large. He needs to be put behind bars."

"Even if he were behind bars, he could still direct his evil plots with the help of others who aren't behind bars."

"You sound like you're talking about a conspiracy."

"I've had experience with this before, and I've learned some things the hard way."

Maybe conventional methods of police work aren't going to work, he pondered. But he still wanted to "stay on the case" whether it helped him academically or not. This girl needed protection, and somebody had to step in. It was out of character for him. Usually, a female was a female, but this girl was different. For want of a better word, he'd have to say she was a lady. Something in his heart wouldn't let him walk out of the picture.

"Please don't think I'm leading you on, but I care about your vulnerability. You can see I'm a pretty big guy, and I already said I'd like to help. Would you consider me being your shadow? Before you refuse, I'll guarantee you I won't get in the way of anything you want to do. I'll just be in the shadows, watching, and making certain that guy doesn't come near you again. Sound like a good deal?" Pete was hopeful she would agree.

Sarah was thinking this stranger was too good to be true, wanting to help her like that. He was pretty good-looking, too, but she chided herself that looks didn't matter. What did he know anyway about hate and about being Jewish? He appeared to be one of those typical All American WASPs. How much should she tell him? Could he be trusted? Maybe if they could talk for a while, she could discern what kind of person he was and if he was genuinely interested in her.

"Yes, that sounds like a good deal, but I'm not sure I'll take it yet. I don't even know you, and you don't know me. Why should you take up a lot of your time, looking out for a total stranger?"

This girl is not a raving beauty. She needs to gain a few pounds, and her nose isn't perfect, but she is very attractive. I am impressed with her courage. Her clear olive complexion, full lips with just a hint of color, her velvety black eyes, and her wavy, shoulder-length dark brown hair add up to about a 'nine' in my book.

"Ya know you got a point there. I can't really answer that. I guess it's like this – I saw a damsel in distress, and I didn't want these muscles I've been punishing myself to develop to go to waste."

In spite of herself, Sarah laughed. Pete rolled up his sleeve, flexed his muscle, and boasted. "Get a load o' that! It cost me some blood, sweat, and tears."

By now Sarah was enjoying the attention of this funny, hand-some guy. His blond hair was the real thing, and his twinkling blue eyes and freckled nose gave him an innocent appearance. Her wari-ness of strangers was waning. Touching his muscle lightly, Sarah exclaimed, "Ooh, what a big, strong man you are, Brutus!"

Pete was delighted that the wall between them was coming down. He extended his hand. "My name is Peter Carson, alias Pete the Crusher."

Sarah clasped his huge hand which was twice the size of hers, and pumped it up and down, laughing. "My name is Sarah Bernstein. And please don't crush my hand. Are you a wrestler or something?"

"Actually no, although I have won a few wrestling matches. My major is Criminal Justice. Part of my motivation in talking to you was to hone my investigating skills, but I'll have to admit I don't care about that now. It seems your type of case may not be in the textbooks anyway. Truly, and I hope you believe this, my only motive is simply to provide some protection for you. Do you believe that?"

"That's a pretty good line. I've never heard that one before." Her eyes twinkled. She needed to test his honesty, although her heart told her he was sincere.

"Okay, you'll probably find out anyway, so I'll tell you. I do have the reputation of being a womanizer, but I swear that was no line. I really meant it. I do want to help you. Please give me a chance," Pete pleaded.

Sarah was convinced this guy was good-hearted and telling the truth. She made the decision to accept his help, sending up a quick prayer to HaShem. "All right, I'll take your offer, but I don't know what kind of recompense you want."

"Please don't think I want some kind of reward. Let's just say this is my community service. You've heard of volunteer work, haven't you?" However, he knew full well he wanted a relationship with this girl. But it would be on a different level from the other girls. He needed to turn over a new leaf.

"You're hired." Sarah laughed. "My own private bodyguard! What will Gloria and Jeff say?"

Pete's eyebrows went up. "Gloria and Jeff who?"

"Gloria Sondheim and Jeff Quentin, the only friends I have at Mississippi State. Gloria and I will be roommates when I move in tomorrow."

Pete was incredulous. "I can't believe this. Jeff is my roommate, but he's moving out!"

"You're letting a nice guy like Jeff Quentin move out? What happened?" Sarah was worried.

"I guess that does cast a bad reflection on me because you're right – Jeff is a nice guy. We didn't have an argument or anything. It's just that we're so different, and....." Pete felt embarrassed.

This really puzzled Sarah and gave her second thoughts about Pete. He could see her expression change from being open to gradually closing. In light of her reaction Pete could see his error clearly. With his head down he apologized. "I need to confess that I've been a jerk. Jeff is as fine as they come, but I've been totally selfish. He's a workaholic, and I've been living like a bum, with no consideration for his needs. Talking to you has changed my perspective. We only made the decision this morning, so maybe I can get him to stay, and I'll promise to be more cooperative. I better go take care of that, Sarah. I want to be a person you can trust. Would you be willing to walk with me to Suttle, so I can at least leave a note for Jeff? He's out and about and won't be there, I'm sure. If I hurry, I can undo what was done this morning."

Sarah was beginning to really like this guy. His transparency was disarming. "Yes, I'll walk with you, and then you can start your guard duty by walking with me to Hamlin," she said, smiling up at Pete.

As they went outside, Sarah's attention turned to the people swarming the campus now that the game was over. She took note of several dark-skinned foreigners, trying to discern whether they were Asians, Indians, Hispanics, Africans, or Arabs. She had not realized until now how many foreign students there were. Some of them had on their native dress. Those were easy to identify. Others could have been home-grown Americans. She wasn't sure.

"Pete, I know that was a Middle Eastern man, probably a Palestinian terrorist, who tried to attack me," she said in a low voice as they walked. "I'm Jewish, and he knew that, but that may not have been his only motive."

"Oh, you're Jewish? I've never met anyone Jewish before."

"Do you still want to protect me?" Sarah searched his eyes for any trace of prejudice.

Pete's brow furrowed. "Of course, dear lady. Don't doubt my chivalry. From the little bit I know about the Jewish people, I'd say it would get me in bad trouble with God to leave one of the chosen race in danger when I had the power to prevent it."

Sarah was ready to tell her story. "I'll tell you what happened. I was leaving the chapel, when I felt someone right behind me close. I ran across the street to the Union. The man was held up by a car, but he was soon on me and grabbed my arm tight. Then he pushed something hard in my side and told me it was a gun, to keep quiet, and he would let me go after he asked me some questions. I suddenly felt very bold, not afraid at all, and I threatened to scream at the top of my lungs, knowing he wouldn't shoot me out in the open. I dared him to run, and I would be quiet. He ran off, and I chased him, but he got away."

"Yes, you really looked fierce chasing him. You put the fear in him, girl. But how do you know he thought you were a Jew?"

"He called me a Jewish slut, and he said he would find me alone. He didn't scare me at all, only made me angry. It was after I sat down in the Union that I went to pieces, thinking what might have happened and what might still happen." Fear was returning to the pit of her stomach.

Pete put his arm around Sarah and looked down into her eyes. "He won't touch a hair of your head, I promise you that, but I'm not sure I'd recognize him if I saw him again. Describe him, everything about him, his height, his clothes, et cetera." Pete gritted his teeth with determination.

Sarah was not ready for this kind of closeness, even if in her best interests, so she unwound Pete's arm and smiled up at him appreciatively. "He was not tall, maybe just a few inches taller than me. Um, let's see… he had a slight mustache, and his hair was jet black. It wasn't combed but stuck up in the back, and he needed a haircut. His skin was very dark, and his white teeth were crooked. He had on a faded red and black checkered flannel shirt, long sleeves, and he was sweating. He stunk! His shoes were black tennis shoes. I can't remember the pants, but they were dark. His voice was high-pitched and full of hate. That's about all I can remember."

"You remembered a lot. If we had photographs, could you pick him out, you think?"

"Possibly."

"Maybe we could find his picture in a yearbook, unless he's a freshman."

"I doubt it. If he's the type I encountered in New York, he has wormed his way in here and probably isn't enrolled as a student."

"You're from New York?"

"Don't tell me you haven't guessed by now, with my accent and all?"

"Yes, I could tell you weren't one of us southerners. I'm bona fide 'south of the Mason-Dixon line,' and I guess you can tell it, right?"

"Yes, I can. Jeff is from Tupelo. Where are you from?"

"I'm from Columbus, just a few miles down the road. But back to the Middle Eastern man… what do you think he wanted to question you about?"

"It probably had something to do with the trial of the suspects in the 1993 World Trade Center bombing. My father was a witness."

"Oh……." Pete was deep in thought. Here was Suttle. He hated to leave Sarah by herself even for a minute, but surely she would be safe in the lobby. Several people were there, and he made sure she

89

sat close to them. He quickly bounded up the steps to the fourth floor. That was part of his fitness regimen.

As Sarah waited, her thoughts went back to the chapel and the Psalm she had read over and over.

"Thou, O Lord, art a shield for me, my glory and the lifter of my head. I cried unto the Lord with my voice, and He heard me out of His holy hill." (Psalm 3:3)

That's what Pete is, a shield! HaShem must have sent him! First the Holy One had given her boldness and courage to fend off her attacker, and then He had sent Pete to act as her shield against her enemies. All that fasting and praying.... and HaShem heard. Yes, He heard. She was not alone here in this strange, new place. HaShem had sent Gloria, then Jeff, and now Pete. "Oh, how good you are, Adonai Eloheynu,"[20] she muttered under her breath. "Whatever I have to face, I know You are with me. I was downcast, but now my head is lifted up!" Sarah began to sing softly, "Hodu L'Adonai, ki tov, ki le'olam chasdo ...."[21]

Pete hadn't been gone two minutes when Jeff Quentin came in the door.

CHAPTER FOURTEEN

THREE FRIENDS FOR SARAH

Jeff was startled to see Sarah sitting in the lobby of his dorm. "Hey, Sarah. What brings you here?"

Sarah knew her appearance in the lobby of a men's dorm must be a little disconcerting to Jeff. She couldn't help blushing as she replied, "Jeff, what a coincidence. Pete just went upstairs to leave a note for you, and suddenly here you are. I was waiting for him. I know your next question is, 'How do you know Pete?' I'll answer before you ask," she said, nervously. "The truth is I've only known him less than an hour. It will take a while for me to explain---"

At that moment Pete bounded back into the lobby. He was surprised to see Jeff talking to Sarah. Putting out his hand to shake Jeff's hand, he said, "Hey, roommate. I'm glad to see you. You know Sarah, right?"

"Yes, I've come to know two beautiful girls in the space of three days, and Sarah is one of them," Jeff said, smiling at Sarah. "Say, what did you want to see me about? Sarah said you were leaving me a note."

"I was trying to stop you from getting that apartment. I have a confession to make. Please hear me out. I've been a lousy roommate, and if you'll stay, I'll reform my ways," Pete grinned, self-consciously.

"Well, pal, I'll be glad to reconsider. I didn't get anything done anyway, being as it's Homecoming. Hmm–it looks like this new lady friend must have had some influence on your life," Jeff suggested.

Pete tucked his head, a little embarrassed. "Let's just say she helped me to see you in a different light," he chuckled.

The sun was going down, and Sarah's hunger suddenly came to her attention. "Guys, I've got to leave. The hunger pangs are getting fierce. Vegetable pizza, here I come! Anyone who wants to join me is welcome!" she shouted over her shoulder as she hurried out.

"Wait, Sarah, I'm coming!" Pete dashed to catch up with her, calling to Jeff, "Come on, let's go have pizza with Sarah." Jeff quickly came to the conclusion that food combined with Sarah's explanation of meeting Pete would definitely be worth his time, so he chased them to the Union.

When they got to the front of the building, Sarah balked and sat down on a bench. Pete and Jeff looked at each other, and Pete voiced the obvious. "Just like a woman to change her mind."

"Sorry, fellas. I'm waiting for the sun to completely set. Then Shabbat will be over. Normally, I don't fast, but since I made a vow not to eat until sundown, I have to carry it out. You two go ahead, and I'll join you in about five minutes."

"No way. I'm not leaving you," pledged Pete. "Besides, I don't like cold pizza, and my mama told me not to start eatin' until everyone was seated and we had the blessin'. Is that what your mama taught you, Jeff?" Realizing Sarah wasn't moving, they sat down.

"My mama didn't even tell me I am Jewish," replied Jeff. He thought it would be interesting to drop a bombshell on Pete.

Pete exclaimed, "You're both Jewish! First I had never met anyone Jewish, and now I find out my roommate is Jewish, and my girlfriend is----"

Sarah looked hard at Pete, and Pete hastened to explain, "I mean 'my new friend who happens to be a girl' – is Jewish."

Ignoring Pete's predicament, Jeff said, "Speaking of girlfriends, I wish mine was here and could join us."

"I think I know where she is," Sarah offered. "She went to the game but planned to leave after the half to work on a history paper at the library. Maybe she will come to the Union for supper."

"That's a coincidence," Jeff marveled. I also have a paper to do for history, due next Wednesday, and I was headed to the library when I saw y'all, as I was stopping by to get my notebook. I have to write about a famous person who made a significant contribution that has affected our lives today."

"Talk about coincidence. That was the subject of her paper, too. You must have the same history professor."

"My professor is Dr. Holder."

"Hey, that's her professor, too. And she wouldn't call this a coincidence, if you know what I mean." Sarah laughed.

Pete felt like an outsider. "Could you let me in on what y'all are talkin' about?"

Sarah rose to her feet. "We can talk about it over pizza, okay? Shabbat is over, and I need to go celebrate the answer to my prayers. I just hope the Union isn't too crowded now that the game is over."

Pete shook his head as he got in step with Sarah. "A celebration? That's something else for you to explain. Looks like we're having a long meal time, but I'm not complainin,'" said Pete playfully.

Jeff's gaze was fixed on a coed coming their way. "Wait a minute. I think this just might be Gloria." It was hard for Jeff to contain his excitement.

"Is it really Gloria?" asked Sarah. All three of them were looking at the approaching figure.

"Looks like a cool chick," commented Pete, as the girl came closer.

"I wouldn't say 'chick,' Pete. That girl is beyond such an ordinary description. She's almost like a goddess, Hey, it **IS** Gloria."

"Another God incidence!" exclaimed Sarah. "How many have there been today? It's like that Christian song, 'His eye is on the sparrow, and I know He watches me–'"

Pete was beginning to catch on, and he marveled that he happened to be in the company of such interesting people. "I can't wait to meet this chick, uh--, I mean goddess."

Gloria's face lit up like the lights of a football stadium when she caught sight of Jeff. He was with Sarah, but who was that tall, blond guy? *I'm thrilled that I don't have to wait till tomorrow to see*

Jeff. I was getting so hungry to be with him again. It looks like I'll have to share him with these other two, though, but God knows best.

"Hello." Gloria greeted them. "Amazing finding you here. Are you guys going to eat? That's what I was doing."

Pete was a people person and knew how to fit in with most any group. He jumped right in. "Yes, it's a God incidence! We just happened to be here at the exact time you walked up. Glad to meet you. I'm Pete Carson, Jeff's roommate." Pete reached out to shake Gloria's hand.

"And I'm Gloria Sondheim, Sarah's roommate-to be." Gloria flashed her gorgeous smile again. Then she shook Pete's hand and reached over and hugged Jeff and Sarah at the same time.

"Sarah, you didn't tell me about Pete. You didn't either, Jeff," she scolded.

Sarah was getting impatient. "Can you hear my stomach growling? It must be drowning out everything you're saying," she laughed. "Let's get some pizza fast, and then we can talk and talk and talk. Thank goodness, it's not very crowded in here."

"Race ya," Pete challenged as he led the way. Gloria and Jeff followed slightly behind Sarah, hand in hand.

The pizza was loaded with all the fixings, except Sarah didn't want meat. And they ate until they were stuffed, with Pete way out in front on the number of pieces consumed. How sweet it was, this care-free college life in the fall of the year in the deep South, where "fish are jumpin', and the cotton is high." The conversation was light and free-flowing, with gastronomic delight the top priority. The Dawgs beat Central Florida, Homecoming was over, and now it was time to relax and enjoy friends. Dessert followed pizza – ice cream for the boys and brownies for the girls. Afterward, the talk gradually shifted gears to more serious topics.

"If God arranged this, does that mean He approves of pizza?" joked Pete.

"Aw, Pete. Don't blame God for our gluttony," reprimanded Jeff.

"I was just jokin'. Actually, I've never heard the expression 'God incidence,' but I like it. It gives you the idea that God is in control," said Pete.

"Well, He is, Pete," assured Gloria. "Ever since I gave my life to Jesus, it has been a wonderful adventure. I can see God's hand in every instance. There's no such thing as luck, but everything that happens to me is being orchestrated by God. It gives meaning and purpose to me. I want to be in the center of God's will and to fulfill His plan for my life. I found out that I am God's workmanship, created for good works that He has already planned for me to do. Isn't that exciting?" Gloria looked at the three of them for agreement.

Pete was obviously affected by what Gloria said. She had some novel ideas, he thought, but ideas worth exploring. Maybe she was right. He would keep listening and try to put it all together in his head before he said anything.

Sarah had a tough time listening to Gloria once the name "Jesus" was spoken. It was hard to get past that point in her thinking, but she did agree that God seemed to be orchestrating her life these past few days. It was just that Gloria kept being personal with the Almighty. That seemed irreverent to Sarah. But how could Gloria be so vibrant, so confident, and so glowing? Undoubtedly, she believed what she was saying with all her heart. A big question loomed in Sarah's spirit.

"It's exciting when all happenings are positive, but what about the negative events? I struggle with that, although I think HaShem just showed me that He answered my prayer," reasoned Sarah.

"Yeah, I wanted to ask you about that. You said you wanted to come in here to eat pizza and celebrate the answer to your prayers," said Pete. "What did you pray?"

"Well, today was Shabbat, or as you call it, the Sabbath, and in my tradition we spend the day resting, studying the Scriptures, and praying from the Siddur, our prayer book. I was at the chapel most of the day. Due to the trauma of losing my parents recently, I spent a lot of time crying out to God for answers and also for deliverance from fear. Pete, you didn't know, but my parents were killed in a suicide bombing in Jerusalem just two months ago," said Sarah with great sadness.

"Gosh, I'm so sorry. What a burden for you, and then to be attacked today! God's eye is on the sparrow? He must have been looking the other way when that fella threatened you," said Pete, indignantly.

"What?" asked Gloria. "What are you talking about?"

"Somebody attacked you?" asked Jeff. *So her parents* **were** *killed by a suicide bomber! And now Sarah herself has been attacked.*

Sarah recounted the incident and the aftermath of horror she felt, praising Pete for coming to the rescue, enabling her to vent her feelings, and then offering his help. She explained that Pete had asked to be her personal bodyguard, since his major was Criminal Justice, and he needed the practice.

Jeff and Gloria thoroughly agreed and complimented Pete on his unselfish offer. This would be a costly commitment of time. Jeff volunteered to "work a shift" and give Pete a break from time to time. The three encouraged Sarah that nothing would happen to her. They would be alert at all times.

"You see, Pete, I had been praying David's prayer in Psalm 3 for the Lord to be a shield to me from my enemies. While I was waiting on you in the men's dorm, God showed me that He had sent **you** to be my shield from danger. As the Psalmist said, God lifted my head. The fear left me, and I felt safe. **You** were an answer to my prayer, Pete." She looked at Pete gratefully.

Pete felt self-conscious as they all three looked at him. He was at a loss for words.

Sarah continued, "I need to share with you more of my situation. That Middle Eastern man could possibly be connected to the men who planted a bomb in the World Trade Center four years ago, resulting in six deaths and more than a thousand injuries. I'm not being paranoid, just alert to the fact that the persecution of my family that started with my father testifying in the trial of those terrorists is still going on, even in Starkville, Mississippi. Evidently, they have trailed me here, knowing that I am the most vulnerable one in the family. They are not only motivated by revenge, but they are trying to keep more evidence from coming to light that could convict others in their terrorist network."

"But do you have more evidence?" asked Pete.

"My parents are the ones who knew the most. We haven't finished going through their belongings. My oldest brother and his family live in Israel, and they are in the process now of settling the estate. It's hard to do across the ocean, family here and family there, plus dealing with bank accounts and all. There are some lock boxes in the U.S. that haven't been opened yet. I'm not sure what my father found out. He was a prolific writer, so his journals may contain condemning evidence. The family plans to get together for Hanukkah at my sister's house in New York and go through everything. We have a lot of decisions to make. Father was an author, and my mother was a wonderful philanthropist. There's much business to take care of in regard to his books and her charities and foundations. I haven't been praying just for myself but for all my family members, and we are a large family," finished Sarah.

"Bless your heart, Sarah," consoled Gloria. "I would never have guessed in a million years that you were carrying all this around. But God knew it, and do you remember that night in the lobby when I couldn't stop crying and groaning? Now I know that's what it was about. The Holy Spirit was praying **through** me for your burdens to be removed, for your heart to be comforted."

"Yes, sweet Gloria. You really are sweet, and God also revealed to me that you and Jeff are answers to my prayers. God sent Pete as a shield, and God sent you two as my closest friends."

Pete felt the conversation was great so far, but he sensed it was getting too serious, and he instinctively knew that Sarah needed the medicine of laughter. Too much of her life the past months and even years had been filled with tragedy.

"Hey, wait a minute. You hurt my feelings," whined Pete in the most juvenile manner, feigning a deep hurt. "I don't mind being called a shield, but I want to be called a friend, too." He turned his mouth down and pouted, glancing sideways at Sarah.

Sarah got tickled at the little-boy look on Pete's face. When he was riled, he could be a grizzly bear, but at heart he was just a big ole harmless teddy bear, thought Sarah. She played along with his charade, reaching over and giving him a motherly hug.

"Little woman," he teased, "you should'na done that." Pete stood to his full height of six feet seven inches, lifted Sarah off the floor in a tight embrace and whirled her around until she squealed. "Be my friend or else. You wanted to reward me, remember?" demanded Pete.

"Go on and kiss her, Pete," cajoled Jeff.

Sarah was out of breath and laughing. Pete pecked her on the cheek, and Jeff and Gloria broke out in applause. Sarah blushed, looking up at her benefactor with undisguised affection.

Sarah pointed at her feet. "Kneel down here, Knight Peter, and I will dub you 'friend forever' by order of the Royal Court, Queen Gloria and King Jeffrey." She was tickled and really having fun.

Pete made an elaborate bow, knelt in front of her, and bowed his head. Jeff and Gloria rose from their "thrones," and together with Sarah struck his head with their drink straws and pronounced him Friend. Then they all broke into paroxysms of laughter, while students looking on were amused at this crazy foursome.

CHAPTER FIFTEEN

Revelations at the Library

Jeff was the first to suggest leaving. His practical side was nagging at him to make tracks. Procrastination was a dreaded foe, and he never entertained such an enemy. As satisfying as it had been in the company of Gloria, Sarah, and Pete, he knew that his history paper wouldn't write itself. Besides, he really was eager to do the research on some famous person and his or her contribution in life. He had not forgotten about the poor among the Filipino people. He determined that he would work toward alleviating their misery. He needed more inspiration to propel him toward that goal, and he felt like he could find it at the library. But why did he have to do it alone? Hadn't he just heard that his sweetheart had the same assignment from the same professor he had? *It wouldn't hurt to ask*, he thought.

"This fellowship has been fantastic. And I don't want to leave y'all, but duty calls. Professor Holder wouldn't hesitate to give me an F, if my paper is one day late. I haven't had time until now to do the research, and my schedule is packed the next three days. It's now or never," he said fatalistically.

"Don't go, buddy," begged Pete. "It's time for you to follow your heart instead of your head. We've got two gorgeous gals here, and there's never been a better party. I've got some ideas up my sleeve for the rest of the evening, so why don't the four of us keep partying?" It made perfect sense to Pete, but he had never been one to take his studies seriously.

"Hey, friend, I thought you promised me you were going to reform. No more late night parties, remember?" teased Jeff. "Besides, I was just getting ready to ask one of these gorgeous gals who has the same assignment from Professor Holder to accompany me to the library. You might say, it would be a 'semi-party', but on the quiet side," he laughed.

Gloria didn't know how Jeff found out, but this was obviously something God arranged – they both had the same professor and the same assignment. It would be the perfect safe environment to continue their relationship, and she also had an urgent need to get started on her paper. Jeff looked straight at her with a questioning look.

"Am I the gorgeous gal you are speaking of?" she responded.

"You bet! Sarah told me you had the same assignment. Would you go with me?" pleaded Jeff, bowing and offering her his arm.

"Ah'd be charmed, ah'm sure," Gloria drawled in a thick southern accent as she curtsied and took his arm. "But wait, honey chile, ah need to go to the dorm and get mah notebook." Gloria's syrupy tone was accompanied by her fluttering eyelids as she waved to Sarah and Pete. "Goodbye, ya'll."

"We know Sarah is in good hands with you, Pete," winked Jeff. "But be sure to get her back to the dorm at a reasonable hour," he said, sternly.

"Oh, Sarah, don't forget about tomorrow – leaving for church at ten o'clock," reminded Gloria.

"I'll pick both of you up at Hamlin," said Jeff.

"I haven't forgotten. In fact I'm looking forward to it. It will be a new experience for me, another one to add to my growing list." Sarah rolled her eyes. "Now you two don't dawdle on the way back to the dorm and find yourselves locked out. I'm expecting you to get tons of work done!" she teased, looking aside at Pete, mischievously.

"Yeah, me, too," agreed Pete, sarcastically.

As Jeff and Gloria walked away, Pete and Sarah had their heads together, most likely making plans for the evening. Gloria could hardly wait for Sarah to move in and give her report on the evening with Pete. So far she hadn't been able to enjoy girl talk with Rebecca, but tomorrow would be a new day. She and Sarah had already bonded, and she cherished this God-sent friend.

Jeff and Gloria headed for the computer room and began to pore over the list of famous people for their history paper. It wasn't a very long list, but it could be endless, considering that the professor had tacked on the optional choice of "a famous person of your ethnic identity." That was the most appealing possibility to both of them, and they could read each other's minds. Without saying a word, they started making a list of famous Jewish people. Jeff got on the internet to search for more names. Gloria looked over his shoulder as he clicked on Stamps of Israel. The categories were Famous Women, Political Leaders, Zionists – the Builders of Israel, Arts & Literature, Rabbinical Portraits, Heroic Lives, Scientists, and Musicians.

"Go to Musicians first, please," asked Gloria. She was a music major, and this piqued her interest. The stamps came up on the screen. She wasn't familiar with the faces, but she picked out several names she recognized. "Arnold Schoenberg, Gustav Mahler, Ernest Bloch.... I remember those names from my Music Appreciation class. Oh, there's one I love! Leonard Bernstein. Hey, wonder if Sarah is kin to Leonard. I adore his music. 'West Side Story' has the most exquisite songs. 'Maria' is so romantic, and I've heard Barbara Streisand sing 'Somewhere.' I get chills when she sings that. Don't you?"

"This is not my field, sweetheart," Jeff replied as he looked up at her. "But I know I would get chills if you sang any of those songs. You put Barbara Streisand in the shade!"

Gloria leaned over and sang softly in Jeff's ear, "There's a place for us, a time and space for us..."

"Watch out, little songbird. You are revving my engine, and I need to stay focused." Jeff squeezed her hand.

"Okay, sweetheart." She loved that term of endearment. Every time Jeff said it, it revved her engine, too. "Anyway, Bernstein's a possibility."

There were plenty of computers available, but it was more fun to work together on one, even if it did take longer. Having Gloria close behind him was a warm fuzzy he didn't want to give up anyway. "Tell you what, Jeff. I'll let you click on a few more for me, and I'll hurry up and decide, so you can browse to your heart's content."

"Anything for you, sugar." Gloria felt caressed by his words.

Under the category of Arts & Literature, Gloria found two of interest. Anne Frank was a teenager hiding in the attic of a Dutch family's house in Nazi-occupied Holland. Her diary became of great value as an eye-witness account of the horrors of the Holocaust.

Then Jeff clicked on Eliezer Ben Yehudah, and at the same time there was a click in Gloria's spirit. "Stop right there. That's the one. I've already heard a little about him. He was the man who almost single-handedly revived a dead language – Hebrew – and now it is the official spoken language of the State of Israel. Just to think, Hebrew is the original language of the Old Testament Scripture, and there is a country of people who speak this language every day. Wow! He made a significant contribution in the late 1800s that is affecting lives today. That's worth writing about, don't you think?"

"I think you're absolutely right. Great choice, Gloria. Do you want to continue on your own at another computer now?"

"I'll go check the shelves first. I can find books quicker that way. Computers paralyze me. If I don't find anything, I'll try the internet. But you go ahead and find your famous person now. Thanks, sweetie, for helping me." Gloria leaned over and kissed Jeff on the cheek. Sparks flew, but with a supreme effort she pulled away and headed for the book shelves.

Jeff stayed on the same site and made the choice of Albert Einstein. It was an easy decision.

"What a genius this Jewish man was. His theory of relativity revolutionized scientific thought, but he didn't even talk until the age of three!"

Jeff continued to find many interesting facts. At five when Einstein's father gave him a pocket compass, he was captivated by the mysterious way the compass needle pointed the same way no matter which way it was turned. He later said, "Something deeply hidden has to be behind things."

So Einstein was religious. I never knew that.

In school Einstein cut classes. *Aha! He was no model student, but then geniuses rarely fit the mold.* He kept reading, "...and used his time to study physics on his own or to play his beloved violin."

Ah, Einstein was a scientist but also a musician. Wonder if Gloria knows that. The man used both sides of his brain, and he thought about God. I'm glad I chose him to write my paper on. I know Gloria will approve.

Jeff was engrossed in his study of Einstein. Writing a three-page paper would be a piece of cake. He could write ten pages easily. And proving that this man made a significant contribution that affects people's lives today would be a simple task. He would write that every time we watch television or go to a movie, we can thank Einstein for his work that produced the photoelectric cell, making these inventions possible.

He could also write that after World War I, Einstein's public support of pacifist and Zionist goals made him the target of vicious attacks by anti-Semitic and right-wing elements in Germany. When Hitler came to power, the Nazi government took his property and deprived him of his positions and citizenship. It was then that he renounced his pacifist stand in the face of the threat to humankind by the Nazi regime. He moved to the United States and became a math professor at Princeton. *Hitler threw a Nobel-prizewinning Jew out, but the good ole U.S.A. took him in!*

Jeff continued to write furiously. Einstein's theory of relativity laid the basis for splitting the atom. In 1939, he wrote a letter to President Roosevelt warning him that Germany was working on nuclear fission. As a result, the United States began the process that led to the development of the atomic bomb in 1945. *That's really heavy*, thought Jeff.

Einstein was offered the position of President of the State of Israel in 1952, but he turned it down. He could have become wealthy, but he was not interested in money. This caught Jeff's attention, but what impressed him most was the statement that "Einstein's nature was deeply religious. Merely to come into his presence was always a profoundly spiritual experience." Einstein did not believe in a personal God, however, but he believed in the universe as one of absolute law and order. He once said, "God does not play dice with the world."

Jeff leaned back in his chair. *I am learning so much. Albert Einstein's life was of great significance, and it is still affecting me today. I had hoped to be inspired, and I am. He's Jewish, too. He championed the underdog. He was not materialistic. He spoke out even when it cost him his academic positions and citizenship. He did something very important in writing Roosevelt that letter. To top it off, he played the violin. He had a heart, not just a head. I can't wait to share all this with Gloria. It's too bad, though, that he didn't believe in a personal God. She will certainly be disappointed in that.*

Gloria came to where Jeff was working. "Let me tell you what I found," she said.

"I'm ready to hear it, sweetheart." Jeff got up from the computer. "Let's go find a study room and compare notes. Your timing is perfect. Just as you walked up, I had completed my research. Now all I have to do is get this written down in essay form. It's going to be a humdinger, but keeping it to three pages will be tough." He smiled with satisfaction.

They sat down at the table, and Gloria said, "You go first, sweetie. I can't wait to hear what person you are writing about."

"Albert Einstein. You won't believe how interesting this man is or was. Bet you didn't know he played the violin."

"He did? No, I surely didn't know. All I know is that he advanced the theory of relativity. If he was musical, too, then that means he used both sides of his brain."

"I can't believe you said that. I thought the same thing. Listen to this – he didn't care about money – that impressed me. And he spoke out when Hitler came to power – he had courage. He lost his positions and his German citizenship, but at least he didn't lose his life. He came to the United States and was a professor at Princeton."

"It looks like the Lord was protecting him, or he would surely have perished in the Holocaust. God preserved his life and used him to bless the world, I'd say," observed Gloria.

"He believed in God, too, Gloria, but I know you won't like this – he didn't believe in a **personal** God." Jeff waited for Gloria's reaction.

"So he was a genius, but, evidently, he didn't really know about the God who gave him such an astounding intellect. That fits with what Jesus said—'I thank You, Father, Lord of heaven and earth, that You have hidden these things from the wise and prudent and have revealed them to babes.'[22] Yes, a lot of smart people haven't figured out that God revealed Himself in a carpenter from Galilee. It doesn't take brains. We just have to come into God's kingdom with the simple faith of a little child. The great people in the eyes of the world often have too much pride to bend down and make it through the narrow gate," concluded Gloria, sadly.

"The little bit I've read so far doesn't indicate he was prideful, Gloria, although I can agree that people with extremely high intelligence often are not religious. But Einstein **was** religious. Oh, I almost forgot to tell you what he said about Jesus. Let me read it to you: 'As a child I received instruction both in the Bible and in the Talmud. I am a Jew, but I am enthralled by the luminous figure of the Nazarene.... No one can read the Gospels without feeling the actual presence of Jesus. His personality pulsates in every word. No myth is filled with such life. — Albert Einstein.'[23] Wow! It is still true, however, that Einstein didn't have a personal relationship with Jesus. Anyway, his life's contributions are still affecting us today."

"I love what he said about Jesus. If only he had gone one step farther and invited Jesus to come into his heart. But it's not like we can find God. He finds us. He has even been called 'The Hound of Heaven.' For us to know God, He has to do the revealing, Jeff. And He **has** revealed Himself. He became flesh and dwelt among us, as the Bible says. I'm talking about Jesus Christ. He said, 'I am the Way, the Truth, and the Life. No man comes to the Father but by me.'[24] So, no matter how great these famous people are, they can't get to God by any other way but through Jesus." Gloria was emphatic.

"That's a pretty bold statement Jesus made."

"You're right. If He wasn't telling the truth, then He was either a liar or a lunatic. You can't say that He was merely a good teacher or a prophet, if these words weren't true. There's no middle ground. C.S. Lewis said to choose who Jesus is – liar, lunatic, or Lord!"[25]

Jeff could see the conviction in Gloria's eyes, and he was attracted to her firm belief. He knew the time had come to make a decision about Jesus. He couldn't keep dodging the issue. Tonight he would offer up a serious prayer. He would really seek the Lord. *If He doesn't answer tonight, surely He will reveal Himself at church tomorrow.*

Jeff was excited about the life of Einstein, but Gloria was drawing his attention to Someone infinitely **more** exciting. He wanted to learn more from this wonderful girl. Her mouth dripped revelation, and it was stirring in him a hunger for the Truth.

CHAPTER SIXTEEN

FORGIVENESS

S arah could hardly wait to tell Gloria about her evening, so when Gloria got back to her room about ten o'clock, she was there. "Surprise! I've been waiting for you. How was your evening?"

"Sarah, I'm so glad you are here. I want to hear all about **your** evening. Mine was great! We accomplished a lot. Our time together was more on an intellectual level this time. The smoldering fires didn't have a chance to be ignited. Hope you played it cool with Pete, too."

"You know I did. Pete is a very enjoyable person. He's just the medicine I needed, and I felt so safe with him. He's kind of like a big brother, but not quite," said Sarah with a twinkle in her eye.

"Well, tell me. I'm waiting."

"Oh, nothing. We just chartered an airplane and flew to Acapulco and back!"

"Ha! Ha! I didn't know you could be such a blast, Sarah."

"I didn't either, really. Anyway, we had a super time. We stayed at the Union and talked and talked. I found out all about him. Pete has a large family. They are Baptists, and—guess what? Pete agreed to go to your church with us tomorrow. Isn't that fantastic?" Sarah was exhilarated.

"Terrific! The four of us are an unbeatable combination. Well, dear roommate-to-be, don't you think we better hit the sack, if we're going to get our beauty sleep and look magnificent tomorrow?"

"Yeah, I'll go now, but I don't think I can go to bed yet. Rebecca is in my room, and it doesn't look like she's leaving any time soon."

"Well, if that's the case, maybe she could stay there, and you can spend the night here. Why don't you go ask her?"

"Sure thing. Be right back."

Gloria began singing and praying as she straightened up the room and changed into her nightgown. *Oh, Lord, thank you for a wonderful evening with my beloved. Please keep working on him and drawing him to Yourself. Thank you for my new roommate. Show me how to whet her appetite for the Messiah. Let tomorrow be a revelation to her, to Pete, and above all, to Jeff. Reveal your warm love to all of us.*

As Gloria was finishing putting night cream on her face, she heard a knock at the door. "Come on in, Sarah. You don't have to knock." The door didn't open. "Come in," she repeated. Finally, Gloria went to open the door, expecting Sarah to have her arms full.

Sarah's face was ashen, and her hand was badly hurt.

"Sarah! What happened?"

"I couldn't turn the doorknob. My hand is killing me! I may have a broken rib, too."

"Come in here and sit down right now." Gloria's brow furrowed with concern as she took Sarah's bag out of her hands.

Sarah was making a valiant effort not to cry, but as soon as the door was closed behind her, she grabbed Gloria like a life preserver and sobbed violently on her shoulder.

"Go ahead and cry, honey." Gloria sat Sarah down tenderly on Rebecca's bed, holding her, stroking her hair, and comforting her. She prayed silently and fervently, feeling like this was the most important intercessory prayer she had ever offered to God. Carefully examining Sarah's hand and side and the bump on her head, she assured her that everything would heal, that no real damage was done.

"You'll have bruises and be very sore for only a day or two, I think. It will definitely heal, honey. Don't worry," Gloria comforted. Gradually, the sobs subsided, and a sweet peace settled over them. Sarah was calm enough to explain what happened now, thought Gloria. "Now take your time and tell me what happened."

"Okay. Prepare yourself. When I opened the door to my room, I saw Rebecca and Jenny kissing! I could hardly believe it. It was sickening, and I know they could see the disgust on my face. Jenny said, 'What's the matter with you? Don't you holy Jews know what it is to have a gay ole time?' I didn't expect a New Yorker to be a prude.'"

"I wanted to get out of there as quickly as possible. I could sense something evil. I didn't reply to their garbage, but I told Rebecca I'd like to spend the night with you and asked if she would like to spend the night in my bed. She said, 'Sure, as long as **you** aren't in it,' and they both laughed."

"I said, 'We can move permanently tomorrow afternoon,' and Rebecca answered in a sarcastic voice, 'Whatever's convenient with **you**.' Jenny said, 'Yes, we don't want to cause any inconvenience. We're in perfect agreement about the roommate swap, dear.' Her voice was also dripping with sarcasm."

"As fast as I could, I crossed the room to the closet to get my clothes, but Jenny tripped me, and I hit the floor hard, bumping my head on the chair! She said it was an accident and pretended to be so sorry. As she and Rebecca reached down to pull me up, Jenny stumbled, and her big foot crushed my hand! She kept apologizing for being such a klutz, but I could see the hidden smiles between them. Before I could get to my feet, a pile of books fell and hit me in the side. Again they said it was an accident, but I knew Rebecca knocked them off the desk. After I got my clothes and things in the bag and got out the door, they were laughing their heads off. And I could hear them say, 'The dirty Jew is gone! At last!' They didn't care if I heard."

Gloria's emotions went from disbelief to shock to hot anger. Then she stood to her full height with her hands on her hips. "I'm going to tell the dorm mother. This makes me furious!"

"Don't do it, Gloria. They are sick. They're going to get away with it, just like most anti-Semites do. There is an unreasonable hatred for Jews throughout the world. I see that I can't escape it even here in Mississippi. It will cause more trouble for me if you tell. Trust me, I know what I'm talking about. And don't forget, you are Jewish, too. Eventually, you will suffer for it, just like me."

"But the dorm mother, Mrs. McClendon, likes me. She will listen to me, I know it. Please let me go talk to her, Sarah."

"No, you can't do it. We just need to keep as much distance as possible between us and them. I've learned how to control my anger, and you need to learn it, too. When Mashiach comes, He will make everything right. The wicked will be punished and the righteous rewarded. Do you know Psalm 37? It teaches us about the fate of wrongdoers, and why we shouldn't get angry, but just trust the Lord. I've got my Tanakh. Let's read it. If we're going to be roommates, we need to start off right by studying the Scriptures together, don't you agree?"

Gloria was delighted. "Of course I agree. We Christians believe in the power of God's Word. That's the way Jesus defeated the devil in the wilderness temptation, by quoting God's Word. You go ahead and read it out loud. I'll follow you along in my Bible."

Sarah read:

Do not be vexed by evil men; do not be incensed by wrongdoers; for they soon wither like grass, like verdure fade away.

Trust in the Lord and do good, abide in the land and remain loyal. Seek the favor of the Lord, and He will grant you the desires of your heart.

Leave all to the Lord; trust in Him; He will do it. He will cause your vindication to shine forth like the light, the justice of your cause, like the noonday sun.

Be patient and wait for the Lord, do not be vexed by the prospering man who carries out his schemes.

Give up anger, abandon fury, do not be vexed; it can only do harm. For evil men will be cut off, but those who look to the Lord—they shall inherit the land. (Psalm 37:1-9)

"I see what you mean about anger not accomplishing anything. We need to see this situation from God's viewpoint. He sees all the injustice, and He will judge evil doers. My translation says, 'Do not fret because of evil doers.' I admit I was fretting. I give up my anger right now. God will vindicate you. That's the truth. God's Word says so!" triumphed Gloria.

Sarah, feeling the need to pray, reached in her bag and drew out a tallit. It was silky white with blue stripes, gold-embroidered Hebrew letters on the top edge, and long white tassels at the corners. "This is my tallit. I hope you don't mind if I wear it when I pray."

"Sure. That's neat. I don't own one, but it would be nice to have one. Papa Sam and Mama Anna wear those."

"The whole nation of Israel wears one because their flag is a tallit," said Sarah.

"Hey, I never thought of that, but you're right. Goodness, I love it!"

"Are you ready to pray? It will be so good to have someone to pray with. I really miss the prayer sessions with my friends in Hebrew University."

"Yes, Sarah. I am honored that you want to pray with me. You believe in Judaism, and I believe in Christianity, but God will make it work," said Gloria, her face all aglow.

"I know your heart is right, and that's what counts. But what about some ground rules, like saying 'Messiah' without saying His identity?"

Gloria sensed that the Lord had already given them common ground, and she surrendered any remaining doubts to Him. "You must know I'll be thinking of Jesus when we pray, but I will respect your wishes and use the name 'Messiah.' But please don't be offended if I use words from the New Testament. I know I can't stop them from coming out of my mouth." Gloria laughed.

"Okay, and I request of you that you won't go to sleep if I start praying in Hebrew. And please don't think I'm *meshugenah!* That means crazy!" Sarah laughed long and hard, and Gloria joined her, both rocking back and forth on the bed and slapping their thighs.

What a relief they felt as they got down on their knees by the bed, holding hands. Gloria deferred to Sarah, and Sarah began the

Shema, the ancient creed of Judaism: "Sh'ma Yisrael, Adonai Eloheynu, Adonai Echad. Baruch shem k'vod malchuto le'olam va'ed."
She repeated it in English: "Hear, O Israel, the Lord our God, the
Lord is One. Blessed be His glorious name Whose kingdom is
forever and ever."

Sarah proceeded to pray for the peace of Jerusalem, and that all
who love her would prosper. She prayed for Mashiach, the Messiah,
to come. Gloria thanked the Lord for all their blessings and prayed
for their protection from evildoers. She prayed that God would
remove their anger, guard them from hate and put love in their
hearts for their persecutors. Sarah thanked the Lord for Pete coming
to her rescue and for giving her Gloria as a friend and roommate.
Gloria asked the Lord to bless Rebecca and Jenny, to show them
His lovingkindness in the face of the Messiah.

Sarah began to squirm, and Gloria sensed that her prayer for
Rebecca and Jenny had made her uncomfortable, so she quickly concluded the prayer, expressing love for the Messiah in song,
"Then sings my soul, my Savior God to Thee, how great Thou art,
how great Thou art. Then sings my soul, my Savior God to Thee,
how great Thou art, how great Thou art."

Sarah was moved as she watched Gloria's radiant face and let
the soaring melody wash over her. "You have a beautiful voice,
Gloria, and I liked that song very much. Will you teach it to me?"

"You liked it? Sure, I'll teach it to you. Wait till you hear the
verses. They are wonderful. But Sarah, I sensed that you thought
it inappropriate to pray for God's blessing on Rebecca and Jenny.
Did I read you right?"

"According to the Scripture we just read, wrongdoers will be
'cut off,' and that means they will be killed. We can't take vengeance, but God will avenge us," explained Sarah.

"That is true, but it is also true that God doesn't want anyone
to perish. He wants all to come to a knowledge of the truth. Jesus
has taught us that we are to forgive our enemies. We are to love
them and bless them. Paul taught that the goodness of God leads

to repentance. Jesus even forgave those who were crucifying him. Forgiveness is at the very heart of a Christian's beliefs. Jesus taught his disciples to pray, 'Forgive us our trespasses as we forgive those who trespass against us.'"

"God is really the only one Who can forgive sins," replied Sarah. "Isaiah the prophet said of Adonai, 'It is I, I who—for My own sake—wipe your transgressions away and remember your sins no more.' Also, the sixth blessing of the *Amidah*, the standing prayer of Benediction, ends, 'Blessed are you, Adonai, who is gracious to forgive abundantly.' So you see, it is up to God to forgive sins."

Gloria didn't feel like she could convince Sarah. Anyway, she was glad that Sarah didn't want to retaliate, and she did want to trust God. That was a victory.

"Sarah, you are right, and I have to say that it is the most wonderful feeling in the world to know that God has forgiven us for our sins. I have experienced that, and it makes me want others to experience it, too. The main thing is that we stay as close to God as possible so that hate and fear won't grow in our hearts."

"The last thing you said I can agree with. I don't want to hate back because then I would be no different from the anti-Semites," reasoned Sarah.

"That beauty sleep is awaiting us, Roommate. Let's 'leave all to the Lord,' as the Psalmist said, and get some Zs!" concluded Gloria.

CHAPTER SEVENTEEN

CHURCH SERVICE

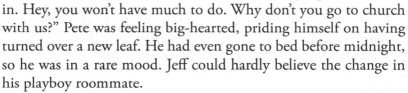

J eff and Pete were at the desk in Hamlin promptly at ten a.m. waiting for Gloria and Sarah. Pete engaged Priscilla Caldwell in conversation. "Hi. Surely the desk doesn't need tending this early on Sunday morning. I bet most everybody is sleeping in. Hey, you won't have much to do. Why don't you go to church with us?" Pete was feeling big-hearted, priding himself on having turned over a new leaf. He had even gone to bed before midnight, so he was in a rare mood. Jeff could hardly believe the change in his playboy roommate.

Priscilla perked up when she saw these two handsome boys come in, wondering what in the world would bring them here at so early an hour. She couldn't remember where she had seen one of them. Before they came in she needed toothpicks to keep her eyes open, but now she was wide-eyed and running on all cylinders. *Surely they haven't come in here just to talk to* **me**. *Well, I'll enjoy it as long as it lasts.*

"You're kiddin' me, right? You two don't look like the church-going type."

Jeff figured Pete could respond to that. Pete moved closer to the desk. "I've always been told you can't tell a book by its cover. Actually, this is not our normal behavior, but we've made some new friends, and hangin' out with them has changed our ways." Pete was unashamedly elated.

"And who might those new friends be?" Priscilla asked, afraid of the answer.

Jeff spoke up. "Gloria Sondheim and Sarah Bernstein. They should be down any minute."

"Oh," was all Priscilla could get out. To cover her disappointment, she hastily added, "That's right, I remember you came for

115

them Friday night, and you said you were going to worship. You two must be Jewish, also, or you wouldn't be going out with Jews." The tone of her voice betrayed her disgust.

Pete's old-world chivalry kicked in. "These girls are first-class, so that makes us first-class. You can join the club if you'd like to."

Priscilla was glad she didn't have to answer because Gloria and Sarah came up, and the four hugged like they hadn't seen each other in months. Priscilla felt the green tentacles of envy creeping all over her and the lead weight of disappointment settling in the pit of her stomach.

Pete glanced over at Priscilla and immediately felt pity for her. She was a pretty girl, but the load of resentment she carried canceled out her beauty. He was drawn to her, feeling a strong impulse to express kindness. "I'm Pete, and you are --?"

Clasping Pete's outstretched hand, she said weakly, "Priscilla--, Priscilla Caldwell."

"Well, Priscilla, I'm leaving you with a standing invitation to attend church with us the next time we go. We'd like to have you along. Just find a substitute for a few hours, okay?" Pete held on to her hand a few moments longer. He was amazed at himself because ordinarily he would have had a smart comeback for her catty remark.

Priscilla was taken aback. She couldn't think of much to say. "Sure. Bye now." The envy and disappointment gradually faded away. Then she found herself smiling at all four of them.

As they waved goodbye to Priscilla, they all felt like a million dollars. This was going to be a great day. Sarah marveled at Pete's way of neutralizing hate, and with her "good hand" she gave his hand an intense squeeze.

Adaton Baptist Church was eight-and-a-half miles west of Starkville. College students made up a majority of the congregation. The church had sent out an elderly couple from Nashville, Tennessee, to begin an outreach on the campus the year before, and through their exciting Bible studies at the Baptist Student Union, many students had been "born again." Now every Sunday they were crowding into the church that had sponsored the outreach.

As they drove up, Sarah viewed the modest red brick steepled church building. *This is a typical church, but there is nothing typical about this situation for me. How am I going to cope with this? If my parents were alive, they would never get over it, my going inside a church, flanked by Christians. Strangely enough, however, I feel safe with these new friends. It's only fair to go with them, since they went with me. It will be an educational experience. I'll try to check all my preconceived ideas at the door.*

Friendly faces and handshakes greeted them, and they received bulletins. Gloria led the way down close to the front in the midst of other college students. Some recognized Gloria, smiled, and nodded. After the announcements came the greeting time. Gloria introduced her friends to several people. Some even crossed the aisle to get acquainted with the new visitors.

"I'm sorry, Gloria," whispered Jeff. "Forgive me for my negative thoughts. I thought we'd be sitting by a bunch of old fogies, but there are plenty of students and a pretty good cross section of people here. I feel right at home."

"I knew the Lord would prepare the way for you, sweetie."

As the auditorium began to fill up, Pete was busy explaining things to Sarah. Even though he thought this church was less formal than First Baptist, he knew each Baptist service had pretty much the same format. "The preliminaries are okay, but the sermon is the part I get the most out of. I hope this preacher is as good as ours. If he's not, I'll take you to my church next Sunday."

"Wait a minute. You haven't even been to temple with me yet."

The choir filed in as the organist and pianist played a stirring arrangement of "Majesty." The song leader motioned for everyone to stand. It was obvious this was the moment he had waited for all week, as he quoted King David, "I was glad when they said unto me, let us go into the house of the Lord!" The joy on his face and on every face in the choir was genuine, and the contagion of joy quickly spread through the congregation.

A young keyboard player joined with the pianist and organist, and the song service was under way as the leader exuberantly waved his arms and sang with all his might. Gloria signaled her charges to join in the singing and quit talking. The words to the songs were in the bulletin. Gloria knew them all, and Pete knew two of them. Jeff and Sarah were in the dark, but they enjoyed observing Gloria singing her heart out and Pete making a valiant effort. The songs went from loud and joyful with fast rhythms to soft and sweet melodies with slow tempos.

As the music moved from boisterous praise to heartfelt worship, Jeff was mesmerized with the look on Gloria's face as she sang. "My Jesus, my Savior, Lord, there is none like You. All of my days, I want to praise the wonders of Your mighty love…."[26] He knew she was unaware of her surroundings and was on some kind of heavenly wave length he had never experienced. There was an intimacy between Gloria and the Object of her worship. He looked around and saw a few other people with similar expressions of adoration on their faces. It made him feel like someone on the outside looking in. In that moment he became jealous. He didn't want to share Gloria with anybody, even if it was God. *But how do you compete with the Maker of the universe?*

As the singing continued for some time, Jeff found himself praying like he had at the temple, forming his troubled thoughts into a prayer. *I admit it. I'm jealous. Gloria has a special relationship with You, and I don't. She's saved, and I'm not. She knows Jesus, and I don't. Won't You please reveal Yourself to me? Jesus is like a real person to Gloria. Can You make him real to me, too?*

Suddenly, the singing rose to a crescendo like giant ocean waves. It was another song, and Jeff could hear Gloria and Pete above the rest. *Oh, I know that song! That's the song Gloria sang to me in the Union that night.* It grabbed his heart, as the words drove the Truth straight to the core of his being. "O love of God, how

118

rich and pure! How measureless and strong! It shall forevermore endure the saints' and angels' song...."

When Gloria sang it, Jeff had never felt the desire for intimacy any stronger, but now the song was having a different effect on him. This was a much deeper experience. A thrill went through his being as he realized it was **God speaking to him**, answering the prayer he had **just** prayed! Now he could see that God wanted a relationship with him as much as he wanted a relationship with God. *He is pursuing* **me**, *not the other way around. You* **are** *real to me, God. Show me about Jesus.*

The words came to his mind, "Just sing." *Are those my thoughts or is that* **God** *telling me to sing?*

The music had become very quiet. Jeff knew it was now or never. He would dive in and test the waters. The song was simple enough – "Alleluia, alleluia ..." over and over. He shyly began singing, self-conscious at first, then gradually singing with all his heart, until he didn't care who heard him. He felt engulfed by total peace and comfort. *Hey, I'm water skiing, and I'm outside the wake. I'm flying on the water! It's so easy, so simple, so fun. I'm worshiping the real God, and I love it.*

He forgot all about Gloria. He was having his own intimate relationship with God. Never had he felt more exhilarated or more inspired. *Now I know what makes Gloria sparkle.*

Jeff became aware that Gloria was tugging at his hand, pulling him down. The song service was over, and he was still standing, lost in wonder at the beauty of communing with the Living God. Quickly sitting down, he squeezed Gloria's hand, looked deep into her eyes, and communicated without words *I've just touched God.* His eyes said it, and he nodded his head with a knowing look.

Gloria had no doubt that Jeff had made contact with the Lord. She could feel the electricity coming from his hand into her hand, up her arm, and into her heart. She feasted on the deep satisfaction of knowing that Jeff and she were becoming one spiritually. She beamed her love at him through her eyes, her tender smile, and her warm handclasp. *This is the best gift you could have given me, Lord. Thank You, thank You for answering my prayer. Please help Jeff to make his decision public. Oh, Lord, is this the man you want me to spend my life with?*

She marveled that the Spirit of God was moving so fast this morning. *What next, Lord? Are you going to touch Sarah the same way you touched Jeff? I know I can't outguess You. Your thoughts and Your ways are so much higher than mine. Please draw Sarah to Yourself, dear Lord, in Your time and in Your way. And bless Pete. I don't know him well yet, but I know You have something good for him, too.*

The offering plate was coming their way, and Jeff hastily reached in his pocket and plunked two twenty-dollar bills in. It was the easiest donation he had ever made. If he had drawn out a fifty or even a hundred-dollar bill, he would have gladly given it. He would give more next time, he thought. Pete hadn't thought of giving anything, but Jeff's example had its effect. He pulled out a ten and smiled to himself, thinking how generous he was. Gloria already had her offering in an envelope.

Sarah didn't feel obligated to give. This was alien territory to her. Nevertheless, she had enjoyed the music, in spite of the name of Jesus in almost every song. She found herself joining in on the repetitive parts that didn't have that name. She didn't feel critical, just cautious. The presence of Pete on one side of her and Gloria on the other gave her a secure feeling, but her guard wasn't all the way down.

Pete whispered to Sarah, "Here's the good part, the sermon." He pointed to the bulletin. "The sermon topic is 'Despised and Rejected.' Oh, I hope this isn't a downer."

Pete nudged Jeff and showed him the bulletin. He whispered, "Hey man, the preacher has your name! Jeff – Jeff James. You don't suppose this would be another..."

Jeff finished the sentence. "Yeah, friend, another God incidence," he whispered, his eyes twinkling.

120

The scripture reading was Isaiah 52:13 through the entire chapter of Isaiah 53. Sarah regretted she had not brought her Tanakh. She assumed only the New Testament would be used. Gloria handed her a Bible from the rack in front of them. She couldn't find the place in this strange Bible, so Gloria turned to it for her. Students at the other end of the pew handed Bibles to Jeff and Pete. Glancing at the page number, they had no trouble finding the right place.

The minister asked everyone to stand, as he read the entire passage.

"See, my servant will act wisely; he will be raised and lifted up and highly exalted. Just as there were many who were appalled at him – his appearance was so disfigured beyond that of any man and his form marred beyond human likeness – so will he sprinkle many nations, and kings will shut their mouths because of him. For what they were not told, they will see, and what they have not heard, they will understand.

"Who has believed our message and to whom has the arm of the Lord been revealed? He grew up before him like a tender shoot, and like a root out of dry ground. He had no beauty or majesty to attract us to him, nothing in his appearance that we should desire him. He was despised and rejected by men, a man of sorrows, and familiar with suffering. Like one from whom men hide their faces he was despised, and we esteemed him not...."

Pastor Jeff James read to the end of the 53rd chapter with deep emotion in his voice. The congregation was unusually attentive.

Pete was impressed. *Whew! That's the longest Scripture text I've ever heard read in a service. But it was worth it, and it makes perfect sense to me. My mind is clearer today than it usually is. Must be because I got eight hours' sleep, and that's a change for me on Saturday night. I know this Scripture is talkin' about Jesus. I hope the preacher does it justice. I can see Sarah's really engrossed in this. I hope she can be convinced that this is a picture of Jesus on the cross. I've got a feeling just hearing a sermon won't do it, but I'm sure God has His ways of getting through to His chosen people. I sure would love to have the privilege of seeing the veil removed from Sarah's eyes.*

The minister was in his element, Gloria could tell. He said this was his favorite passage in the Bible, and he needed a week to properly teach it. Today he would zero in on the physical suffering of the Messiah. Gloria was amazed that he kept saying "Messiah" instead of "Jesus." *Has the Holy Spirit told him that there is an unbelieving Jew in the congregation? This sermon is perfect for Sarah. I remember that she mentioned Isaiah 53 and said that this was not about Jesus, but about Israel. Lord, please help the preacher to show that this refers to Jesus. Please convince Sarah, Lord. And help me to hear Your message for me. What are You speaking to **me** today?*

Jeff James had a strong voice. He boomed out his introduction, "The nation of Israel did not recognize the Messiah because he appeared as an ordinary man. The Jews were expecting a conquering King on a white horse to come in and vanquish their Roman oppressors. They had overlooked the prophecy that he would enter the world as a baby, although he was Emmanuel, meaning 'God with us.' He was a Jew but was not extraordinary. Most likely he blended in with his countrymen."

Humph! He's trying to say that the Messiah has already come, and that he's Jesus. If that's so, why is the world still in such a mess? Sarah put her guard up.

Pastor James continued, "As the Scripture says, 'He had no beauty or majesty to attract us to him.' God sent him to be a Suffering Servant. The twelfth verse says, 'he bore the sin of many, and made intercession for the transgressors.' Many do not believe that the Messiah bore our sins and that he suffered for us. These people think they can do enough good deeds to be accepted by God, but if that is so, then the Messiah didn't have to die. That's like saying his death was in vain. However, He **did** die for our sins, and he was horribly disfigured by the cruel torture. They killed Him. He was a perfect sinless sacrifice, the Lamb of God who took away the sins of the world."

Sarah was resisting this interpretation of the prophet's message because she knew better, or so she thought. She had steeled herself, waiting to be told that this was about Jesus and his crucifixion, but those words hadn't actually been mentioned thus far. *What does the preacher know? Isaiah describes what the Jewish people have had to endure throughout history, this rejection and torture and death. This passage refers to Israel in general, not the Messiah. But I know the rabbis also teach that Messiah ben Yosef will arise, do mighty deeds, go to battle with his enemies, and be killed. Then Messiah ben David will come and resurrect him. That confuses me though. Is it Israel or is it Messiah ben Yosef, this Suffering Servant?*

Pete could sense Sarah stiffen as Pastor James continued. "From chapters forty-two through fifty three of Isaiah there are four passages dealing with God's suffering servant. Sometimes the prophecy marks Israel as the suffering servant, and other times it indicates the Messiah. That's because Israel is a **TYPE** of the Messiah. Just as the Christian is intimately identified with Christ as part of his Body, so the Messiah identifies with and embodies national Israel."

Sarah was shaken with this revelation. Never had she considered such a concept. Her hunger for truth was increasing with every word from the minister's lips. *Okay, I'm going to take this all in. Real truth can withstand the onslaught of lies. I'm not afraid to consider this.*

She was offended, however, with the next part of the sermon. "In Isaiah forty-nine the third verse says, 'You are my servant, Israel, in whom I will be glorified,' but listen to the sixth verse: 'And now the Lord says, It is too light a thing that you should be my servant to raise up the tribes of Jacob and to restore the preserved of Israel; I will give you as a light to the nations, that my salvation may reach to the end of the earth.' How can Israel raise up Israel? She can't raise up herself. You can see this passage refers to the Messiah. But once Israel believes in the Messiah, she can then perform her calling of being a light to the nations as the Messiah is now."

123

Believe in the Messiah? Of course, I believe in the Messiah. I pray for his coming every day, but I don't believe this Jesus is the Messiah! Sarah fumed within herself.

The remainder of the sermon focused on the physical and mental suffering endured by the Messiah. The minister read a doctor's description of the crucifixion, and how the victim died a slow, terrible death. "'He was wounded for our transgressions, he was bruised for our iniquities; the chastisement of our peace was upon Him, and by His stripes we are healed.'"[27]

Hearing the word "bruised," Sarah looked down at her hand and began to relive the incident back at the dorm when she was cruelly attacked.

The congregation was visibly moved as the preacher emphasized the ways in which Jesus was despised and rejected before and during the crucifixion. "'He came unto His own, and His own received Him not...' Yes, 'He was despised and rejected by men, a Man of sorrows and acquainted with grief...' but 'Surely He has borne **our** griefs and carried **our** sorrows...' Yes, friends, the Messiah not only bore your sins, but He bore your sorrows – your disappointments, your mental anguish, your griefs, your anxieties, your heartbreak, your rejection. He experienced all of it, and He is 'touched with the feeling of your infirmities.' He wants to lift the load you are carrying. He has already paid for all of it. You don't have to carry it around anymore. That's what the Messiah is for. Let Him save you. There's nothing He can't rescue you from. There's no sorrow He can't soothe. There's no pain he can't erase. Put your trust in Him today."

Sarah's mind was resisting, but her heart was beginning to respond to the message. *If only this were true. It is so appealing, but it's too good to be true. Yes, the Messiah will come one day and make everything right, but in the meantime we must endure much suffering.*

Pastor James continued, "Some of you may doubt that this passage in Isaiah depicts the crucifixion and identifies the One who was crucified for our sins, but not only does Isaiah prophesy the crucifixion of the Suffering Servant, the Messiah, but in Psalm 22, King David described the crucifixion also. This Psalm was written a thousand years before crucifixion was a method of execution. Listen to this: 'They pierced my hands and my feet; I can count all my bones. They look and stare at me. They divide my garments among them, and for my clothing they cast lots.' In his gospel Matthew describes what happened at the foot of the cross with the soldiers casting lots to divide up Jesus' garments, and he says this is a fulfillment of Psalm 22.

"On the cross Jesus cried out to God, and his words directly quoted this Psalm, the first verse, 'My God, My God, why have You forsaken me?' The nineteenth verse prophesied this crying out, 'But You, O Lord, do not be far from me; O my Strength, hasten to help me!' Verse twenty-one says, '**You have answered me**.' Yes, God answered His Son Jesus. He cried out for help, and the Father God raised him from the dead! The resurrection was prophesied over a thousand years before the fact right here in Psalm 22:21!"

Sarah could hardly take it all in. When the gospel of Matthew and the name of Jesus were introduced, it became increasingly difficult for her to concentrate. She actually could not hear it.

Pastor James walked to the front of the stage as he made his final conclusions. "Isaiah 53, verse 10 says 'When You make His soul an offering for sin, He shall see His seed, He shall prolong His days, and the pleasure of the Lord shall prosper in His hand.'" The preacher had proved most convincingly that the Suffering Servant of Isaiah 53 was the Lord Jesus Christ. His voice rose in triumph as he proclaimed the message of salvation through the death, burial, and resurrection of Jesus. Then he gave an invitation to all present to surrender to the Lord and be saved from eternal death and receive the gift of eternal life, asking that they make it public by coming forward and kneeling at the front of the stage.

Pete was quite familiar with this part of the service. At his Baptist church every service was concluded in this way. He had gone down to shake the preacher's hand and join the church when

125

he was fourteen, so he was immune to further pressure from calls for salvation. He always spent this time in observing those around him to see who would go forward. He sensed this was probably an affront to Sarah, and he wanted to lessen her discomfort, so he grabbed her hand and patted it.

"Ouch!" Sarah's hand hadn't recovered from Jenny's stomping it. People around them looked to see what had happened. Pete then noticed the bruise on her hand and looked apologetic and questioning.

"Oh, I'm sorry," he whispered.

"I'll tell you later," Sarah whispered back.

Leaning over, he said, "That was a good sermon, wasn't it? Right out of your Bible, too."

Gloria and Jeff glanced at Pete and Sarah, wondering what was going on and hoping Sarah wasn't turned off. The hymn of invitation was "I Surrender All." Gloria held the hymn book up to Jeff and began to sing, determining she wasn't going to think about Jeff and Sarah, but just her own relationship with God. She put all of her heart into the words, "....Worldly pleasures all forsaken; take me, Jesus, take me now....Make me Savior, wholly Thine. Let me feel the Holy Spirit, truly know that Thou art mine. I surrender all..."

Several people who looked to be college age went down to the front and knelt. It was a holy moment. The pastor led them in prayer, asking that the rest of the congregation say the prayer aloud with those at the altar. "Dear Jesus, I ask You to forgive me of my sins. Thank You for dying for me. Thank You for forgiving me and giving me the gift of eternal life. I open my heart to You and ask You to come in and be my Lord and Savior. Thank you for writing my name in the Lamb's Book of Life. Please lead me in paths of righteousness that I may bring honor and glory to Your name. Amen."

The service was over after the benediction. Gloria had spotted a girl down front that she knew from the BSU meetings, Grace

Thomas. Grace was the one who had invited Gloria to her first BSU meeting and who faithfully picked her up for church each Sunday morning. Gloria rushed down to give her a big hug. The organ and piano were blasting away the hymn, "Victory in Jesus," as more people went down to congratulate those making commitments. The hugging seemed to be contagious, as most people in the church were reaching out to someone close by to hug.

Jeff turned to Pete and said, "That was a fantastic sermon, and I learned so much. I can feel the joy in this place, can't you?"

"You bet," Pete agreed, but he wished he felt it as keenly as Jeff obviously did.

Sarah felt lost and alone in the midst of the celebration. She didn't know how to respond. She had so many questions. Pete's attention turned to her as he realized she was not in tune with everyone else.

"Hugging is a regular way of life at this church, I can see. Now I've got the excuse I've been waiting for, little woman." Gleefully, he grabbed Sarah up in his strong arms and pressed her tightly to his chest, holding her face close to his cheek.

Sarah was surprised but also relieved to hide herself in Pete's secure grasp. It felt good to be loved, and it helped her to put all her agonizing thoughts about the sermon on the back burner of her mind. She allowed Pete to hold her for several minutes, neither one speaking. *I've always been an intellectual. Now I see I've been missing something. This physical pull I'm feeling is terribly exciting, and I feel so blessed by God that this big, sweet guy seems to really care about me. I care about him, too. He's truly wonderful. I don't know if this is love or not, but I love these feelings. Yes, I think I love Pete.... But wait a minute, he's a goy! I can't fall in love with a goy. As my mother always warned me, a nice Jewish girl must marry a nice Jewish boy. I agree with that, too, but what am I going to do with these feelings? He's my friend, okay. And it's good to have feelings for your friends.*

Sarah tried to convince herself that it wouldn't lead to marriage anyway, but in her heart she couldn't be sure of that. She finally decided that if HaShem had led her this far, she could trust Him to continue leading her, especially in something as important as marriage.

CHAPTER EIGHTEEN

FELLOWSHIP

Pete and Sarah were standing beside the SUV when Jeff came out the front door of the church with his palms up and eyebrows raised, shrugging his shoulders. "I can't drag Gloria away from her friends, guys. I guess we'll just have to wait."

"Okay with me, pal," replied Pete cheerfully. "Just unlock the car for us." Jeff unlocked the car and went back inside the church. Pete and Sarah scrambled in the back and sat together as close as possible. *H-m-m-m! This little woman is just right for me, and I think she is warming up to me at last. I wonder if holding her hand and putting my arm around her is in order.*

Pete slowly eased his arm around Sarah and reached down to lightly touch her bruised hand. "Oh, you were going to tell me how you got that bruise."

"My roommate stepped on my hand last night."

"How in the world did that happen?"

"Well, I was getting my things out of the closet to go spend the night with Gloria, and she tripped me. Before I could get up, she crushed my hand with her big foot."

Pete started getting red in the face and demanded to know all the details. He had to pull it out of Sarah little by little because she wanted to forget about it. Pete was as upset with himself as with the meanness of the roommate because this had happened not long after he had pledged to guard and protect Sarah. He was supposed to be her shield, and this made him feel helpless and tremendously frustrated.

Sarah's thoughts turned from herself to Pete, when she realized that he couldn't deal with his anger, and it was getting the best of him. She was touched by his unfeigned sympathy and genuine concern for her. Cradling his face in her hands, she looked deep into his eyes and said, "Pete, I can't handle this, and you can't handle it either. I can see you really meant it when you said you would protect me, but sometimes you won't be able to. Only HaShem can do anything about it. So when you're not with me, just pray for me, okay? And right now I want to give you some medicine for your anger."

Pete began to cool down, when this sweet girl put her gentle hands on his face. He was drinking in every word she said and tracing every inch of her face with his eyes. *What medicine could she possibly mean?* Much to his surprise her lips were covering his, and her arms were around his neck before he could figure out what was happening.

Ooh! I like this medicine! Sarah is not like all the other girls I've had. She is miles apart from any of the others. Oh, Lord, don't let this moment end.

Jeff and Gloria broke the spell when the door flew open, and Gloria said, "Sorry to keep you waiting." Noticing what she had interrupted, she added with a laugh, "Well, I can see you two are not sorry you had to wait!"

Pete regained his composure and freely admitted, "Hey, you've got bad timing, and also God didn't answer my prayer. I just prayed for this moment not to end. Oh, well, I guess He did answer. He just said, 'No.'"

They all laughed, and Pete caressed Sarah and thanked her for the "medicine."

"Am I the only one who is hungry?" asked Jeff. "It seems the rest of you are enjoying visiting, but I'm about wild with starvation setting in!"

"Oh, really?" said Gloria sarcastically. "I saw you talking to two blondes while I was down front with Grace. Aha! You thought I didn't notice, didn't you? You weren't dying of hunger then, unless it was the hungry wolf type." Gloria pretended to be greatly offended, turning away with pouting lips.

"Now, Gloria, don't mistake my intentions. They wanted to talk to me, not the other way around, and it was hard to get away. They were just making sure I felt welcome, and they invited me to come back. Anyway, I was waiting on **you**."

Pete horse laughed. "Sure you were, you hungry wolf. I didn't know you had it in ya, friend. Your lines are almost as good as mine."

Gloria turned around and holding back her laughter, made a fist at Pete. "I'm standin' by my man and **you** quit giving him such a hard time. Let's go eat. I'm ravenous, and not like a wolf either." She burst into laughter which soon became contagious with the four of them.

"Okay, you guys, I'm gonna do penance by taking the four of us out, and I'm the one paying. We're going to Harvey's. I'm a frequent customer, Pete, both in Columbus and Starkville, so I can vouch for the food. Is everyone in agreement?"

All agreed, and they were on the way.

After the waitress took their orders, Gloria directed the conversation to the church service. "Well, what did you all think of my church?"

Jeff was the first to answer. "If I had known that going to church was that exciting, I'd have been going long before now. The people were friendly, the music was great, and the preacher really had everyone in the palm of his hand."

Pete was the next to comment. "Well, folks, I've found that most Baptist churches have a lot to offer, but this one was unique. First of all, I was impressed that three-fourths of the congregation were college students, or at least they appeared to be about our age. You'd think that the students would prefer a downtown church. I go to Columbus First Baptist downtown, but the MUW students make up only about a fourth of the congregation, if that much. Yes, there's something going on at Adaton Baptist. I could feel it."

"That was the Holy Spirit you felt," said Gloria. "Brother James has said many times that he wants our worship to be led by the Spirit and not by the flesh, not by a lot of hype. He honors the work of the Holy Spirit, and he encourages everyone to yield to the moving of the Spirit. He says you don't work it up, you just let it flow. Does that make sense?"

Jeff needed to say something. "I don't know anything about spiritual things, but I do know that I felt something in church today. Y'all don't know this, but I've never been one to sing along in a group, and I sure don't ever sing by myself, not even in the shower. However, this morning I wanted to sing for the first time, and I think it was God who told me to start singing." Jeff looked right at Gloria and smiled, knowing that a singer like her would value what he was sharing.

"That's great, Jeff! I wish I had heard you, but I was so caught up in the worship that I didn't even notice whether you sang or not."

"Anyway, something happened to me while I was singing, and I think it changed me. Maybe it was the Holy Spirit that touched me."

Gloria was anxious to assure him that it was. "Yes, Jeff, I could feel the electricity from your hand when I tugged on you to make you sit down." She giggled. "You were still standing after everyone else sat down."

Pete didn't want to be outdone. "Hey, I know about the Holy Spirit. Back before I was saved – and I was fourteen – I used to feel like I would die if they sang one more verse of 'Just as I Am.' A lot of church services ended with that hymn, but during revivals it was worse than ever. When the preacher started warning sinners about hell and urging them, or rather us, to repent of our sins and accept Christ, I'd hold on to the pew as tight as I could to keep from going down front. The preacher always said that the Holy Spirit was convicting the sinners of their sins, and they, or rather we, wouldn't get any sleep until we surrendered to God. I dreaded that time in the service because I knew what a sinner I was, and I was forced to think about the fact I'd bust hell wide open, if I didn't get saved. To me, getting saved meant giving up all the fun things in life and just spending the rest of your life being bored and doing stuff you didn't want to do to please the Lord. The conviction of the Holy Spirit made you miserable until you surrendered your life to God." Pete's expression looked pretty desperate as he relived those experiences.

"Well, did you get saved, Pete?" asked Gloria, anxiously.

Pete gave a sigh of relief. "As a matter of fact, I did!" he crowed, triumphantly. "I was fourteen. It was at a revival, and my best friend answered the call to accept Christ. I saw it as my chance to make things right with God, so I followed him down front. Both of us shook the preacher's hand and told him we repented and wanted to accept Christ as our Lord and Savior. The preacher made us get down on our knees, and he prayed for us to be assured that Christ had saved us and would give us the power to walk the Christian life daily." Pete sat back, smugly.

Sarah had not said a word during this whole conversation, but now she ventured to ask some questions. "As an observant Jew I must say that what all of you have been saying is pretty confusing to me. I have a lot of questions, but first let me say that I, too, felt something in that worship service. We call the Holy Spirit the Ruach HaKodesh, and I haven't experienced Him very often, but when I did know that He was near me, it was very much like what I felt this morning. Now for some questions. What do you mean by the terms 'get saved' and 'accept Christ'"?

Pete, ever vigilant in his assignment as Sarah's shield, could see red flags. He was looking forward to a good meal and good fellowship with friends, and he didn't think this was the time or place to try to get Sarah saved. An idea quickly popped into his head, and as carnal a Christian as he was, he still recognized it as divine wisdom, not his own thoughts.

"Sarah, that's a good question, but I see our salad coming, and how about we finish it off first, then go for the discussion on theology? Hey, I thought of something even better. Did you read the flyer in the bulletin about a special service at Trinity Church this Wednesday night? A Messianic Jew is the speaker, and I bet he is just the person to give you some answers. You've seen that church, haven't you? It's between here and Columbus. Why don't we go hear this guy? I'd be happy to pick everyone up on my Chevy. Whaddya say?"

The waitress was serving the salad as Pete made his proposition. Sarah seemed puzzled by the term "Messianic Jew," but Gloria was delighted at this suggestion and looked at Jeff to see if he agreed. Jeff didn't hesitate. He wanted more of what he had just experienced in the church. "Sure, I don't see why not. What about you girls?"

Gloria looked at Sarah. "Do you want to go, Sarah? We're still planning to go with you to temple on Friday night."

"Well, I, uh, well, uh...," stuttered Sarah. Everyone was looking at her, waiting for an answer. *Oh, why resist when Pete is so irresistible,* she concluded within herself. *It would be great for the four of us to be together again, and I don't have to buy into anything. I can just listen and weigh all the rhetoric.*

"Okay, I'll go." Sarah felt like she'd lost the play but not the whole ballgame. "Now go ahead and eat your salad. It's getting cold!" she laughed.

They dug into the salad with a vengeance. With his mouth full, Pete said, "Can you believe we'd rather talk than eat? We're turning into a bunch of weirdos!" Everybody laughed at this and nodded their heads, stuffing in the salad and crackers.

"Well at least we can be weirdos together." said Gloria. "I really love being with you guys."

The fellowship was truly sweet. During the main course the talk revolved around school and extra-curricular activities. Gloria shared about her music courses, required attendance at concerts, and upcoming voice and piano recitals. She drew some laughs with her imitation of the eccentric choral conductor and the embarrassing methods used by her voice instructor for reaching high notes.

134

Pete shared about his first speech in public speaking class and about his strange classmates in sociology. Sarah shared about the antics of her instructor in French and how he tried to corner a blonde bombshell in his office. She told about the anti-Semitism of her accounting professor.

Jeff felt like all his academic experiences were colorless in comparison to the others, but he delighted in telling about the rewards of his birthday cake operation. His freshman year he made an effort to sell stadium seats and student directories, he said, but the slim profits from those sales were not worth all his efforts. He dropped that and concentrated on selling birthday cakes to the students' parents to surprise their children. This brought joy and satisfaction to all, including Jeff.

"Hey, dude. I didn't know your life was so exciting. I thought you were more machine than human, even though you have the movie star looks. Proves you can't know a person just by being his roommate, right? Fellowship at the heart level is what counts, man."

"So true," replied Jeff, ignoring Pete's backhanded compliment. "Spending time together is what bonds people together – you know, having common experiences."

"Well, we were an uncommon bunch to start with, but I see real possibilities for us now," remarked Sarah, grinning at Pete.

Pete gave Sarah a seductive look, then immediately felt ashamed and hid his face with his hand, looking sheepishly at Sarah between parted fingers. Sarah got the message, shyly smiling back with lowered eyes.

The waitress came with the bill, asking if anyone wanted dessert. Gloria hoped to prolong the conversation, so she asked for another cup of coffee, but no dessert. The rest took her cue and asked for drink refills.

Jeff wanted to pursue the line of conversation about common experiences, so he suggested that Pete join them on Friday, making deliveries of the birthday cakes at MUW. He had been thinking about the gap of time between this project and the temple service, and he knew just the thing to fill it with, a short jaunt over to Tupelo to introduce his new friends to his parents.

Sarah was the first to respond. "First, I had zero social life at Mississippi State, and now since I met you three people, I can hardly catch my breath for all the social activity. It's a literal whirlwind, but I love it."

"Don't say it's all social because it's business, it's academic, and it's spiritual. You're right though, if we're doing it together, it's social," commented Jeff. "Hey, I love it, too. I've been an all-business guy ever since I got out of high school, and I didn't know how starved I was for friends and fun."

Pete felt privileged to be included with these three special people. "My life has been one long party since about the eleventh grade in high school, so I know about having fun. However, the fun I'm having with y'all is a different kind, and I much prefer it. I'm makin' a public announcement right now that I've left my old way of life behind. I want my life to count for something, so, therefore, I'm taking church more seriously from now on, and I'm spendin' my time with people like you who do the same thing."

"Well, Gloria, you haven't said anything. What do you think of these weekend plans?" asked Jeff.

"I'd like to say something awesome, but all I can say is I'm tickled pink!" exclaimed Gloria. "It's almost too good to be true that we can have this kind of fellowship in the year 1997. Most college kids I've met, except for the ones at BSU, have worldly things on their minds. Trying to live their lives to glorify God is an alien concept to them. So, yes, let's deliver the birthday cakes, go to Tupelo to meet your parents, and come back to attend temple in Columbus. Everyone in favor, say 'aye!'"

All raised their hands with enthusiastic "ayes."

"Jeff, don't forget I'm willing to help you do the bookwork for your business enterprises," volunteered Sarah. "It won't take me long to move my stuff to Gloria's room this afternoon. Would you like to bring the books to the lobby, say around four o'clock, and you can show me what to do?"

"Sounds like a winner," agreed Jeff.

Pete snapped to attention when he realized that Sarah would be re-entering a danger zone. Those despicable roommates of hers and Gloria's may try to give them trouble again.

"Look, Sarah, you need to remember that I'm your shield, and I have strong arms." Pete flexed his muscles. "Surely there's a heavy trunk or piece of furniture you need me to move for you. Or maybe you have one of those little refrigerators." He knew he had to get up on that third floor and be a buffer between Sarah and the cruel roommates.

Sarah had been pushing fear back into a far corner of her mind, but now the memory of her recent attack came surging back. "Yes, Pete, I do need your help. If you could come to my room and move the heavy things, then you could stay in the lobby until I do the rest. I'd feel safe knowing that you are on the premises, and we could make it clear to Jenny and Rebecca that you will be waiting for me in the lobby. Maybe you could do some studying while you're waiting, so your time won't be wasted."

"Waiting on you is definitely not a waste of time, sugar." It was the first time he had ventured a term of endearment, and he was happy to see that Sarah seemed to like it.

Gloria's wheels were turning. "We've made a lot of plans here today. This is all very exciting. Since we're going to be seeing a lot of each other, maybe we better call a fast on fellowship until Wednesday night so we can get our studying done. And I've got to put my time in practicing piano and voice. There's also a concert on Tuesday night I'm required to attend, so that means getting my paper ready for Professor Holder before Tuesday night. How is yours coming, Jeff?"

"I'm almost through. If I'm not going to be seeing you until Wednesday, I'll have plenty of time to finish it. By the way, are we still meeting on Thursday to study Economics?"

"Of course, sweetie." She had already figured out that her private time with Jeff was dwindling, so she definitely wanted to hold on to their Thursday night tryst.

The waitress came back with Jeff's credit card and receipt. It was time to go. On the way to the door, Gloria spotted Rebecca and Jenny at the far corner table. She grabbed Sarah's hand and started toward them. Unfortunately, it was the bruised hand, and Sarah yelped.

Rebecca and Jenny looked up and were startled to see the two Jewish girls they so hated. Before Sarah could retreat, Gloria took her other hand, and they walked right into the hateful stares of Rebecca and Jenny. Gloria was determined to go on the offense against hate, and, contrary to her natural feelings, she willed herself to speak kindly. "Hello. Hope your food was good. We really enjoyed ours."

Rebecca reluctantly responded, "It was okay, nothing to write home about. Who are your friends?"

Sarah could hardly bear to stand there. She marveled that Gloria could have anything to do with such obviously wretched people.

"Those guys went with us to church today – Jeff Quentin and Pete Carson. We've recently become friends with them. Would you like to meet them?" asked Gloria.

Rebecca felt intimidated by such astonishingly good-looking men because she had never even had a date. *What have I got to do with men anyway?* "That's okay. We wouldn't want to steal them from you," Rebecca teased.

Jenny was beginning to see Sarah in a new light, realizing that if one of those guys was dating her, then maybe there was something to her after all. She wondered if it was the brunette or the blonde. If men appealed to her, she would have felt more attracted to the blonde. "Sarah, I hope you aren't too sore from your fall last night. I'm sorry it happened."

Sarah knew Jenny was not sincere, but, taking her cue from Gloria's attitude, she replied, "Just a little bruise on my hand. It's all right."

The hateful stares had softened somewhat by now, and Gloria felt like her mission was accomplished. "We better go – time to study, ya know."

Sarah was hopeful at this point that her move would be un-eventful. "Jenny, I'll be getting my things as soon as we get back to the dorm. I'll try to leave everything neat for you."

Rebecca piped up, "I've already moved my things in the room, so I hope you don't have trouble getting your things out. I tried not to block anything of yours until you got it moved."

Rebecca didn't lie well, but Sarah took her words at face value and managed a kind response. "That was thoughtful of you. Thanks."

"Bye now. See ya around," said Gloria, cheerfully. She and Sarah smiled and left to rejoin their men.

Jeff and Pete had been looking on curiously. Gloria steered them to the SUV, and they were belted in before she explained. "Those were our roommates. I thought we needed a little closure, so this was the perfect opportunity."

"**What!**" Pete was furious. "What were you doing talking to those creeps? They are out to cut your throats! You should avoid them like you would poisonous snakes!"

Gloria figured that Sarah had told Pete what happened while they were waiting on her to come out of the church. "Pete," Gloria cajoled, "Jesus said to love our enemies and pray for those who persecute us. We're just trying to overcome evil with good."

Jeff was puzzled by Pete's violent reaction. "What's going on here? What do you know that I don't know? What's the deal with your roommates?"

Sarah and Gloria both explained what had happened the night before. Then they had **two** angry men on their hands. Jeff shook his head in disbelief. "This is horrible. Sarah, you were attacked **twice** in twenty-four hours, and you did absolutely nothing to deserve it! It seems to stem from your being Jewish. Gloria and I are Jewish, too, but it hasn't happened to us."

Gloria had to interrupt. "Wait a minute. I have experienced some prejudice for being Jewish, especially in elementary school, but it doesn't compare with what you've been going through, Sarah. And Jeff, you haven't even 'come out of the closet' yet, as they say!"

"I seem to be the odd man out, here," said Pete. "In my lifetime I may have been the persecutor, especially in regard to blacks, but I've never been the persecuted. Now I feel like it's happening to me if it's happening to Sarah. And I am **mad!**"

Gloria felt a responsibility to defuse the anger aroused in Pete and Jeff. "We're going to pray. Only God can help you deal with these strong emotions," she announced with authority. Grabbing hands, they bowed, and Gloria prayed. "Lord, please cool us off. Please take away the hurt, fear, anger, and resentment. Show all of us how to handle hard situations. Help us to do it like Jesus would. In His name, amen."

The air was cleared. Pete took a deep breath, letting the anger drain out. Then he gave Sarah a warm embrace. Jeff turned the key in the ignition, then reached over and squeezed Gloria's hand. "There's safety in numbers. One for all, and all for one."

The other three chorused, "One for all, and all for one!"

CHAPTER NINETEEN

MOMENT OF TRUTH

Gloria and Sarah were already in the lobby at Hamlin by six o'clock on Wednesday, eagerly waiting for Jeff and Pete to show up. They hadn't seen each other since Pete helped Sarah move to Gloria's room, and Jeff transferred his bookkeeping records to Sarah on Sunday. It had been three whole days of "fasting," as Gloria called it. Absence did make the heart grow fonder they both had discovered. It had been good for them, however, because it gave them time to reflect on all that had happened thus far in their relationships. It was mind-boggling to think that Gloria had met Jeff just a week ago, Sarah six days ago, and Pete four days ago! The lives of all four of them had drastically changed in that short time, and it all got started when Gloria ventured to approach Jeff in the library that night.

Since Sarah moved in with Gloria, they had done some heart-to-heart sharing, finding out about their experiences growing up, their parents, their school life, the fun times, and the sad times. Their personalities made a good match. They studied together, ate together, read the Bible, and prayed together. Gloria had faithfully made her piano practice time at the music building each day, attended the concert the night before, and completed her history paper on Ben Yehuda. Sarah had done all her assignments and also the book work for Jeff.

They had not run into Jeff or Pete on the campus, and they had not had a phone call from them either. Gloria marveled that everyone had been abiding by her suggestion for a "fellowship fast." Trying to keep Jeff off her mind, Gloria began to think about her parents, and how she had been neglecting them. Usually, she called them every Saturday, but it had been two weeks since she called, and she hadn't written. Neither had they. Feeling guilty about it, she called home as soon as the concert was over last night.

She told them about her new friends. She wanted them to be happy for her that she now had a Jewish roommate and a Jewish boyfriend, but she could hear the disappointment in their voices, even though they said it was good. When she told them that she had been to the temple in Columbus and was going with her friends to a church to hear a Messianic Jewish speaker, there was silence on the other end. She knew she had touched a nerve, so she changed the subject and told them about helping Jeff deliver birthday cakes at MUW. Her father was delighted when she gave a good report on her progress in Economics, and he promised to reward her with an extra deposit in her bank account.

Alvin and Sylvia Sondheim were proud of their daughter's musical accomplishments, but they especially wanted her to be well-known socially at the University. Her father kept asking if she was getting involved in activities on campus, especially in student government. Gloria had to admit she had no interest in that. She wanted to share with them her excitement about the Baptist Student Union, the people she was meeting there, and the enriching Bible studies, but she knew they wouldn't understand. They may even object to her involvement. They knew she was attending church because she always had, but they would not have approved of her going to a rural Baptist church. They would expect their daughter to attend First United Methodist Church or at least one of the big churches downtown, so she didn't mention Adaton Baptist.

Gloria's parents had not seen her since late August, and they really missed their only child. They planned for her to fly home for Thanksgiving. Gloria tried to talk them into visiting the campus before then, but they had to say no. Her father was busier than ever with his campaign for City Councilman of Port Jefferson, and the election was right around the corner. Gloria really wanted them to meet her new friends, and she wanted her friends to meet them. *Oh well, God will make a way.*

"I'm a little nervous about going to this Trinity Church tonight," admitted Sarah. "A Messianic Jew is speaking. I know that means a Jew who believes in Jesus, or else he wouldn't be speaking at a church. But I could say I myself am a Messianic Jew because I believe the Messiah is coming. I pray for it every day."

"Hey, I hadn't thought of calling myself a Messianic Jew, but that's exactly what I am, too!" exclaimed Gloria, trying on this new identity for size. "I've been calling myself a Christian, and I am, but maybe I'm better described as a Messianic Jew. On the other hand, I've also heard the term 'Hebrew Christian.'" Throwing up her hands, she said, "Well, whatever I'm called, I love Jesus. He's Jewish, and I'm following Him, no matter what."

Sarah looked at Gloria with admiration. "You are so sure of what you believe, and I like that. But even after hearing Pastor James' sermon, I still can't understand why you think Jesus is the Messiah."

Gloria took Sarah's hand and looked her right in the eye. "Sarah, I'm not going to let anybody coerce you into believing in Jesus, BUT will you promise me that you will keep an open mind tonight? And if you hear enough evidence, biblical evidence, to prove that He truly is the Messiah, will you believe in Him?"

Sarah was touched by the love in Gloria's eyes, and she savored the feeling of love that was washing over her as Gloria continued to hold her hand and look into her eyes. Waiting a full minute to answer, Sarah said quietly, "Yes, I will open my mind and my heart and listen. I appreciate your love, and I will give your god a chance."

Just as Sarah reached out to embrace Gloria, Rebecca and Jenny slipped up behind them and held their heads together. "Aha! We caught you, you hypocrites!" accused Jenny. "I thought you were too holy for such unholy love."

Sarah was about to protest, when she saw Jeff and Pete enter the lobby.

Gloria felt like they had been rescued just in time. She didn't know what to say to Jenny, and now she didn't have to say anything. She wasn't depending on her own defense anyway because she knew they were innocent, and God would vindicate them in His way and time.

Pete didn't hear Jenny's words, but he didn't like it that "the enemy" was standing so close to his girl, so he moved quickly to grab Sarah's hand and lead her out to the car, not even acknowledging the presence of "that girl." Jeff did the same with Gloria. Rebecca and Jenny had a short-lived victory. They scowled at Pete and Jeff, then turned their backs and left for their room.

Pulling up into the parking lot of Trinity Church, Pete was pleased he had been the one to instigate their outing. He had always been curious about this church. Construction began four years ago, and he had watched its steady progress as he drove back and forth between Columbus and Starkville. He wondered who would want to build a church in the middle of a cow pasture. He didn't think people would drive so far to church, but evidently it was thriving, judging from the cars in the parking lot. *It isn't a Baptist church, or the sign would have said so. It's probably one of those non-denominational churches. This is an adventure, and I'm expecting something great to happen here. I feel an excitement, especially for Sarah to be here. Maybe this is where she will see Jesus as the Messiah.*

"Well, what do you think?" asked Pete, indicating the building itself.

"I like it," answered Jeff. "This architecture is neat, and these massive front doors look hand-carved."

"Yes, it is beautiful, and whoever designed these doors with a cross built into the handles is very gifted. I like the way you are entering through the cross when you grab the handles to open the doors," said Gloria. "I'm glad you suggested coming here, Pete. I've got a feeling we're going to really enjoy the service. How do you feel about it, Sarah?"

Sarah needed to express herself before they went inside. "To be honest with you, I'm scared. If Abba and Imma could see me now, they would be very disapproving, almost outraged. I was never a rebellious child, and I had great respect for my parents, wanting to please them in every area of my life. Unfortunately, they are not around now, and I have to make my own decisions. It's true that HaShem seems to have put you three people in my life, so I have to consider that the places we go together are part of His plan for me. However, maybe I'm not the only one making big changes. Have you considered that God may be using ME to be an influence on you three?"

"Yes, I've considered it. You are leading me back to my Jewish roots, and I thank you," said Gloria.

"I don't need to answer that question, sugar. It's obvious that I'm 'under the influence' around you!" laughed Pete. "Hey, let's go in. It's almost time for the service to begin."

There was a circle of dancers – men, women, and children – on the stage, dancing to "Shaalu Shalom Yerushalayim." The congregation was singing with the dancers, first in Hebrew, then in English – "Pray for the peace of Jerusalem, shalom, shalom… Jerusalem shall live in peace." This was a bittersweet experience for Sarah as she reflected on her parents living in Israel and dying in Jerusalem. There was anything but peace in that strife-torn city, the Holy City of Scripture.

None of the four had ever experienced worship like they did at Trinity. It took some getting used to because they hadn't expected drums and guitars. The praise team consisted of four ladies singing, including the one at the piano, and a man leading the singing. There was a bass guitarist, another guitarist, and a drummer. There was no organ, which was quite unusual to them. They found them-selves joining in the clapping, and Gloria raised her hands without self-consciousness as the music moved into an intimate level of worship. Gloria was the only one who knew the songs, but the others made an effort to join in on the repetitive choruses.

After about twenty minutes of worship, Jeff began to have the same sensations he had at Adaton Baptist, and this time he didn't hesitate to yield to the Holy Spirit. Before he realized what he was doing, he was raising his hands to the Lord in complete abandon.

Pete didn't see the need of raising his hands, and he wondered why Gloria and Jeff did. *This isn't something Baptists do. I am not sure my parents would approve.*

At her synagogue in New York, Sarah had seen some pretty lively dancing on special occasions, such as weddings, so the drums and guitars didn't bother her, but she still felt way out of her element in this church. It was even more threatening than Adaton Baptist.

Dr. Michael L. Brown was the Messianic Jewish speaker,[28] and this was the first night of a three-day conference he was leading at Trinity Church. His testimony was quite dramatic. He was saved at the age of sixteen at a Pentecostal church in New York City in 1971. He was not a religious Jew and thought Jesus was for the Catholics, but God got ahold of his heart at that church service. He had been a heroin-shooting Jewish rock drummer and was radically transformed and started preaching on a regular basis at the age of eighteen.

Sarah could not identify with this type of Jewish person, even though she had to admit that his changed life was surely the result of a powerful encounter with HaShem. More powerful, however, than Dr. Brown's own story were the stories of miracle healings he recounted. He told about mighty men of God who knew how to pray, and whole cities and countries were shaken and changed. Sarah had never even heard their names before, and yet their exploits were the stuff of award-winning movies and best-selling novels. She marveled at all she was hearing and wondered how so much had been hidden from her. She, too, believed that HaShem answered prayer, but her experiences of answered prayer were dwarfed in comparison to the stories Dr. Brown was telling.

All four of them were rapt with attention, but Sarah was being impacted the most. At the very beginning of his sermon, Dr. Brown had said God told him to change what he was planning to preach and to preach on Jesus' crucifixion. He knew that the people who had come for the conference were already familiar with the details of the crucifixion, but he would have to be obedient. His exhortation to repentance was hard-hitting, and Sarah felt more and more uncomfortable. The Jesus that Dr. Brown painted was hardly a Gentile or Western God. He was a Jew of Jews in a Jewish setting.

Sarah found herself on the side of Jesus as he battled his opponents, the religious leaders in Jerusalem, and was even identifying with Him. She was actually feeling for him as he endured the mocking, spitting, beating, and finally the excruciating pain of the nails, the thorns, the humiliation, and the torture of trying to breathe. This sermon was affecting her in a more emotional way than had the Adaton Baptist Pastor's sermon. After an hour of preaching, Dr. Brown built to a climax, driving the knife of his words straight into the hearts of the congregation. He pointed his finger and shouted, "Those Jewish leaders and the Roman soldiers crucified an innocent man, and **you** would never have done that, right? You would have followed him down to the foot of the cross, right? You would never have betrayed him or deserted him in his hour of need, right?" Then suddenly, Dr. Brown leveled his charge in a loud, threatening tone, "**Wrong! You** were there when he was crucified, and **you** put him on that cross! **Your sins** caused his torture and death! You have no hope until you admit your sin, and you can't be forgiven unless you **repent** and turn your back on sin. Jesus would never have had to suffer and die if it were not to pay for **your sins. You** crucified Him! Admit it! Confess it! Repent! Feel the agony he suffered for **you.** He died for **YOU.**"

Since Sarah had become emotionally involved with the story of Jesus' crucifixion, she was also becoming involved in this challenge, especially when Dr. Brown came closer to the front of the stage and softened his voice in a final appeal. "Jesus has already forgiven you. What He said to those present at the cross that day 2,000 years ago, He was saying to you down through the centuries: 'Father, forgive them, for they know not what they do.'[29] He is right now making

147

a personal invitation to you to admit your guilt, so you can receive His pardon. He says, 'Come unto Me, all you who labor and are heavy-laden, and I will give you rest. Take My yoke upon you, and learn of Me, for I am meek and lowly, and you will find rest for your souls. For My yoke is easy, and My burden is light.'"[30]

The only lights turned on in the sanctuary were those on the stage, but Sarah noticed there was a light on Dr. Brown's head when he bowed and began to pray for the people. It was a strange glow, and she began to wonder if it had been there all along, or if it just now appeared. People started coming to the front, kneeling before the steps to the stage. The pianist played softly, and the congregation bowed in silent prayer. Dr. Brown prayed for each kneeling person, and he gave each a different message. What really stunned Sarah was when he put his hand on a person's head and prayed, the man or woman would crumple to the floor. This happened with about half of those who had come forward. Some looked like they had touched an electric wire, and others appeared to have fainted. No one showed any alarm, but sometimes a person from the congregation would go up to pray over someone who was lying on the floor. Some showed no emotion, and others cried softly or sobbed violently. Each reaction was different. Sarah was mesmerized by all the strange things occurring, wondering what her friends thought about it.

She glanced at Pete, and he looked just as puzzled as she did. Gloria and Jeff were whispering to each other. Jeff asked Gloria if she had seen this kind of thing before. She had not, but she was clearly moved by all of it. She told Jeff that she felt the Lord wanted her to go kneel at the altar and pray. Jeff said he wouldn't let her go by herself, in case she fell out, too.

Pete and Sarah quietly walked to the back and down the side aisle to go out to the hall and find a water cooler. While they were in the hall, they spotted a large room with food spread out on a table. The room was decorated with an Israeli flag, and Judaica items were placed all around. Some ladies in the kitchen saw them and beckoned to them to come in and have some punch. Beautiful taped music with a Jewish flavor was playing. There was a book table, and the ladies encouraged them to browse.

"Hey, these refreshments look inviting," drooled Pete. "Too bad we have to wait until the service is over, but I'm glad we found this place. I was getting spooked in there."

"Don't say that, Pete," responded Sarah. "I think something holy was going on in there. It was strange, but that doesn't mean it wasn't a work of the Ruach HaKodesh. Dr. Brown is quite a speaker. He almost convinced me that Jesus is the Messiah, but, of course, he couldn't be because the world is in a bigger mess now than when he was on earth. And I surely don't believe that he was raised from the dead. His disciples came and stole his body and started the rumor that he was alive. That's what the rabbis have always taught us.[31] Anyway, I'm not scared of Christianity any more. I admire the people he talked about who gave their lives for what they believed in, some of them even burned at the stake!"

Pete and Sarah looked at the books, most of them written by Dr. Brown, and they sat down and continued their conversation about the things they had experienced in the service at Adaton and here. The time passed quickly as they enjoyed each other's company.

People started coming in for refreshments, children the first in line. "Surely Jeff and Gloria will be here any minute," said Pete. "Let's get in line. I'm hungry."

"No, I think we ought to wait," said Sarah, keeping her eyes on the door. After a few minutes the room was filled with people, and still Jeff and Gloria had not come. Everyone was friendly to Pete and Sarah, trying to get them to take refreshments, but they explained they were waiting for their friends.

Pete got a strange look on his face as he leaned over and whispered to Sarah, "Hey, you don't think Gloria is in there stretched out on the floor, do you? Like those other people Dr. Brown prayed for?"

"Oh, no, I hadn't thought of that. Let's go back in there." They walked into the sanctuary and were relieved to find Gloria and Jeff with Dr. Brown, sitting in chairs and engaged in serious conversation. They were the only ones in the sanctuary.

Gloria saw Pete and Sarah coming. She stood up and flashed her beautiful smile to them. "Dr. Brown, I want you to meet Sarah Bernstein, my roommate, and Pete Carson. In only a week's time the four of us have become fast friends."

Dr. Brown and Jeff stood as introductions were made. Dr. Brown extended his hand to Pete and Sarah. "It's a real blessing to meet you. Have a seat. Here, let's make a circle with these chairs."

Jeff was clearly excited, and Gloria's face was lit up like a football stadium as she looked at him. "I wish you had been here a few minutes ago," Jeff said, breathlessly. "Let me tell you what happened. I came up here to the altar just to look after Gloria, never expecting anything for myself. Well, Dr. Brown was praying for everybody, and when he came to me, he read my mail! It was like he had been snooping on me and knew all about me. He told me stuff about myself, my family, my dreams, my ambitions, things he could not possibly have known. Then I caught on – it wasn't **him**, it was the Lord speaking to me **through** him!"

Pete's eyes were getting bigger and bigger, and Sarah was feeling fearful. Jeff continued, "He even said that I would be seeing my parents soon, and the Lord was preparing me for a painful encounter, but that my friends would help me weather the storm. I thought of our visit this Friday. He said that He, the Lord, would give me an understanding heart for my mother, and He would use **me** to bring her into His sheepfold. He also said that He, the Lord, had given me power to get wealth in order to establish His covenant."[32] Jeff stopped talking, dumbfounded that God would say these things to him, when he had ignored God his whole life until the past week.

"Wonderful!" was all Pete could say, as he pondered Jeff's words.

"I can't remember what He said to me after that because at that point I lost it! Grown men don't cry, as they say, but I did. I know it was God. It was Jesus. Now what am I supposed to do, Dr. Brown?"

Dr. Brown had been praying quietly as he observed Pete and Sarah receiving Jeff's report. "Jeff, have you ever publicly confessed Jesus Christ as your personal Savior and Lord?"

Everyone looked at Jeff. "Uh, well, I think the Holy Spirit touched me last Sunday at church, and now tonight, I know God spoke to me."

Dr. Brown wouldn't let him off the hook. "That's not what I asked."

"Okay, I have to say no."

"Well, would you like to do that right now in front of your friends?"

"Yes, I would, I really would."

"Okay, Jeff. Let me share this Scripture with you, ask you some questions, and then we can pray. The Bible says that if you confess with your mouth the Lord Jesus and believe in your heart that God raised Him from the dead, you will be saved. That's in Romans 10:9. Also, the prophet Joel said, 'Whoever calls on the name of the Lord shall be saved.'[33] That's pretty clear, don't you think?" Jeff nodded yes. "Do you believe Jesus was and is the Son of God, and that God the Father raised him from the dead? Do you believe Jesus was telling the truth when He said, 'I am the Way, the Truth, and the Life. No one comes to the Father but by me'?"[34]

"Yes, I do," answered Jeff.

"So do you want to pray now and receive forgiveness for your sins and eternal life that Jesus has purchased for you by His death and resurrection?"

"Yes, I do," answered Jeff.

"Well, let's pray and seal the deal, and then you can confess with your mouth to your friends that Jesus is your Lord and Savior," directed Dr. Brown. He asked the others to join them in prayer, affirming Jesus' sacrifice on the cross for their sins, His resurrection to give them eternal life, and the Holy Spirit to convict, guide, teach, empower, and comfort them in their everyday lives.

Jeff prayed, self-consciously at first, then louder and bolder, "Thank You, Lord Jesus, for bringing me here tonight, for showing me Your truth, for Dr. Brown, and for my friends here. Thank You for dying for me, for forgiving all my sins, for saving my soul and for eternal life. I want to follow and obey you the rest of my life. Amen." Jeff looked up into Gloria's eyes, which were wet with tears. Pete looked at him admiringly, and Dr. Brown was grinning out from under his bushy moustache. But Sarah's eyes were downcast.

Jeff wasn't finished sealing the deal yet. "Friends, this reminds me of the end of a wedding when the preacher says, 'I present to you Mr. and Mrs. Smith,' or whatever, and then he says, 'You can kiss the bride!' So let me make my similar announcement --- I want you all to know from this moment on that Jesus is my Savior and Lord!" Then Jeff breathed a deep sigh of relief. The deal was sealed.

Dr. Brown was chuckling. "No, you can't kiss him, just hug him." It was Adaton Baptist all over again with marathon hugging. Sarah's confusion melted away as soon as Pete put his arms around her and held her close.

"Time to celebrate, folks!" proclaimed Dr. Brown. "They tell me there are some delicious falafels back there in the fellowship hall. Let's go eat." He led the way.

"What's a falafel?" asked Gloria. Sarah perked up. Finally, she was back in the ballgame. As they walked down the hall, she informed her friends on the subject of Mediterranean cuisine.

CHAPTER TWENTY

A NIGHT OF MIRACLES

Driving away from Trinity Church, Pete was deep in thought as Jeff held forth in the back seat, replaying his dramatic encounter with Truth, the Lord Jesus Himself. Gloria was hanging on every word, so delighted for Jeff to have center stage. Her hero was taking on angelic proportions as he re-preached Dr. Brown's sermon.

Sarah's mood matched Pete's, but with a more troubled dimension of thought. Dr. Brown's use of the New Testament was reverberating in her mind. When he quoted Jesus' claims of divinity, she was unnerved by the weight of authority the words carried, and she was fighting to quell the emotional attachment to Jesus that had been called forth from her inner being during the horrible depiction of His crucifixion. Yet she knew she was obligated to ferociously resist these fabrications of truth. She felt so outnumbered, but at least Pete was somewhat of an ally. She could tell he had not wholeheartedly embraced the things that went on tonight at Trinity Church.

Jeff's sudden loud proclamation intruded on her thoughts. "I'm going to the Christian book store and buy me a really good Bible, a new translation I can understand. I vow not to continue in my biblical illiteracy. I feel like a starving man. What Dr. Brown preached was like an appetizer to me, and now I am ravenous for Truth. I think I could literally **eat** a Bible!" he laughed.

Gloria clapped her hands in approval. "Jeff, you really did get saved tonight. What you said is the greatest proof – being **hungry** for the Word of God. I've been learning at BSU that the first sign a person has been born again is this desire to study the Bible and grow as a Christian."

Pete felt like the air was getting stuffy, so he turned on the air-conditioning full blast. "Hey guys, I got this great new tape. Listen to this. Pink Floyd is one of my favorites. Why don't we just chill for a while? People will think we are religious freaks, if we get too far out with all these church meetings." He didn't wait for agreement but started the tape full volume. It was about time he asserted himself, he thought. After all, wasn't it **his** car and **his** idea to go to Trinity Church in the first place?

Gloria was alerted immediately that all was not well with Pete, but she sensed the Holy Spirit telling her to be silent. Jeff picked up on Gloria's leading, and he decided to simply trust the Lord, not taking offense at Pete's abrasiveness.

"Friend, you've got an idea I can go with," joked Jeff. "It is chilly in this car, and if I'm not mistaken, there's a little lady next to me who needs some warming up. I'm just the man to do it, too. Come here, honey," he coaxed as he drew Gloria into his outstretched arms.

Sarah was relieved that the conversation had changed gears. Looking at Pete gratefully, she said, "I'm cold, too." Pete was delighted he had gained control of a threatening situation. He peered into the darkness of the back seat to see what level of affection might be employed with his cherished Sarah. Unfortunately, the bucket seats presented an obstacle to his affectionate advances.

Sarah started screaming at the top of her lungs, "Watch out! Stop! Stop, Pete! There has been an accident!" Police cars were blocking the road. Two cars had evidently collided, and paramedics were on the scene, pulling bodies from the cars. Pete slammed on brakes and turned the music off.

"Oh, gosh!" gasped Gloria. "I hope it's not somebody we know."

Without a word Jeff got out of the car and purposefully walked over to a young man lying on the ground who was unattended. He knelt down and took the man's hand, leaned over him, and bowed his head in prayer. Then he began to talk to the man, and the man went from crying to laughing, as Jeff knelt by his side for about fifteen minutes. During all this time none of the medical people had come near them. Neither did the state troopers. Pete, Sarah, and Gloria stayed in the car at the direction of a deputy, but Gloria wanted so badly to see what was going on. She saw Jeff helping the young man to his feet, and here they came toward the car.

As they approached, Pete recognized Gary Grayson, one of his foremost party friends. Gary was grinning from ear to ear, sticking out his bloody hand to Pete. "Hey friend. Boy, am I glad to see you and to thank you for bringing Jeff with you! I'd be a dead man if Jeff hadn't showed up. See this blood on my head and my arms, and my leg was nearly severed from my body! I was bleeding to death until Jeff started praying for me. Thank God you guys came along! The paramedics had so many to work on, they hadn't gotten around to me yet. I think I wasn't long for this world, until your buddy Jeff appeared on the scene. I can't thank God enough for Jeff's question…"

Gloria was speechless, until she saw Priscilla Caldwell come running toward them. Her clothes were torn, and her face was badly scratched and bleeding. "Hey, Priscilla, what happened? I'm so sorry you're hurt." Gloria got out of the car, intending to be of some help, but Priscilla grabbed Gary's hand and pulled him away. She was so dazed, she had forgotten what she saw minutes ago – Gary lying there with blood gushing from his leg!

"I'm not really hurt bad, but some of our friends are in serious condition. The rest of them are loaded into the ambulances, and we need to go. They say we've got to be strapped to the backboards with the collars on, even if we're okay. Come on, Gary." Then suddenly she "woke up" and realized Gary was on his feet, and he was walking on the leg that she feared might have been severed! Clapping her hand over her mouth and bending to feel of Gary's leg, she finally yelled out, "It's impossible! I know what I saw just a few minutes ago! What happened to you? Am I delirious?"

Gary pulled Priscilla close to him and assured her he would fill her in on all the details, but they better obey the medical people and go in the ambulance. Giving one last hug to Jeff, Gary waved to the others and said, "Tell them what happened, Jeff, how Jesus saved my life. I'm a walking miracle!"

Jeff got back in the car and collapsed in Gloria's arms. His chest was heaving, and his eyes were closed. The others could tell he didn't want to speak, so they backed off and let him unwind. Pete had a flurry of questions charging through his mind. Sarah's mind was a complete blank. Her dropped jaw made her appear almost catatonic. Gloria was privately worshiping the Lord in the depths of her spirit. After about five minutes of total silence, Sarah blurted out, "What was the question, Jeff?"

Like Rip Van Winkle waking up, Jeff sat up and began to relate the incredible miracle he had just participated in. "Sarah, it's hard to remember everything, but I know the first thing I did when I got to Gary's side was to pray for the Lord to come right there as Physician, Healer, and Savior. Then all I could think of to say was to ask him, 'If you died tonight, where would you spend eternity?'"

Pete interrupted, "Where did you get a question like that, man? Here's my friend nearly bleeding to death with a leg almost cut off, and instead of giving some love and comfort, you try to scare the hell out of him!"

Jeff was unruffled. "I don't know why I said that either. No one has ever asked me that question, and I had not heard it before. But it came out of my mouth, and as soon as I said it, I knew it was God speaking to Gary. Those weren't my words."

"They have told us about different methods of evangelism at BSU, and that question is one way to approach people," offered Gloria.

Pete was mad. "Well, I still think it's cruel."

"Please finish the story," urged Sarah.

Jeff continued, "I didn't know Gary, so I couldn't guess how he would answer the question. It really opened him up, like a surgeon's knife. Tears flooded his eyes in a greater way than the blood flowing from his wounds. I had to cry with him, it was so powerful. He began to confess some pretty terrible things. He really was afraid he would die and go to hell. It was obvious he didn't have long to live, and he felt totally hopeless. At that point some words poured into my mind, and also joy poured into my gut! I heard the Lord say to me, 'Open your mouth.' I did, and what I said to Gary was definitely straight from the Lord because I could not have thought it up. A lot of it I knew was from the Bible, although it wasn't something I had memorized. And other things I said were very personal, things I didn't know about Gary, but the Lord did. The whole time I was talking to him, it was like a river coursing through my body, and I felt an incredible joy. From the time I started until the time the faucet was turned off, I watched Gary being healed from the inside out. It was awesome! He stopped crying and started laughing and saying, 'Thank You, Jesus! Thank You, Jesus! I believe in You! Thank You for forgiving me! Thank You for saving my soul!'"

"We both were so excited that Gary was saved and going to heaven, but we nearly went ballistic when Gary discovered that his leg was healed! Wow! I've never seen anything like that before in my life. I never prayed for his leg. It looked like God just threw it in extra. The main thing was Gary was born again! And now he's gonna live and tell everybody about Jesus!"

Pete felt like the air was taken out of his sails, but he had to say something. After all, a good friend of his was brought back from the brink of death and healed at the same time. He should be ecstatic, so why was he feeling depressed and even a little angry? Hadn't Jeff done the right thing? Wasn't Gary happy? So what was the matter with him? Was he jealous that Jeff had tapped into a power he had never experienced? Reluctantly, he said, "That's good, Jeff. I'm glad you helped my friend. Maybe we better follow them to the hospital."

As Pete drove into the emergency room parking lot at Baptist Memorial Hospital in Columbus, he spotted Gary Grayson and

Priscilla Caldwell being carried on stretchers inside. "Hey, there are Gary and Priscilla on the stretchers, guys. I wonder who else we know was involved in the accident. Let's sit here in the car until the people crowding around the doors are all inside. The relatives need to be first."

Gloria knew what to do. "Yes, this would be a good time to pray. We just memorized a great verse at BSU about group prayer. After I quote it, let's act on it, okay?" Gloria didn't wait for an answer. "If two of you on earth agree about anything they ask for, it will be done for them by my Father in heaven. For where two or three gather in my name, there am I with them.'[35] That's Jesus talking. I am going to ask for healing for all the injured and also for everyone, including the doctors and nurses, to recognize God's power and presence. Please join me."

This was a totally new experience for all of them, to pray for healing, but they knew there was no way they could refuse Gloria's request. So they bowed their heads and let Gloria say the prayer for them. After Gloria prayed, she urged, "Does anyone else want to make their own prayer?" Pete and Sarah looked uncomfortable.

Jeff had a question. "I have something to ask." He quickly bowed his head again and prayed, "Lord, I can't thank you enough for using me as your mouthpiece to deliver healing and salvation to Gary tonight. Now, Lord, would you please help him to grow in the faith and to tell others about Your power to heal and save? Thank You! In Jesus' name I pray."

Gloria beamed from ear to ear. It was time for them to go inside and ask about the accident and who else was hurt. Once inside the hospital, they found out all they could about the accident and the people involved. It seemed that Gary and Priscilla were the only ones they knew. The doctors were checking Gary over thoroughly, so they didn't get to talk to him, nor were they allowed to talk to Priscilla because she also was being examined. Fortunately, no one was killed. Jeff breathed a sigh of relief. "Let's go. I think we did what we were supposed to do, and now we are just going to trust that God heard our prayers and is answering them. The sun will be coming up before we know it." Everyone agreed.

That night Gloria and Sarah could hardly get to sleep they were so wound up about the events of the evening, especially the miraculous healing of Gary Grayson. Sarah had a lot of questions about everything that happened, starting with the church service. She felt very comfortable talking to Gloria because nothing she said seemed unacceptable to her, even when Sarah would not give the credit to Jesus for Gary's healing. They covered every subject, including her feelings for Pete and Gloria's feelings for Jeff. The romance angle was common ground for them, and it was so good to share and give voice to their exciting feelings. Finally they drifted off to sleep around 3:00 a.m.

CHAPTER 21

HOLOCAUST CONNECTIONS

Gloria and Jeff called off their Thursday night study time at the Chapel, but on Friday morning after their early classes the four companions were more than ready for the trip to MUW in Columbus to deliver birthday cakes for Jeff. Then they would go on to Tupelo to meet Jeff's parents and in the evening attend Temple B'nai Israel in Columbus. Jeff picked them up and greeted them with a name for their association – "Good morning, Holy Rollers! Let's roll!"

Sarah was puzzled, and Gloria was embarrassed, but Pete was shocked. "Where in the world did you get that 'handle,' friend? I don't think it's a compliment at all. I know some of those kind of people, and they are 'holier than thou' types. We certainly aren't like that."

Gloria agreed with Pete. She had heard some of her BSU friends describe church services at the local Assembly of God about people jumping up and down and shouting out during the worship services. Sarah shook her head. "Well, I assumed you were giving us that name because we are always traveling, or rolling on wheels, to Columbus and now Tupelo."

Jeff threw back his head and heartily laughed. "Hey, guys! What's the matter with your sense of humor? Why do we have to let weird people steal all the good adjectives? Sarah nailed it because we are 'on a roll' for doing exciting stuff together. And why not call us the 'Holy Rollers'? Or would you rather we call ourselves 'Wheelers and Dealers'? Don't you want to be holy? Well, I do. I read the Holy Bible, and I serve a holy God!"

Gloria's face regained her usual glow. "Well, when you put it that way, Jeff, I say yes. I am ALL IN, a 'Holy Roller'!" The others laughed and vowed they, too, were all in. They were Holy Rollers!

After a few seconds of laughter, a quietness came over them, and they yielded to the wonderful feeling of peace and calm. Not only their minds, but their bodies began craving rest. No one wanted to talk. Jeff's thoughts turned serious. *I DO think there is something 'holy' about the four of us. After what happened last night at Trinity Church, followed almost immediately by the accident and God using me in the salvation and healing of Gary, I believe God is saying He has something special for the four of us. We will do something together for Him. Yes, that's it, holy, we are holy. I always disdained that word, but someone told me it means "set apart." And just to think, we met a powerful man of God, Dr. Brown, who is a Messianic Jew, and now Gloria and I have become Messianic Jews. It seems we have a divine destiny as God's chosen people who believe Jesus is our Messiah. But what about Sarah? Lord, I believe she is being drawn to her Messiah, and Pete is turning away from his old life. And it is happening as the four of us are together, together for Your service.*

Jeff knew it was time to break the silence and proclaim this revelation from the Lord. "Listen up, Holy Rollers. God has shown me that we really are HOLY. That word means we are 'set apart' for HIS purposes, not OUR purposes. And He showed me that we are holy TOGETHER."

On the way to Columbus, Jeff explained to Pete his Quentin Services Unlimited operation, delivering the birthday cakes. Pete was more than glad to go inside a **women's** dormitory at Mississippi University for Women for this job. If it had to do with women, it was right down his alley! With all four of them making the deliveries, the job was accomplished in a short time. Then they drove toward Tupelo.

On the way Jeff briefed them on his parents' background and what to expect. He had called two days before and asked his mother if she would prepare a simple lunch for them. They had a very large house, so there was plenty of room for everyone to find a place to nap after lunch. Then they could drive around town and see the "sights" and learn about the place where he grew up. Of course, the most important part of the visit would be the conversation with his parents, Jeffrey and Leah Quentin. "I was born in Tupelo, but my mother Leah grew up in Chicago. She moved to Tupelo and met my dad. I am named after him, and he expects me to come into his company, Jeffrey M. Quentin Wholesale Grocery, as a full partner after I graduate."

"Pete, when I told Gloria and Sarah the names of my grandparents, my mother Leah's parents, Sarah told me I was Jewish! Their names are John and Rachel Cohen. Sarah said that the name Cohen is a Hebrew word for 'priest.' Here is the sad thing – I loved Papa Cohen dearly, but my mother argued with him all the time, especially when he put on his little hat – now I know it was a kippah. He would put on a prayer shawl and read his Bible, then rock back and forth to pray. It really set her off, especially his reading the Bible. She hid my Jewishness from me all these years. Evidently, she rejected her Jewish heritage. Anyway, Papa and Mama Cohen were killed in a car wreck, when I was only five years old. My mother would not allow me to go to the funeral! Looking back on that now, it makes me feel angry and deeply sad. Maybe this visit is for a reason. I need to forgive my mother, and I didn't realize it until now, but I still have a wound from losing my grandparents so suddenly. You are my friends. Please, please, pray for me and also for my mother. Remember what Dr. Brown told me last night? He said I would be seeing my parents soon, and the Lord was preparing me for a painful encounter, but that my friends would help me weather the storm. I am counting on your support. God spoke through him, so I would be prepared. You need to be prepared, too."

Pete's heart was touched with his friend's traumatic childhood experience. "I hate that happened to you, but we are here for you, buddy." The others agreed.

Gloria shared that her grandparents, her father's parents, Samuel and Anna Sondheim, also lived in Chicago. Every year at Passover, her parents took her to visit them, but they usually visited at other times in New York. "You may not know, Pete, but Jeff and I both have no siblings. I am an only child, and so is he. My father is Alvin Sondheim, and Mama Anna and Papa Sam are his parents. My mother's name is Sylvia. Her parents, Levi and Ruth Bloomberg, died a few years ago. Both she and my father are not trying to hide their Jewishness, but on the other hand, all their friends are Gentiles, and they are fully invested in the Gentile culture and want me to be, also. My dad is running for City Councilman in Port Jefferson, Long Island, and appearing non-Jewish will help him. My mother values their wealth and standing. Her parents never kept Passover like Mama Anna and Papa Sam do. One day I was looking in an old scrapbook at Mama Anna and Papa Sam's house and found some awful black and white pictures of people behind a fence who wore striped clothes and looked like they were starving. I was a child then and didn't realize what that meant. Years later I understood these people were Jews in Hitler's concentration camps. I still didn't catch on that Mama Anna and Papa Sam may have had relatives in the Holocaust! But now, as I think about it, I am sure they must have. Maybe that explains why my father wanted to protect me from all that connection with our Jewish history, not speak of it, and encourage me to appear as a Gentile."

Gloria continued, "Sarah has taught us, Pete, that Jeff's grandparents, John and Rachel Cohen, must have been Orthodox Jews, and his mother Leah wanted no part of that religion. She married Jeff's father, who is a Gentile, and she wants to be seen as a Gentile, too. Sarah said that Jeff's mother would be considered an 'assimilated Jew,' especially since she married a 'goy,' which is Hebrew for 'Gentile.' Sarah also said that many of the children and grandchildren of Holocaust victims turned against God and became 'assimilated' into the Gentile world, except for attending church. They became atheists or agnostics because the Church persecuted the Jews. That got me to wondering if both Jeff and I have been deprived of knowledge about our Jewish roots and about the Bible for that very reason."

Pete didn't really want to think about the Holocaust and the possible connection with the families of his new friends. That was heavy stuff. He knew they expected him to say something, so he was forced to respond. "I guess all three of you can't escape the effects of that horrendous time in history, the Holocaust. I know so little about it because it was never mentioned in our Baptist church, and my parents didn't mention it. We never knew any Jewish people. Please accept my apologies for ignoring something that has devastated your ancestors. I will start to learn and pay more attention, even to what is going on in Israel. Sarah, did you say that the Church persecuted the Jews? Surely, you don't mean Hitler and the Nazis and lots of the German people were Christians!"

Jeff interrupted. "Hey, wait a minute. I remember seeing one of Dr. Brown's books on the book table at Trinity Church that was titled, *Our Hands are Stained with Blood: the Tragic Story of the "Church" and the Jewish People*.[36] I read the back cover, and it shocked me to find out that anti-Semitism actually **began** in the Church, even as early as the fourth century! That is awful!"

Sarah was about to open the eyes of these three Christians regarding the complicity of the Church throughout history to the present in the persecution of Jews, but she didn't get a chance.

Jeff announced, "My friends, the Holy Rollers are now entering the Deep South territory of Tupelo, Mississippi, my good old home town. It is only a few minutes to my house, so we better pray about this visit. Pete, why don't you lead us? It's your turn to pray."

Pete swallowed hard and began, "Dear Heavenly Father, we thank You for this time together. I am really glad You gave me these new friends. This visit with Jeff's parents is important, and I ask You to give us the right words in our conversation and also keep us from speaking the wrong thing. Show us when to speak and when to remain silent. We acknowledge Your presence, and we ask this in Jesus' name." Jeff and Gloria joined in the "amen." Sarah inched away from Pete on the back seat, but she couldn't help but smile at him for getting out of his comfort zone and praying. He reached out and drew her back close to him. "My little Jewish filly is not getting away from her shield and defender." Sarah made a pretense of resisting, but only for a moment.

CHAPTER 22

CONFRONTATION

Jeff turned in the long driveway of his home, as Gloria was exclaiming, "This is where you grew up, Jeff? It is gorgeous, and so big! All the homes in this area are beautiful and have outstanding landscapes. I'm glad I didn't know you were rich when I met you, or I would have been intimidated. However, I have to admit, my parents are wealthy also, but they don't have a mansion like this. I can't wait to see the inside."

It was right at 12:00 noon, and the Holy Rollers were ready for lunch. Sarah said, "Jeff, I am glad you asked your mother to prepare us some lunch. I am famished."

Pete agreed, "Yeah, and even hours ago I could have bit into one of the birthday cakes." They were all laughing when Mrs. Quentin opened the front door and welcomed them in.

Jeff made introductions, and Gloria hugged his mother. Then she could see that wasn't the right thing to do. Mrs. Quentin was clearly uncomfortable. Gloria hastened to say, "Oh, Mrs. Quentin, I am just a hugger. Don't mind me. I will calm down now, but I was so excited to meet you and be in your beautiful home."

Jeff reached down and hugged his mother, too. "It's really good to see you, Mom, and I want to thank you for letting us visit and have lunch. I just had to bring my new friends to see where I grew up and to visit with you and Dad. I will come right out and say it – "Gloria is my girlfriend. And Pete is the perfect roommate. Sarah is Gloria's roommate. And the last week we have formed a close friendship. It's amazing how it all happened."

Leah Quentin had a guarded expression as soon as she heard Gloria and Sarah's last names. They were no doubt Jewish, and that was not what she wanted for her son. Nevertheless, she would be a good hostess and hide her displeasure. "Jeffrey," she called up the stairs. "They are here, and lunch is ready."

Mr. Quentin hurried down with a newspaper in his hand. Jeff embraced his dad and introduced him to Gloria, Sarah, and Pete, saying the same things he had said to his mother, giving a few more details. "Dad, I found out that Mom's parents and Gloria's grandparents both are from Chicago. That's a coincidence, isn't it? But Gloria's **parents** are Yankees from New York. They sent her south to Mississippi State University, so now she is a Southerner like us. Ha! That is sort of like Sarah because she came from New York, too. Now good ole Pete was born and bred in the South only a little distance away in Columbus."

Jeffrey Quentin extended his hand to Pete, but, surprisingly, he reached out and hugged Gloria and Sarah. "Well, we are very glad to meet your friends, Jeff, and now we will make our way to the dining room where some good Southern food awaits us."

Pete was not used to such elegant formality, but he liked it. Sarah felt like she was in a "foreign land," as her relatives all had modest homes and plain Jewish food. Gloria was right at home, and Jeff was delighted his mother had "put on the dog." Fine china, crystal, the works, not to mention the beautiful roasted turkey, cornbread dressing, black-eyed peas, broccoli casserole, candied sweet potatoes, tossed salad, rolls, and sweet iced tea with lemon. "Wow, Mom! I only requested a simple lunch, and you have laid out a banquet for us. I can't thank you enough."

"Well, son, since you haven't been home in a while, I figured you needed a change from college cafeteria food. Am I right?" Pete, Gloria, and Sarah joined in with "oohs and ahs" over the lavish meal set before them, as Jeff went over to his mother, enfolded her in his arms, and gave her a big kiss on the cheek.

Very little conversation took place as the young people concentrated on eating big servings of every dish set before them. Leah felt great satisfaction to observe their obvious enjoyment of her cooking. A maid soon appeared from the kitchen to refill drinks and bring out the dessert, Jeff's favorite, pecan pie, along with hot coffee. As they ate the dessert, Jeff filled in his parents about his courses, grades, and his birthday cake business. His dad had always loved the name of the business, Quentin Services Unlimited. Jeff told them how Gloria was majoring in music and was a wonderful singer and how he had been helping her with her Economics class. Pete told about his Criminal Justice classes. Sarah said she was taking the basic curriculum and majoring in accounting. They finished off the last bite of the pecan pie, and Jeff and his friends gave high compliments to Mrs. Quentin. Now it was time to retire to the living room and talk some more before they found a place to nap.

They were comfortably seated, and Jeff opened up the conversation, hoping he wasn't opening up "a can of worms." He had silently prayed for wisdom and receptivity from his parents as he began to speak. He knew Gloria would be praying as he broached some "sticky" subjects. "Mom and Dad, I can't leave here today without telling you that some life-changing things have happened to me since I first met Gloria and soon afterward met Sarah. Through our sharing, I discovered that I am Jewish!" Jeff paused to let it sink in and to gauge his mother's reaction. Red flags went up in Jeff's spirit as he saw his mother slightly flinch. But he couldn't stop now. "I have to ask you, why did you never tell me I am Jewish, and that you, Mother, are Jewish?" Now he had done it. He had put her on the spot, but he was encouraged to know his friends were silently supporting him at this moment.

Leah controlled her anger and responded to the question. "Jeff, I was trying to protect you from some of the things I experienced as a young Jewish girl, growing up in Chicago. I was not happy in a Yeshiva primary school, so I convinced my parents to put me in a public high school. That's where I was attacked. I was called names and made to feel like an outcast. Most of the ones attacking me were Christians. When I told my parents, they said that anti-Semitism was everywhere in Chicago, not just in my high school. I felt trapped, and right then I determined that as soon as I graduated I would move South and hide my Jewishness. I married your father. He knew I was Jewish, but he respected my wishes when you were born, Jeff, not to tell you that you were Jewish. My parents were deeply disappointed in me. My father, John Cohen, was a respected rabbi in the Petersen Park area of Chicago, and it shamed him that his daughter would reject her Jewish heritage. My mother Rachel was more understanding, but my father and I continually argued, especially when he tried to read Scripture to me. They came to visit us on special occasions, but we stopped visiting them. It was so painful when we tried to communicate. I resisted my father's efforts to instruct me from his Bible."

Jeff was grateful that his family history was finally out in the open. He hastened to assure his parents that his friends already knew about his quest to understand these things, so his parents could feel comfortable in talking openly. "Mom, I have to know why you didn't allow me to attend Mama and Papa Cohen's funeral when I was five years old. I really loved them, and it hurt me so bad that you made me stay home when they were buried! I have to admit that I have held it against you, Mom. I want to forgive you, but I have to know why. Maybe it will be easier to forgive you when you tell me why." Tears started as Jeff slipped back into his five-year-old mind, reliving the agony of this tragedy.

Leah was visibly moved by her son's plaintive "Why?" As she looked at him, she saw him as a vulnerable, weeping child once again. Summoning her courage, she decided to be candid in front of all of them. "Oh, Jeff, again I had to protect you, my beloved only child. We never wanted you to know that the car wreck that resulted in the death of my parents was not accidental." Jeff and his friends gasped. Leah struggled to keep her voice even. "No, they were actually murdered!"

Jeff stood to his feet. He couldn't form words for an instant. "Oh, Mom! How awful! Who would want to kill Mama and Papa Cohen? They would never harm a fly. Oh, Mom!" Jeff quickly embraced his mother as they both cried. Gloria was crying with them but stayed in her chair. Sarah and Pete were shocked but knew they should stay quiet, feeling honored that they could be present when a 15-year-old misunderstanding was about to be cleared up.

Leah continued, "It was terrorists, Islamic terrorists!"

Besides Jeffrey Quentin and his wife, no one else in the room understood at the heart level, except for Sarah. Before Pete could stop her, Sarah ran out of the room, looking for the bathroom, so she could give vent to the flood of tears needing release. Pete suddenly realized that the same fear he saw in her eyes the day he met her was raging in her again. He thought, *Sarah was attacked most likely by an Islamic terrorist also. Gloria and Jeff haven't experienced the terror that I witnessed in Sarah's face, but now they are seeing terror in Mrs. Quentin's face. I feel like there is something I must do, but I don't know what it is. Oh, yes, I do. I know Gloria is praying her heart out right now, and I am going to do the same thing. Only God saw the Cohen's murder, and only God knows what was behind Sarah's attack. He has a reason for involving me in all this. Oh, Lord, show me how I can help.*

Mrs. Quentin regained her composure and continued, "It was the year 1983. Men from the Islamic terrorist groups were threatening my father and other rabbis and Jewish leaders in the city because they were outspoken about the land of Judea and Samaria in Israel belonging to the Jewish people. Most American Jews at that time had no regard for the nation of Israel, and they didn't keep up with the news and understand the political conflict. I was like that. My father told me of a time when he was in prayer one day, and God revealed to him that He Himself had caused the nation of Israel to be reborn. So my parents started thinking about moving to Israel. I was shocked. He kept reading to me from the Bible, trying to convince me it was the right thing for Jews to do. When you saw us arguing, Jeff, it was about that. I didn't want my parents leaving me. How could they leave America for Israel, a people and a country hated by the world? Jews call it 'making aliyah,' the Hebrew term for immigration. They wanted to settle in the heartland of the country, which the world calls the 'West Bank,' but, actually, it is Judea and Samaria. They wanted to claim their biblical inheritance, my father would say. He would also say that he was not afraid to stand up in the synagogue or to stand up in the Community Center and say that Jews everywhere should make aliyah and do it soon! 'America has always been a haven for the Jews, but now the safest place for Jews is Israel,' he would say. Isn't it ironic that he and my mother died in America? It was the proof of his warning! Anyway, two Islamic terrorists overheard my parents planning a trip out of the city, and they planted a bomb in their car. They timed it to go off when my parents had driven many miles, giving the terrorists time to be far away from the scene of the crime. Since these terrorists had threatened a lot of people, resulting in more fatal attacks, the police found them. During the trial, they said they would kill all of Mother and Daddy's relatives! Jeffrey and I were sitting in the courtroom, and we felt stark terror when those two men stared at us!" At that point, Leah broke down in sobs, and Mr. Quentin took her in his arms.

Jeffrey rushed to comfort his mother also. "Oh, Mom, now I understand, I understand! At last I understand. Yes, you did want to protect me, and I thank you for it. You have suffered so much. Please forgive me for doubting you. Forgive me!"

Leah embraced her son. "Jeffrey, you also must forgive **me** for hiding your Jewishness from you. I see now that it was wrong. I was motivated by fear. That is just what the terrorists want – to terrify us, paralyze us, and rob us of our glorious Jewish heritage."

Pete couldn't help but interrupt. "Yes, Mrs. Quentin. I can see it clearly. Well, I for one am going to do all I can when I finish my criminal justice degree to help bring these kinds of evil people to justice and help alleviate the fears that Jewish people have. I think God has already given me an assignment to watch over Sarah since she was attacked."

Leah's eyes got wide. "Oh, where was she attacked? By whom?"

172

Pete could see that this line of conversation had to be derailed immediately. "Don't worry, Mrs. Quentin. Sarah wasn't hurt at all. In fact she chased after the attacker, and he ran off like a scared rabbit. Anyway, she isn't worried about it now and feels safe with me looking out after her." Stretching to his full height and flexing his muscles, Pete said, "You see I am 6 feet 7 inches tall, and look at these muscles! No worries." Everyone laughed.

Jeff sensed the need for the presence of the Lord to bring healing to his mother's heart. "Gloria, how about coming to the piano, playing something, and singing for us? Then maybe we can get that nap I promised y'all." Gloria gladly obliged, sending up a quick silent prayer, and sat down at the piano. She knew just the Spirit-filled song to sing to welcome the Prince of Peace into the room. She began to play and sing:

When peace like a river attendeth my way. When sorrows like sea billows roll. Whatever my lot, Thou hast taught me to say, "It is well, it is well with my soul." (Chorus): It is well, it is well, it is well, it is well with my soul....[37]

Jeff looked around the room as Gloria was singing and noticed the serene expression of his mother and the half-smile on his father's face. He saw Pete's expression of awe and Sarah's relaxed posture. His heart was bursting with love for Gloria, for His Savior, for his parents and for Pete and Sarah. This beautiful music was just the medicine each one of them needed. Gloria sang all three verses of the hymn. Then before anyone might try to applaud, she said, "Let us all pray together." And she touched heaven in her inspiring words to the Lord. None of them would ever be the same again.

CHAPTER 23

I Was Glad When They Said Unto Me

Leah told Jeff and his friends to pick a sofa, maybe girls in the living room and boys in the den, and she would leave them undisturbed for as long as they wanted. Sarah said, "Thank you, Mrs. Quentin. I could really use a nap. We are planning to go to the temple in Columbus tonight, and I want to feel rested for that."

"Right, Mother. Pete is the only one of us who has never been to a Jewish house of worship. Since it is in his hometown, he is eager to experience the service and meet the people, aren't you, Pete?"

How can I deny it? "Yes, since I met Sarah, I am getting a real education, and this is part of it. I called my parents to meet us there, but they had a prior engagement. I wish you could get to know each other. You would love them, and it would make them happy to know their son is friends with some quality people."

"You are quality yourself, Pete," Gloria said. "Maybe the next time we deliver birthday cakes, we can visit them, and they could go to Temple with us, too."

"After our nap, Mom and Dad, I am going to drive my friends around and tell them about my life in Tupelo."

Mr. Quentin responded, "Jeff, be sure to take them through our business, and show them all you will be in charge of before long."

Jeff tried to hide his anxiety and smile at his father, but he began to feel an urgency to talk to him before much time went by. "Okay, Dad."

Pete was the first one to awaken from his nap, and he was surprised that it was already four o'clock. He calculated the time they may need to go see Mr. Quentin's Wholesale Grocery business and see a few other places, then get on the road to Columbus. They could get some fast food and be on time for the temple service at 8:00, he hoped. So he roused the others and told them the schedule.

Jeff woke up from a deep sleep, a little bit alarmed. "Pete, you won't believe it. I think God gave me a dream. I won't go into the details, but the message I got from God is that my parents need to go with us to that temple service. My mother could come home to her Jewish roots, sort of like 'getting back up on the horse and riding it.' My SUV is pretty big. We can fit them in, or they can follow us in their car. What do you think? If only they would say YES." Pete heartily agreed with Jeff's plans. "Now let's go wake the girls and tell them our plans for tonight."

Gloria and Sarah were in instant agreement, and Gloria whispered, "Please, God. Please cause them to say YES. In Jesus' name."

The four of them went to the bottom of the stairs, and Jeff called out. "Mom and Dad, can you come down quickly, and let us tell you the great idea we have?"

Neither Jeffrey nor Leah had been napping. They were enjoying a movie on television, and it had just ended. Leah called out, "We're coming."

"Mom and Dad, I **know** you will not refuse us when you hear the plans that involve YOU." Jeff laid it all out, feeling the strong presence of God. His mother saw the shining hope in his face and only hesitated a moment. Miraculously, Jeff thought, Leah found herself agreeing. Before anything negative could be voiced, Gloria, Pete, and Sarah clapped their hands. Mr. Quentin was outnumbered, they realized, and everyone grinned.

Pete's plan stayed on schedule with the six of them piling into Jeff's SUV. Jeffrey Quentin was in his element, giving them a tour of his cherished business, ending with the executive suite that Jeff would inherit. Gloria, Sarah, and Pete were impressed and said so. They also were impressed with the Tupelo schools and the really nice churches, especially those downtown. It was a quick tour but expertly carried out by Jeff. His parents decided to follow them to

Columbus and agreed to get the fast food with them, afterward going to Temple B'nai Israel.

As Leah and Jeffrey followed their son to Columbus, Leah was deep in thought. *I am making a sacrifice to fulfill Jeff's wishes. I dread going inside the temple, but I feel I owe it to Jeff to help make up for the hurt I have caused him by hiding his Jewish identity from him and not telling him the circumstances of his grandparents' death.* "Oh, Jeffrey, it did me good today to tell Jeff about the persecution I received as a child and teenager because I was a Jew. I feel we are closer now, since I shared that. Now it is time for me to help him connect with his Jewish roots. But I just can't do it by myself, Jeffrey." Her husband looked at her tenderly and patted her arm.

In about an hour they were at McDonald's, getting their hamburgers, and eating. Jeff looked again at his watch. "Well, we have enough time that we don't have to eat fast. We will probably even get to the temple at least 20 minutes early. That way we can meet some people."

Pete was wondering who would be there. "I remember a few Jewish people in high school, but they probably won't be there. Their parents might be though. It's just a fact in the late 20th century that most young people aren't interested in religion."

Gloria said, "That's just the problem, Pete. 'Religion' is boring, but having a personal relationship with Jesus Christ is exciting! Jeff and I can vouch for that."

Jeff knew what was coming. Gloria had now opened the second "can of worms." Leah looked puzzled and a little angry. "Oh, no, Jeff! I was relieved that our secret was out in the open at last, the fact you and I are Jewish. But don't tell me you have become a Christian! Surely you know that Jesus is not the Messiah. You don't need to 'jump from one frying pan into another.' It is the Christians who have persecuted the Jews down through the centuries. What do you think the Holocaust was all about?"

Pete foresaw that this visit to the temple was about to wind up in a disaster, and he took it on himself to save the day. "Mrs.

Quentin, we four had a unique experience on Wednesday night, when we visited Trinity Church. That's a new church out in the country between here and Starkville, close to the airport. The speaker was a Messianic Jew, and he opened our eyes to things in history, including the Holocaust. He could answer your objections a lot better than we can."

"Yes, Mom. This man is Jewish, and yet he believes that Jesus is the Messiah. He pointed out that Jesus was born in Israel to Jewish parents, and all His disciples were Jewish. As a matter of fact, every author of the books of the Bible, including the New Testament, were Jewish, except for one. He called Jesus by His Hebrew name, 'Yeshua.' Anyway, Mom, please let's don't argue now. Sarah doesn't believe Jesus is the Messiah either, but she respects our beliefs, and we respect her beliefs. Our friendship is growing closer all the time. Mom and Dad, don't worry about me. Let's just accept each other, 'warts and all,' as they say."

Gloria believed that God was in complete control. "We better get moving, you guys, if we want to get to the temple a little early."

Sarah was more than ready to leave McDonald's. Her family would be disappointed in her, being in such a place that Orthodox Jews did not enter. She silently prayed for forgiveness for breaking the Jewish food laws, as well as breaking the Sabbath again by riding in a car. But in her heart she knew that HaShem loved her and wanted her in a house of worship. "Yes, I can hardly wait. I felt so at home last time, and I want to talk to those people who gave us a warm welcome. Maybe we can talk to the rabbi this time. I identify with the words of King David, 'I was glad when they said unto me, 'Let us go into the house of the Lord.'"[38]

CHAPTER 24

PROPOSAL

No sooner had they entered the door of Temple B'nai Israel than a short young man came up to Pete with an outstretched hand. Pete was shocked to see his high school friend, a fellow football player at Columbus High School. "Bryan Green! I didn't know you were Jewish. It's great to see you. This is my first visit to your temple. And I brought my new friends with me. Let me introduce you to them."

Bryan was wearing a kippah, but he still didn't look Jewish to Pete. Bryan said, "My grandparents changed our last name from Greenberg to Green to hide our Jewishness, and my dad never changed it back. That's why you didn't know I was Jewish. I will be joining you at State next year after I graduate. I am so glad you came."

Pete made all the introductions and said to Bryan that he and Mr. Quentin were the only Gentiles in the bunch. Bryan went and got his parents and introduced them, adding, "I am ashamed to say that Mother and Dad had to bribe me to get me here. Ha! Like you, Pete, I always have partied on Friday night."

Leah could hardly believe it. She and Delia Green had been friends for years. Neither one knew the other one was Jewish! They became acquainted through their membership in the Mississippi Historical Society. Delia was delighted that Leah had come. "Oh, Leah! This is wonderful. I have so much I would like to talk to you about, now that it is obvious we are both Jewish. Recently, I have become active in the Institute of Southern Jewish Life which is connected with the Historical Society, and I am having a ball. I want you to come with me to the next meeting in Jackson. It's in November. What about it?"

Leah was taken aback. The cat was surely out of the bag now, and she would just have to resign herself to being known as Jewish, at least in Columbus. *Oh, well, with Jeff running around with a Jewish girlfriend and being proud of his Jewish identity, I will just step out of the boat. At least I won't have to become a Messianic Jew like Jeff. I will become a member of Temple B'nai Israel, that's what I will do. The news will take a while to get back to Tupelo, but if I become exposed among my friends, I will cross that bridge when I come to it.* "Yes, Delia, I will put it on my calendar and attend the conference with you." She handed Delia her calling card. "Here is my contact info. You can give me all the details. I will be glad to take my car." Delia was delighted.

While Leah and Delia were talking, the others were engaged in light conversation with the friendly temple members, all but Jeff and Gloria. They found a seat on the back row which afforded a little privacy, and they scooted close to each other, heads touching, eyes downward, feigning interest in the prayer book while they had intimate conversation. "Oh, Jeff," Gloria cooed. "This is all so exciting, what is happening with your mother, and I am deeply grateful that she has cleared up all the misunderstandings you were struggling with. But, honey, I am starving for some time alone with you." Her heart began to beat wildly as Jeff squeezed her hand and brushed her cheek with his lips. She could hardly contain herself and was relieved when the organ started playing and people found their seats. For sure no one was looking at them, and she snuggled up to him as close as she dared and squeezed his hand three times, meaning "I love you."

After the temple service was over the four friends and the Quentins said their goodbyes and promised to return for the next services. Jeff hugged his parents fiercely. "Mom, I cannot thank you enough for your gracious hospitality today, the perfect and delicious meal, and for explaining all the mysteries concerning my grandparents' death. I needed to know how you have been hurt because of your Jewishness."

Leah replied, "I am relieved it is out in the open now and no more secrets. Because of you, I am determined to return to my Jewish identity and make no apologies for it. In fact, I am going to learn more about my heritage." Jeff's heart overflowed, and he embraced his mom again.

Jeffrey clasped his son warmly. "We are proud of you. The girl you have chosen is high quality. If you continue in your relationship, we would be honored to welcome her into the family." With a chuckle, he added, "You know, I am beginning to be a little jealous of all you Jews!" Gloria, Pete, and Sarah crowded around them, thanking them profusely for their hospitality, as the Quentins got in their car.

Waving till they got out of sight, Gloria said, "Oh, Jeff, I am so full of joy I can hardly stand it. You all could not have missed the fact that God answered all our prayers tonight!" Jeff, Pete, and Sarah loudly agreed and had a group hug. "Victory in Jesus!" Gloria shouted, as she put her arms around Jeff and kissed him on the lips.

Pete exclaimed, "Whoa! Public display of affection around here. Better call the cops." Everyone laughed. Pete was emboldened more than ever. "Hey, that's me, and I am a sympathetic cop. Come here, Sarah." Pete grabbed her up, whirled her around and attempted to plant a kiss on her cheek without success.

Sarah headed toward the SUV. "Pete, you are embarrassing me. What will these people think?" But her grin was so big, it was easy to see she loved "the display of affection."

They were back at Hamlin dorm by 10:15. The girls hurried inside. Jeff drove off with Pete, dropped him at Suttle, and went back to Hamlin Hall. Gloria was waiting outside for him according to their secret plan whispered to each other during the temple service. "Jeff, we've got at least an hour before I have to check in. Let's walk. I want to show you a nice, private place we can sit and talk for a while." The weather was slightly cool but still comfortable, and the dark area back of the chapel was a perfect rendezvous point. Gloria had brought cushions, and they sat down on the concrete

181

bench. "Oh, Jeff, we're alone at last. I just want to rest in your arms and relive the answers to prayer we witnessed this afternoon and tonight. Wasn't it obvious that God orchestrated everything?"

Jeff agreed. "Gloria, how can I ever thank you enough for your prayers, for your love, for every word you said today and for the beautiful song you sang for all of us? And I am glad that you blurted out that you and I have a personal relationship with Jesus Christ."

"Well, it just came out before I could stop my mouth. Ha! I am glad I said it though. Let's have no more secrets from your family."

"I wish you could have heard what my dad said as I told them goodbye. He said the girl I have chosen is high quality, and if we continue with our relationship, he would be honored to welcome you into our family."

Gloria could feel a tingle from the top of her head to the tips of her toes. "I truly love your dad. He is so sweet, so caring and sensitive to your mom's needs. I think you are a lot like him. And I want you to know that I love you with all my heart, Jeff Quentin. As Julie Andrews sang in the movie, 'Sound of Music' – *Somewhere in my youth and childhood I must have done something good.* I am blessed by God in many ways, but YOU are the greatest blessing I could have ever hoped for."

Boldness rose up in Jeff. He wanted to shout. *Why should I wait one minute longer? I know this is God's will.* "Gloria Anna Sondheim, I love you. Will you marry me?" Not waiting for her reply, he embraced her tightly and kissed her so deep and long, they almost quit breathing.

With all the passion she could summon in her breathless state, Gloria loudly whispered, "Yes, yes, yes, my awesome, wonderful sweetheart. Yes, I will marry you." Deep conviction filled her heart. She stood to her feet. "Tonight is fine with me. Jeffrey M. Quentin Junior. I, Gloria Anna Sondheim, accept your proposal to be your wife with my whole heart. I want you to be my husband now and forever!" Then she drew him to his feet, reached up and encircled his neck with her arms and kissed him very lightly and tenderly, gradually increasing her kisses until again neither one of them could breathe.

They sat back down on the bench, exhausted, but Jeff's mind began working overtime, trying to figure out a way they could become man and wife as soon as possible. He needed to purchase an engagement ring right away. They were both silent and were savoring the tremendous feelings they had stirred up in each other. After a few minutes, Gloria caught a glimpse of her watch. "Oh, Jeff, we have barely enough time for me to make it back to the dorm before I am locked out." Quickly, they put their feelings on hold and walked back to Hamlin Hall.

CHAPTER 25

MEETING THE SONDHEIMS

A MONTH LATER

Gloria and Jeff were settled in their seats on Delta Airlines, about to take off for New York. Thanksgiving was the perfect holiday to be celebrating at this time in their lives when they would be having a feast with Gloria's parents and her grandparents to express thanks for blessing their upcoming marriage. At least they believed it would turn out that way, since God had given them numerous signs that He had prepared the Sondheims, and He had paved the way for their startling announcement.

"Oh, Jeff, this is November 26th, and we met in the library that night on October 22nd, so we have only known each other a little over a month. And here we are preparing for marriage! It has gone by so fast I feel like I'm dreaming. But if I am, I don't want to wake up."

Jeff squeezed her hand. "Nope, you are not dreaming, but YOU are a dream. This is real. You know what, Gloria? My life has been turned upside down since I met you. I used to be so material-istic, and now I am more interested in spiritual things. Remember the night God used me to bring salvation and healing to Gary Grayson? Participating in a miracle like that is more intoxicating than being a millionaire. But that would not have ever happened had you not told me your story with Jesus at the library that night. Then that led to visiting a little rural church, Adaton Baptist, where God stirred my heart even more. After that, I was ripe and ready for what happened at Trinity Church when Dr. Brown preached and then counseled me as an individual. I became a bona fide believer, a Messianic Jew like him and like you! God's power was working through me to reach Gary shortly after that."

"Yes, Jeff, I had a conversation with Priscilla Caldwell at the dorm a few days ago, and she was just glowing. Gary is telling everyone about his experience. Some are writing him off as a 'religious nut,' but others are joining him at the BSU. Priscilla has been saved. She had a similar experience there like I did. She and I are friends now. I know you haven't had the time to come to BSU, and I have missed some meetings, too. But maybe we can go together when we get back. I guess nobody has come looking for you to pray for them like you did for Gary, or you would have said something about it. Is that right?"

"No, Gloria, and I am glad. That miracle was all God's doing. He set up the whole thing. I was picked as the one to funnel His power through for reasons only He knows. It is not MY power, and if people come to me expecting a miracle like Gary's, they may be disappointed. On the other hand, I am available for God's use at any time. I meant it when I gave my life to Jesus."

"It has been a whirlwind since I met you, Jeff. We keep seeing 'God incidences' and changed lives. Now your own mother has a changed life. God really demonstrated His power when He healed your relationship with her."

"Another miracle!"

"Having Sarah and Pete along for the ride has been a bonus blessing, hasn't it?" Jeff agreed. "Sarah and Pete are being used by God, too, and He is doing a work in them. I am praying that Pete will sincerely surrender ALL to Jesus. I also pray that Sarah will quit 'kicking against the goads' and have a dramatic encounter with Jesus like Paul did.[39] It's too bad she couldn't be on this plane with us, but she has plans to fly to New York to her sister's house for Hanukkah in December and wrap up things in her parents' estate. In the meantime I am praying that Jenny and Rebecca will not give her any trouble. And they won't, if Pete has anything to do with it."

"Honey, you and I both have got to calm down. I know we want our lights to shine before your parents and grandparents, but if our lights are as bright as search lights, they may think we are the police and they are about to be captured! Let's turn our wattage down, whaddya say?"

"Jeff, darling, you are exactly right. Besides, I suddenly feel very tired. We have time to get in a good nap before we get to the JFK airport. Nighty-night," Gloria whispered, as her eyelids were closing. They got their pillows, adjusted their seats, and both of them were soon asleep.

———◆———

Sylvia Sondheim was feeling blissful as she finished up dusting the living room furniture while singing along with Simon and Garfunkel's "Bridge Over Troubled Water"[40] playing on the stereo. The music took her back to her courtship days with Alvin. *It's amazing how a song can reach the deepest place in my heart. I love these romantic feelings. If only I could feel like this all the time, carefree and living for the moment, when I can see him again and feel his arms around me. He called me his "silver girl," like in the song.* Sylvia began to sing with deeper emotion, "Sail on, silver girl, sail on by. Your time has come to shine. All your dreams are on their way, see how they shine. Oh, if you need a friend, I'm sailing right behind. Like a bridge over troubled water, I will ease your mind…." *Alvin was always saying he would be that bridge for me over troubled water. He would lay himself down.* She indulged herself in calling up from her memory bank the many nights they had found a secluded parking space and …

"Sylvia, Sylvia!" called Alvin from upstairs. "I can't find my purple-striped tie. I've got to have it. Can you find it for me?"

Sylvia's euphoric mood immediately changed. She turned off the stereo and complained within. *What am I thinking? There is no romance in our marriage any more. Not since Alvin got political ambitions. Being the wife of a City Councilman is a small step on the ladder, and I am really glad he won his race, but still it is outside my comfort zone. Now he will start climbing another ladder, trying to be in the State Senate. Oy! Well, at least I can live vicariously through Gloria and her boyfriend's romance. I can't wait to see what he looks like. I hope they are not getting serious though because Gloria must get her music degree and set up a piano studio.*

"I'm coming, honey," shouted Sylvia. "I guess you heard that song playing on the stereo, 'Bridge Over Troubled Water.' Isn't it great that those two men who wrote it are Jewish, and it was the number one popular song in 1970? It was our favorite song when we met in high school and fell in love." Sylvia knew she better get up those stairs fast.

Alvin looked a little irritated as Sylvia walked in the bedroom, still talking about the song. "I read an article about Paul Simon writing it.[41] His words, 'silver girl,' were about his girlfriend who was finding gray hairs in her head, and Paul meant it as a joke. But he called the song a 'little hymn' and said he didn't know where it came from. It became a hit fast, and it won five Grammy awards. Something about it really touches my heart. While I was singing, it fanned the flames of my love for you, Alvin. Do you suppose God inspired it?"

"Oh, I guess it's a pretty good song, but it doesn't matter if Jews wrote it, does it? It was so long ago. We were only 14 when we first met, and the song was popular. That was 27 years ago, and at 41, you are still as pretty as ever, Sylvia. But please find my tie."

Sylvia didn't expect that, Alvin giving her a compliment. He hardly ever noticed when she had a new dress or a new hairdo. Nevertheless, she knew she had to receive his compliment if she wanted a closer relationship. "Alvin, I will find that tie for you, but first, I want you to know that you were definitely the handsomest man in high school and college, and you are still handsome. You called me your 'silver girl' from the words of the song." Sylvia then took a chance by reaching for Alvin. *It is now or never.* She kissed him hard on the lips. Alvin seemed a little shocked but quickly recovered and kissed her back, holding her closer. "I love you, darling," Sylvia murmured, choked with emotion. Then, while she was 'ahead,' she quickly reached deep in the closet and pulled out the purple-striped tie.

"Sylvia, I love you, too, and you are a good wife. You are the best City Councilman's wife there has ever been! I think that's how I got the votes." Both of them grinned and embraced. It was going to be a good day.

The doorbell rang. "I wonder who has arrived first, Alvin – your parents or Gloria and her boyfriend? I'll go down. Please hurry."

"Oh, Gloria, at last you are here!" Sylvia grabbed her daughter in a fierce embrace and kissed her on the cheek. "And you must be Jeff." She almost hugged him but then decided to just shake hands.

"Mom, you look wonderful, even younger than when I saw you last. This is Jeffrey M. Quentin, Jr., the love of my life. And it will be okay, Jeff, if you hug my mom."

"Mrs. Sondheim, I agree with Gloria about your youthful appearance, and I have to hug you for bringing Gloria into the world. She means everything to me." Jeff almost picked up Sylvia off the floor in a bear hug. Ma'am, I have to ask you if you would mind if I call you Miss Sylvia."

"Yes, I like that name. You may certainly call me that. And you may call Gloria's father 'Mr. Alvin.' I guess that is typical of greetings in the South." Sylvia grinned.

"Yes, ma'am, it sure is."

"But now that 'Mr. Alvin' won his race for City Councilman of Port Jefferson, you can also call him 'Councilman Sondheim.'" Sylvia was obviously proud of her husband and reached out to hug him as he came down the stairs.

"I hope your flight was comfortable, Gloria, and I welcome you, Jeff, to our humble home. Let us sit down, and you both can bring us up to date on your college life in the Deep South."

"Thanks so much, Dad, for underwriting our plane trip. We both loved the first-class seats. Give me a hug, Dad. I love you and Mom so much."

Alvin quickly reached out and embraced his daughter and warmly shook Jeff's hand. He ushered them into the living room, and Jeff opened up the conversation. "First, Gloria and I want to congratulate you on winning your race for City Councilman."

Sylvia slid over closer to Alvin on the sofa. "And who knows? Alvin may run for the State Senate one day." She winked at Alvin, and he pecked her on the cheek.

"Mr. Alvin and Miss Sylvia, your home is so beautiful. I knew it would be because Gloria told me you are a successful caterer. My dad is also successful and is a food distributor. Food is the world's number one necessity, so it does give our families a foundation of security. I thank God for that."

"Yes, Dad, I am very proud of you for providing everything I need. Both Jeff and I are the only child of our parents, so we have had an easy and fantastic life. We both have been brought up in homes where love abounds. I enjoyed being in the home of Jeff's parents very recently. Love truly makes all the difference. I believe that whether a family is rich or poor, love is the most important thing. Jeff and I have found the real **source** of love is God, and that is what **our** love is built on. We both have given our lives to Jesus Christ." Gloria paused to let that announcement sink in, since she knew her parents thought Jews had nothing to do with Jesus Christ. She held Jeff's hand tight and looked at him adoringly.

Sylvia was the first to respond. "Well, dear, I can't say I am too surprised, and maybe I am responsible for your defection from your Jewish roots because I have always encouraged you to go to church and make Gentile friends. But, as I noticed your face when you said you have 'given your life' to Jesus, I see that you have gone too far. I honestly have to say that it alarms me. I know Alvin feels the same way." Alvin reached for his wife's hand and brought her closer, showing agreement.

Jeff had to say something. "Mr. Alvin and Miss Sylvia, please don't be alarmed. I have to tell you a little of my story. I was brought up in a non-religious home without a Bible and didn't even **know**

I was Jewish. The friends of my parents and me were all Gentiles. It was Gloria's new friend at MSU, Sarah Bernstein, who figured out from our conversation that I am a Jew. I mentioned the names of my mother's parents, John and Rachel Cohen, and she told me that Cohen is a Jewish name, meaning 'priest.' I was bowled over. Then Sarah explained to Gloria and me that from our descriptions, it looked like both sets of our parents were 'assimilated Jews,' except for my dad. That term means Jews who have concealed their Jewish identity in a world of Gentiles." Jeff hastened to add, "But, unlike my mother, I know you are proud of your Jewishness, even though socially you move in Gentile circles. Gloria told me that. It gives me joy that my own mother is now trying to reconnect with her Jewish roots. But to finish my story, I want you to know that Jesus Christ – and the name 'Christ' means Messiah – is my personal Lord and Savior. It is all because of your awesome daughter Gloria who showed through her life and her words that Jesus really is the Jewish Messiah and the Savior of the world."

Gloria stood up. "Mom and Dad, I have to stand up to say this. Jesus is Jewish. Sixty-four of the sixty-six books of the Bible was written by Jews. All of Jesus' disciples were Jews. And the first church was entirely Jewish. I will end my declaration by thanking you that you encouraged me to go to church. It was in a church organization on campus, the Baptist Student Union, that I asked Jesus to come into my heart to save me and to be my Lord. I have never been happier and more fulfilled since that moment of divine encounter. Jesus IS the SON of God and the Messiah of Israel. He died on the cross as a sacrifice, to forgive the sins of all people who would believe in Him and to give them eternal Life."

Sylvia and Alvin were shocked. Alvin could see that his plan for any further political advancement had gone up in smoke. He didn't know what would happen next. His daughter was a religious fanatic. The doorbell rang.

CHAPTER 26

THE BIG ANNOUNCEMENT

Everyone stood to their feet, as Alvin and Sylvia opened the door and welcomed Alvin's parents. Jeff had been looking forward to meeting them. From the pictures Gloria had shown him, he expected them to be as tall as his Jewish grandparents, John and Rachel Cohen, according to his memory as a five-year-old, but they were shorter. Before he could extend his hand in greeting, Gloria ran into Papa Sam's outstretched arms, nestling her head on his shoulder.

She waited for her father to quit hugging his mother before grabbing Mama Anna with squeals of delight. "Oh Mama Anna, I am so glad you and Papa Sam are here! Please, both of you, meet my sweetheart, Jeff Quentin from Tupelo, Mississippi. We have only known each other a little over a month, but we have an exciting announcement for all four of you. I know you, Mama Anna, will be the happiest of all to hear our good news. It's something God has been doing in our lives."

Suddenly, the room seemed to be electrified, as Gloria led them to the sofas, and everyone was seated. "Please forgive me for being so abrupt, but I can't hold it back any longer. Jeff, hold my hand and steady me so I can give our big announcement." Gloria stood up, and Jeff came alongside her. Alvin and Sylvia looked at each other with worried looks. Samuel and Anna had questioning looks, but they were smiling with anticipation.

Gloria looked up at Jeff and whispered, "Let's say it together." Jeff nodded. It felt like jumping off the diving board in the deep end of the pool for the first time. Gloria started, "WE..." with Jeff in sync to finish the sentence: "... ARE GOING TO BE MAR-RIED!" Gasps went up from Alvin and Sylvia. Sam and Anna chuckled. No one ventured to say anything for at least 20 seconds.

They're not even asking permission! What do we know about this young man? This is crazy. They just told us they believed Jesus is the Messiah, and now this. Sylvia's thoughts went wild. "Okay, I see you are determined. Well, you are just too young to know what you are doing. You are still teenagers. And I don't see an engagement ring."

Alvin hastened to speak calmly before Sylvia said too much. "Now Sylvia, we were the same age when we got married, only nineteen. And Gloria, my sweet daughter. I see how happy you are, and that has always been my foremost desire, to see you happy. However, before your mother and I give our blessing, we need to know a whole lot more about this young man and what his future plans are, especially how he will support you."

Sylvia stood up. "Yes, Gloria, absolutely! And we want Papa Sam and Mama Anna to hear about your religious fanaticism and abandoning Judaism for Christianity. I realize this is an inflammatory subject, and Thanksgiving dinner is waiting for us. If you can get ahold of yourself, and let us have light, ordinary conversation over our meal, then afterwards we can talk about these startling revelations you have spoken to us so quickly after arriving here!" Sylvia caught her breath. Her face had turned red.

Alvin knew what his role must be, so he quickly reached out to his wife and whispered in her ear, "I love you, darling. Please be calm. We will get through this."

Sam tried to break the tension. "You young folks probably don't realize that Anna and I can identify with your dilemma as a Messianic Jewish couple. If it's okay with your parents, Gloria, we would like to tell our story during the dinner hour, and then you can tell yours and Jeff's story after dinner. Is that all right, Alvin and Sylvia? I promise to make it as short and sweet as possible."

Alvin had his own announcement as the host. "Get ready for another shock. We are not having a traditional Thanksgiving meal with turkey and the trimmings. My parents run one of the top delicatessens in Chicago, Sondheim's Delicatessen, Jeff, and they suggested the menu. It is the type food both Sylvia and I had growing up in a Jewish neighborhood of Chicago. Sylvia bought the food from the nearest Jewish delicatessen on Long Island, one that sells both kosher and non-kosher food, and she and Madeline have it all ready for you. Food is the way to the heart, as the saying goes. In my campaign events in certain Jewish venues on Long Island I offered this Jewish cuisine. I had to be careful though because where many Orthodox Jews were in attendance, I had to serve **only** kosher food. I catered to both gastronomic delights and Talmudic delights!" Alvin laughed. "I think my accommodations may have helped me get elected as City Councilman of Port Jefferson." Now Sylvia laughed.

"Pardon the pun, Mr. Alvin, but you are 'a man after my own heart,' and I look forward to joining ranks with the who's who of New York." Jeff chuckled. "Gloria and I have a lot in common. We are both Jewish. Each of us is an only child. Our grandparents are both from Chicago, and neither of us will ever go hungry with my parents and you and your parents in the food business!" Jeff was "making points" with Alvin. The conversation really flowed after that.

Jeff and Gloria couldn't help but silently compare the meal at the Sondheims with the meal at the Quentins. Maids were on hand, and the tables were lavishly set at both places. The food would not be the same, however. After the maid brought the food to the buffet, Alvin motioned everyone to come over, and he named each dish, emphasizing their kosher or non-kosher rating. "You can taste everything here, if you want to, and then come back and load up on the dishes you especially like. Tell our maid Madeline what drink you would like. We have soft drinks, coffee, iced tea, and two kinds of wine."

Jeff's eyes got really big. He decided every dish was "kosher" for him because "ignorance is bliss!" The bountiful fare consisted of braided loaves of Challah, Noodle Kugel, Potato Knish (stuffed with kale, leeks, and cream cheese), Corned Beef Hash, Cabbage Rolls, Matzo Ball Soup, Pastrami Cheese Fries, and smoked Lamb

Strip. The desserts were Rugelach cookies, Chocolate (bitter-sweet)-Dipped Coconut Macaroons (pareve), and Cheese Blintzes with Blackberry Syrup.

"No waiting for the blessing," Alvin announced. "We are Jews. We will have a prayer at the **end** of the meal. However, since it is Thanksgiving, and we are thankful to be Americans, the land where the Jews have found refuge from oppression in Europe and Russia, I will ask my father to offer up a prayer of thanks now."

When Sam finished his prayer, he and everyone else was crying, except Alvin and Sylvia. Even the maid was crying.

CHAPTER 27

ANTI-SEMITISM AND ZIONISM

Samuel decided he would not say a lot about his life as a child of the Holocaust at dinner because the conversation was supposed to be "light and ordinary" as Sylvia requested. He would first tell them about his and Anna's recent trip to France. They had also been to Israel, but he would save that for later. "Jeff, have you or your parents ever been to France?"

"No, we haven't, but we have been to the Philippines, and I was greatly impacted by the poverty I saw there. Ever since we were approached by the beggar children at the airport, my heart has been stirred to do something. I haven't told my parents yet, but I am considering not going into my dad's business after college, as he expects me to do. I feel called to some kind of mission work and even more so since I gave my life to Jesus Christ."

Sylvia caught her breath but managed to stay silent. *So, how does he plan to support our daughter? He and Gloria need to wake up to the real world.*

Anna broke in. "Oh! That is the best news of the day! Even more than your declaration of marriage. Sam and I were also in college when the Lord made Himself known to us. We were in astronomy class together, and one day the professor took a Bible and taught about the creation of the world in the Book of Genesis. Sam and I weren't religious, so we didn't even have a Bible. We bought one and began reading it together. We were like starving beggars as we hungrily consumed every page and discussed it. Eventually, we came to the New Testament part, and the fireworks started!"

Samuel interrupted, worried that Anna would tell about his father Isaac snatching the Bible and tearing up the New Testament pages. "Yes, children, Anna and I gave our lives to Jesus Christ also. The Bible convinced us that He is the Messiah of Israel. We call

Him by His Hebrew title, Yeshua HaMashiach. We finished college and were married, and not long afterward we went to Israel because we wanted to see firsthand all the things and places we read about in the Bible. And mainly, we wanted to 'walk where Jesus walked,' as the saying is. We have more to tell you later about our future plans related to Israel."

Alvin had never heard his parents speak so openly about their belief that Jesus was the Messiah. He wondered if they felt insulted when Sylvia said Gloria was a religious fanatic and had abandoned Judaism for Christianity. *All these years has my wife not realized my parents believe in Jesus? Did she not hear my father identify the afikomen[42] as the body of Yeshua at their Passover Seder each year? I guess she must think if we don't talk about it, then it isn't so. I have never felt threatened by their beliefs. Evidently, Sylvia is in a state of denial.*

"Mom and Dad, you went to Israel before I was born, so I missed it. Maybe one day Sylvia and I can accompany you back there. I have always been an advocate for Israel, the Jewish State. I hope I can advance her cause in the political arena. I really want to travel there, and I think Sylvia does, too."

Sylvia agreed. "Yes, I had not been born when Israel was declared a nation in 1948, but I remember hearing my parents talk about it when I was a child. They said it was a miracle, a fulfillment of Bible prophecy."

Samuel could see that the conversation was leading back to the things he wanted to tell them about France. "Yes, what I want to share that Anna and I learned in France has a direct bearing on the rebirth of Israel. Anna majored in history in college, so she wanted to visit museums in Paris. We learned that in Paris in 1894, Captain Alfred Dreyfus, a French artillery officer, who was Jewish, was convicted of treason. He was accused of passing French military secrets to the German Embassy and was imprisoned in Devil's Island in French Guiana, where he languished for five years. The real culprit was Major Esterhazy, but Dreyfus was made a scapegoat by high-ranking military officials using forged documents. All this happened in the virulent anti-Semitic climate in France. Mobs rioted against the acquittal of Dreyfus. A famous French novelist, Emile Zola, who wasn't political at all, was urged to use his influence on behalf of Dreyfus. In 1898, Zola wrote an open letter published on the front page of a liberal newspaper, addressed to the French prime minister under the headline 'J'accuse (I accuse).' He accused the French State and the army of injustice and anti-Semitism and pleaded for Dreyfus' innocence. No one had openly discussed anti-Semitism in France or in the world at large prior to this, except for the Jews. In 1899, Dreyfus was brought back to trial again, pardoned and released. In 1906, he was exonerated and reinstated as a major in the French Army. Justice was done because of the writing of Emile Zola. This writer reshaped France!"[43]

Gloria was caught up in the story. "But Papa Sam, you said this history of France was connected to the rebirth of Israel. How?"

Samuel continued. "Another writer, Theodor Herzl of Vienna, was outraged as he witnessed the trial of Dreyfus. Only a few months later he began writing his book, *The Jewish State*, in which he proposed the organized exodus of Jews to a land of their own, not necessarily Palestine. His experience of watching the Paris crowd baying for the blood of Dreyfus profoundly affected him.[44] Herzl is considered the 'Father of Zionism,'[45] and at his First Zionist Congress in 1897 in Basel, Switzerland, he laid the foundation for the Jewish State of Israel."

"He actually made a prophecy without knowing it!" Anna drew a piece of paper out of her purse. "I copied it and kept it in my purse. Let me read you what he said – 'In Basel I founded the Jewish State.' To which he added: 'If I said this aloud today, I would be answered by universal laughter. Perhaps in five years, and certainly in fifty, everyone will agree.'[46] Amazing, isn't it? In 1947, the United Nations passed the Partition Plan for the Jews and the Arabs to have two states in Palestine. From Herzl's conference in 1897 to the U.N. Partition Plan in 1947 is 50 years, just like he said! And when we were in Israel, we visited Independence Hall in Tel Aviv, and there was Herzl's picture on the wall!"

Samuel and Anna apologized that they had done all the talking, but everyone laughed and assured them they loved learning about the "Dreyfus Affair," Emile Zola, and Theodor Herzl.

"We have had an awesome history class, starring Jewish people, today," declared Jeff. "I myself haven't been touched by anti-Semitism, but what Papa Sam and Mama Anna have told us has whetted my appetite to learn more about what my people have suffered. And it makes me want to go to Israel. But I have a question about your vocation, Papa Sam. Why didn't you pursue astronomy, and how did you wind up becoming the owner of a Jewish delicatessen?"

"Jeff, it was because my father Isaac had the store, which had belonged to Anna's uncle. My father worked for him. When he died, my father inherited it because Anna's uncle had no other heirs. When Anna and I finished college, my father brought me alongside him to run the store. I never dreamed it would be such a success, but it was. Anna and I had already given our **lives** to Yeshua, and we knew we had to give the **store** to Him, too. **He** made it a success."

"And it was in that very store that I first met you, Alvin, wasn't it? You helped your dad after school. One day my mother and I shopped in there, and you caught my eye," Sylvia teased. "I thought you were so cute. And I saw you again in high school."

"And the rest is history," Gloria chimed in. "Oh, this is the richest conversation I have ever had around the dinner table. Somehow we have all managed to consume lots of delicious food during all the talk, especially me. I have only listened. Papa Sam, did you have enough to eat, since you were the main 'orator'?" About that time Madeline came in to clear away the dishes and see if anyone wanted more to drink.

Sam patted his full stomach. "Yes, I really enjoyed the food. But, as Yeshua said, 'I have food to eat of which you do not know.... My food is to do the will of Him who sent me and to finish His work.'[47] That's when He was telling the Samaritan woman at the well how to get the Living Water that He offered her."

"Now you're talking 'Greek' to me, Papa Sam." Sylvia laughed. If you want to talk about Jesus, let's do it in earnest in the living room. I did agree to hear about Gloria and Jeff's newfound religious ideas."

CHAPTER 28

OUT OF THE ASHES OF THE HOLOCAUST

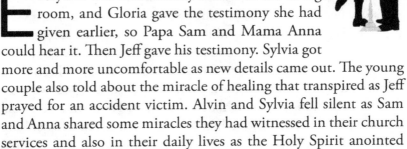

Everyone was comfortably seated in the living room, and Gloria gave the testimony she had given earlier, so Papa Sam and Mama Anna could hear it. Then Jeff gave his testimony. Sylvia got more and more uncomfortable as new details came out. The young couple also told about the miracle of healing that transpired as Jeff prayed for an accident victim. Alvin and Sylvia fell silent as Sam and Anna shared some miracles they had witnessed in their church services and also in their daily lives as the Holy Spirit anointed them.

Sylvia had a burning question that had to be answered. "But why has the Church persecuted the Jews and called them 'Christ killers' down through the centuries since Jesus was crucified? Christians in Europe and Russia primarily, but also in other countries, have justified all manner of atrocities against the Jews because they believe we were responsible for his death. I know that none of my Christian friends believe that, but still they have their 'Jewish jokes,' and they look down on Jewish people. That is why Alvin and I have kept a low profile when it comes to our Jewishness. I will come right out and say it – Hitler and the Nazis claimed to be Christians, and look what they did! He exterminated six million Jews during World War II, which included one-and-a-half million children! These Jews were guilty of nothing except being Jews." Sylvia had wanted to shout that out for years, and now she felt drained. But still she hoped there was some explanation she had missed.

Gloria was glad her mother had raised this awful question, and she had one of her own. "Papa Sam and Mama Anna, I remember one time when I was a child, and we visited you for Passover. I was looking in a cabinet in your bedroom and found a scrapbook. In there were some awful black and white pictures of people behind a fence who wore striped clothes and looked like they were starving. Years later, I knew those were pictures from the Holocaust. Were those people related to either one of you? I have always wanted to ask you about it."

"I am glad you asked, Gloria. It is time for us to tell you that sad story because it is part of your own history. I was born in Germany to Isaac and Ruth Sondheim, your great-grandparents. We were there when Hitler came to power and immediately began the persecution of the Jews. For a few years we managed to keep from being taken to a concentration camp, but then in 1942 we were discovered, hiding in a neighbor's basement. I was nine years old when we were loaded into a boxcar and taken to the Flossenburg concentration camp in Germany. Miraculously, I was not separated from my parents like most of the children were. Actually, I managed to hide so well, that the guards didn't know I was there. I won't describe the horrors we suffered. Most people have seen film clips and magazine pictures. The Holocaust is well-documented. I made friends with Anna in that hellish place. She, too, escaped separation from her parents. Together we dodged the Nazi guards. And, believe it or not, we experienced love in those circumstances. Looking back, we both realized that Yeshua was there in our midst, suffering with us. Both our parents became very close, as together they did hard labor in the stone quarries. Anna and my parents and I were devastated when Anna's parents died. They were weak from starvation, and they kept stumbling and falling in the quarries. The Nazi guards' brutal whippings killed them! Papa and Mama were sick and weak, when later the Nazis moved the other prisoners out on a 'death march,' and they were left behind with a few hundred others, including Anna and me. Shortly after this happened, we were liberated! Praise God for the Americans! On April 23, 1945 at the end of the war we were free![48] Again, I won't go into detail about the months of transition and physical recovery that followed.

It was like a fog, but when we got on the ship to America, my parents, Anna and I felt like we were being born again. I was twelve years old and had never experienced such exhilaration. We actually TASTED freedom. Oh, freedom! We had heard that America was the 'land of the free and the home of the brave.' We could hardly wait to start our lives over."

"Anna's aunt and uncle were waiting for us in New York when the ship docked, and through a miracle that cut through the red tape, we were on a plane to Chicago within a few hours. Before we knew it, we were sitting down to a midnight snack with them in their beautiful home. It was a humble apartment in Chicago, but to us it was a mansion, and we had our own bedrooms."

Everyone was on the edge of their seats. "So were those pictures I found in your scrapbook, were they pictures of you and your family and Anna's family, Papa Sam?"

"No, Gloria. These were given to us later. Those are memories we **needed** to preserve, but we didn't **want** to preserve them. I have a little more to add to my story about being in the Holocaust. This is a heavy subject, but I have to tell you that my father became very bitter and hated Christians. When Anna and I were reading the Bible together in college one night, he came up behind us, snatched the Bible out of our hands and began tearing out the pages of the New Testament! We had not even gotten that far in our reading, but we were learning that the Bible is the history book of the Jews. What a revelation that was to us. My father did this just as we were saying our first prayer. I have often pondered why we were attacked right in the middle of a prayer. Since then the Holy Spirit has taught me so much. I know, as strange as it sounds, that attack was kind of like God's answer. I now understand that it was caused by Satan, the enemy of our souls. He was angered by the faith that was budding in mine and Anna's hearts, especially because we are Jews, God's chosen people. I was deeply hurt, of course, but I knew I had to pray for my father's wounded spirit to be healed. He was being consumed by hatred. I learned later that Yeshua bore all the world's hatred in a moment of time on the cross."

"Tell them, dear, the happy ending for your father." Anna reached over and warmly clasped Samuel's hand.

"My prayers were answered, but it took years. Shortly before my father died, he accepted Yeshua as his Messiah. Anna, Mama, and I were in the room when he passed away. We saw his eyes open wide, looking upward with his hands raised and a smile on his face. My mother had already met Yeshua several years before. We cried, but we also rejoiced and began to sing. My father had made it home before us. Satan thought he had the perfect plan, using Hitler, but out of the ashes of the Holocaust came new life. The hatred against Christians was defeated in our family. I know of some Jews who met Yeshua in the work camps and the extermination camps. Of course, there were others who could never let their bitterness go. If only they had realized that Yeshua not only suffered unjust persecution and physical torment in a greater way than they or anyone ever had, but in his death He suffered **eternal** damnation for all who would accept His atoning sacrifice on the cross."

"And Samuel, another good thing that came out of the ashes of the Holocaust was the rebirth of Israel." Anna knew it was time to reveal their plans. "We want you all to know that Samuel and I are planning to make aliyah!"

Jeff was the first to respond. "I know what that is. It means immigrating to Israel. The Hebrew means 'going up.' My grandparents, Mama and Papa Cohen, my mother's parents, were also planning to make aliyah. Sad to say, they never made it. Some Islamic terrorists planted a bomb in their car in Chicago. It exploded when they traveled outside the city, and they died."

Gloria added, "And our friend at MSU, Sarah Bernstein, is grieving over her parents' death in Israel. Only a few months ago after making aliyah, they and others in a bus in Jerusalem were killed by a suicide bomber! Papa Sam and Mama Anna, are you sure God wants you to make aliyah?"

CHAPTER 29

VISIONS OF A HONEYMOON

The rest of the evening was rich in conversation, with Alvin plying his parents for more information about their experiences in Germany and in the concentration camp. He also wanted to hear more about his grandparents, Isaac and Ruth, as well as his parents' college life. Gloria was drinking it all in. As the six people fellowshipped, strong bonds of love and understanding formed, and Jeff felt like he was now grafted into this wonderful family. Reluctantly, Papa Sam and Mama Anna said their goodbyes and returned to their lodging at Three Village Inn.

Jeff was assigned to the Sondheim's guest room, which was immaculate and elegant. Gloria would spend the night in her old bedroom. Jeff took her suitcase in. "I'm glad Madeline has put everything in order since I left here in September to return to MSU. What do you think of my childish décor, Jeff?"

"As far as I can see, this room has the mystique of a mature woman of God, even though you had not realized your true identity until that night at the Baptist Student Union. Ooh! I love this feminine boudoir. Just think, when we return here after our marriage, we will have this love nest together. No more guestroom for me, darling."

"Now Jeff, if we copied the lifestyle of most of the students on campus, we would both be spending the night in my room now. But, you know, that isn't even a temptation to me because Jesus lives on the inside of me, and He is holy. He is pure. And He is love personified. I am very satisfied to wait until we are married."

Jeff hastily agreed. "But we can have some conversation here tonight, can't we sweetie, before we retire?"

"Of course, and I can't wait to talk about what happened today. Sit down on the loveseat with me. The thing uppermost in

207

my mind now is that I wish Sarah could have heard all our conversation. And Pete also. Sarah is not planning to come up here to New York until Hanukkah, and that is weeks from now, beginning December 23rd. I would be home for Christmas, but I would give anything if she would come to New York while we both are here now. We could meet each other's families, and that would include Papa Sam and Mama Anna because they are staying around for a week. Sarah's parents made aliyah, and my grandparents are talking about it, too. We "holy rollers" have not even been to Israel, the ancient homeland for the three of us. Do we dare make plans to go on a tour of Israel? Pete could connect with his Jewish roots because, according to Paul, he is a 'wild branch' grafted into the Jewish olive tree!'[49] I never thought about it until now."

"Gloria, can you believe I was thinking the exact same thing? Wow! Honey, we are so on the same wavelength. I can hardly wait until we complete our relationship by becoming one physically. Nothing thrills me more ever since I read God's design for marriage in the second chapter of the Bible. Eve was joined to Adam, and they became 'one flesh.' He said, 'bone of my bone, and flesh of my flesh!' And they were naked and not ashamed.[50] Whoa! I better calm down."

Gloria's face turned red, and her heart started racing. *We haven't set a date yet, but I hope it's soon. I guess we have got to at least complete our sophomore year first. Maybe we could marry in the summer and apply for the married housing. God has put us on a roller coaster timeline so far.* "Why would He change now?"

Jeff was puzzled, "Huh? What do you mean – 'Why would he change now'?"

Gloria laughed and reached out for Jeff, holding his face in her hands. "First things first. I want to kiss you, dear fiancé." Gloria centered her lips on Jeff's as he enveloped her in his arms tightly and pressed in. A full thirty seconds passed. Gloria pushed away and squealed. "I love you so much I don't trust myself on the same sofa with you." Gloria stood up and went over to sit down in a chair.

"What I was thinking was about the date of our marriage, thinking about how God has put us on a roller coast timeline so far in our relationship, and why would He change now? I even envisioned us marrying this summer and applying for married housing on the campus."

"Here we go again. I was thinking the same thing. But I want to add to that vision. Let's do it, and let's go on our honeymoon to Israel!"

"Your kiss took me to heaven almost, sweetheart, and now you have blown me away with a glorious idea for our honeymoon. I can't stand it, I'm so excited! Let's call Sarah and Pete right now, and let's contact a travel agent and plan it."

"Wait a minute. You don't take other people with you on a honeymoon, my naïve little future wife."

"But, Jeff, we could start out together alone, and they could join us at some point. Would that work? But, of course, they would get separate rooms. H-m-m-m... wait a minute.... Oh, my, I just had an epiphany!"

"Epiphany? What's that?"

"I will blurt it out, honey. It's a revelation. Maybe Sarah and Pete will get married, too. It surely would cut down on the cost of our trip. Double occupancy price is cheaper for the rooms. Ha!"

"Where is that 'mature woman of God' I called you? You have got us both so revved up, we will never be able to sleep. I can hear your parents. They are still up. Maybe we could go down to the living room and listen to some soothing music to relax us. We need to put all of this on the back burner and chill out, okay? Just planning for a wedding is enough to take on right now."

"Maybe you're right, but if I am enthusiastic, it only means I am 'IN GOD.' That's what the word means that 'enthusiasm' comes from, 'en theos' – 'in God.' I have always been a sponta-neous person. Is that wrong? Look at the fast-moving relationship of Ruth and Boaz in the Bible.... I can't believe that popped into my head.... See? God helped me think of that as a way of putting

His seal of approval on these unorthodox plans. Remember when I spontaneously burst out with an announcement of marriage, Papa Sam and Mama Anna loved it! Now what do you think?"

"Okay, okay, okay. I am learning that I must 'go with the flow' when you have visions." They both chuckled and went downstairs. It was only 11:00 o'clock.

We can cap off our glorious tete-a-tete with music. Let me see what's available on this stereo. H-m-m-m, I know that one. It's old, but I guess it must be a favorite with Mom and Dad. They must have been listening to it lately because it's on top. If Jeff doesn't know it, he still will be blessed by it, 'Bridge Over Troubled Water' "Get ready for a blessing, Jeff. I am spinning this record, 'Bridge Over Troubled Water.' Mom and Dad have kept all of their old records. Do you know this song?"

"Sure I do. It's a favorite of Mom's. I like it, and I found out that Paul Simon and Art Garfunkel are Jewish. That didn't mean much to me until now. Let's hear it. Come over here, and we can snuggle up as we relax."

The quality of the recording was excellent, and peace filled the room, as the lovebirds rested in each other's arms. *"When you're weary, feeling small, when tears are in your eyes I will dry them all. I'm on your side. Oh when times get rough, and friends just can't be found, like a bridge over troubled water, I will lay me down, like a bridge over troubled water, I will lay me down.... I will ease your mind...."*

They both yawned as the music finished. Jeff whispered in Gloria's ear, "I will be your bridge over troubled water. I will lay me down. I will ease your mind. I love you, and I'm always there for you. I am so sleepy though, that I won't attempt to carry you upstairs, but you can lean on me as we go up."

"Yes, wonderful man, let's go get a good night's sleep and be ready for the morning. We have a God of surprises, and I am on tiptoe to see what happens next."

CHAPTER 30

SURPRISE PHONE CALL

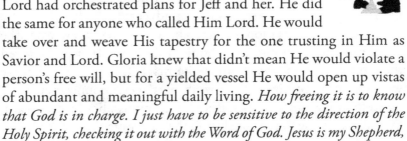

Gloria had set her alarm clock for 7:00 a.m. She wanted to be sure not to miss anything that would transpire today because she knew the Lord had orchestrated plans for Jeff and her. He did the same for anyone who called Him Lord. He would take over and weave His tapestry for the one trusting in Him as Savior and Lord. Gloria knew that didn't mean He would violate a person's free will, but for a yielded vessel He would open up vistas of abundant and meaningful daily living. *How freeing it is to know that God is in charge. I just have to be sensitive to the direction of the Holy Spirit, checking it out with the Word of God. Jesus is my Shepherd, and He is Jeff's, too.*

Gloria read her devotional for the day and spoke the Scripture out loud. Then she bowed her head in prayer, first worshiping her Lord in song. Today she thought of singing "The Lord's Prayer." In case someone was still asleep, she sang it as softly as she could, but the high A-flat was loud. Quickly, Gloria made her petitions with thanksgiving. She figured Jeff would be coming to the door when he heard her singing. Sure enough, there was a light knock on the door.

"Jeff, don't come in. I am not dressed yet."

"It's not Jeff, dear. It is your mother." Sylvia laughed. "He has been downstairs for thirty minutes, looking for some food! I came up to tell you that breakfast is ready."

"Okay, Mom. I know how to get ready fast. I will see you in about 15 minutes."

Gloria walked into the kitchen and sat down by Jeff at the small table set for four. Her dad had cooked patty sausage and was now fixing pancakes. Her mother had poured the hot coffee, and orange juice was on the table, as well as fresh strawberries, blueberries and maple syrup. "M-m-m! My favorite breakfast. Thank you so much, Mom and Dad."

"It's my favorite, too, Mr. Alvin and Miss Sylvia. You don't fool around. I like an early breakfast, so I can get on with the day. At school I adhered to my routine pretty rigorously because I had to sandwich in my birthday cake business while attending classes and studying. No extra-curricular activities for me, that is until I met Gloria. She turned my world upside down, and now I follow her like a puppy dog, having exciting adventures!"

Alvin and Sylvia looked at each other. They knew what the other one was thinking. Their smiles told it all. They really loved their future son-in-law. Alvin spoke first. "Jeff, you saw that we were shocked last night about your marriage announcement, and our response was not proper. But after thinking about it afterward, Sylvia and I came to the conclusion that we couldn't ask for a better son-in-law! So, you have our blessing."

Sylvia stood behind the young couple and patted their shoulders. "I heard some beautiful music wafting up the stairs last night, and I knew you were listening to a record on the stereo. You may not know it, but that song was our favorite, when Alvin and I first fell in love in high school. We don't ever want to forget what young love felt like. That music sort of connected me to you at a heart level right then. So, let me say we are behind you all the way. It's true that we still don't understand your interest in Jesus, but we won't let that hinder our full acceptance of your decision."

The phone rang in the kitchen. Sylvia was surprised to hear that the caller wanted Gloria. "Gloria, it's for you. Someone named Sarah. You can take it on the extension in your bedroom if you would like more privacy."

"Hello, Sarah. Let me go to my bedroom and put the phone on speaker so Jeff can hear, okay?" Sylvia held the phone while Jeff and Gloria bounded upstairs. They looked at each other, worried.

"We are both listening. Is everything all right? I am glad I gave you my parents' phone number. I bet you are lonely on the vacated campus."

"Oh, no, everything is fine. More than fine! But you are right. When everyone cleared out for the Thanksgiving holidays, I was feeling lonely. There are only a few students here. Unfortunately, that includes Jenny and Rebecca. I told Pete, and he arrived very early yesterday to take me to his parents' house for Thanksgiving. He dropped me off at the dorm late last night, made sure 'the coast was clear,' and said he would be back this morning to check on me."

"I knew your 'shield' would take care of you, Sarah. Good ole Pete. Well, what are your plans for the rest of the weekend? Is Pete taking you to temple tonight?"

"Oh, Gloria, I am about to bust at the seams to tell you what has happened. Last night in Pete's car at the dorm, he kissed me! I did not resist. It really lit my fire. He told me he loves me! I am aware that he has been a womanizer, but I have no doubt that he has changed, and he really does have feelings for me. We had a long conversation before the curfew, and you won't believe what we hope to do today!" Sarah waited for that to sink in. "And…" Thirty seconds went by.

"Oh, you mystery woman. Don't keep me hanging. Tell me everything!"

"We are flying to New York TODAY!" She could hear Gloria's loud gasp. "Pete's parents have a travel agency, and they are booking a flight for us. After our discussion last night about all the possibilities of a visit to meet your family and for you to meet my family, guess what we did. We held hands and prayed for God to open the doors if this was His will."

In the background Sarah could hear Jeff saying, "Praise the Lord!"

"Go ahead. Jeff and I are listening. Did you go up, pack, and go to bed? Maybe you called your sister. Did you?"

"Gloria… and Jeff, can you hear me well?"

213

"Jeff practically shouted. "Yes, Sarah, coming through loud and clear."

"Yes, I called my sister. I got her out of bed, and at first she was alarmed. But then she realized how happy and excited I sounded and said, 'Sarah, you haven't called me since you have been at that college. I know it is important. I am all ears.' Well, Gloria, if this doesn't qualify as a God incidence, I don't know what does!"

"Sarah, I will say what my dad has said many times: 'Hurry up and tell me before I wet my britches!'" Gloria and Jeff roared with laughter, and so did Sarah.

"Can you handle it? Here it is almost verbatim. My sister – her name is Chaya – SAID, 'I was going to call you in the morning early and see how you were making out during the holiday. All of our family, at least most of the family, has decided to go to Israel for Hanukkah. This year is the 50ᵗʰ anniversary of the State of Israel. I am so excited! And we want you to go with us! We are having to settle Mom and Dad's estate before then, so we can be in Israel for Hanukkah. The money will come out of the estate for all of us to make the trip.' Gloria, I was so overjoyed to hear that. I said, 'That's great, Chaya, but I am coming to New York TOMORROW to see all of you! And I am bringing a friend with me.' I was surprised she didn't ask a lot of questions, but there was a long pause."

"I can't believe this! Jeff and I talked about calling you, and you beat us to it. We said how wonderful it would be if you and Pete could come to New York, and we could meet each other's families. God is giving us our hearts' desires without our even asking Him. We have room for you at my house. My grandparents aren't staying here. They are at a neat place called Three Village Inn. Pete and Jeff can room together, and you and I can have my bedroom. Oh, wait a minute, I must ask Mom, but I know she will say yes."

"I know this is sudden, but slow down, Gloria. Listen, if it all works out and we actually get to New York, Pete and I will stay with Chaya and Max. She has a really big house. Wait a minute, you said you and Jeff were going to call me last night. Was it only about wanting us to be with you this weekend?"

"I will tell you when you get here. But you didn't say if Chaya fainted when you told her you were flying to New York today and bringing a friend! Did you tell her it was a **male** friend?"

Sarah giggled. "Oh, Gloria, you know I did. I better go. Pete may be trying to call me. Pray that he got us a flight leaving this morning. Chaya will pick us up at JFK Airport, and we've got to be at her house before sundown, or we will defile the Sabbath. I am all packed. As soon as he calls, I will hurry to the lobby. See you soon."

"Wait before you hang up, Sarah. I am going to ask Mom and Dad to host us for lunch tomorrow. I can't wait for you to meet each other and also for my grandparents to meet you. Please say yes!"

"Gloria, I have already violated the Sabbath twice by riding in a car back from the temple service in Columbus. HaShem may be losing patience with me! Pete and I can't come to your parents' house until after sundown tomorrow. Please don't be disappointed. If it's not too long a drive, maybe you and Jeff can come to Chaya's house in the morning. From there we could walk to a restaurant, or Chaya could fix us lunch."

Jeff and Sarah looked at each other, and both were downcast. Jeff took the phone. "Sarah, that is A-okay. Give Gloria your sister's address and phone number. We will do it!"

Gloria almost dropped the phone when Sarah told her Chaya's address. "Sarah, my house is in Port Jefferson, Long Island, and the address you gave me is VERY close by. Stony Brook is only about five miles from here. This is **definitely** a God incidence! We can possibly use Mom's car. Sarah, it is clear as crystal that the Father God is orchestrating our visit. Here is a good Bible verse that fits what is happening to us: 'A man's heart plans his way, but the Lord directs his steps.'[51] God is setting this up. But I know you are waiting for Pete's call, so I will get off the phone. Shalom for now."

Gloria and Jeff held hands and thanked God for bringing Sarah and Pete to New York, and they prayed for God to lead them step by step in His plan for their visits. They acknowledged that He wanted Sarah to come to know Yeshua as her Messiah more than they did, and they promised to trust Him.

Gloria and Jeff scampered down the stairs to the kitchen to break the news to her parents. "Mom and Dad, I am so glad you two love to entertain and have the gift of hospitality." Sylvia and Alvin looked at each other with a mixture of alarm and bewilderment. Gloria continued, "Jeff and I have invited our very best friends, Sarah and Pete, who are flying to New York today to visit her sister and also to visit us, to come to our house for dinner tomorrow night. Do you agree to that?" Not waiting for an answer, Gloria said, "Jeff and I will go out to the grocery store or go get some restaurant food and bring it home. We will take the work off of you. We just want you to meet our friends. And we want Papa Sam and Mama Anna to meet them, too. More than that, we want **them** to meet YOU. Sarah and Pete mean everything to us." Gloria was shooting silent prayers heavenward.

Alvin put on a smile. "Children, we will definitely welcome them. You may not know it, but there are tons of food in the refrigerator, freezer, and cabinets that are available for a banquet. Included is food left over from yesterday's Thanksgiving meal. We will mix up Jewish and Gentile cuisine, won't we, Sylvia?"

Sylvia's expression conveyed joy coupled with anxiety. "Yes, Alvin is the food guy, and whatever he says we will do."

"I was amazed to find out that Sarah's sister Chaya lives in Stony Brook! Can you believe it? It's so close, Jeff and I could almost walk there. All this time I thought she lived in New York City proper. Jeff and I want to meet Sarah's family. Mom and Dad, you could rest all day. We will be back to help prepare and host the dinner."

"My head is in a spin, child! Where did you get all this energy? You and Jeff seem to be on a roller coaster." Sylvia walked in the living room and sprawled on the sofa. "I need to rest. This youthful zest is challenging my stamina." Alvin, Gloria, and Jeff had a good laugh. "I will just have to learn to go with the flow." Sylvia laughed longer and harder than the rest.

CHAPTER 31

PLANNING THE DAY

"**M**om and Dad, Jeff and I are going upstairs to my bedroom to map out our plans for the day. And don't be worried – my door will be open, and I won't even sit on the loveseat with Jeff."

Alvin couldn't resist commenting. "Well, Jeff, I do trust my daughter, but what about **you**? It is not debatable that she is the most gorgeous girl anywhere around here, or for that matter, anywhere in the known world! And yes, you two need to do whatever you wish today. Sylvia and I have a catering job, and I was hoping it wouldn't disappoint you if we are gone most of the day."

"But we don't have to leave until you both go out the door to enjoy your day," Sylvia added.

"Now, Mom, are you saying you don't trust us?"

"No, Sylvia didn't mean that. She only meant that you can take her car which is parked behind my food truck, dear." With a twinkle in his eye, Alvin reached out to give Gloria a bear hug and to shake Jeff's hand.

"Mr. Alvin and Miss Sylvia, I will be Gloria's shield and protector while you are gone. We will be back downstairs in probably thirty minutes or so and drive the car out, so you can get to your catering job."

With the door open and comfortably seated away from each other, Gloria and Jeff earnestly began planning the day. "Jeff, it just popped into my head that we will have some time to visit with Mama Anna and Papa Sam at Three Village Inn. Why don't we drive around the area, so you can see where I grew up, like we did in Tupelo to see where **you** grew up? Then we can go visit with them."

"I am all for it, but there is only one problem. What if Sarah calls back, and there is no one here to take her call? Does no news mean good news?"

"I tell you what, do you know the name of Pete's parents' travel agency? That is a good way to keep in touch with them if they are already en route." Jeff shook his head. "Let me get information on the phone and find the name and number. Maybe the name is Carter Travel Agency."

Gloria sent up a quick prayer. It didn't surprise Jeff that in a few minutes Gloria had Mrs. Carter on the phone and was questioning her. Paper and pen were in her hand, and she began to write furiously. As her facial expression indicated success, Jeff came up behind her and embraced her warmly. Gloria hung up the phone. "Good news! Sarah and Pete are on their way to the Golden Triangle Regional Airport outside Columbus. I have the number, and in a few minutes I will call and have them paged. They don't board the plane for another forty minutes. Terrific! Having parents with a travel agency is a blessing. Mrs. Carter said they would arrive at JFK at 3:30 p.m."

"Maybe you don't even need to page them. All we wanted to know is if they got a flight, and they did. Not only were you praying, I bet they were, too. I say we go on the tour of your stomping grounds and then get on over to Three Village Inn. I am excited about talking to your grandparents because I have so many questions."

Gloria felt irresistibly drawn to her tall, dark, and handsome sweetheart and didn't even care if her parents happened to walk by the door. She encircled her arms around Jeff's neck, and kissed him all over his face. Jeff looked warily at the open door, but what could he do? He was literally captivated by the amorous advances of his passionate fiancé. *How can I wait until the wedding next summer? Oh, how much I want the date to be moved up. I need to put a ring on her finger as soon as possible, and we need to set a date. Down, boy, come down to earth. I don't even know how I can support a wife. I thought I wanted to drop out of school, but now I don't know. Maybe our parents will support us as a married couple if we continue on and get our degrees. Then maybe we will go together as missionaries to the*

Philippines in a humanitarian work of some kind. My heart is bursting with love for Gloria, and that's all I can think about right now.

"Darling, you are holding me so tight and so long, that I don't think you realize Mom and Dad might see us. I know I started it, but now I feel an urgency to leave this bedroom."

Jeff snapped to attention. "You are right. Let's get out of here and get on the road. Let me go to my room, get spruced up for the day, and get better dressed."

"Honey, how can you look any better? I can hardly contain myself now! But I need to do the same thing to match the appearance of my Greek god fiancé." They both laughed and blew kisses as they parted.

CHAPTER 32

LEARNING ABOUT HANUKKAH

I t was a beautiful fall day on Long Island. Gloria delighted in giving Jeff a tour of her neighborhood in Port Jefferson, Belle Terre Village, and pointing out the homes of her girlhood friends, all of whom she left behind when her parents sent her south to Mississippi State University. Gloria knew Jeff would be impressed to see The Knox School, one of the best college preparatory boarding and day schools in New York. Her parents had sacrificed financially to enroll her there, but they felt it was well worth it. Gloria knew she got an excellent education and was grateful, but she wasn't totally accepted by a lot of the girls. Maybe it was because she was Jewish, although only her name identified her as Jewish. They enjoyed the thirty-minute drive to the school, but Gloria decided to only show Jeff the exterior and not go inside.

"Sweetheart, how in the world did you keep from being a snooty aristocrat after attending an exclusive school like that? Not to mention that your home is a mansion. You don't have a proud bone in your body, thank goodness. I would never have guessed that you were so rich because you have a humble spirit, and you treat everybody the same, no matter their social or economic status. You are kind toward all you encounter at MSU."

"Thank you, Jeff. I look at you the same way. You are rich, too, you know, but you have a wonderful down-to-earth personality. I bet you were the most popular guy at Tupelo High School."

Then Gloria figured she better show Jeff her church, First United Methodist of Port Jefferson, because that is where they would be married. It was also a thirty-minute drive, so Gloria was getting worried that Papa Sam and Mama Anna may have left before they ever got to Three Village Inn. *Well, I won't take Jeff inside the church. We don't have time.*

"I bet they will be surprised to see us. I hope our visit won't be an inconvenience." Gloria parked, closed her eyes, and quickly reached for Jeff's hand, "Dear Lord, please let us be a blessing, and don't let us interrupt their plans for today. May Your purposes be fulfilled in this visit."

"I agree, in Jesus' name." Jeff squeezed Gloria's hand. At the desk they got the room number and walked down the hall to the right door and knocked. "This will not be a shock but only a surprise," Jeff confidently asserted.

"Yes, it will be another God incidence," Gloria added. The door quickly opened, and Mama Anna squealed with delight.

"Children, you happened up at the perfect time. Sam and I were sitting on the sofa, reading the Bible and wishing you were here to share what the Holy Spirit is showing us. Come in."

Papa Sam grabbed Gloria in his arms and kissed her on the cheek. He shook Jeff's hand and pointed to the loveseat across from the sofa where they were sitting. "Sit down. Let me give you Anna's Bible, so we can read and discuss together."

"So where are you reading, and what did the Holy Spirit show you, Papa Sam?"

"We are reading the book of Daniel in the Old Covenant. Your grandmother and I have been in a study of the end times in our Messianic Jewish congregation in Chicago, the Olive Tree Congregation. In the 24th chapter of Matthew in the New Covenant, Yeshua referred to something Daniel the prophet said. Anna and I decided we would read that quote in the Old Covenant but also read the whole book of Daniel and see what we could learn. How fascinating it is."

"Yes, dear, I am deeply interested in eschatology because the time is drawing near for Yeshua's return," Anna exclaimed.

"Wait a minute. You all are way over my head. We didn't even have a Bible in our house, and I have only owned a Bible for a short time, ever since God changed my life. The Holy Spirit has given me a burning desire to know it from cover to cover. Where is that word, 'eschatology,' in the Bible, and what does it mean?"

Anna grinned. "Oh, I didn't mean to throw around such big words, but it means 'the study of the end times.'"

Jeff was alarmed. "Do you mean to say the world is coming to an end soon? I hope that question doesn't show my ignorance. Thank the Lord I got in under the wire before the world burns up! At least I know I will go to heaven."

Papa Sam stood up and walked over to Gloria and Jeff. He patted Jeff on the shoulder. "Yes, we are possibly living in the end times before Yeshua returns. However, the Apostle Paul believed the same thing in his day, almost 2,000 years ago. But I have some good news to tell you now, even though I was waiting to tell you when Alvin and Sylvia are with us. Anna and I are making our second trip to Israel just a month from now. We will be there during Hanukkah, and it is also the 50th anniversary of the State of Israel. We are preparing ourselves spiritually by reading the Book of Daniel, along with the apocryphal books of First and Second Maccabees because they tell the story of Hanukkah."

"Hallelujah! That is phenomenal, Papa Sam. Our friend at MSU, Sarah Bernstein, is going with her family to Israel at Hanukkah also. We just found out, talking to her on the phone. She and her boyfriend, Pete Carson, are flying here to Long Island this very day. I can't wait for them to meet you. We are going to Stony Brook tomorrow where Sarah's sister Chaya lives and visit with them. And then Sarah and Pete are coming to my house tomorrow night for dinner. You will get to meet them!"

"You see, ever since Gloria and I gave our lives to Jesus, He is orchestrating everything that happens to us. For some reason He wants to grow us up **fast**, and it looks like He is giving y'all to us as mentors and teachers. That must be why we are here talking to you. Tell us everything. But first, what does 'apocryphal books' mean? I never heard of the Maccabees. Have you, Gloria?"

"Yes, tell us, Papa Sam. I don't know either. Jeff and I will just sit back, and you and Mama Anna teach us."

"Well, I will begin by saying that Christians and Messianic Jews have strongly differing opinions about the end times. Anna and I do our best to just stick with Scripture and to compare different passages. Of course, God has given teachers to the body of Messiah, as well as apostles, prophets, pastors, and evangelists.[52] They help us grow. I think the Holy Spirit has given me the gift of teacher, so He uses me as a vessel to teach His people. First, 'apocryphal books' are those books that chronologically come between the Old and New Covenants, but they are not inspired and not included in the canon of Scripture. Nevertheless, they are true history, and the events of Hanukkah are recorded in them. First and Second Maccabees, plus other books, are to be found in the Catholic Bible, not in Protestant Bibles. Anna and I bought a Catholic Bible, so we can read Maccabees."

"This is brand new to me, so please go slowly," pleaded Jeff.

"Yeshua celebrated Hanukkah in Jerusalem, as recorded in John 10:22. It is called the 'Feast of Dedication,' commemorating the rededication of the temple in Jerusalem after the Maccabees won it back from the Syrians. Hanukkah is a Hebrew word for 'dedication.' It was in the wintertime. At the feast the religious leaders demanded that Yeshua tell them if He was the Messiah. Yeshua affirmed that He was, and that He and the Father were ONE.

"Hanukkah is a story about a wicked ruler named Antiochus Ephiphanes who profaned the temple, claiming he was God. This man was a foreshadowing of the 'anti-Messiah' or the 'anti-Christ.' Daniel called him 'the abomination of desolation.' Yeshua warned His followers, 'When you see the abomination of desolation spoken of by the prophet Daniel, standing in the holy place (let the reader understand), then **let those who are in Judea flee to the mountains** …For then there will be great tribulation, such as has not been from the beginning of the world until now, no, and never will be.'[53] Matthew continues in this chapter to describe the events preceding the coming of Yeshua the Messiah back to the earth. Some of the signs that Yeshua gives in the first part of Chapter 24 are signs that we are seeing today! That is why many people believe we are living in the end times before the Lord comes back, when He will destroy the wicked and set up His throne in Jerusalem."

"Children, you may not remember all of this, but the Lord will bring it to your memory when you need to know it," interjected Anna. Later, you can study the parts of the New Testament that tell about the end times. Try to remember where to find them. The primary sources are Matthew 24, Mark 13, Luke 21, 2 Thessalonians 2 and 3, 1 Thessalonians 4 and 5, and the Book of Revelation. Here is some paper and a pen, so you can write that down. But since we are telling you the story of the first Hanukkah that is found in Daniel and the Maccabees books, let us resume that history. Before Sam tells it, I want to point out that Yeshua was giving very practical advice to His followers about actions to take when the 'abomination of desolation' would stand in the holy place. This came to pass shortly before A.D. 70, when the Romans conquered the city of Jerusalem. "Josephus [the foremost first century historian] says that Titus entered the Holy of Holies with his generals in A.D. 70. Shortly thereafter, Titus was worshipped in the Temple … as was customary of someone declared imperator in fulfillment of 2 Thessalonians 2:4: **'He sets Himself up in God's Temple displaying himself as a god.'**"[54] Then in A.D 70, the Romans destroyed the temple. Thousands of Messianic Jews heeded the words of Yeshua and had fled to the Judean mountains to Pella and were saved![55] Children, it pays to listen to prophecy. But here is something that is important to know. A prophecy can have more than one fulfillment. Yes, part of Yeshua's prophecy in Matthew 24 has already come to pass, but not all of it. There is more to be fulfilled at the end of time before Yeshua returns to the earth. Paul prophesied to the church at Thessalonica that the 'man of lawlessness,' (the anti-Messiah) would sit in the temple and proclaim himself to be God!"[56] So, the Syrian ruler, Antiochus Ephiphanes was the first 'lawless one,' and Emperor Titus was the second 'lawless one.' There is another evil man who is coming as the 'abomination of desolation,' the one who will precede the second coming of Yeshua."

Jeff's and Gloria's eyes were getting wider and wider. Gloria was breathless. "I am on the edge of my seat, Mama Anna. I never knew that Bible study could be so exciting. But wait! Please don't tell any more, until we have Sarah and Pete with us at dinner tomorrow night. Papa Sam can tell the story of Hanukkah then. Pete will not have heard **any** of it, and probably Sarah only knows **part** of it. It will blow her away that thousands of Messianic Jews were saved because they heeded Jesus' words that referred to Daniel's prophecy! Just think, she will be in Israel at Hanukkah, too. Her brother and his wife live there, so maybe they can tell her what to expect in the Israeli celebration of that holiday."

Jeff gasped. "Gloria, you and I must go also. I know I promised you a trip to Israel for our honeymoon, but that will be in June, and it's too far away. I can't wait for you and I to go visit our ancient homeland, the reborn nation of Israel. How special to be in the Holy Land on Israel's 50th birthday!"

"I was thinking the same thing while Papa Sam and Mama Anna were talking. Yes, honey, let's do it. But that's a lot of money our parents would have to fork out, and what about missing school?"

"But won't you be on your Christmas break from college at that time?" Anna asked. We are planning to fly there on December 21st because Hanukkah will begin on the 23rd. Our return flight is on the 30th. Surely you won't start back to school until after January 1st."

Papa Sam spoke up. "Before we all 'flip out,' as the young people say, we better take care of our growling stomachs. Mirabelle Tavern is the original part of Three Village Inn. It was built long years ago as a tea house. Then rooms for the guests were built. Their food is excellent. Anna and I take all our meals right here. We can keep talking about the end times or change to a lighter subject."

"We were thinking the same thing," exclaimed Gloria and Jeff in unison. "Can you believe it, Jeff? We said that together. Before you know it, we will be finishing each other's sentences. Ha!"

"Lead the way, Papa Sam. I am hungry."

CHAPTER 33

RECALLING FAMILY HISTORY

D uring lunch, questions were forming in Jeff's mind, things about Gloria's parents. He wanted to know how her parents got from Chicago to New York. They went to high school and college together, Miss Sylvia had said, and they met in Papa Sam's delicatessen in Chicago. "Papa Sam, please tell us how Gloria's parents wound up in New York after growing up in Chicago."

"Jeff, my son Alvin fell deeply in love with Sylvia in high school. Both of them experienced persecution from the students because they were Jews. There were many Jewish students, but they were outnumbered by Gentiles. Worst of all, the neo-Nazis rallied and marched in Chicago. They painted swastikas on Jewish graveyards and vandalized synagogues and Jewish community centers. One day Sylvia was walking near Marquette Park where the neo-Nazis were having a rally.[57] She walked beside a protestor carrying a flag, saying, 'Smash the Nazis!' The protestors emboldened Sylvia, and she yelled out, 'Hitler was defeated. Jews and blacks have freedom here!' One of the neo-Nazis came off the platform and got up in her face. He threatened her, saying, 'We will finish the job Hitler started!' It was at that point she decided to leave Chicago after her high school graduation and go to the City College of New York. Her parents went along with her wishes."

"Alvin had not suffered as much persecution as Sylvia, maybe because of his physical appearance. He could pass for a Gentile. Nevertheless, because he loved Sylvia so much, he felt he had no choice but to enroll with her in the same college. They were already talking about marriage after graduation and living in New York. I wanted him to inherit my store, and he actually wept when he told me his decision. Of course, Anna and I financed his education and were glad to do so. The same was true of Sylvia's parents. Alvin and

Sylvia determined to make Gentile friends in New York and stay away from Jewish activities. Anna and I had not been able to persuade Alvin to go to our wonderful Messianic Jewish congregation in Chicago. They said they would stay away from religion, period. They would not attend church or synagogue in New York. Even in spite of that, they did not disavow their Jewishness, and they always kept Passover. But they were happy to appear as Gentiles."

Gloria responded, "I am glad Jeff asked you that question. Thank you, Papa Sam, for explaining. I wish my mother had told me how she was persecuted. Jeff only learned recently of his Jewishness because his mother was also persecuted in school, and she determined to protect her son from persecution by hiding the fact they were Jews. It makes me feel bad for both our mothers. Dad and Mom never talked to me about it. I could see that their guidance of my development as a child and a teen did not include my ethnic identity. I was fine with it, but now I know the motivation behind it. I am sad that they have deprived themselves of enjoying their rich Jewish heritage. Since I have reconnected with my Jewish roots, I believe the Lord will use me to help them reconnect also. More importantly, I want to see them receive their Jewish Messiah and know the joy of walking with Him daily in the power of His Holy Spirit."

"Child, you don't know how ecstatic Sam and I felt when you told us yesterday that you had been born again in the Messiah. Ever since I first set eyes on you as my grandchild and held you in my arms, I prayed that the Lord would reveal Himself to you. Sam and I prayed that prayer together many times. Now you can join us in praying for your parents, that they, too, will have the scales removed from their eyes and know Yeshua."

"Papa Sam and Mama Anna, let's pray right now and include my parents, too. I think my mother has come to believe, but I am not sure about my father." Jeff reached out, and the four of them held hands right there in the restaurant and prayed quietly, as the waitress and customers looked on. They felt no embarrassment, and even if they did, they could not let this moment pass without making corporate intercession for the eternal souls of their loved ones. After some customers kept looking at them, they knew it was time to go back to the room, so their conversation could not be overheard. The meal was soon finished.

Back in the room, Gloria had another question. "Papa Sam and Mama Anna, I have a question, too. When you were in Jerusalem, did you go see the Holocaust Museum? There is also one in Washington, D.C. I missed the opportunity to go on a tour with my high school classmates because at that time I wasn't interested, sad to say."

"I will answer that question, dear. I think it may be a little easier for me to talk about it than your grandfather. Yes, we did go through the Holocaust Museum in Jerusalem. It is called Yad VaShem, which means 'a memorial and a name.' It commemorates individually the six million Jews who were killed during World War II by Hitler and the Nazis in many extermination camps. Also, there is a building for honoring the one-and-a-half million children who were murdered. Sam and I were among the children who escaped, and we praise the Lord every day for that. The Righteous Among the Nations are honored also. These are the Gentiles who risked their lives to hide Jewish people. Trees are planted in their memory. In recent years I read the story of a Christian Dutch family of Righteous Gentiles in a book by Corrie ten Boom, *The Hiding Place*.[58] Her family hid Jews in a tiny hiding place in Corrie's bedroom. One day the Ten Booms were caught and arrested, but the Jews went free. It is a sad story but also a victorious story. When Corrie was released, she was given a ministry by God to both the victims and the perpetrators of the Holocaust. She herself was approached by a Nazi guard at one of her meetings whom she recognized as the guard who had treated her sister so cruelly. He held out his hand, wanting assurance of God's forgiveness. Corrie reluctantly shook his hand, and God's love spread up her arm and poured into Corrie's heart!" Anna began to cry, as the awful memories came rushing back.

Sam held her close and wiped the tears away. "Yes, children, both of us suffered in that camp, but the suffering was not as bad for us as children as it was for the adults. We were never detected because children weren't supposed to be there. It was a miracle that we slipped in, and it was easier for us to get by the guards and steal food and other things for us and our parents. Like Corrie ten Boom, Anna and I had to learn to forgive those wicked Nazis, or we would have been crippled for life. My parents never released the bitterness until the end of their lives, when Yeshua changed their hearts. They received His forgiveness and eternal life. It was when Anna and I read the New Testament together that it happened for us. When we got to the part about the crucifixion of Yeshua, it was like a movie. We were reading, and yet we became part of the actual story. In our minds we were back at the camp, seeing the torture of the inmates by the Nazi guards. As Yeshua was being beaten, we felt it! We felt it when the nails were driven in His hands and feet, and blood came streaming down His face from the crown of thorns. We were cut to the heart when He said, 'Father, forgive them, for they know not what they do.' We both started crying so hard the pages of our Bible were wet. We stopped reading and started praying out loud. 'Father, forgive us for hating the Nazis, for hating Hitler, for all the wicked things we did even before we were in the camp.' And you know what? While tears were running down our faces, we felt a warm rain on the inside. We felt cleansed. We felt forgiven. We felt free! All the hate was gone. That is when Anna and I were born again!"

Jeff and Gloria were stunned and couldn't say a word. Finally, Jeff broke the silence. "I feel privileged to be in your presence. I feel honored to have heard you open up your hearts and tell of your experiences in a concentration camp and what you suffered. I just pray that if I am ever called on to suffer like that, I will not let bitterness enter my heart. I want to be like Jesus and forgive.

Also, I won't forget the example of Corrie ten Boom, and I plan to read that book, too." He looked at Gloria. "Honey, we are definitely going to visit Yad VaShem. I have heard people say that the survivors of the Holocaust are dying out, and others need to tell the story. 'We must never forget,' they say."

"That's right, Jeff. When my classmates came back from touring the Holocaust Museum in Washington, D.C., they reported what General Dwight Eisenhower said when our troops liberated the Ohrdruf concentration camp in 1945. The Russians liberated the worst killing camp, Auschwitz, and the British also liberated some camps. But what impressed my classmates the most were Eisenhower's words, which are engraved on the entrance of the museum. Can you believe that I have that quote right here in my purse? It impressed me so much when I heard it that I copied it down and kept it with me. And now, knowing my own grandparents went through the Holocaust, I want to learn all I can about it. Let me read it to you." Gloria quickly retrieved the note from her purse. "'The things I saw beggar description…The visual evidence and the verbal testimony of starvation, cruelty and bestiality were so overpowering…I made the visit deliberately, in order to be in a position to give first hand evidence of these things if ever, in the future, there develops a tendency to charge these allegations to propaganda.' This quote was condensed from a paragraph in a letter that General Eisenhower wrote to General George C. Marshall on April 15, 1945."[59]

"Eisenhower made a prophetic statement without knowing it," Sam exclaimed. What he said MIGHT happen HAS happened. Holocaust denial is becoming more common all the time. The Palestinians say it is all propaganda. Even so-called intelligent people believe that lie. Yes, we must always have witnesses to speak out about this horrible time in history. We must learn from it and vow it will never happen again!"

Gloria stood up. "I can't wait until we get to Israel for Hanukkah. We have had a crash course in history and Bible from you two in only two days so far. And we are getting together again with you tomorrow night at Mom and Dad's. You are preparing us for a trip of a lifetime, Israel at Hanukkah. Jeff and I better hit the road for home though. We have to get near the phone so we won't miss a call from Sarah and Pete. They may have already landed at JFK. I am excited about being with them tomorrow morning and also tomorrow night. This visit to New York is being packed with un-forgettable experiences! Jeff and I better leave. I love you so much." Gloria embraced her grandparents, and so did Jeff.

CHAPTER 34

A NEW WORLD FOR PETE

Gloria pulled in her driveway. The food truck was not there. "Honey, your parents aren't home yet. Do you think we should go inside or just sit here in the car until they return? What was it you told me the other day that you learned at BSU – that we should avoid even the appearance of evil?"[60]

"Jeff, you learn fast. I am impressed." Gloria leaned over and kissed him lightly on the cheek. "Yes, it's very true, but I'm sure Mom and Dad will be back any minute. They haven't mentioned supper. I don't think we'll have dinner, meaning they will be too tired after a long day catering, and we will probably have a light meal. They call it 'supper' in the South for almost every evening meal, don't they?"

"I am proud of you, Gloria. You are learning about 'southern.' You are becoming quite a Southern Belle already, even before we are married. That deserves some 'back seat smooching' in the front seat!" Jeff reached for Gloria, but she had quickly opened her car door and got out just in time.

"Come on, Jeff. You got 'my motor running,' and you are not trustworthy whether we are inside or outside the house. Let's go in. We can sit in the kitchen or living room and wait for Sarah's call."

As Gloria turned her key in the lock, she heard the phone ring and picked it up in the kitchen. It was Sarah. "Jeff, get on my extension. It's Sarah." Jeff bounded up the stairs to Gloria's bedroom. "Sarah! Jeff and I just got back home in the nick of time. I am so glad we didn't miss your call."

"We have deplaned at JFK, and I have called Chaya. She said she is on her way. So Pete and I are going down to claim our baggage. After we get our bags, we will keep a lookout for Chaya. Maybe there will be time to call you again before she arrives. Pete and I have had a ball, flying first-class, courtesy of his parents. Wonderful! I know you are saying it now: 'It's a God incidence.'" Gloria and Jeff could hear Pete laughing in the background.

"Sarah, we have a lot to tell you, and it will blow your mind! I guess we will have to wait until tomorrow to see you both in person. Tell Pete that we really love his parents. Also, tell him that Jeff and I are going to need their services very soon. Wish you had time for me to tell you more, but I will hang up, and you and Pete can go get your luggage. Bye, sweet friend."

Sylvia and Alvin returned home. They were relieved to find Jeff and Gloria in the living room, only talking. Jeff had already formulated a plan in his mind. "Mr. Alvin, can we go outside? I have a business proposition I want to talk over with you, just the two of us."

Sylvia was glad for them to have a talk, even though she was curious to know what business proposition Jeff could possibly discuss with Alvin. "Go ahead, Alvin. I am going upstairs and take a quick nap before I prepare supper. That was no easy catering job. Gloria, I will be back down in no more than an hour."

"Mom, you go rest. I myself need a nap."

It was late afternoon, and Jeff felt an urgency to carry out his plan with Alvin's help. "Mr. Alvin, I know you are tired, and it is late in the day, but is there any way you could take me downtown? I want to pick out an engagement ring for Gloria, and I want to surprise her with it tomorrow night. You do remember that we invited our friends, Sarah and Pete, for dinner, don't you?"

"Yes, Sylvia and I have it covered. And Mom and Dad will be coming also. Sylvia and I were wondering if you were really serious about marrying our daughter, since you haven't given her a ring. This is good news to me, and I will be glad to help you get that ring."

"Oh, thank you, thank you, Mr. Alvin. I will stick my head back in the house and tell Gloria we are going downtown, and we are going to look at birthday cakes in the various bakeries." *Lord, please forgive me for lying.*

They got in the car and headed downtown. Jeff felt like he had the perfect plan, but if the ring didn't fit, he wasn't sure she could get it sized in Starkville. *Father God, You surely inspired this idea, and you have given me favor with Mr. Alvin. I want to ask one more thing – could You help me pick out a ring Gloria will like and one that fits? I have faith You will. Right now I pledge to You that Gloria and I will put Jesus first in our marriage.*

Gloria was too sleepy to ponder what Jeff was trying to accomplish. *He must be milking my dad for all the advice he can get to make his birthday cake business more profitable. If anyone would know, it would be my dad. Birthday parties probably bring in more money than all the other parties Mom and Dad cater. Anyway, I am glad they will be alone. Oh, Lord, cause them to bond together, and also cause Dad to see Jesus in Jeff and to want what Jeff has found. And what I have found, dear Lord.*

No sooner had Gloria closed her eyes than the phone rang. *Oh, that's got to be Sarah.* She didn't know that it was Pete calling, and he only planned to talk to Jeff. Pete disguised his voice to make Gloria think it was a wrong number. She hung up and went back to bed, quickly falling asleep.

Alvin took Jeff to a jeweler he knew well, and in a short time Jeff had chosen the right ring for Gloria. Alvin agreed it was perfect. Jeff paid with his credit card, and they were on their way home. They both remarked they were looking forward to getting a short nap before supper.

No sooner had Jeff laid his head down on the pillow than the phone rang again. Sylvia was in the kitchen and picked up. "Yes, Jeff is here. He is up in his room. I will go get him."

Jeff decided to take the call in Gloria's room, since there was no extension in his room. He would just have to wake her up, so he knocked on the door lightly. "Honey, Pete is on the phone. I'm sorry to bother you. Your mother said he specifically wanted to talk to me and in private. I'm sorry to disturb you. Do you mind switching rooms with me for a few minutes? I can't imagine why he only wants to talk to me."

"Sure, I don't mind at all. I think I can get right back to sleep." Gloria yawned.

"Okay, Pete, shoot. I am in Gloria's bedroom, and she is not here. What's on your mind? By the way, welcome to New York, the home of the New York Yankees!"

"Jeff, I'm sorry I am in no mood to have small talk. I've got to make this quick. There's hardly any privacy around here, even though this is a big house. They only have one phone extension, and it's in the back hall. I have the doors closed. First, let me say that when I picked up Sarah at the dorm, my eyes bugged out. She was so lovely, I was speechless. She was wearing makeup, which she never does, and her bright red lipstick showed off her white teeth. I could tell she had curled her hair, and it lay so gently on her shoulders. Her dress must have been silk, which really displayed her curves! There was no one in the lobby, so I took the bags out of her hands and put them down. For a few seconds my eyes just feasted on this gorgeous girl. Amazingly, my thoughts weren't unholy, and I didn't feel the lust that had driven me in the past. I grabbed for her. She came into my arms with delight, seemingly. I held her as close and kissed her as deep as I dared. We had our first kiss the night before, and she and I both must have kept savoring it! Whew! That's enough description, but I wanted you to hear it because my response to her beauty only shows how much I have really changed since I started hanging out with you guys and attending religious services. Let me get on with it. The flight was great. In first class I could hold hands with Sarah easily, and we even had some delicious but discreet kisses. I am afraid to say that I really have fallen in love with her. Now her family is another matter. I feel sort of cornered here in an orthodox Jewish household. Everything has to be just so, by the book, you know. Chaya drove so fast to get here before sundown that it scared even daredevil me. Sarah said I don't have to

240

wear that little hat, a kippah, but she expects me to wear my finest to Shabbat dinner. I didn't bring a suit and tie, but I do have a sleek pair of pants and a dress shirt and shiny loafers. I have never been to a Shabbat dinner, and I hope I don't make any glaring mistakes in the Jewish etiquette. Just say a prayer for me, buddy. You are my good ole roommate, and you know my sinful past, but maybe God will have mercy. I don't want to mess this up. As clueless as I am about the real Christian life, I know I can't seduce Sarah. Jeff, I confess I really do want to, and I could probably succeed. But I love her too much to have my way with her before marriage. Oh, my! I didn't mean to say that word, 'marriage.' It slipped out."

"Well, Pete, you won't believe it, but Gloria and I made our announcement of marriage to her parents and grandparents on Thanksgiving soon after we arrived! Her parents were shocked, but her grandparents chuckled. I can't wait for you to meet them all tomorrow night, especially the grandparents. But let me continue. In some conversation Gloria and I had privately, Gloria said she hoped you and Sarah would get married, and we could all four go to Israel together for a honeymoon! But since talking to her grandparents, we now want to go to Israel for Hanukkah, just a month from now. We can't wait to talk to you about it. My life since meeting Gloria has been like a jet taking off!"

"Yep, buddy. That fits my life right now, too, and my head is spinning from what you just said about a honeymoon in Israel. Well, it won't be long until dinner. I better go. Say that prayer for me. And also, pray that Max and Chaya will like me, and we can find something in common to talk about. After all, I will be in their house until we fly out Sunday morning. Goodbye. Thanks, Jeff, for hearing me out. I don't mind if you share with Gloria, but please don't include the sensual part." Jeff laughed.

"Wait, don't hang up. Gloria and I are coming to see you and Sarah tomorrow. We want to meet Max and Chaya, too. Then we will take you away from them and treat you to lunch, so we can talk. Gloria showed me the area today. The four of us can actually walk to a good restaurant, okay?"

"That is certainly good news to me. You and Gloria come on around 10:00 in the morning. Good talking to you, buddy. Good-bye." *I can see deliverance coming. But now I need to focus on making Sarah happy. If we are to have a future together, it is imperative that I learn to be comfortable in her Jewish Orthodox family. And that goes both ways. She has got to feel at home in MY family. She can already see what great parents I have because they got us on a plane in a hurry and even paid for our first-class seats. Come on, Pete, you can do this.* Pete got dressed and groomed and admired himself in the full-length mirror in his bedroom. Max was tall, too, so Pete couldn't dazzle them with his impressive height. He wouldn't dazzle them with his personality either, he feared. He surely was counting on Jeff's prayers.

CHAPTER 35

THE TRIP OF A LIFETIME

I t was a peaceful and harmonious time in the Sondheims' home on Friday night, although Sylvia and Alvin did not observe a traditional Shabbat meal for Gloria and Jeff. They had been called upon occasionally to cater this meal in a Jewish home in the Stony Brook area, and they knew all the elements of the traditional observance from their youth. However, they had chosen not to bring their daughter up in the Jewish way, so they usually found themselves at sports events on Friday nights during Gloria's high school days. They would grab a hot dog at the concession stand, aware that it broke the kosher laws, but they had long ago ceased to care about that.

Jeff and Gloria and her parents relaxed and had light conversation during the simple meal. Jeff didn't say much, however, because he was trying to envision what Pete might be going through at a traditional kosher Shabbat dinner. He offered up a heartfelt silent prayer for his friend. After about an hour, the young couple excused themselves from the table. They were anticipating their visit with Sarah and Pete in the morning and wanted to go to bed early.

It was nice to sleep later than usual. Gloria and Jeff enjoyed a light breakfast and leisurely conversation with Sylvia and Alvin, telling them of their plans for the day. Sylvia graciously offered them her car to drive to Stony Brook. Gloria said, "Mom, we appreciate your generosity. We will be back in the late afternoon to help you and Dad prepare for dinner tonight. I can hardly wait for you to meet Sarah and Pete. I know they will love all that variety of food you told us about, Dad. And it will be an education for Pete, although he was exposed to some Jewish cuisine last night."

"Now y'all rest today, Miss Sylvia and Mr. Alvin. You deserve it. You worked so hard yesterday. Anyway, it's the Sabbath. And Mr. Alvin, remember the dessert we discussed yesterday, okay?"

Alvin replied, "I won't forget, Jeff. Everybody, especially my parents, will really love it!"

They were about to leave. "Shalom, Mom and Dad!" Gloria yelled up the stairs. "Let's go, Jeff. We've got to find Chaya's house, go inside to meet Chaya and Max, have a little conversation, and then on to another restaurant. Our lives seem to revolve around food. But Jesus loved to be with people at mealtime, too. There's a great verse in Revelation 3:20 about it: 'Behold, I stand at the door and knock; if any man hear my voice and open the door, I will come in to him and sup with him and he with Me.' Or you could say 'dine with Him.' I love that."

"And both our parents and grandparents have vocations to do with FOOD. Ha!"

"Yeah, and you yourself sell birthday cakes, the most delicious kind of food, honey!"

As soon as they were in the car Gloria quizzed Jeff about his conversation with Pete. "You surely didn't tell me much about that conversation you had with Pete."

"Well, the only thing I didn't tell you was that when he picked up Sarah at the dorm, he was stunned by her appearance. Let me see if I can remember what he said. M-m-m, she had on bright red lipstick, her hair was curled, and she had on a silk dress. You can guess what happened. He kissed her, and she liked it! Then Sarah wiped the lipstick off his mouth! Sweet Gloria, when I kiss you and your lipstick gets on me, I just savor it for a while. I even sport it around campus. I'm not going do that around your parents though." Jeff chuckled.

"Jeff Quentin, you are trying to distract me. I know how members of the opposite sex like to brag to other men about their romantic exploits, so I forgive you for not telling me the whole story. We both know that Pete has had experience with women. I just hope Sarah restrained him."

"Gloria, trust me. It was a beautiful thing. But the main thing he said was to pray for him that he would act right at their Shabbat meal, since he isn't familiar with the ritual. I will lead us in a retroactive prayer right now."

"You funny guy! You didn't pray right then, and now you want to pray and think God will apply it to last night?"

"Well, why not? He is the Great I Am, Who is, Who was, and Who is to come! I learned that from reading Exodus. He can make things happen in the past, present, and future, can't He?"

"Now that is something I need to chew on. In our Bible study at BSU, we were studying the first chapter of Revelation, and the Spirit opened my eyes to see JESUS AS GOD more than I ever had before. Jesus said, 'I am the Alpha and the Omega, the Beginning and the End, says the Lord, Who is, Who was, and Who is to come, the Almighty.'[61] That amazed me."

"I did pray last night, but I want us to pray together right now. We can pray a blanket prayer, covering the whole day and include Pete's request." Jeff felt a boldness and proceeded to pray loudly in detail, forming a prayer that God would be glorified and His purposes fulfilled.

"Honey, you blessed me. Your prayer made me remember that your grandfather, John Cohen, had a name that means 'priest.' I think you just made a priestly prayer. Beautiful! And when we marry, you will be the 'high priest' of our home, carrying all the needs of your wife and children to the throne of the Lord."

Stony Brook was coming in sight. "Here we are, Jeff. We don't have to stay long, but I am interested in meeting Chaya and Max."

Pete was looking out for his friends and was the first to meet them and welcome them into the house. "Chaya, here are our friends, Jeff Quentin and Gloria Sondheim. I already told you a lot about them. As I said, I am Jeff's roommate. Then I met Sarah." Sarah looked up at Pete adoringly, as she held his arm. "Together we met Gloria who had already captivated Jeff. I am sorry that Max isn't here because I really wanted him to meet my best friends."

"Welcome to our new home, Gloria and Jeff. It's not really new, but it is new to us. We moved from Queens only a month ago. Max got a new job here. Unfortunately, he not only has to work sometimes on Shabbat, but he is on call most all the time. He is with a security company. He installs and repairs house and business alarms in this whole area. At least Pete got to meet him last night. Please sit down, so we can visit."

Sarah was all smiles. "I am going to have another niece or nephew in about six months! If Chaya has to hurry out of the room, you will understand." Jeff looked puzzled.

"What Sarah is saying is that Max and I are going to be parents! We are very excited, especially because it has been four years since our marriage. My brothers and sisters have lots of children, and they were worried about me."

Gloria had to know. "But isn't your whole family flying to Israel for Hanukkah in less than a month? Will you be able to go, if you are still having morning sickness?" Now Jeff understood fully.

Sarah spoke up. "Don't doubt my sister. Chaya would not miss the trip for anything. She will manage. Besides, you guys know how to pray and get your prayers answered. So please get on this case."

Gloria and Jeff looked at each other. Gloria whispered in Jeff's ear, "Should we tell them that my grandparents are going to Israel for Hanukkah, and it is possible that we may go, too?"

Jeff whispered back, "I told Pete on the phone that you and I were thinking about the four of us going to Israel on our honeymoon in June, if Pete and Sarah get married."

Pete was getting uncomfortable. "Hey, guys, it is not polite to whisper. Please tell us what's going on."

Jeff stood up. "Okay, I will reveal our big secret." All eyes were on Jeff. "Aha! I knew you would now hang on every word. Pete, when I talked to you on the phone last night, I told you that Gloria and I had discussed going to Israel on our honeymoon in June. That's not all I said, but let's save that for later. Well, Gloria and I had a visit with her grandparents, and they told us they have a trip planned to Israel for Hanukkah. This year. As you said, it's only a month away. This was in the context of a Bible lesson that Papa Sam gave us about the first Hanukkah, the story of the Maccabees, and he tied it into what Jesus said when He talked about the end times."

Gloria chimed in. "Yes, and Jesus celebrated Hanukkah Himself. Sarah, you and Chaya may not know that. Anyway, Jeff and I got so excited during the Bible lesson, that we said we wanted to go, too! And especially since it is the 50th anniversary celebration of the State of Israel. Mama Anna said we should go, that we will be on Christmas break and won't miss school."

Sarah was jubilant. "Oh, how wonderful! I hope you do go. Chaya, Max, and I are planning to stay at our brother's house in Jerusalem. Maybe you could stay with us. Do your grandparents already have a hotel booked? If so, you may want to stay in the same hotel with them, separate rooms, of course." Sarah looked at Pete, and everyone got quiet.

Pete felt his heart racing. Did he dare to suggest a plan that included him? He knew zero about Hanukkah and almost zero about Israel. What he did know was if this was an opportunity to get closer to his beloved Sarah, he better not miss it. Nervously, he put forth a proposal in a shaky voice. "Jeff, you know we are getting along great as roommates now that I have rededicated myself to the Lord. Do you think you would consider me for a roommate somewhere else besides Mississippi State?"

Everybody laughed because it was obvious what Pete was proposing. "You said it, blessed roommate! I officially invite you to room with me in the Jerusalem hotel where Papa Sam and Mama Anna will be staying."

Gloria was feeling left out. "Well, I guess I could get a single room at the hotel."

Sarah moved over beside Gloria on the sofa. "You, Gloria, are MY blessed roommate, and we should not be separated. My brother will have a full house as it is, so I will room with YOU at the hotel! That way the four of us can be together." The four embraced each other.

Chaya was enjoying their camaraderie. She had only made one friend in Stony Brook, but she never saw her because she had been too busy since the move. After unpacking and decorating the house, she began to work on the nursery. She had doctor's visits and other domestic duties. Soon the family in the U.S. would be coming together to settle the estate. There was little time to do it because she and Max had to get ready for the trip to Israel. She was feeling tired, just thinking about it. "Sarah told me you four had dubbed yourselves the 'Holy Rollers.' I feel a morning nap coming on, so you couples better roll on along to the restaurant for lunch." Chaya broke out into laughter, and it felt good. She had been weighed down with sorrow ever since her parents were killed.

"Yes, sweet sister. You deserve a nap after all the hard work you did for our Shabbat meal and for breakfast, too. I say you are a stellar hostess." Sarah loved on Chaya, and Pete showered her with compliments.

"I will hug you easy, mother-to-be," Pete promised. "We will see you late tonight. Gloria told me we should go back with Jeff and her to Port Jefferson after lunch and loll around in the afternoon. Then she won't have to drive back here to pick us up for dinner."

Gloria convinced Sarah she could make another exception to the prohibition against driving anywhere on the Sabbath, and she drove them to the restaurant. They ordered quickly. All four of them had a lot to talk about, and food didn't matter.

Pete was the first to start the conversation. "Jeff, I already told Sarah about asking you to pray for me last night that I wouldn't make a great big faux pas at the Shabbat meal. I want to report that, according to Sarah, I was the model guest. Hoorah!"

Sarah chuckled. "I kept kicking Pete under the table so he would loosen up and relax. He got tickled and almost spit his food out, trying to keep from laughing. But it worked. He and Max hit it off right away. In fact they monopolized the conversation because they are great big strong guys and had to top each other's stories about encounters with gangster types. Don't worry. Pete did not mention about my being attacked on campus by a terrorist. If he had, Chaya would have exerted pressure on me to leave Mississippi State. I could never do that. I found Pete there, and I won't abandon him and the relationship we have."

Pete didn't care who watched. He reached over and kissed Sarah on the lips. "I'm glad I got that kiss in before you had your mouth full of food!" Sarah playfully punched him in the arm.

"Okay, lovebirds, cool off. I want to know more about the conversation with Chaya and Max," Jeff insisted.

"Max told me something I had never heard before. We were talking about El Al, the Israeli airline that flies out of JFK. It is the most secure of all the airlines. You know how the nation of Israel has the best intelligence and security of any nation. Well, El Al was hijacked!"

Gloria was shocked. "Not El Al! I was hoping we could fly to Israel on El Al."

"And you still can. This happened in 1968 and was the first and only successful hijacking of an El Al plane. On July 23, 1968, their plane was en route from Rome to Tel Aviv. It was hijacked and flown to Algeria. There were 38 passengers on board, plus ten crew members. The three hijackers were members of the Popular Front for the Liberation of Palestine (PFLP), a Marxist group. They burst into the cockpit with guns. Max has an amazing memory and gave all the details. I determined to remember what he said. The passengers and crew were turned over as captives to the Algerian officials. This ordeal lasted 39 days. The pilot as commander told everyone that they were to behave as if they were prisoners of war. Israel was at war with Algeria, so as POWs, they would be treated better. In 24 hours, 23 non-Israeli passengers were released and flown to France. Four days later Israeli females and children were released. Only 12 Israeli men remained, and they were taken to a villa. Israel planned a military rescue operation. The PFLP demanded that 1,000 Palestinian prisoners be released, and they would return the hostages. There was a global effort to get the hostages freed. On September 1, 1968, the 12 Israeli hostages were flown to Rome and then, within hours, on to Tel Aviv. The $6 million

Boeing 707 was also returned to the Israelis. No one had lost their lives in the 39-day ordeal. After five months 24 Palestinian prisoners were released by Israel. But the era of political hijackings and other terror attacks had just begun."[62]

"Wow! How did you remember all that, Pete?" Jeff wanted to know.

"I have no idea. But I was riveted to Max's voice as he gave all those details. You know, he and I are a lot alike. We want to catch the bad guys. He is in security, and I am majoring in criminal justice at MSU. If I could get my hands on that Islamic terrorist that attacked Sarah, it would be curtains for him!"

Gloria was determined that fear would not stop their plans for flying to Israel. "Okay, fellas, you are big. Sarah and I are small. But all four of us have a BIG GOD living on the inside of us. We will look fear in the face and make a reservation right now on El Al Airlines for Tel Aviv, to be in Jerusalem and celebrate Hanukkah and the 50th anniversary of the rebirth of the State of Israel. There! Now I said it. This will be the trip of a lifetime. Let's do it!"

Jeff reached for Gloria, squeezed her, and declared, "Gloria has made a motion. I second it. Hear ye! Hear Ye! The motion is before you. All in favor, say 'Aye.' There will be none opposed. Ha! Come here, gorgeous. In front of all these people. I will seal this vote with a kiss."

Pete banged his fist on the table lightly. "The meeting is adjourned." Luckily, there were only a handful of customers in the restaurant. Jeff put down a big tip on the table, smiled at the waitress, and they all smiled and waved as they went out the door.

Sarah's conscience bothered her. Traveling by car was a violation of the Sabbath laws. But she consoled herself that it was a situation similar to "getting an ox out of the ditch"[63] and qualified as an exception to the rule.

CHAPTER 36

FAMILY AND FRIENDS BONDING

I n the car Pete got right to the business at hand. "Holy Rollers, do you realize that it will be an absolute miracle if we can get plane reservations in time to arrive in Israel for Hanukkah? I did the math. Today is Saturday November 29th, and Hanukkah begins on Tuesday, December 23rd, just a mere 24 days from now! My parents run a travel agency, so I know it will require a miracle to get tickets. Many a time I have heard my mother complain when she had to deal with a cantankerous customer who wanted a flight to some foreign country in only two weeks. She would come home saying, 'Who does he think I am, a miracle worker?'"

"Well, at least Sarah has her ticket. Now we need three tickets more," Gloria reasoned. "Jeff, why don't you lead us in a prayer?"

"Okay, let's pray. Mighty God, Lord of heaven and earth, I saw You do a miracle of healing that night when I prayed for Gary Grayson. This is a different type miracle we need now, but I have faith in You to answer this prayer that somehow the four of us can be in Israel on Hanukkah just three weeks away. Lord, if you have another plan, we will be happy to follow it, but we feel You are leading us already, and we ask You to give us a sign today that this is Your will. Then I know you will grant our request. In the wonderful name of Jesus. Amen."

Gloria felt the presence of God as Jeff prayed. "Pete, I feel that you are supposed to call your mom and dad and ask them to get a flight for the three of us to Israel on whichever airline they can." "We will be out for Christmas on December 19th. We could stay in our dorms over the weekend and on Sunday, the 21st, fly out of the Golden Triangle, going through Atlanta and then up to JFK to board El Al."

"Brilliant, Gloria. But as an alternative to staying in our dorms until Sunday, I bet Mom and Dad would love to have us stay at our house in Tupelo." No sooner had he said this than Jeff realized they were taking a lot for granted, making their plans without first talking to their parents about it. "Wait, guys. Not so fast. We are getting carried away with our travel plans and have not even considered that in order for us to go to Israel, we need the money. And who is paying for our college education and practically all our needs? Yes, you guessed it – our parents. They have to agree to this and write the checks. And if they don't agree, we need to be respectful of their wishes and not try to force them to agree. We know our parents have plenty of money, but we don't need to treat them like ATM machines."

A few moments passed, as they realized their self-centeredness for not even considering their parents' wishes. Pete felt it more keenly. "Yeah, can you imagine my calling Mom and Dad and asking them to get us flights to Israel without first asking them if they would agree to it and buy my ticket, not to mention pay for other expenses?"

"Oh, Pete, maybe I didn't hear from God after all." Gloria felt like crying.

"Now Gloria, remember that when Jeff prayed, he asked for a sign that God wanted us to be in Israel together on Hanukkah. But if God had another plan, we would be happy with it. And I felt His presence when Jeff prayed."

"Yes, Pete, I did, too. I want us to go so badly, but only if it is God's will. Maybe the sign that we are supposed to go will be our parents' response when we tell them."

Pete was in a "take charge" mood. "Okay, I will call Mom and Dad just as soon as we get to your house, Gloria, first asking for their permission and next for their funding. If I get two positive answers, then I will ask that they book our flight. Then Jeff can call his parents."

Sarah interrupted. "Listen! I just thought of something. You may not know this date in history, but my parents used to talk about it a lot. Today is November 29th, and it is the very day in 1947 that the United Nations voted for the Partition Plan, which would divide Palestine into two nations, one for the Jews and one for the Arabs. The Arabs rejected the plan because they didn't want half the land, they wanted it all. The Jews accepted the plan. Do you get it?"

"Yes, I get it!" Gloria answered first. Today, which is the Jewish Sabbath, is the 50th anniversary of the Jewish State! So we don't have to wait until we get to Israel. We can celebrate TODAY!"

Pete's eyes got big. "So today is HISTORIC! It looks like we are going to receive our miracle, guys. God is orchestrating our every move. Do you feel it?"

Sarah continued. "Yes, my dad taught me a lot about the re-birth of Israel. After this legal action by the U.N., things didn't seem to change. The Jew-Arab conflict still raged in Palestine. But then David Ben Gurion, who became the first Prime Minister, decided to take action. He called for a meeting in Tel Aviv, and he officially declared that Israel was a state among the nations of the world. President Harry Truman was the first to call and congratulate him. This happened on May 14, 1948. The very next day the fledgling State was attacked by six Arab armies. It was David and Goliath all over again. With God's help, Israel won her War of Independence, and it was a miracle! My dad told me all kinds of stories about how the Israeli soldiers experienced supernatural victories!"

Gloria pulled in her driveway. "Amazing! Thanks for teaching us, Sarah. Papa Sam said they visited Independence Hall, the building where Israel was declared a nation. Mama Anna told us how a man named Theodor Herzl prophesied it fifty years before, back in 1897, and they saw his picture on the wall. Well, here we are. I am excited for my parents to meet you two, Sarah and Pete."

After Pete and Sarah were introduced to Mr. and Mrs. Sondheim, Gloria told them that Pete and Jeff had urgent calls to make.

Gloria helped Sarah get acquainted with her parents. Then she was ready to talk to them about their hopes to fly to Israel for Hanukkah. However, Alvin and Sylvia quickly excused themselves and went upstairs, saying that they really needed a nap before dinner.

Gloria and Sarah gave each other puzzled looks. "I guess it's not God's timing to ask them now. Well, let's go up and see what Pete and Jeff are finding out."

Sylvia and Alvin retired to their room. They were curious about the urgent phone calls, but they knew they would find out later.

Pete talked to his parents. They didn't hesitate to give their approval for the trip and said, of course, they would pay for Pete's expenses. They would go back down to the office, work on the flight and call him back as soon as they made the reservations, that is, IF they could get a flight. Then Jeff talked to his parents. His mother had a lot to share about the things she was learning about her Jewish heritage, and she was thrilled at this opportunity for Jeff to go to Israel. His dad was happy about it, too. Gloria told them she didn't have the opportunity to talk to her parents yet. Then the four friends held hands and prayed with faith, rejoicing that the Carsons would get their flight for them, and Gloria's parents would agree and pay for Gloria's expenses. All their emotional energy was spent, so Jeff invited Pete to his room for a nap. Sarah stayed with Gloria, and they also got a nap.

The foursome awoke to find that it was almost time for dinner. Papa Sam and Mama Anna had arrived, and the Holy Rollers went downstairs to meet them. Alvin and Sylvia were in the kitchen.

Gloria greeted her grandparents and embraced them with exuberance. "Papa Sam and Mama Anna, please meet our dearest friends, Sarah Bernstein and Pete Carson, our roommates at MSU. We haven't known them long, but it feels like we have known them for years. Sarah is from New York, and Pete is from Mississippi."

"We've heard a lot about you, and it is an honor to meet you," said Pete as he and Sarah shook their hands warmly.

Gloria explained, "Pete's parents have a travel agency, and we just called and asked them to get us three tickets to Israel for Hanukkah. Sarah already has her ticket and will be traveling with her sister and her sister's husband. YOU are the ones who set Jeff and me on fire to go to Israel for Hanukkah and to celebrate Israel's 50th birthday! We can't thank you enough. Now I've got to ask Mom and Dad for their permission and if they will pay for it."

Anna squealed with delight. "Children, I told Sam after you left us yesterday afternoon that I saw God doing a fast work in your lives, and that I wouldn't be surprised if you didn't act immediately on your desire to go to Israel for Hanukkah. So we stopped and prayed that God would give you your hearts' desires."

Jeff hugged her and Papa Sam. "Thank you, Mama Anna. When the phone rings, I am believing for good news. Pete says it will have to be a miracle to get tickets with Hanukkah only 24 days away. But we prayed, so we are expecting that miracle."

"What miracle?" asked Alvin as he came in the living room and motioned everyone to sit down. "Sylvia is right in the middle of preparing for dinner, but she will come in here soon. Go ahead and tell ME now. I could hear your excited talk, and I must know what it's all about."

Gloria told her father about their hopes to go to Israel for Hanukkah. With her most endearing smile, she humbly asked if he would agree to let her go and pay for her trip. She added that it was a really historic time because Hanukkah would begin the celebration of Israel's 50th birthday.

Alvin called to Sylvia in the kitchen. "Sylvia, come in here. You won't believe what Gloria is asking for. Sylvia hurried to the living room, eager to hear of their daughter's latest escapade. "Sylvia, should we allow this? Gloria, tell your mother what you told me."

Jeff, Pete, and Sarah crowded around Gloria and her parents, knowing their support was needed. Gloria went through the whole story again, saying that her grandparents had inspired Jeff and her to go, and they were also going.

Alvin suddenly became alarmed. "Gloria, don't you know the danger of Saddam Hussein in Iraq firing missiles into Israel while you are there? I heard it on CNN about two weeks ago that even though intelligence says he won't attack, the Israelis have been getting three times more gas masks now than the last time Iraq attacked Israel in 1991."[64]

Sylvia was clearly afraid. "Being so young at the time, you kids probably weren't aware of that crisis during the Persian Gulf War in 1991. Saddam fired 39 SCUD missiles into Israel. The Israelis did not even retaliate. They just let it happen because the United States told them to show restraint. They put on their gas masks and got in their sealed rooms. I was so mad. At least only two Israelis were killed, but thousands were injured and left homeless!"[65]

"Yes, honey, but I heard a lot of Christians around here say that God protected them because it was a miracle that there were no more deaths than those two."

Jeff was ashamed he knew so little about this war. Did he dare comment on something he was just now hearing about? Faith rose up in him. "Yes, it must have been a miracle of God. He DID protect His chosen people, and I believe He will protect us, too."

The phone rang. Pete and Jeff bounded up the stairs to answer it. Gloria told her parents that Pete's parents had a travel agency and had been trying to get them a flight. Everyone became silent, straining to hear the phone conversation upstairs, but they couldn't make it out. Then they heard a loud yell from Pete. He and Jeff skipped some steps coming downstairs.

Pete was beaming. "WE ARE GOING! Someone canceled! Someone canceled!"

Jeff was just as excited as Pete. "Yes, it is a miracle! Pete's mother first told Pete that there were no more seats left on any plane going to Israel on December 20th through the 26th. While they were still on the phone, another phone in the office rang, and Pete's father answered it. He shouted to Mrs. Carson, and we both could hear him, saying there had been a cancelation of two seats! Two seats on El Al for December 21st and returning on the 30th. The agent suddenly had to get off the line, but she said she would call him back with details. He is waiting for her to call him back. And Mrs. Carson said she wouldn't have any trouble getting us a flight out of Columbus to JFK in New York."

Sarah looked bewildered. "But you need three seats. I agree it is a miracle that two seats are available, but not one of you three should be left out. I have seen God answer everything you have prayed so far, but maybe it is not His will for one of you to go. Had you thought of that?"

Pete's joy instantly changed to sadness, as everyone could see. "Jeff and Gloria, those two seats are definitely for YOU. I know we all agree. I will just keep believing that a third seat will come available for me somehow. Do you think we could pray about that?"

Gloria looked at her mom and dad and wondered what they were thinking. She knew they didn't know the Messiah, and they didn't even read the Tanakh, so she didn't know if it was right to ask them to join in a circle of prayer to request that third ticket from God.

Sylvia took Alvin's hand and headed toward the kitchen. "I see that you have a problem, and I hope it is solved. But in the meantime a good meal will cheer you up, and maybe it will work out, if you don't worry about it. We will soon be ready to call you to dinner."

God knew Gloria's thoughts, she realized, and He had made a way for them to petition Him once again. "Pete, you are unselfish about giving Jeff and me those two seats. I believe God will make a way for you, too, so let's join together in believing prayer."

Papa Sam felt the Lord wanted him to lead the prayer. As the anointing of the Holy Spirit came upon him, he spoke confident words, quoting promises from Scripture. The hearts of all in the prayer circle, including Sarah, were deeply moved, and there was a knowing in each heart that God would answer their petition. Alvin came back in the room and invited them to take their places at the table in the dining room. Then he explained the choice of cuisine, named all the dishes on the buffet, and designated them as kosher or non-kosher. Then he motioned everyone to get up and help themselves.

Sarah cringed when she heard Mr. Alvin name the Jewish dishes. She had been taught never to mix meat and dairy at the same meal. *My parents would be shocked that I am in this pseudo-Jewish environment, eating non-kosher food. HaShem, what am I supposed to do? Is this another exception You are allowing me to make besides traveling in a car on Shabbat? Perhaps You are testing me. But surely You want me to show love and gratitude. If I refuse to eat the food, I will be hurting everyone here! Unless You stop me, Adonai, I will just pick out the kosher food items. I love You so much and would never disobey you, but I guess "the ox is in the ditch" again.* Sarah felt a sweet relief sweep over her. She knew that HaShem was giving her His blessing. Her countenance brightened.

Everyone piled their plates high, including Sarah. They took their seats and looked at their host. Alvin said the same prayer he had learned as a child, and everyone said "Amen." As soon as the eating got underway Sylvia took charge. She had decided to start the conversation and steer it away from Hanukkah and Israel. Since she had not heard a progress report from Gloria about her music classes, she picked that subject to begin with. "Gloria, tell us about your courses, especially music."

"Mom and Dad, I am blessed. I have the best piano teacher anywhere in the South, Mrs. Pagani. She has a television program, and I have been asked to play two of my pieces on her program in February. I love the Chopin piece and the Liszt piece she gave me to learn, but what I don't like is having to practice extra time in a tiny practice room. I almost get claustrophobia. However, I have survived last year and this year so far. Music majors are required to go to concerts. Some of them are excellent and some are boring as all get out. Lately, Jeff attended one with me, and it was more fun. I have to tell you, that I have trouble playing with rings on my fingers, so I take them off and put them on top of the piano. My first day in the practice room this semester I forgot to put them back on. Two hours later I realized I didn't have my rings on, and I panicked! I ran back to that little room. Thank goodness, there they were. I wasn't a Christian when that happened, so I didn't even pray. God was just merciful, that's all.

Jeff could hardly believe his ears. It was obvious that God had arranged the perfect setting and timing for his formal proposal of marriage in front of Gloria's family and their friends. He looked at Mr. Alvin, and Alvin winked, as he reached in his pocket and handed a little gift-wrapped box to Jeff under the table. He had made sure he was sitting beside Jeff, so it was as smooth as glass.

Gloria couldn't help but notice her father's smiling face. She sensed something was about to happen that he was involved in. Then she looked at Jeff, and her heart started thumping in her chest. Jeff stood up before the diners could go back to the buffet for second helpings. "I have an announcement to make, everyone." No one moved a muscle. All eyes were on Jeff. He pulled Gloria to her feet, walked her away from the table and then knelt in front of her. She began to cry as Jeff gave his little prepared speech: "My dearest Gloria, the love of my life, the one I want to live with forever, here in the presence of your family and our friends, as well as in the presence of our Lord Jesus Christ, I ask you to marry me! You said yes when I asked you that night on the campus, but now I am making a formal proposal with this ring to officially seal our engagement. I await your answer."

Gloria was too choked up to speak for a minute. Then wiping tears away, she answered with conviction. "Yes, my darling Jeff. I thank our Lord that He brought us together. It will be a great honor to become your wife. I love you with all my heart!" Jeff slipped the ring on her finger. Tears started again while she took her time to admire the sparkling ring. Her shimmering eyes were beaming as she showed it to everyone. "I love this ring. It is gorgeous, and it's a perfect fit."

Pete had to say what was obvious to everyone. "What are you waiting for, pal? Kiss your fiancé. We won't blush. We are happy for you."

Jeff overcame his self-consciousness in front of the Sondheims and swept Gloria off her feet, wrapping his arms around her and kissing her passionately.

"I'm timing you, roommate," Pete bantered. "You better come up for air!"

Alvin was proud to have had a part in this special moment. "Okay, break it up, you two. Let's go back for seconds, and help yourself to dessert. And as for me, I want to know more about the trip to Israel for Hanukkah. I will make it mine and Sylvia's early wedding present to you, Gloria and Jeff, but you've got to get separate rooms, of course. I assume your wedding will wait until summer, right?"

Everyone was looking at Sylvia. She put on her brightest smile. "Yes, Alvin and I will give you a wedding the likes of which no one around here has ever seen before. Congratulations, Gloria and Jeff. So now tell us more about the trip to Israel. You only have three weeks to plan it. You will have to have lodging, of course."

Sarah spoke up. "I am flying over there with my sister Chaya and her husband Max. We plan to stay with my brother Abe and his family. Gloria could stay with us. Hopefully, Jeff could get a room in the hotel where Gloria's grandparents are staying."

Jeff added, "Yes, I will get a double room, so Pete will have lodging when he gets a ticket. I have faith in God that he WILL get that ticket. I'll get the name of the hotel from you, Papa Sam, before you leave."

Gloria looked admiringly at Jeff. It was obvious how much he had grown in the Lord. "And I wholeheartedly agree. But right now I am eager to hear what Papa Sam promised to tell us tonight, the story of Hanukkah, the actual history."

"Okay, let's go in the living room and get comfortable. Sylvia and Alvin, you served us the most delicious food I have had in a long time. Thank you, thank you." Each one expressed thanks and showered Alvin and Sylvia with compliments.

"Okay, I will give you the story in short form because I think some trip-planning is in order for these young people while they are together tonight. They will be on separate flights going back to their college tomorrow."

CHAPTER 37

SACRIFICE

Samuel silently prayed that the story he was about to tell would be used of God to draw Alvin, Sylvia, and Sarah to the reality of the God of the Hebrew Scriptures and His Messiah who longed to have a personal relationship with them.

"We find the story of the first Hanukkah and the valiant Jewish warriors called the Maccabees in the period between the Old and New Covenants of the Bible. Syria had control of the Holy Land, and an evil ruler named Antiochus Epiphanes wanted to remove every trace of Hebrew worship. It was 168 B.C. when he demanded to be worshiped as God. He erected an idol of Zeus, which bore the face of Antiochus, on the holy altar in the courtyard of the temple in Jerusalem. On the 25th of the Jewish month of Kislev, the birthday of Zeus, Antiochus offered a pig on the altar. This was an 'abomination.' He sprinkled its blood in the Holy of Holies in the temple and poured its broth over the holy scrolls before he cut them in pieces and burned them!

"Faithful Jews were outraged! A Jewish remnant fled to the mountains, carrying with them copies of the book of Daniel. Daniel was a prophet in the court of King Nebuchadnezzar of Babylon and then in the court of King Darius the Mede, and he had prophesied about these terrible times. In warring against the Syrians the Jews studied the Scriptures and saw what Daniel wrote. Antiochus had pigs sacrificed on altars all over Israel and forced the people to eat the sacrifices. In 167 B.C. his soldiers came to the town of Modi'in and demanded that Mattathias the priest sacrifice a pig on the altar. He refused, and he killed the Syrian soldier and another Jew who attempted to make the sacrifice. Then Mattathias took his five sons and ran to the hills from where they waged war against the mighty Syrian army. Other Jews joined them who were 'zealous for the law and supported the covenant with God.' Mattathias was the leader for one year. On his deathbed he turned over the leadership to his son Judah, surnamed 'Maccabeus' which meant 'hammer.' Before each battle the Maccabees fasted and prayed, and God gave them victories. It was obviously a supernatural thing that a tiny band of warriors could be victorious over the huge army of the Syrians!

"The Maccabees defeated the Syrians and rededicated the temple on the 25th of Kislev, 165 B.C., exactly three YEARS after the desecration of the temple by Antiochus. This 'resurrection' of the temple was a foreshadowing of the resurrection of the Messiah in three DAYS after His death on the cross. You may know the Scripture in the New Testament book of John, which is Yeshua's statement: 'Destroy this temple, and in three days I will raise it up, meaning HIS BODY.'[66] Yeshua rose from the dead and then ascended to heaven. On the Day of Pentecost, His Holy Spirit was poured out on the Apostles and many others. Later the Apostle Paul taught that the followers of Messiah are His body because His Spirit lives inside them. And each individual believer is a 'temple' of God and should not defile his temple but should live a holy life.[67]

The Jews had a big job cleaning out the temple after the horrible desecration by the Syrians. It was time to celebrate the Feast of Tabernacles, but they had a problem. They searched but could not find enough holy oil to light the menorah. They only found one small vial of oil, not enough to keep the candles burning for eight days. In faith they lit the wicks, and as tradition has it, the oil miraculously burned for all eight days! The temple was rededicated to the God of Abraham, Isaac, and Jacob, and the Jews finally were an independent nation. This independence lasted for 100 years, until the Romans took over Jerusalem in 63 B.C."

Sarah was becoming confused and had to interrupt. "Mr. Sondheim, you are telling the story of the Maccabees very well. My father educated his household faithfully, and we also learned the story in the synagogue. But I have never heard what you said

about Jesus calling his body the temple and about the Ruach HaKodesh – that's the Hebrew name for 'Holy Spirit' – living inside the
Christians' bodies! Of course, I know about Pentecost. It is called
'Shavuot' in Hebrew. You said the Spirit was poured out on the
Apostles on that feast day. I once tried to read the New Testament,
but I had to put it down. To me it was shocking to read, and I only
read a few pages."

"May I give you my extra copy of the New Testament? The
title on the front is in Hebrew, *Brit Hadasha, the New Covenant*.
I didn't know any Hebrew to start with, so this book really helps.
It has English on the opposite page of each Hebrew page. You can
read what I was just talking about in the Book of John, chapter
two, verse 19. Anna, please dig down in your purse and find that
copy to give to Sarah."

Anna was excited to give this holy book to Gloria's Orthodox
Jewish friend. She felt like it would not be long until Sarah yielded to the drawing of the Holy Spirit to her Messiah. Sarah was a
little hesitant to receive the book but decided she could always
stop reading, if it was blasphemous. "Thank you very much," she
said politely. Gloria was ecstatic, but managed to be silent as she
smiled at Jeff.

"I will continue," Sam said. "As it is with any war, many
sacrifices were made. Of the Jewish martyrs during the Syrian oc-
cupation, there was a woman named Hannah who had seven sons.
Refusing to eat swine's flesh, they were tortured, then boiled alive!
Their mother encouraged them, saying they would be resurrected.
She also refused to apostatize and was put to death. These faithful
Jews are described in the book of Hebrews in the New Testament:
'Others were tortured, not accepting deliverance, that they might
obtain a better resurrection ... of whom the world was not worthy.
They wandered in deserts and mountains, in dens and caves of the
earth. And all these, having obtained a good testimony through
faith, did not receive the promise.'[68] Remember that Abraham was

looking for a city whose builder and maker is God. He saw it far up ahead, but he did not inherit it on earth."

Sarah commented, "So these Maccabees are talked about in the New Testament? I did not know that. I have heard about the Romans persecuting the Christians, even throwing them to the lions. I am glad that Christians can learn about the Jews' persecution in their New Testament."

Anna ventured to make a comment without sounding condescending. "Sarah dear, almost all the people in the New Testament are Jewish, starting with Yeshua and His parents, then His Apostles, and then the first church that was birthed on Shavuot. Besides Yeshua's warnings about the persecutions to come, the Apostle Peter warned the Jewish believers who had been scattered in the Dispersion or Diaspora to **expect** persecution." Sarah's eyes got bigger and bigger.

Sam was intent on showing that sacrifice was required to follow Yeshua and seek the kingdom of God. "Yeshua said, 'Your father Abraham rejoiced to see My day, and he saw it and was glad.'[69] Yes, the believers in Yeshua did not necessarily live 'happily ever after.' All the Apostles died terrible deaths except for the Apostle John, but they were confident of the promises of God. They knew they would have great rewards in eternity, especially because of their sacrifices. Even today many Christians and Messianic Jews are being persecuted and some killed for being loyal to their Savior."

Everyone was mesmerized by Sam's story. Sarah was impressed that Mr. Sondheim who believed in Jesus knew more about this Jewish holiday of Hanukkah than most Jews did. Gloria was waiting for him to say that Jesus celebrated Hanukkah. "Papa Sam, you said yesterday that Jesus celebrated Hanukkah. How do you know that?"

"Gloria, it is told in the book of John, chapter ten, verse 22. He was at the Feast of Dedication in Jerusalem, and it was winter. Most Christians don't realize that the English word, 'dedication,' is 'Hanukkah' in Hebrew. The temple was dedicated back in the days of the Maccabees, and the Jews have continued to observe the miracle of Hanukkah every year since. Of course Yeshua observed it; He was Jewish. It was that particular year at the feast that the Jews asked Him if He was the Messiah. Yeshua was almost stoned on that occasion. It is true that all the Apostles were Jewish, and the first church was Jewish. It was primarily the Jewish religious leaders who would not believe that Yeshua was their Messiah. All the healing miracles did not impress them. Their political power in the temple must be preserved at all costs, so they plotted to have Yeshua killed. When they saw Him suffer and die on the cross, they were convinced more than ever that He could not possibly be the Messiah. They knew that the Messiah would bring world peace. They only paid attention to the passages in the Tanakh that showed the Messiah as King over the world. They overlooked the passages about the suffering of the Lamb of God as depicted in Isaiah 53, as well as in Psalm 22. Even today the rabbis refuse to believe that Isaiah 53 is a description of the crucifixion of Yeshua."

Sarah couldn't hold back any longer. "Mr. Sondheim, I hate to disagree with you, but Isaiah 53 is a picture of the 'suffering servant,' and that is Israel, not the Messiah."

Anna felt like it was her time to be a spokesman for the Spirit. She prayed silently that God would open Sarah's understanding and touch her heart. "This chapter in the Bible is so important that I have memorized it, so let me point out a few things I believe will help us all to see that Yeshua's person and His crucifixion is described here. I will quote it as I go along. 'He is despised and rejected by men, a **MAN of sorrows** and acquainted with grief.' This is not a nation being described, although I will agree that the Jewish people have been hated and persecuted down through the ages more than any nation. This is a MAN, as Isaiah says. 'Surely HE bore our griefs and carried our sorrows. Yet we esteemed Him stricken, smitten of God and afflicted, but He was wounded for OUR transgressions. He was bruised for OUR iniquities. The chastisement for OUR peace was upon Him, and BY HIS STRIPES we are healed.' Do you see those words describe the horrible beating of Yeshua by the Romans? They lashed Him 39 times with a whip that ripped off pieces of flesh from His back! All Jews are aware that blood must be shed for them to receive forgiveness. At Passover there must be a blood sacrifice of a perfect lamb. Yeshua was that perfect lamb, and it is amazing that He was sacrificed on the cross at the precise time that the priests were killing the Passover lambs in Jerusalem that day!"

Sarah was stunned. Pastor Jeff James at Adaton Baptist had given a detailed sermon on Isaiah 53, but what Mama Anna was saying now was mind-boggling. Everyone in the room was taken aback. Sylvia and Alvin had never heard this. Pete had heard it from Pastor James, but now he began to feel it.

Sam could not resist taking over the teaching. "Gloria and Jeff, did you realize that not only is this Man of sorrows described as a 'lamb being led to the slaughter' and as 'a sheep before His shearers is silent,' but Isaiah says, 'For the transgressions of my people He was stricken!' To me, that proves that this chapter is not about the nation of Israel. How can Israel be a sacrifice for Israel? The Man of sorrows is bearing the transgressions of Israel on Himself. He bore their sorrows. He was wounded for their transgressions. By His stripes Israel can be saved! Because He, Yeshua, is the Lamb of God who takes away the sins of the world!"

Anna broke in. "And the resurrection of Yeshua is shown also in this chapter of Isaiah 53. 'When You – which means Yahweh – make His soul – the soul of Yeshua – AN OFFERING FOR SIN, He shall see His seed, He shall PROLONG HIS DAYS, and the pleasure of the Lord shall prosper in His hand.' So, that means that after Yeshua presented His body as a sin sacrifice and died on the cross, He came back alive to see His seed, those He had saved. He would prolong His days. He was alive and would never die! I have to say, 'Hallelujah!'"

Jeff and Gloria were so excited they jumped up and joined in the hallelujah! Sam joined them. Then Pete pulled Sarah to her feet, and also joined in the hallelujah. Alvin and Sylvia stood up, but they couldn't quite say 'hallelujah.' Sarah could only manage a half-smile.

The phone rang.

CHAPTER 38

BITTERSWEET NEWS

Gloria, Jeff, Pete, and Sarah looked at each other. "Here is our miracle!" exclaimed Jeff. "Let's go hear the good news." They sprinted up the stairs. Sam and Anna held hands and prayed silently.

Sylvia welcomed a lull in the conversation and was content to sit close to Alvin. *This evening has really sapped my energy. That story about the Maccabees and Hanukkah and then the Bible lesson on Isaiah was too heavy for me. But maybe that is because almost everything Papa Sam said I had never heard before. My head is about to burst with all that information. I have got to get me a good Bible and try to catch up with my own daughter. I want to be able to make intelligent conversation. It was a cut and dried issue for me, that Jesus is NOT the Messiah. But now I am not one-hundred per cent sure. I wonder how this affected Alvin tonight. We must talk about it later when we are alone.*

Minutes passed, and there was no news forthcoming from upstairs. Finally, Jeff and Gloria walked slowly down the stairs. Gloria broke the silence. "Well, we have bittersweet news. Sarah's sister called. She is going to cancel her reservation on El Al to Israel for Hanukkah. She began to have some pain, and although they aren't supposed to drive on the Sabbath, Max took her to the emergency room of the hospital. Her own doctor happened to be on call. He examined her and told her it wasn't serious, that the baby was fine, but that Chaya could absolutely not get on an airplane her entire pregnancy. Sarah took the news badly and started crying. Pete is trying to console her. Sarah is worried about her sister. Chaya wants Max to go on to Israel, but Sarah is worried that something could happen to Chaya."

Pete and Sarah came downstairs and took their seats in the living room. Consolation poured forth from everyone. Alvin ven-

271

tured to say something. "Sarah, isn't there someone who could look in on your sister while you and your brother-in-law are in Israel?"

"Chaya said that she has made only one good friend since they moved to Stony Brook not long ago. She barely knows the other people in the synagogue. All her other siblings will be in Israel for the feast. She has been talking to that friend ever since she got back from the doctor's. Her name is Frieda. She is about Chaya's age, is married, but has no children. Since she is between jobs, she has the time to keep tabs on Chaya and will be glad to do so. But I want to be there, too!"

Gloria held Sarah's hand. "Worry is not going to help, Sarah. If you don't go to Israel, then it will be no fun for us. We were looking forward to meeting all your family and maybe even going places with them. Please just trust God. He wants you to have peace of mind."

Sylvia had an idea. "If your sister has not yet canceled her reservation, Sarah, would it be possible for her to cancel it and then buy that available ticket for Pete Carson? I know the airlines don't make transfers of reservations to another name, but maybe a cancelation followed by purchase of that ticket is possible."

Pete's countenance brightened. "I can't believe I haven't already thought of that. Thank you, Mrs. Sondheim. Hey, guys, didn't we pray that God would get me a ticket? Do we believe in answered prayer? Of course we do." Then it dawned on him that Sarah may feel differently about it. "Sarah, would it be okay with you if we ask Chaya to do that? I will reimburse her."

Sarah dried her tears. "It's worth a try. Maybe Chaya hasn't called and canceled yet. Shall we go call her?" The foursome went back upstairs. It wasn't long before the Sondheims heard the good news.

The young people's faces were wreathed in smiles as they descended the stairs. Pete blurted out the news. "Chaya had not called yet! I have to say, 'Praise the Lord!' She is calling El Al now, and she will cancel her reservation and then buy that available ticket for me. I will send her a check for it right away. Oh, boy! I can see myself on that plane, seated right beside Sarah."

No one spoke, but there were some white knuckles that said it all. Fifteen minutes passed before the phone rang again. "Get it in the kitchen, Sarah. It's closer," advised Sylvia.

They could hear Sarah's voice clearly. "Oh, Chaya, I am thrilled that Pete can take your seat. He will send you a check for the cost promptly. He will be taking your seat, but he can never take your PLACE. Hopefully, it will lessen the pain of your having to stay behind though, to know that you made it possible for Pete to go. I promise to write down everything we experience and to take lots of pictures. I love you, and I believe you will be well cared for by HaShem. Please call your friend Frieda right now."

CHAPTER 39

JOY UNSPEAKABLE

Alvin was trying to process all the exciting developments taking place in his house in the space of a few hours. *I need to follow through on my promise of an early wedding present for Gloria and Jeff. And do it now! Pete said his parents had been notified by El Al of the two cancelations on the flight to Israel for Hanukkah. My goodness! I don't need to waste any time paying for those tickets, as well as the tickets for Jeff and Gloria's flight from Columbus to New York. I will call the Carters right now.* "Pete, please accompany me to the telephone in the kitchen. I need the number of your parents' travel agency."

"Just a minute, son. Anna and I have something to say." Everyone looked at Papa Sam.

"Yes, you tell them, Sam," squealed Anna.

"Alvin, just sit back down. Anna and I are making the El Al flight to Israel for Hanukkah OUR gift to Gloria and Jeff. You can still pay for their flight from Columbus to JFK. I hope you don't argue with me. Think about the fact that you will have the wedding to pay for! That is no small sum of money, my son."

"Father, please don't do that. You have your own Hanukkah plans, which also add up to no small sum of money."

Anna had to explain. "Here is why we are doing this. Gloria and Jeff visited us at the Three Village Inn yesterday, and we had a glorious Bible study about Hanukkah from the Book of Daniel and from the apocryphal books of the Maccabees. The Holy Spirit came on me powerfully as I observed these young people, sitting there, drinking it all in. When they expressed the desire to go to Israel for Hanukkah, I knew what the Lord wanted Sam and me to do."

"That's right. After they left, Anna and I talked about it and felt it strongly that we should cancel our reservations with El Al and buy new tickets for Jeffrey Quentin and Gloria Sondheim. We knew that the plane would be filling up fast, especially since it will be the 50th birthday of the State of Israel. We acted immediately, and after it was done, great joy flooded our souls! We have been feeling that joy increase since we came here tonight."

Gloria and Jeff were dumbfounded. "So you mean, Papa Sam, you two aren't even going? Oh, no. We are deeply grateful for your gift, but I don't think we can receive it." Jeff shook his head.

Anna held their hands. "Children, we have already been to Israel once, and, after all, we are planning to move there very soon. We will have plenty of Hanukkah celebrations in Israel after that. Don't take away our blessing from the Lord by not receiving our freely-offered gift."

Jeff was amazed. "Oh, I see. Those two cancellations we just heard about were yours and Papa Sam's seats! The El Al agent's conversation with Mr. Carter was interrupted. The agent will be calling him back, she said. Now I know she will tell him that new tickets have been bought for Gloria and me. As it turned out, God answered our prayer through you two. But you are making such a sacrifice." Jeff and Gloria embraced Papa Sam and Mama Anna with heartfelt tears.

"There is more to our gift," Papa Sam announced. "We have also changed our reservations at the Dan Panorama Hotel in Jerusalem and put them in the name of Gloria Sondheim. Jeff, I will let you take it from there. Our room is for double occupancy. I just heard you say that the girls would have a room, and the boys would have a room. I know you and Gloria can work it out. I have the number of the hotel. If you call right away, I bet you can get a reservation for the second room. Now we must go. Anna and I will drive our rental car back to the Inn. We are getting some age on us, and all the excitement will take a little time to process before bedtime. Also, we always have our prayer time with the Lord before we retire. But let me say that the things that have transpired here tonight with the eight of us have thrilled our souls. It is definitely a highlight of our sojourn on earth."

Anna nodded in agreement. "What I am feeling now is best expressed through the Apostle Peter's words: '... the appearing of Jesus Christ: Whom having not seen, ye love; in whom, though now ye see him not, yet believing, ye rejoice with joy unspeakable and full of glory.'[70] Amen! That's how I feel. I am rejoicing with joy unspeakable and full of glory!"

Everyone rushed to embrace Anna and Sam. There were expressions of love and gratitude, tears and kisses and hugs and handshakes until the old couple finally walked out the door.

Alvin needed to make a phone call, and so did Jeff. Pete needed to reimburse Chaya. Time was of the essence. Alvin went first, making his call from the kitchen. The four young people went upstairs to Gloria's room to handle all the other arrangements. Meanwhile, Mr. and Mrs. Carter had already planned to stay late at the office. Things were popping fast, and Pete had begged them to hang around. His dad called to say that El Al had called him back to inform him that the two people who canceled their tickets had bought two new tickets for Gloria and Jeff. They were mailing the tickets to Gloria in Mississippi.

After another hour, the four friends felt like the plans had been completed. It was late, and they needed to get a good night's sleep because their Sunday flights back to Columbus were early in the morning. Sylvia and Alvin had gone back to the kitchen to finish cleaning up.

Sylvia reached out, wrapped her arms around Alvin, and gave him the most passionate kiss she had given him in a long time. "Alvin, this has been a glorious evening! I treasure every moment, and I will be thinking about it for weeks, savoring what happened in our home tonight. I honestly think I will never be the same again. And you know what? On Monday morning, I am going downtown and find a store that sells Bibles. I will buy a nice one with big print. I plan to read all of it, and that includes the New Testament. Now don't argue with me, please."

"Honey, you feel so good in my arms, and your delicious kiss made me want more. How could I ever argue with an angel sent from heaven who happens to be my very own wife? As for the Bible, it's amazing I was thinking the same thing, how I really want to read it and understand it. And yes, including the New Testament. Maybe I should get my own copy. We could read them together like my papa and mama do, before bed each night. What do you think?"

Before Sylvia could answer, their daughter, Jeff, Pete, and Sarah came in the kitchen, profusely thanking them for an excellent dinner and for being so gracious and involved in their plans to go to Israel. Love had already flooded the living room, and now the presence of the Lord was so strong in the kitchen that they were leaning on each other to keep from falling down! No one wanted to leave.

Finally, Pete and Sarah said their goodbyes. Jeff and Gloria said they wouldn't be long, taking them back to Stony Brook and returning. They needed to pack before they went to bed because of their early Sunday morning flight back south.

Sylvia summed up the evening with her parting words. "I felt the Lord Himself visit us tonight. Who would have ever thought that mine and Alvin's home would be 'holy ground'? We love all four of you dearly. And rest assured, we will say many prayers for you from now on, and especially when you go to Israel. Maybe Alvin and I will plan a trip there one day."

CHAPTER 40

DANGER AT THE AIRPORT

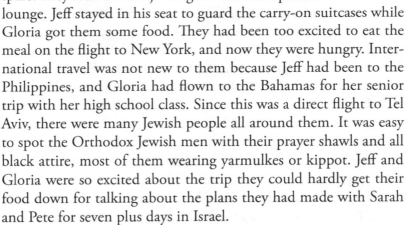

Jeff and Gloria got to the airport hours early, checked in, went through customs, and then walked down to the Gate with plenty of time to spare. They found five adjoining seats in the departure lounge. Jeff stayed in his seat to guard the carry-on suitcases while Gloria got them some food. They had been too excited to eat the meal on the flight to New York, and now they were hungry. International travel was not new to them because Jeff had been to the Philippines, and Gloria had flown to the Bahamas for her senior trip with her high school class. Since this was a direct flight to Tel Aviv, there were many Jewish people all around them. It was easy to spot the Orthodox Jewish men with their prayer shawls and all black attire, most of them wearing yarmulkes or kippot. Jeff and Gloria were so excited about the trip they could hardly get their food down for talking about the plans they had made with Sarah and Pete for seven plus days in Israel.

They would be going up to the Galilee, including Nazareth and Cana, and up to the Golan Heights. They would visit Yardenit and be baptized in the Jordan River. They would tour Masada and Qumran and go floating in the Dead Sea. But most of their days would be spent in Jerusalem. They wanted to see Yad VaShem and try to envision what Papa Sam and Mama Anna had gone through during the Holocaust. Their next priority would be to see the Temple Mount, the Western Wall and the tunnels, the Jewish Quarter of the Old City, and all the places Jesus walked, beginning outside the city when he rode into Jerusalem on a donkey. They wanted to visit the Upper Room, the Garden of Gethsemane, and see where Jesus was tried before the Sanhedrin and before Pilate. Then they would surely walk on the Via Dolorosa and up the hill where Jesus carried his cross and was crucified.

In their studies of the burial place of Jesus, they found that two sites were claimed, but that the most authentic and worshipful site was called "The Garden Tomb." They would take Communion there. Most Christian tourists ended with this climactic event. But there would be more to see from the Orthodox Jewish viewpoint, and Sarah's brother Abe would guide them to those places that most Christians don't tour. The highlight of the trip, however, would be the official lighting of the menorah on the first night of Hanukkah. That would happen at the end of their first full day in Jerusalem.

"Oh, Jeff! I can hardly wait to see them light the first candle at the Western Wall in the Old City! I read about their plans. An Israeli youth will run with a torch to President Ezer Weizman's house, which he and Prime Minister Benjamin Netanyahu will use to light the first candle of Hanukkah. This ceremony will kick off the eight-day observance of the Festival of Lights and a celebration of Israel's 50th anniversary next May. And listen to this. The orthodox Habad movement has built a 66-foot tall menorah made of metal pipes, and it will be lit each night, using a crane![71]

Pete and Sarah walked into the waiting area and quickly spotted Gloria and Jeff. "Watch this, Sarah." Pete sneaked up behind the couple and tapped them on their shoulders. Gloria let out a yell, as she and Jeff jumped up and turned around.

"Pete! You nearly scared me to death! I wondered what was keeping you and Sarah. Here are the seats I saved for you. Now go get your boarding passes."

Sarah started looking all over the waiting area. "We should start boarding in about forty minutes. I don't see Max. He better hurry up and get here." Sarah's eyes suddenly got big. She gasped and grabbed Pete's arm, moving behind him.

"Honey, what's wrong? You look terrified!"

Sarah loudly whispered in Pete's ear. "Look right over there four rows back on the left end. That's the guy who attacked me on campus. Remember? I described him to you. I would never forget that hateful face, but he is not dressed like he was that night. He is obviously trying to pass himself off as an Orthodox Jew. He is even wearing a kippah on his head and a tallit under his coat."

Gloria and Jeff heard Sarah and looked around to see, as Pete walked Sarah over behind a big post. "Sarah, you are perfectly safe with me. I'm your shield, remember? Jeff and I are a lot bigger than this shrimp. We will do what we have to do. He might see me watching him, but it doesn't matter. I will talk to Jeff. Both of us will watch him like a hawk. If he truly is an Islamic terrorist, however, I don't see how he got through customs to get on El Al, the most secure airline in the world. He certainly couldn't have a weapon on him after the thorough screening they put you through in customs."

Sarah looked from behind the post to see if the man was still sitting there. "Look, Pete. Did you see that? A man wearing a white robe just brushed by him, and I saw the terrorist covertly take something from him and put it under his coat. It might be a gun!"

Pete saw Max walking up. He quickly introduced him to Jeff and Gloria, then bent down and whispered to Jeff that he and Max would formulate a plan, while he should stay seated by Gloria and keep an eye on the terrorist and pray. Pete knew he couldn't let Sarah out of his sight, so he walked both Max and Sarah over to an area out of the terrorist's line of view, so they could talk more freely. "Max, we are in trouble, and I have to give you the back story why. Sarah was attacked on campus back in October."

Sarah interrupted. "Pete, I have already told Max and Chaya all about it."

Pete took charge quickly. "Max, the thing is this – the attacker is sitting four rows behind our seats on the left end of the row, dressed as an Orthodox Jew. Sarah is sure it's the attacker because that night she got a good look at him close up. And now she and I both saw a man in a white robe hand him something that he put in his coat. It could be a gun."

281

Max walked over to glance at the seats and saw the man Pete and Sarah described. "I have no doubt he is trailing Sarah. You know that Sarah and Chaya's father was a witness to the 1993 World Trade Center bombing, and he testified in the trials of the terrorists. Even though Abba Nathan and Imma Naomi are no longer alive, these thugs are going after our family. That is why Chaya and I moved out of Queens and chose to live in the quiet area of Stony Brook where few Jews live. I have been following the trials of all those Islamic terrorists. It is clear what their motivation was for bombing the towers. You probably know that six people were killed, and thousands were injured. But did you know that if their plan had fully succeeded, the North Tower would have fallen on the South Tower, and **tens of thousands** of innocent people would have died? In March of 1994, four men were convicted of carrying out the bombing, but just **one month ago** two more were convicted. They were Ramzi Yousef, the organizer, and Eyad Ismoil, who drove the truck carrying the bomb. Before the attack Yousef had mailed letters to the New York Times making three demands: an end to all U.S. aid to Israel, an end to U.S. diplomatic relations with Israel, and a pledge not to interfere with Middle East countries' internal affairs. He stated that this would be merely the first attack of many, if his demands weren't met. Yousef justified this terrorist act because he said Israel is a terrorist country, and America is giving her aid."[72]

"And here we are, about to fly to Israel, the country they hate!" Pete knew that boarding time would be in about twenty minutes. They had to act fast. "Max, you are a security guy. What do you say we walk up to the ticket counter, with you as the spokesman, and ask for the closest security guard? Three of us, including Jeff, could easily take this thug. We could turn him over to security and let them hold him until they make a thorough search of the baggage."

Sarah was alarmed. They had not thought of something. "But you might get shot! And if he does **not** have a gun, you guys could be arrested instead of him! Wait. Gloria seems to always know what to pray for. Let's go over there and talk to Jeff and her and then join them in prayer before anyone does anything. Please."

Pete hesitated. Max was shaking his head. "We men will handle this. Let's get underway, and Gloria can pray while it's happening."

Pete looked at Sarah. They knew Max did not understand. More than ever, they felt that Gloria had to pray on their behalf BEFORE they took action. Sarah spoke up. "Max, we are not going to do anything until we have had a chance to pray and then listen for HaShem's guidance."

Sarah made a beeline for Gloria and Jeff and filled them in quickly. Pete and Max followed. Gloria reached out for Sarah and Jeff's hands. Sarah grabbed Pete's hand. Max knew he was outnumbered, so he joined the circle of prayer, holding Pete's and Jeff's hands. Gloria could feel the Holy Spirit strongly. She could barely speak, but she knew if she opened her mouth, the Lord would fill it like He always did. "Holy Lord, God of Abraham, Isaac, and Jacob, and the Father of our Lord Jesus Christ, Yeshua the Messiah ..."

Max stiffened and looked up. He saw tears running down Sarah's cheeks. Her eyes were closed. *Sarah is moved, but I cannot participate in an idolatrous prayer. I am withdrawing my hands now. What? Are my hands glued? I can't get them loose. But what is that I feel? It's like electricity! I can tell that Sarah and her friends are feeling it, too. The more Gloria prays, the more I feel power in my hands. I give up. For some reason HaShem is using this Christian girl in her prayer. I will listen.*

".... Oh, Lord, I know you hear me. You see and You know. You have already started your plan through our strong men, Jeff, Pete, and Max. I trust that You will make the apprehension of this terrorist quick and without a gun being fired. I claim Your promise that 'no weapon formed against us shall prosper.' We are taking our refuge in You. We will not be afraid of the terror by night, or the bullets that fly by day, or the destruction that lays waste at noonday. Only with our eyes will we look and see the reward of the wicked. We are calling upon You in trouble, and You are answering us. You, our mighty HaShem, are delivering us! With long life You will satisfy us and show us Your salvation. Amen."[73]

Everyone's hands fell limply to their sides. Max was stunned. "You were quoting our Torah, Gloria. How did you know it so well? Those words are not in your Bible."

Gloria was beaming. Her heart was full of faith and hope and love. She reached over and grabbed Max's hands, and he felt the electricity again! "Oh, Max, those words are from Isaiah and Psalms. I recognized them as they came out of my mouth, but I had not memorized them. It's amazing. That had to be God Himself speaking. He is answering my prayer. We Messianic Jews have your part of the Scripture, as well as the New Testament, the Brit Hadasha. That's the whole Bible."

Sarah nodded her head vigorously. "Yes, Max. Now you guys, go do what you have HaShem's power to do. Do it, now."

Jeff, Pete, and Max walked up to the counter. Max spoke. "Please direct us to the closest security guard."

A man standing near the counter heard and stepped up. "I'm your guy. How can I help you?"

Pete looked behind them and saw the terrorist walking quickly to the restroom. Boarding had already started. The girls were at the back of the line, watching them. "Follow us, sir. We are headed to the restroom to disarm a terrorist. I will begin the explanation as we head that way. Time is of the essence." Jeff and Max had seen the terrorist, too, and came alongside Pete.

The security guard got out in front. "I have on a bulletproof vest and a gun. I will go in first."

The terrorist had to be in one of the stalls. Max gave a warning. "There could be accomplices who have been waiting for this man, and they could be positioned in a stall or two so their feet don't show."

The terrorist's feet were showing. Pete's thoughts went crazy. *What if this man is drawing us away, so another terrorist can board the plane and plant a bomb? We need to get back to Sarah and Gloria.*

Okay, worry is not helping. I am going to trust God. I will wait for the security guy to make his move.

"You in there! Come out. I know you have a gun. But if I am mistaken, you can prove it by opening the door and letting me search you."

The El Al ticket agent came hurrying to the rest room. "Everyone has boarded except you three men and whoever is in the stall. What are your names? Quickly." Pete, Jeff, and Max showed him their boarding passes. "Okay, that means the guy in that stall is Felix Becker." Pete knew the Jewish name was not the man's real name.

The security guard said to the agent, "I'll take it from here. Felix Becker, come out!" He pushed the door open, ready to shoot. The man was trembling violently and came out with his hands up. Pete grabbed him while Max took his jacket off and examined all his pockets, pants included. The security guard pushed open the other stalls, and they were empty. Then Jeff saw the gun! It was in the adjoining stall, obviously having been pushed by the terrorist behind the metal waste receptacle.

Jeff retrieved the gun and handed it to the security guard. "Here is his gun. I suppose he thought he could get on the plane with it. We have reason to believe it was our friend he was targeting. Thank the Lord we aborted his plan!"

The security guard checked it and found it was loaded. Pete's heart started racing. *If I was a girl, I would faint now!* Pete found his voice. "Sir, I know you are going to lock this man up, but don't forget there is another dangerous guy in a white robe on the loose somewhere in the airport. I saw him give the gun to this man." Jeff held the man until the security guard could go over and call for a cart and another guard to take the prisoner to the airport jail. As soon as the terrorist was handcuffed, the security guard told the men they better go board the plane.

Jeff took the lead. "I am going, but I am thanking God on the way. Hallelujah, mission accomplished! You did it, Lord. Thank You, thank You!" Pete and Max were rejoicing, too, with shouts of

"Amen, thank You, Lord!" Passengers in the other adjoining lounges heard the commotion and looked their way, a few standing up and cheering them on. The airport personnel at the counter were smiling and complimenting them on helping with the arrest. The flight attendants saluted them as they walked through the jet way to board the plane. One said, "I want your autographs. You will be all over the news tonight!"

As they craned their necks to find Gloria and Sarah, the whole cabin erupted into enthusiastic applause. Pete decided he would get out of his comfort zone and give credit where credit was due. "Thanks, everyone. But the glory goes to God. We prayed before we acted, and our mission was accomplished." The passengers clapped even louder. As the men located their seats, they found two adoring women holding out their arms for a victory embrace. Max looked on enviously as Jeff drew Gloria in his arms and kissed her hard, and as Pete passionately kissed Sarah. Max longed for Chaya. A shadow crossed his face as he thought about her being alone. At that moment two middle-aged Orthodox Jewish women without husbands felt they must perform a mitzvah[74] for the single man. So they kissed him sweetly, one on each cheek. Max smiled bigger than Sarah had ever seen him smile.

CHAPTER 41

ISRAEL BOUND

The takeoff was delayed a short while because of a thorough check in the baggage compartment by security. Gloria began to sing. "Off we go into the wild blue yonder."

Jeff joined in. "Flying high into the sky. Song over. That's all I know. No news is good news, I suppose. Evidently, security didn't find a bomb. Thank the Lord!"

"I wasn't worried for one minute. Oh, Jeff, we are on our way to Israel. Can you believe it?" They had seats close to the front of the cabin with Jeff on the window side. Sarah, Pete, and Max were in the mid-section. All the excitement had drained them of energy, so after getting settled in their seats, becoming familiar with their surroundings, and listening to the safety instructions, they reclined and began to unwind. Jeff fell into a deep sleep. Gloria finally relaxed but didn't go to sleep.

After about an hour, Jeff suddenly sat straight up. "Gloria, I just had a disturbing dream. I dreamed that there was a bomb aboard this flight! You know, that guy in the white robe may have boarded the plane minus his robe and holding a ticket with a fake Jewish name."

Gloria felt such a deep peace that Jeff's dream did not upset her at all. She took Jeff's face in her hands, and looked deep into his eyes. "Thou wilt keep him in perfect peace whose mind is stayed on Thee, because he trusts in Thee."[75] Jeff looked at Gloria dreamily, turned his head to the side, and went back to sleep. Gloria had to put her hand over her mouth to keep from laughing out loud.

Sarah had rested, and now she was ready to share something with Gloria, so she walked up the aisle and knelt beside her. At that point Jeff began to snore, and Sarah and Gloria giggled. Gloria told her about Jeff's dream and the Scripture she quoted to him.

It didn't scare Sarah at all. "I don't think I told you, but after your grandparents gave me that Brit Hadasha, I have been reading it along with my daily reading in the Tanakh."

"Oh, Sarah, that is fantastic. How far are you?"

"Well, I have read the 'Sermon on the Mount,' and it's wonderful, but I do have questions. However, that is not what I wanted to tell you. I think the Lord spoke to me when I was reading my Tanakh. It was in Shemot – you call it Exodus – but the books in the Torah are named for the first Hebrew words. In this case the book begins, 'These are the names of the sons of Israel.' Shemot means 'names.'"

"While you are explaining that, tell me what 'HaShem' means. You say that name instead of 'God,' don't you?"

"Yes, we Orthodox Jews believe the name of God is too holy to say. Instead we use 'Adonai' for 'Lord' and also 'HaShem,' which means 'THE Name.'"

"Sarah, I have a lot to learn. Thanks for teaching me."

"Let me get to the point because my knees are hurting, and I know I am blocking the aisle. Anyway, the Lord wants all of us to know His promise for this trip to Israel. HaShem showed it to me from the 23rd chapter, the 20th verse – 'Behold, I send an Angel before you to keep you in the way and to bring you into the place which I have prepared.'"

"I love it, Sarah. Let's share it with the men later. That gives me even more confidence that the Lord is leading us on this trip. I plan to memorize that verse. Thank you so much." Sarah squeezed Gloria's hand and went back to her seat. Gloria determined to tell Jeff this when he woke up. *Dream or no dream, Jesus is our Shepherd. And that's that. No worries and no fears. I stand on the promises of God, including the one about the Angel leading us to Israel.* Gloria finally dozed off.

About ten minutes later, Jeff woke up, and gently shook Gloria awake. "Oh, Jeff, that's not fair. You got a good nap, and I only got a few minutes."

"Trust me, sweetheart, you will be glad when later at the right time you will go out like a light. I should have waited. In the Philippines I had a bad case of jet lag. Changing the subject, I have got to thank you for something. Your insistence that the four of us go to the Baptist Student Union meetings has meant the world to me these last three weeks. Never having read the Bible, each message that I heard was like food to a starving man. And my private reading of the Bible has given me purpose and guidance in my daily life. Maybe I should have started reading at the beginning, but someone at BSU, your friend, Grace Thomas, suggested I start with the book of John. Oh, I love it. After you quoted that verse to me about peace, it reminded me of the last chapter I read, Chapter 14. Jesus starts off with the words, 'Let not your heart be troubled,' and then later in the chapter He says to His disciples, 'Peace I leave with you, My peace I give unto you. Not as the world gives, give I unto you. Let not your hearts be troubled. Neither let them be afraid.'[76] Bomb or no bomb, I truly am not afraid."

"Amen. I am not either. And while you were snoring away, Sarah walked up and knelt beside me. She wanted to share a verse from Exodus the Lord gave her for us. It reinforces what you just quoted. 'Behold, I send an Angel before you to keep you in the way and to bring you into the place which I have prepared.'" Gloria turned around to look back and see if the others were napping. She saw Pete beside the window fast asleep. Max and Sarah were walking toward the restrooms. "Jeff, there is another verse in John, chapter 14, that I have memorized, verse 6, which makes it plain that there is no other way to God but through Jesus. I want Sarah to know this truth and that she must put her faith in Yeshua to be saved, to have eternal life. Please join me in prayer that it will happen soon. She is very close, but she has not made that commitment yet." Jeff agreed and led the prayer, as they bowed their heads.

Max took Sarah to a nook beside the restrooms where he could talk to her privately. "Sarah, you must listen to me. Gloria led us in a prayer of idolatry. Remember our creed: 'Sh'ma, Yisrael, Adonai

Eloyheynu, Adonai Echad.'[77] God is One, Echad! The Christians seem to believe in three gods, and that is idol worship. Also, God does not have a Son. They call Jesus the Son of God."

"I thought the same thing, and I brought it up with Gloria. She really surprised me when she showed me a verse in Proverbs I had never noticed before. It stunned me. Let me get my Tanakh and read it to you." Sarah quickly retrieved the book, brought it back, and turned to the passage. "'Who has ascended into heaven, or descended? Who has gathered the wind in His fists? Who has bound the waters in a garment? Who has established all the ends of the earth? What is His name, and what is His **SON'S** name, if you know? Every word of God is pure...' This is obviously the Creator, and He has a Son! It sounds like this was written for people who would doubt that HaShem has a Son, people like us. Can't you see it?"

Max was caught off guard. No one had ever challenged him on this basic tenet of Judaism. "I still don't get it. It is clear in our creed that HaShem is One."

"Yes, Christians would agree, but they would also say that HaShem is One in three persons. They call it the Trnity of the Godhead: Father, Son, and Holy Spirit. Gloria showed me another verse that got me to thinking. I am not swallowing everything she says, but she is making some good points. Here it is: Bereshit 1:26 – 'Then HaShem said, 'Let **Us** make man in **Our** image, according to **Our** likeness...' Did you hear those three plural pronouns for HaShem? What do you think of that? One more thing – did you know that Jesus said – 'I and the Father are One'?"[78]

"Sarah, you are on a slippery slope. When we get to Abe's house, you will get your head on straight. I think you need to be deprogrammed. For heaven's sake, Christians think that the Jews are Christ Killers!"

"Oh, Max. I know how anti-Semitic the history of Christianity is, but I met a Messianic Jew, Dr. Michael Brown, who owns up to it and apologizes for it. He wrote a book, *Our Hands Are Stained with Blood: the Tragic Story of the "Church" and the Jewish People.* He calls the Church to repent for the sins of their forefathers. I heard him preach, and when he described the crucifixion of Jesus, it cut me to the heart, and I cried. Think of this, too, Max. When Gloria prayed about the terrorist in the airport, she was overcome with the Holy Spirit. That had to be the Ruach HaKodesh. And her prayer was answered. The terrorist was arrested without a shot being fired!"

Max couldn't think of a reply. The wind had gone out of his sails. "Max, we need to get back to our seats because the food carts are coming down the aisles." They moved back beside Pete, and he woke up.

Pete stretched and yawned. "That nap was just what I needed. Too late to run to the restroom though. Here come the food carts. Y'all made it just in time. Max, I was dreaming about that white-robed man. It's not that I am worried about it, but I was just wondering if you think he may have sneaked on the plane and maybe, just maybe, he planted a bomb somewhere."

"There is a U.S. air marshal flying with us. They are not on every flight, but I think I spotted the air marshal on this flight. Typically, they take an end seat and look like an ordinary passenger, but they carry a gun and can make arrests. Look over there." Max pointed him out to Pete.

"I see him. Okay, I am making a decision. I refuse to worry about it, Max. And that's it. What happens on this plane is beyond my control. And there's one thing I have learned these past two months in our Holy Rollers group, you have to trust God. Thinking about all the great things that have happened, I know it wasn't luck. I am getting used to calling these blessings, 'God incidences.' Bomb or no bomb, I am at peace." Max couldn't argue with that. He smiled at Pete and nodded his head.

CHAPTER 42

WALKING WHERE JESUS WALKED

JERUSALEM, DAY 3 OF HANUKKAH

Their second breakfast at the Dan Panorama Hotel was even more delightful than the first.

After a quick trip to their rooms, the four travelers gathered in the lobby to find out the itinerary for the day. Jet lag was now a thing of the past. Everyone's eyes were on Jeff. Gloria didn't want to waste a minute of their time in the Holy Land. "I can hardly wait to continue walking in the footsteps of Jesus today. Jeff has really been holding his cards close to his chest. The only thing I could get out of our handsome tour host last night was that we are going to the Galilee where Jesus began His ministry. It was back at the airport that Jeff and I talked about the usual itinerary that tourists have in Israel, but Jeff said it might not happen exactly as we expect. Hurry up, Jeff. You are keeping us in suspense."

Pete broke in. "Halt! First, I have to have your signatures on a letter I have written to fax to our parents about our experiences so far. Maybe you have used your phone cards to call, but I wanted to get it in writing. Listen to this, and see if you have any additions or corrections. I wrote in small letters to get it all on one page. A nice lady at the hotel desk said she would be glad to make faxes for us at a minimal fee."

Sarah was impressed. "Pete, that is so thoughtful of you. I will give you Max's work number, and I'm sure someone will take the letter to Chaya or mail it."

"Papa Sam and Mama Anna don't have a fax machine, but my father does. He can mail a copy to them. Also, fax a copy to Adaton Baptist, in care of Grace Thomas. I have the number."

"Pete, that's great. Now I know why you were up late last night. I will give you my dad's number at the Wholesale Grocery. Okay, go ahead and read it."

Pete cleared his throat. "Don't worry, I didn't mention the terrorist at the airport. We can tell them in person when we get home. Here goes:

Dear family and friends, Had a safe flight. Our ride in the sherut from the airport to Jerusalem was fun, trying to converse with Hebrew and French speakers who only knew a little English. Had good night's sleep. Rested first day until evening, then went to lighting of the first Hanukkah candle by P.M. Netanyahu at the Western Wall. Beautiful and inspiring. Second day we took taxi to Yad VaShem to tour, then to Sarah's brother Abe's house to visit all her family and have lunch. They are Orthodox Jews. Learned Jewish customs and Hebrew phrases and enjoyed new but delicious food. We loved them, and they loved us and thanked us for watching over Sarah at MSU. Abe took us to the Old City after lunch, first to the Western Wall, where we had awesome prayers. Then he pointed out how to go up the ramp to the Temple Mount. He didn't go because the Muslims or even the Israeli policemen might force him to leave. (Explain later.) Today we continue our tour. Jeff is our tour host and is about to tell us the itinerary. All four of us want to thank you, our parents, Gloria's grandparents, Chaya, and our friends for praying for us. The financing of our trip by our kinfolks is a lavish gift, for which we are deeply grateful. We can see the Father God's hand in everything that has happened. May Jesus be glorified in our lives. Sending all our love. Signed _____,
_____, _____, _____.

Gloria began to clap, and the others joined her, not caring that people stared at them. They put their signatures on the letter, and Pete went to the desk to get it faxed. He left it with them.

Jeff leaned in to his friends. "Here goes. First, I have a startling announcement. This is my gift to you. My money was burning a hole in my pocket since I didn't have to pay for the hotel rooms or the plane tickets. I have paid for a tour guide, and she is a Messianic

Jew. She will drive us all over the land and make the Bible come alive as she shows us places and teaches us. I called Dr. Michael Brown and asked him who he would recommend. He didn't hesitate but immediately recommended a woman named Kelila. He even had her phone number. I called her, and she is available this week. She will pick us up – (Jeff looked at his watch) in about forty minutes. I have another surprise. We are not staying here tonight and maybe not tomorrow night either, although we are keeping our rooms here for the rest of our stay. Kelila is taking us to a nice hotel in Tiberias. I will cover that expense also. You don't need much luggage. Just bring your carry-on and maybe a tote bag, so everything will fit into Kelila's vehicle. Oh, and be sure to bring a notebook and pen with you. Kelila got an extra supply of water."

The group went upstairs and quickly gathered their sweaters, coats, hats, gloves, water bottles, and bags. They could hand carry everything, so Jeff led them in a prayer outside their rooms before they went to the elevator. "Dear Father in heaven, we claim Your promise to send Your angel before us and keep us in Your way until You bring us to the place You have prepared. We acknowledge that Your Holy Spirit has brought us safely thus far, and we love You and praise You. In the mighty name of Jesus we pray." Everyone said, "Amen!"

Kelila had just arrived in the lobby when the friends got off the elevator. Looking at the group of four with their bags, she knew these were her tourists. She walked up and introduced herself. "Shalom. I am Kelila, your tour guide for a few days."

Jeff introduced himself and the others. They took a few minutes for mutual admiration. Kelila was of medium height and a slim figure, had curly copper hair, little makeup, dark eyes, light freckles, and a wide smile with pretty white teeth. She shook each extended hand vigorously. "Jeff told me that your group is all Jewish except for one goy. And I can guess who that is!"

Pete stuck out his chest. "Yes, that's yours truly, the Gentile in the group. Shalom!"

"I love your southern accent, Pete, and yours, too, Jeff. You two girls sound like you are from up north in the U.S. I myself made aliyah from there. I lived in Queens, New York, and I came here in 1990."

Gloria reached out to shake hands. "Sarah and I are from New York, too. I am glad Dr. Brown knew you and could recommend you to Jeff. We want to hear every word you say. We all love Jesus like you. I mean Yeshua. And we want to walk where He walked. I am excited we are starting out in the Galilee where Yeshua began His ministry."

Kelila led the way, and they all piled in her van. "Jeff trusted me with the itinerary. I prayed, and I believe the Spirit said to take you first to the Golan Heights." Jeff got in the front passenger seat. The girls sat in the middle seats, and Pete got in the back.

Sarah gasped. "The Golan Heights? That is where my parents lived after they made aliyah two years ago. They lived in the city of Katzrin. Are you going to take us there, by any chance?"

"Ken. I mean 'yes,' we are going there first." *Thanks, Yeshua, I thought I heard you say "Golan Heights."*

The four were quiet, pondering how the Lord was directing their every move.

CHAPTER 43

THE GOLAN HEIGHTS

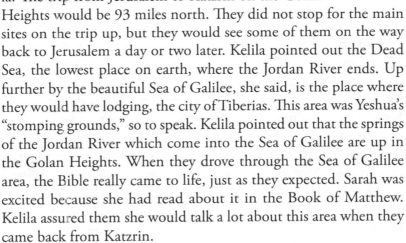

Kelila kept up a commentary all along Highway 90, the longest highway in Israel going from north to south along the Jordan River which separates the nation of Israel from Jordan and Syria. The trip from Jerusalem to Katzrin on the Golan Heights would be 93 miles north. They did not stop for the main sites on the trip up, but they would see some of them on the way back to Jerusalem a day or two later. Kelila pointed out the Dead Sea, the lowest place on earth, where the Jordan River ends. Up further by the beautiful Sea of Galilee, she said, is the place where they would have lodging, the city of Tiberias. This area was Yeshua's "stomping grounds," so to speak. Kelila pointed out that the springs of the Jordan River which come into the Sea of Galilee are up in the Golan Heights. When they drove through the Sea of Galilee area, the Bible really came to life, just as they expected. Sarah was excited because she had read about it in the Book of Matthew. Kelila assured them she would talk a lot about this area when they came back from Katzrin.

As Kelila explained how valuable the Golan Heights was to the defense of Israel, she was really in her element. This land, part of which overlooked the Sea of Galilee, was a buffer zone for them. When Syria controlled it, they were sitting ducks. Israel captured the Golan Heights in the Six Day War of 1967. In the Yom Kippur War of 1973, the Syrians tried to recapture it, but Israel won the war. Kelila described some of the supernatural interventions that God did for Israel in that war. She repeated the eye witness accounts!

The trip did not seem long at all to the four tourists, and they were soon in Katzrin. Sarah could hardly contain herself. "Oh, I did not tell you until we got here that I wrote down the address of Abba and Imma's house. I must see it. Maybe whoever lives there now will let us go inside. Kelila, we have to take time for this. Please." Sarah gave the piece of paper with the address to Kelila.

Kelila found the address and pulled in the driveway. A car was in the carport, so the people were at home. Sarah went up to the door and knocked. A very attractive elderly couple came to the door and introduced themselves as Rabbi Leonard and Miriam Katz. Sarah told them why they had come. Observing Sarah's excited reaction and the broad smiles of the elderly couple, the others got out of the van and came up beside Sarah.

Sarah turned to Gloria, her face wet with tears, and melted in Gloria's arms. She seemed to be joyful and sad at the same time. The rabbi quickly explained to Gloria, Jeff, and Pete. "I am Rabbi Leonard Katz, and this is my wife Miriam. Sarah's parents were in my kehilat. After their deaths, when their house was up for sale, we bought it. So we haven't lived here but a few months."

Shock registered on each face. Kelila joined them to see what was going on. Pete put his arm around Sarah and turned her face toward his. "Darling Sarah, why are you surprised? Hasn't HaShem orchestrated our whole trip? He is giving you a way to find out what life was like for your parents living in Israel in this beautiful town of Katzrin. It is almost like a gift to you from your parents beyond the grave."

Miriam came close and held Sarah's hands. "This young man is speaking for the Lord. What wise words." Pete smiled. "Please, all of you, come inside. It seems our Shepherd Yeshua has led the five of you right to our door. Sarah, you are welcome to look throughout the house. We enjoyed visiting your parents in this home, and now we are proud to own it."

Being the tour host, Jeff led them all inside, following Rabbi and Mrs. Katz. "You said it right, Miss Miriam. Yeshua is our Shepherd, and he made me the 'Undershepherd' of these sheep today. We have been calling it 'God incidences' when things like this happen. But this incident deserves a more magnificent description. I say it is 'Divine Destiny!' And I have to ask, what is a kehilat?"

Miriam showed them into the spacious den, and they were seated. Then she left for the kitchen to prepare a snack. The Rabbi answered. "Kehilat is Hebrew for 'church' or 'congregation.' We are Messianic Jews. I am the rabbi of our kehilat, which is a satellite of HaCarmel Kehilat on Mount Carmel in Haifa. We also have goyim, Gentiles, who worship with us. Miriam and I are sabras. That means 'native Israelis.' Both our parents made aliyah from the U.K. in 1928, so we were born here. Our parents were Orthodox. Miriam and I rebelled against that and really had no religion. We married and were living in Haifa when some friends invited us to go with them to HaCarmel Kehilat one Sabbath. The pastor was an American. His testimony was so powerful that our hearts were cut to the core. That very day we gave our lives to Yeshua, and we never looked back, even though our Orthodox parents disowned us." Sarah was drinking in every word, trying to envision her parents living in this house. She tried but could not envision them worshiping with Christians and Messianic Jews.

"We are identified as Messianic Jews because we believe that Yeshua is our Messiah. Of course, most religious Jews believe in the coming of the Messiah, but we believe Yeshua has already come, and we are awaiting His second coming. We read and believe both the Tanakh and the Brit Hadasha, the New Testament, which both testify that Yeshua came the first time as a Lamb to suffer and die for our sins, and that He rose from the dead and ascended back into heaven. The Scriptures show that He is coming here a second time to rule as King of kings and Lord of lords over the whole earth from His throne in Jerusalem. Later you can check out chapters 12, 13, and 14 of the prophet Zechariah. He describes the second coming and how the Jewish people respond to it." Gloria was quick to write this on her note pad.

Sarah's heart began to race. She wanted to know everything. "Rabbi Katz, you said my parents were in your kehilat? Are you telling me that they believed in Yeshua as the Messiah?"

"Yes, child, most definitely they believed that Yeshua was the Messiah."

Sarah didn't know what to think. One part of her was angry, and one part of her was happy. "None of my family know this. And if I were to tell them now, they would be very upset."

"I understand completely, Sarah. I think their experience was similar to mine and Miriam's. Someone they knew and trusted invited them to visit our kehilat. They were there one Sabbath when the Holy Spirit really moved among us in power. It felt like electricity! Nathan and Naomi were deeply touched. They came to the altar and asked me to pray for them that Yeshua would come into their hearts and save them. It happened only a few months before they were tragically killed in Jerusalem. Our kehilat loved them so much, and all of us grieved deeply."

Sarah put her head in her hands and sobbed. Miriam could hear from the kitchen. She stopped what she was doing and rushed to embrace this distraught young woman. Jeff, Gloria, and Pete also came beside her to comfort her. Sarah's sobs gradually subsided, and Miriam returned to the kitchen.

In a few minutes, Miriam brought out hot peppermint tea, ice water, small sandwiches, and decorated candies. Everyone helped themselves. It was close to lunch, and they were starving. "These look like Christmas candies, Miss Miriam. And they are delicious." Pete filled his plate and demonstrated his satisfaction. "H-m-m good!"

Gloria suddenly realized what day this was. "People, this is December 25th, Christmas Day! I had forgotten, even though I noticed some decorations in Jerusalem. It seems to me there is something significant about this particular Christmas Day. Of course, it is always significant because it is the birthday of our beloved Lord and Savior Jesus Christ. But there is something more this time – I can feel it."

Sarah began to cry harder than ever. Everyone was puzzled, stopped eating and focused on her. **"Oh, I see it now! I know it's true!"** She jumped up, and her words were coming fast. "I remember what I read in Matthew. The angel told Joseph to name the baby Yeshua because He would save His people from their sins. The word 'save' makes sense now. Yeshua, Jesus, He's the Savior. In Hebrew His name means 'Yahweh is salvation.' You friends keep saying He is your Lord and Savior. You say you are '**born again.**' **Christmas** celebrates that Jesus was BORN. I am ready right now. My parents believed in Yeshua, and from all I have seen and heard ever since I met you friends, I want what you have. I have seen our prayers answered in Jesus' name. The gun wasn't fired! We were **SAVED!** Oh, I can feel my heart opening wide. **I want to be saved. I want to be born again!** It is not luck, it is a God incidence. We have been led right to this place, so I can be born again like my parents. Please Rabbi, say a prayer over me like you must have said over my Abba and Imma."

"Wait! I want you to pray for me also, Rabbi Katz." Pete was overcome with the conviction of his sins. Even though he thought he was already saved, he wanted to make absolutely certain that he was born again. There couldn't be a better day to do it, nor a better person to be born again with.

Miriam was crying now. "I was in the Christian Quarter of the Old City in Jerusalem a few days ago and bought those Christmas candies. I never use Christmas goodies in the celebration of Yeshua's birth, but now I know why I bought them! It seems God has used them as a type of 'spark plug!'"

Kelila wasn't crying, but she was clapping. "Oh, thank goodness I obeyed the Spirit in coming to Katzrin today for our first day of touring."

Jeff and Gloria knelt beside Sarah and Pete. Jeff spoke. "Rabbi, Gloria and I are sure we have been born again, and we love Jesus with all our hearts. But after you pray over Sarah and Pete, please pray over us that we will be baptized in the Holy Spirit and refilled every day. We want to carry out the purposes God has for our lives, so we can harvest souls for Jesus the way it happened on the Day of Pentecost in the Bible."

Rabbi Katz quickly opened a drawer and pulled out his tallit and anointing oil. Miriam came beside him, and they laid their hands on the heads of Sarah and Pete. They were open to the Holy Spirit to lead them, and they began to sing. "Jesus, Jesus, Holy and Anointed One, Jesus. Jesus, Jesus, risen and Exalted One, Jesus. Your name is like honey on my lips. Your Spirit like water to my soul. Your Word is a lamp unto my feet. Jesus, I love you, I love you...."[79] Gloria knew the song, and she sang with them from the depths of her being. They sang it again using the name "Yeshua." The fragrance of His presence filled the room.

Kelila came up behind the four friends on their knees and held them steady as they began to sway under the power of the Spirit. Rabbi Katz anointed their foreheads with the fragrant oil. "Relax while I read two portions of Scripture. Then I will pray for you." He read Romans 10:8-13. "The word is near you, in your mouth and in your heart" (that is, the word of faith which we preach): that if you confess with your mouth the Lord Yeshua and believe in your heart that God has raised Him from the dead, you will be saved. For with the heart one believes unto righteousness, and with the mouth confession is made unto salvation. For the Scripture says, 'Whoever believes on Him will not be put to shame.' For there is no distinction between Jew and Greek, for the same Lord over all is rich to all who call upon Him. For 'whoever calls on the name of Yahweh shall be saved.'"

Then the Rabbi quoted Yeshua's words to Nicodemus, a religious leader, from John 3:14-17: "As Moses lifted up the serpent in the wilderness, even so must the Son of Man be lifted up [on the cross], that whoever believes in Him should not perish but have eternal life. For God so loved the world that He gave His only begotten Son, that whoever believes in Him should not perish but have everlasting life. For God did not send His Son into the world to condemn the world, but that the world through Him might be saved."

"Now I will pray over you two, Sarah and Pete. Repeat after me – 'I believe that Yeshua died on the cross for my sins --- I am forgiven, and He has given me eternal life ---. I am now saved and born again by the Spirit, according to the Word of God ---. I invite you Yeshua, My Messiah, to come into my heart --- and lead me in paths of righteousness for Your name's sake ---. Thank You for saving me. --- Amen. ---"

Sarah and Pete collapsed on the floor, still aware of their surroundings, but filled with awe at the Holy Presence all over them and now inside them. They couldn't move.

Jeff and Gloria received the anointing of oil, laying on of hands by the Rabbi and his wife, and then a powerful prayer based on Acts 1:8 – "But you shall receive POWER when the Holy Spirit has come upon you; and you shall be WITNESSES to Me in Jerusalem, and in all Judea and Samaria, and to the end of the earth." Miriam continued the prayer, "Lord Yeshua, enable Jeff and Gloria to win many souls for You and to be very fruitful in their lives as a couple wherever you send them. May they prosper and be in health as their souls prosper."[80]

Jeff and Gloria were also slain in the Spirit and felt like heaven was enveloping them. Strange words formed in their minds and spilled out of their mouths as they yielded to the movement of the Holy Spirit inside them.[81] Leonard, Miriam, and Kelila were touched by the Spirit and shakily walked over, sat down and quietly worshiped the Lord. No one was aware of the passing of time.

CHAPTER 44

DAYS OF ELIJAH

Jeff was the first to emerge from the dream-like state. "I have been walking with Jesus, everyone. He is the top tour guide of all because this is His land. We are His people, and He has brought us here to give us basic training as His disciples, to go and tell the world about Him." He looked at his watch. "Amazing! I had no idea that an hour had passed since the Rabbi prayed."

Gloria sat up. "Oh, Jeff. I experienced the same thing after Rabbi Leonard placed his hands on my head and prayed. It is like we are being commissioned here today at the highest point in Israel."

Sarah stood to her feet. "Yes! I am ready for the basic training, so I can go out and witness for Yeshua."

"Pardon me, folks. I've got to let this girl know what I think of her becoming a disciple." Pete enfolded Sarah in his arms. "Go ahead, Sarah, witness to me. What happened to you here today?"

"I am saved! I am born again! I am happy! I am free! I love my Messiah, and I love all of you!" Everyone cheered.

"Best witness I have ever heard, girlfriend!"

Miriam was elated. "This has been the most glorious day I've had serving the Lord since we came to Katzrin. I can't thank you enough for coming here and for letting us be a part of the magnificent work the Lord is doing in your lives. Leonard and I will tell our kehilat what happened here today, especially the salvation of Nathan and Naomi's daughter. And we will be backing you up in prayer."

Gloria embraced the elderly couple. "Rabbi Leonard and Miriam, we are very grateful for your ministry to us and your hospitality. But like Yeshua said, we need to move on to other towns with His message." Gloria turned to Kelila. "Where did the Lord tell you to take us next? We need to practice witnessing there."

"After what happened today, there is one place we definitely will emphasize on the way back to Jerusalem, and that is Yardenit. Sarah needs to be baptized. And the rest of you may want to do it, too, even if you have already been baptized in a church. Jesus commanded water baptism and, more importantly, baptism in the Holy Spirit. That gives you the power to make disciples for Him."

Sarah was ready. "Oh, yes, I want to be baptized in the Jordan River like Yeshua was. I read about it in the third chapter of Matthew." Back at MSU, Jeff had been telling Gloria that he needed to be obedient to the Lord and be baptized. Pete was ready for a "second dunking," as he called it.

"Jeff has given me free reign, and I think while we are up here we should go visit Har Bental, which was once a volcano. This mountain is on the border with Syria. It is a watch post for the Israel Defense Force, the IDF, and there are army bunkers you can go down into. From high up you can view the Hula Valley. It is really beautiful, and it's easy to see the road to Damascus. If some of you don't know what happened there, you can find it in Acts, the ninth chapter. To put it briefly, the Apostle Paul met Yeshua there in a blinding light. Also, you can see Mount Hermon in the distance. It is snow-capped and is the highest point and the most northern point in Israel. On the slopes is Caesarea Philippi, where Yeshua took His disciples. Maybe we will have time to go there, but probably not. It was there that the Apostle Peter made his astonishing statement to Yeshua, 'You are the Messiah, the Son of the Living God.'"[82]

Kelila continued. "There is another mountain, Mount Tabor, close to Nazareth where Yeshua spent His boyhood. Tradition has it that this is the Mount of Transfiguration, where Peter, James, and John saw Yeshua transfigured, shining so brightly they couldn't look on His face. A cloud came over them, and they HEARD the booming voice of God from heaven, saying, 'This is My beloved

Son in Whom I am well pleased. Hear Him.' They saw Moses and Elijah speaking with Yeshua.[83] However, Mount Tabor is probably not the right location for that event. More likely, this happened on the slopes of Mount Hermon."

Sarah was getting more excited. "I read about both those events in Matthew. I want to read them again. And I also want to read about the man who met Yeshua on the road to Damascus in Acts 9."

"Okay, your Undershepherd says it is time to get going on our tour." Jeff shook Leonard's hand and hugged Miriam, expressing his gratitude for their life-changing ministry. The others followed suit. Then they all headed for the van.

"Wait, children. I took so long in the kitchen when you first came because I knew you would be needing some food on your trip. I have packed sandwiches and other goodies in paper sacks, and I am sending some cold soft drinks in a disposable cooler with you." A cheer went up for Miriam, and the five travelers began another round of profuse thanks and goodbyes.

On their tour of Har Bental, they witnessed to every tourist they saw that Yeshua was the Jewish Messiah, and He had changed their lives. Then they headed straight south for Yardenit. All were thankful it was not a cold day, and there were few tourists getting baptized. They put on the white baptismal robes and approached one of the areas provided to have their private service of baptism. Kelila said she would be the audience. Pete and Gloria had already been baptized, so it was agreed they would act as ministers to Jeff and Sarah. Then Jeff and Sarah would turn around and minister baptism to them. It was agreed to have Scripture and singing. Pete was designated to read the story of Yeshua's baptism. Gloria sang. "*Amazing Grace, how sweet the sound, that saved a wretch like me. I once was lost but now am found, was blind, but now I see.*" Pete gave a loud "Amen!" Gloria and Kelila sang a familiar chorus, and they all felt the moving of the Holy Spirit. "*Spirit of the Living God, fall afresh on me. Spirit of the Living God, fall afresh on me. Melt me, mold me, fill me, use me. Spirit of the Living God, fall afresh on me.*"[84]

The four friends eagerly went down into the water of the Jordan. It was a beautiful baptism. Pete exclaimed, "I feel totally clean now!" Sarah shouted, "I am saved, I am born again!" Kelila read more Scripture: "Therefore we were buried with Him through baptism into death, that just as Messiah was raised from the dead by the glory of the Father, even so we also should walk in newness of life."[85] The euphoria the friends were feeling would not dissipate for days.

"Okay, little tourists, let us go get checked in to the Moriah Plaza Hotel in Tiberias. We will stay there one night. Our plans for tomorrow are to check out early and take a boat ride on the Sea of Galilee. I will talk about Yeshua calling His disciples, ordinary fishermen, whom He would teach to fish for men. Then we will go up on the Mount of Beatitudes where Yeshua preached His 'Sermon on the Mount.' There is an octagonal shaped Catholic chapel there, its eight sides symbolizing the eight Beatitudes, and the interior is saturated with the Holy Spirit. The nuns will greet us and direct us to the circular altar where we can kneel and pray. We can sit on the mountainside and take turns reading Jesus' words to the large crowd that gathered that day." The four expressed to each other that they could hardly wait to walk where Jesus walked, hear Him speak, and pray in the chapel.

"There are so many other important sites on the way back, but I want to save time to visit two Christian ministries in Jerusalem, at least one of them, before we check back in the Dan Panorama tomorrow afternoon. You will have a special Hanukkah Shabbat dinner at the hotel if we make it back in time. I want to take you to Christian Friends of Israel and Bridges for Peace. It is amazing how many outreaches they both have. Their ministry recipients include Holocaust survivors, immigrants, terror victims, poor Christians and Messianic Jews, bridal couples, and soldiers in the IDF. The Bridges for Peace ministry operates a Food Bank, and both ministries do home repair."

Jeff was elated to hear this. "Oh, Gloria, remember what I told you about wanting to have a ministry to the poor in the Philippines. I see now that there are overpowering needs right here in our Jewish homeland."

Kelila continued. "Jeff, I can put you in touch with Inge, a German lady who has dedicated herself to the Holocaust survivors, trying to make recompense for the atrocities by Germans against Jews during World War II. You can go with her on her visits to their homes, if you would like to."

Jeff looked at Gloria. "Let's do it, honey!" Gloria was just as excited about it as Jeff.

After getting settled in their rooms and resting for a while before dinner, the four friends met in the girls' room to reflect on their awesome day. Gloria knew that everyone would have a lot to share, but she felt strongly that she should first teach them a new song and make it their theme song in Israel. They agreed to hear it and try to learn it. It was "Days of Elijah."

Gloria had read about how Robin Mark was inspired by God to write the song, so before playing it, she gave them a full description of the lyrics:

"Robin Mark wanted to show that we believers in the Messiah today need to be like Elijah in the way he stood up against the prophets of Baal. We have to be preparing the way of the Lord in these dark days like he and John the Baptist did, calling people to repentance. And we should be like Moses, calling those who follow Jesus to be holy. The

Listen to
Days of Elijah

church today needs to be like the prophet Ezekiel who spoke to the dry bones to come together and come to life! Those bones referred to the whole house of Israel being restored, and the Church also needs to be restored in unity. King David wanted to build a temple of praise to God, but his son Solomon carried out David's dream. Today we believers must rebuild that temple of praise with our spiritual worship, because the Messiah is coming soon! It is our job to get out in the harvest fields and bring people to Yeshua.

He will be coming in the clouds. The trumpet will sound in the year of Jubilee. We are to lift up our voices and sing in these days of Elijah! Our salvation is coming! Now, let's get quiet and allow God to speak to our hearts while we listen."[86]

Gloria played the CD in her small portable CD player. The friends were mesmerized, and their faces showed their enthusiasm for the music.

Sarah clapped enthusiastically. "I love it! This doesn't sound like a Christian song though. Elijah, Moses, Ezekiel, and David are all Jewish, and they are in the Tanakh. Oops! I forgot. Yeshua is Jewish also, and most of the people in the Brit Hadasha are Jewish. It's amazing how us Orthodox Jews have been programmed against belief in Yeshua and the New Testament. But I am brand new now and can see things I could not see before. It was right under my nose that morning in Adaton Baptist Church, and when Mama Anna talked about it. Now I believe that Isaiah 53 describes the crucifixion of Yeshua. It is very clear to me. And this song is about the coming of the Messiah, which I understand now is His SEC-OND coming. He will be 'shining like the sun' as He did on the Mount of Transfiguration, and Moses and Elijah were right there with Him. The words, 'year of Jubilee,' make me think of the time we are in now, the 50th birthday of Israel. It is their Jubilee. Hey, what do you know about that? It is just another 'divine destiny' that HaShem has been unfolding in our lives!"

"Sarah, you amaze me. And I adore you. Come to Papa." Pete didn't care what anybody thought. He had to kiss his wonderful Sarah. Everybody cheered and rejoiced with them.

Not to be outdone by Pete, Jeff reached for Gloria. "Turn your head, Kelila. But after I kiss Gloria, I will give you a brotherly kiss, if that's okay with you."

"Don't make that kiss too long because it is time for dinner. I think you 'Holy Rollers' better wind up here and get to rolling. You can save MY kiss, Jeff, for the conclusion of the trip because I will be on my own time then. Ha!"

The dinner was very different from the meals they had enjoyed in Jerusalem, but all agreed the food was totally satisfying. After the last bite of dessert, Kelila restated their itinerary for the next day, Friday, and then gave them a preview of the itinerary for Saturday and Sunday. "From Jerusalem, we will go to Tel Aviv. On the way I will show you the Judean hills where the Maccabees hid and from where they made their attacks on the Syrian forces. Their leader Judah was nicknamed 'the hammer,' and the name Maccabees is derived from it. They would keep hammering those Syrian troops and defeat them. But at first they were losing the battle because the Syrians attacked them on Shabbat, and they would not fight on the Sabbath. Mattathias decided to change the law and permit defensive warfare on the Sabbath.[87] It is interesting that I will be showing those hills to you on the Sabbath. Our army, the IDF, does fight on the Sabbath."

Gloria was excited. "Oh, I wish Papa Sam and Mama Anna were with us. They are so precious. I will never forget all they taught us about Hanukkah. Papa Sam is an anointed teacher, and Mama Anna knows history."

"Well, you Jewish tourists are going to love Independence Hall in Tel Aviv because you can learn all the history about the founding of the modern State of Israel there. We will travel on to Haifa and see Mt. Carmel where Elijah had his contest with the prophets of Baal. It might be a good idea for you to study that story in 1 Kings 18 beforehand, and especially since you Holy Rollers have adopted a theme song, 'Days of Elijah.'"

Pete groaned. "Stop, Kelila! I am already about to burst from all this gourmet Bible food! Also, my head won't hold any more facts. You can tell us about the Sunday itinerary tomorrow. This is still Thursday. I need to crash. Come on, Jeff, let's hit the hay."

Gloria felt the Lord was saying to wait. "But Pete, this is Christmas Day, although it seems like a week ago, since this one day has been crammed with so many awesome experiences. We haven't sung one Christmas carol yet. I know you don't sing them,

311

Sarah, but now, I think it would be highly appropriate for us to sing one. Let us gather back in our room before we get ready for bed and sing the chorus, 'O Come Let us Adore Him.' It's not that we **ought** to, but my heart **longs** to take time to worship the One who made our trip possible through our generous family members. We can also hold them up before His throne of grace in gratitude."

Kelila stood. "Jeff's sheep, you have been a delight to guide today. The whole day has been wonderful, but my heart was moved by what happened in Katzrin. I have to do some tasks before bed-time, so I can't gather with you. But what I would like to do now is to bless you by praying the Aaronic priestly blessing over you in Hebrew and then in English. Just close your eyes and receive the blessing." Kelila quickly retrieved her tallit from her tote bag, draped herself and raised her hands over them. "Yevarechecha Adonai Ve'yishmerecha. Ya'er Adonai panayv eylecha vi'chuneka. Yissa Adonai panayv eylecha ve'yaseym lecha shalom. The Lord bless you and keep you. The Lord make His face to shine upon you and be gracious unto you. The Lord lift up His countenance upon you and give you peace."[88]

"Amen! Shalom, Kelila. We all love you." Jeff stood up from the table. "Sheep, follow me. We are going to Gloria and Sarah's room and stand on holy ground. We will sing praises to the King of kings and the Lord of lords and offer Him thanksgiving and worship, basking in His holy presence in this holy Land."

EPILOGUE

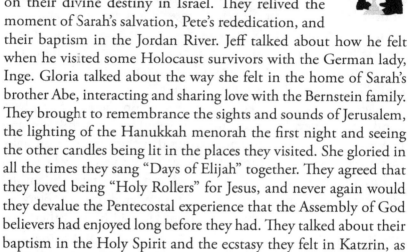

As the big El Al jet lifted off the runway and leveled out, Jeff and Gloria held hands, looked into each other's eyes and reflected together on their divine destiny in Israel. They relived the moment of Sarah's salvation, Pete's rededication, and their baptism in the Jordan River. Jeff talked about how he felt when he visited some Holocaust survivors with the German lady, Inge. Gloria talked about the way she felt in the home of Sarah's brother Abe, interacting and sharing love with the Bernstein family. They brought to remembrance the sights and sounds of Jerusalem, the lighting of the Hanukkah menorah the first night and seeing the other candles being lit in the places they visited. She gloried in all the times they sang "Days of Elijah" together. They agreed that they loved being "Holy Rollers" for Jesus, and never again would they devalue the Pentecostal experience that the Assembly of God believers had enjoyed long before they had. They talked about their baptism in the Holy Spirit and the ecstasy they felt in Katzrin, as they yielded their tongues to a strange language and then later felt such a powerful anointing, witnessing to people they encountered.

They expressed their hopes and dreams for the future together and vowed they were coming back to their roots as soon as possible, perhaps for their honeymoon. Jeff brought up the subject of making aliyah and continuing their education at Hebrew University. Gloria said they needed much prayer together and prayers from their family and friends about making such a radical decision, reminding him that he was an only child, and so was she. There was always the possibility their parents would make aliyah, however. They rejoiced that the Land of Israel was their biblical inheritance, and it was the place of the Messiah's throne where He would return and rule the earth one day. Oh, what a glorious future they would have as man and wife, taking part in the harvest of souls, wherever they were, back in Mississippi and New York or somewhere in Israel. They grew silent and pondered in which part of Israel they would make their home, if they did indeed become citizens.

Jeff ended this time of reverie, saying that his greatest and most overriding desire of all they had discussed was not far in the future. He was going to marry the most gorgeous, loveable, Spirit-filled woman on the planet. Gloria responded with her own declaration of deep admiration for the handsomest, most adorable, and most brilliant man in the universe that Yeshua the Messiah had chosen especially for her. She declared that she passionately desired to belong to Jeff and looked forward to becoming one. Like Yeshua said, "The two shall become one flesh."[89]

Pete and Sarah settled into their seats on the plane and held hands. Max knew his sister-in-law was in love with this goy, and he was getting used to it, anticipating that they would eventually marry. He tried to put himself in Pete's place to see how he would feel as a Gentile surrounded by Jews and was totally unfamiliar with Jewish customs and beliefs. As he pondered this, his tolerance of Pete grew into outright admiration. He told himself there was one thing he had to consider above all else, and that was that Pete truly loved Sarah, and she loved him. So he made a vow to himself that he would not be a hindrance to Pete's entrance into their family circle. In fact he would do all he could to make it easy for Pete. Then Max's thoughts turned to Chaya and how she would feel about it. He had been keeping her up to date in the faxes he sent home. Her replies encouraged him that her health was stable, the baby was fine, and she felt cared for not only by Frieda but by their synagogue family.

Sarah and Pete dived into Sarah's New Testament together. After reading Acts 9, they decided to read some of the Apostle Paul's letters to churches he had founded. Sarah knew right away she needed a teacher. It was just too deep for her, and the terminology was foreign. Pete suggested they scan some of the pages and find a place they understood. Sarah's eyes fell on the first words of Chapter Ten of Romans. She read it in a soft voice to Pete. "Brethren, my heart's desire and prayer to God for Israel is that they may be saved." "Isn't that something, Pete? When he said 'Israel,' I know he must have meant all Jews, and I am one of them. I am part of the answer to his prayer. Oh, thank You, Lord."

Pete took Sarah's Bible. "Honey, this is neat, having the Hebrew on the opposite page from the English."

"I really love it. Papa Sam and Mama Anna were so kind to give it to me."

"Let me get my Bible. I want to find out stuff I have been thinking about." Pete got his carry-on out of the bin above and retrieved his new Bible. Sarah continued to read her New Testament. Pete found Romans 10:1 and kept reading. Max was fast asleep beside them. After a few minutes, Pete had to share.

"Sarah, did you read the eleventh chapter yet? Evidently, the Roman church was full of Gentiles, and Paul was teaching them that they are wild branches grafted on to the Jewish olive tree. They should not boast that some of the natural branches, the Jews, were cut off."

Sarah interrupted, "That means they didn't believe in the Messiah that God sent them. But from what I have read, it was the religious leaders who hated Him and had Him crucified. The common people loved Him, listened to His teaching, and He healed crowds of them."

"That's right, Sarah. But the unbelieving Jews were cut off, so there would be room for the wild branches, the Gentiles. And then he says that if the unbelieving Jews, the natural branches, would say Yeshua is their Messiah, He would graft them back in. You, my adorable angel, have just been grafted back in! At last I see where I myself fit in. I'm not sure if it happened when I was a teenager or if it happened on the floor of your parents' former house in Katzrin. The one thing I do know is I am a wild branch growing right beside YOU, a natural branch. Now how is that for a theological speech? Ha!"

Sarah giggled. "Yes, honey, you are surely a WILD branch, but I have fallen madly in love with you."

Pete pulled Sarah close. "Let me finish. The Jewish olive tree is ONE tree, and Jews and Gentiles are united in the Messiah. I am a 'chosen people,' too. I have to quietly say, 'Praise the Lord.' I don't want to wake up Max."

"This is exciting. I see how that fits in to God's call on Abraham back in Bereshit 12. He said that through Abraham's 'Seed,' all the families of the earth would be blessed. We Jews are the seed of Abraham, but our Jewish Messiah Yeshua is THE Seed. It is in HIM that all mankind is blessed. And that is because Yeshua is the Savior of the **world**. He is Jewish, but God sent him to die for Jews **and** Gentiles. Oh, Pete, I wish my family understood this."

"In our room at the hotel last night, Jeff and I talked about how we want to come back to Israel. He thinks he could work with Bridges for Peace,[90] and I think I could find a job in security. I have to look into it, but maybe there is a possibility that I could become an Israeli citizen, even though I am not Jewish."

Sarah laughed and looked deep into Pete's eyes. "Yes, you surely ought to look into it. Do you think it would help if your wife was Jewish and had citizenship?"

Pete whooped, then clapped his hand over his mouth. Max woke up. Pete waited for him to go back to sleep. "Sarah, is this a proposal of marriage? I am ready anytime you are. Jeff said he could transfer to Hebrew University. Maybe all four of us could." He studied Sarah's face to see if she was serious.

"Pete, you are my shield. How could I ever live without you?" They began to dream together, figuring how everything could be worked out to have their hearts' desires. They knew that Jeff and Gloria were doing the very same thing. It was only a matter of time.

END NOTES

1. Tanakh, an acronym, TNK, for the three-part Hebrew Bible, the same as the Old Testament: Torah (T - first 5 books, the Law), Neviim (N - prophets), and Ketuvim (K - writings, beginning with Psalms). See Jesus' words in Luke 24:44.

2. Genesis 15:5-6.

3. Genesis 26:4.

4. Genesis 35:11-12.

5. Isaiah 55:8-9.

6. Psalm 81:10.

7. "The Love of God" by Frederick M. Lehman, 1917.

8. Matthew 18:19.

9. Talmud is a collection of Jewish law and tradition consisting of the Mishnah (oral law of Moses) and the Gemara (commentary on the Mishnah).

10. Ephesians 2:10.

11. Psalm 23.

12. Hebrew for "The Name." Orthodox Jews use this name for God.

13. Elmer A. Josephson, "Backbone of the Bible" (Ottawa, Kansas: Bible Light International Publications).

14. "I Worship You, Almighty God" by Sondra Corbett-Wood (Integrity's Hosanna! Music, ©1983).

15. http://law2.umkc.edu/faculty/projects/FTrials/scopes/ussher.html

16. https://en.wikipedia.org/wiki/Ussher_chronology

17. https://en.wikipedia.org/wiki/Israeli_citizenship_law

18. https://archive.jewishagency.org/education/israel/achievements/summary-definitions-who-jew

19. https://mishpacha.com/the-road-less-traveled/

20. Hebrew for "the Lord our God"

21. Give thanks to the Lord, for He is good. His mercy endures forever.

22. Matthew 11:25 KJV.

23. "What Life Means to Einstein: An Interview by George Sylvester Viereck," The Saturday Evening Post, Oct. 26, 1929, p. 17.

24. John 14:6.

25   https://www.lewisquotes.com/quotations/jesus/jesus-lord-liar-or-lunatic.html

26   "Shout to the Lord" by Darlene Zschech, Hillsong Music Australia, 1993.

27   Isaiah 53:4-5.

28   https://askdrbrown.org/library/users/michael-l-brown

29   Luke 23:34.

30   Matthew 11:28-30.

31   Matthew 28:9-15.

32   Deuteronomy 8:18.

33   Joel 2:32; Romans 10:13.

34   John 14:6.

35   Matthew 18:19-20.

36   Michael L. Brown, *Our Hands are Stained with Blood: The Tragic Story of the "Church" and the Jewish People* (Shippensburg, PA: Destiny Image Publishers, ©1992).

37   "It is Well With My Soul," words by Horatio Spafford, tune by Phillip Bliss, 1876

38   Psalm 122:1.

39   Acts 26:14.

40   "Bridge Over Troubled Water," Paul Simon and Art Garfunkel, ©1970.

41   https://www.songfacts.com/facts/simon-garfunkel/bridge-over-troubled-water

42   At the beginning of the Passover Seder the leader will lift up the tri-compartment matzoh bag [representing Father, Son, and Holy Spirit] and remove the middle board of matzoh. This middle piece is then broken. The larger part is wrapped in a white linen napkin, and becomes known as the *afikomen*, which is then hidden somewhere in the home. After the meal the children will search for the afikomen, and the finder is rewarded with a gift.

It is the middle matzoh, representative of the Son, that is removed and broken, just as Jesus left heaven, became a man, and died for the sins of the world. The larger piece of matzoh is then wrapped in a linen napkin, which becomes the afikomen [Greek *aphikomenos* meaning, "He has come"]. The afikomen represents the Messiah, as Jewish sources establish. The afikomen is then hidden, and the child that finds it receives a reward or gift. After his death Jesus was hidden away (buried), but rose from the grave, and those who find Him, accept Him as their personal Messiah, receive the gift of eternal life (Romans 6:23). http://www.jewishawareness.org/the-significance-of-the-afikomen/

43   https://en.wikipedia.org/wiki/Dreyfus_affair

44   Impact of the Dreyfus Affair on Hertzl ------ Cohn, Henry J. "Theodor Herzl's Conversion to Zionism." *Jewish Social Studies*, vol. 32, no. 2, 1970, pp. 101–110. *JSTOR*, www.jstor.org/stable/4466575. Accessed 16 Apr. 2021.

45   "Zionism was a national movement for the return of the Jewish people to their homeland and the resumption of Jewish sovereignty in the Land of Israel." https://www.jewishvirtuallibrary.org/a-definition-of-zionism

46   https://zionism-israel.com/hdoc/Theodor_Herzl_Zionist_Congress_Speech_1897.htm

47   John 4:32-34.

48   https://www.jewishvirtuallibrary.org/flossenb-uuml-rg-2

49   Romans 11: 16-24.

50   Genesis 2:23-25.

51   Proverbs 16:9.

52   Ephesians 4:11-12.

53   Matthew 24:15-16, 21.

54   "The Man of Perdition, Titus" https://bit.ly/3rlHswu

55   https://www.hope-of-israel.org/chariotsinthe%20sky.html

56   2 Thessalonians 2:1-4.

57   https://www.chicagotribune.com/opinion/commentary/ct-neo-nazi-skokie-march-flashback-perspec-0312-20170310-story.html

58   https://www.christianbook.com/the-hiding-place-corrie-ten-boom/9780553256697/pd/56696?event=Homeschool|1012903

59   https://newspapers.ushmm.org/events/eisenhower-asks-congress-and-press-to-witness-nazi-horrors

60   1 Thessalonians 5:22.

61   Revelation 1:8.

62   https://www.haaretz.com/jewish/.premium-this-day-the-first-and-only-el-al-hijacking-1.5298481
     Also https://www.iaf.org.il/5642-37791-en/IAF.aspx

63   Deuteronomy 22:4 – exception to law of not working on the Sabbath.

64   http://www.cnn.com/WORLD/9711/16/iraq.israel/index.html

65   https://www.jpost.com/Features/In-Thespotlight/This-Week-in-History-Saddam-terrorizes-Israel

66   John 2:19.

67   1 Corinthians 3:16-17.

68   Hebrews 11:35-39. https://israelmyglory.org/article/the-world-was-not-worthy-of-these-hebrews-1132-40/

69   John 8:56.

70   1 Peter 1:7-8 (KJV).

71   http://www.cnn.com/SPECIALS/1997/hanukkah/hanukkah.israel/index.html

END NOTES

72   https://en.wikipedia.org/wiki/1993_World_Trade_Center_bombing

73   Isaiah 54:17; Psalm 91.

74   A good deed. Primary meaning is a commandment of God.

75   Isaiah 26:3, KJV.

76   John 14:27.

77   Hear, O Israel, the Lord our God, the Lord is One" (Deut. 6:4).

78   John 10:30.

79   "Holy and Anointed One," by John Barnett, ©1988.

80   3 John 2.

81   Acts 2:1-4.

82   Matthew 16:13-18.

83   Matthew 17:1-5.

84   "Spirit of the Living God" by Paul Armstrong, ©1984, Restoration Music.

85   Romans 6:4.

86   "Days of Elijah" by Robin Mark, © 1994, https://robinmark.com/the-story-behind-days-of-elijah/.

87   1 Maccabees 2:29-41, https://www.biblicalarchaeology.org/daily/hanukah-maccabees-and-apocrypha/

88   Numbers 6:24-26. http://www.hebrew-streams.org/works/hebrew/birkat-aharon.html

89   Matthew 19:4-6.

90   https://www.bridgesforpeace.com/

Also by Nancy Petrey

Jewish Roots Journey

Why Christians Should Care About Their Jewish Roots

Habitation of Honey

The Honeycomb Is Waiting

Letting My Light Shine

www.energiondirect.com

From Dr. Michael L. Brown, who appears as a character in this novel

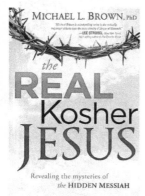

https://shop.aer.io/ncs/p/Real_Kosher_Jesus_Revealing_the_Mysteries_of_the_H/9781621360070-909

https://shop.aer.io/ncs/p/Our_Hands_Are_Stained_with_Blood_The_Tragic_Story_/9780768451115-909

Also by Nancy Petrey for Amazon Kindle:

https://amzn.to/2J5AI3B